THE FAMILY BUSINESS

Hania Allen

CONSTABLE

CONSTABLE

First published in Great Britain in 2020 by Constable

1 3 5 7 9 10 8 6 4 2

A CIP catalogue record for this book
is available from the British Library.

ISBN: 978-1-47213-166-9

Typeset in Bembo by Photoprint, Torquay
Printed and bound in Great Britain by Clays Ltd. Elcograf S.p.A.

Papers used by Constable are from well-managed forests and other
responsible sources.

MIX
Paper from
responsible sources
FSC
www.fsc.org   FSC® C104740

Constable
An imprint of
Little, Brown Book Group
Carmelite House
50 Victoria Embankment
London EC4Y 0DZ

An Hachette UK Company
www.hachette.co.uk

www.littlebrown.co.uk

Kathleen Gunn

Hania Allen was born in Liverpool, but has lived in Scotland longer than anywhere else, having come to love the people and the country (despite nine months of rain and three months of bad weather). Of Polish descent, her father was stationed in St Andrews during the war, and spoke so fondly of the town that she applied to study at the university.

She has worked as a researcher, a mathematics teacher, an IT officer and finally in senior management, a post she left to write full time. She is the author of the Von Valenti novels and now lives in a fishing village in Fife.

By Hania Allen

THE
FAMILY
BUSINESS

CHAPTER 1

'I've found something!' the uniform shouted. 'Over here!'

He straightened, transferring the stick to his left hand. They had been combing the fields since dawn, and it was now midday. And this was just the first of what would be many searches, if recent history was anything to go by. The sun was slamming down on his head, and temperatures were expected to touch the high twenties. He wiped his face with his hand. He was already regretting not bringing his cap.

'Everyone stay where you are,' Sergeant Munro said, as people started to move towards the uniform. He hurried over, stopping short as he saw something poking out of the grass.

'It's a shoe,' the uniform said quietly. 'A lassie's shoe.'

The sergeant parted the blades of grass with his stick. 'Oh, Christ,' he murmured. 'Aye, it's hers, no question.'

The low-heeled court shoe was made of sparkly white material and had a plastic bow on the toe. It had last been worn by little Euna Montcrieff when she'd been a flower-girl bridesmaid at her sister's wedding. She'd disappeared from the reception after the photos were taken.

The wedding, the day before, had been a huge affair in Redwood Manor, a newly built country-house hotel outside Inchture, a village that stretched back from the A90. When Euna had vanished from the group of children playing in the hotel's garden, someone had immediately raised the alarm. A search of the hotel and grounds had revealed nothing. Which was why the uniforms, forensics officers and a large number of volunteers had got up at sunrise to search the grassland around the village.

Suddenly, a man broke from the group and ran towards them. He was tall, with a full head of brown hair falling over his forehead. 'Is that my Euna?' he shouted, emotion choking his words. 'Is that my wee lass?'

The sergeant blocked the man's path and threw his arms round him, holding him fast. 'Please, Mr Montcrieff. Leave this to us. Forensics will deal with it,' he added into Montcrieff's ear, repeating the words as the man's legs buckled and he collapsed on to the ground, his body racked with sobs.

Two uniforms came forward and gently helped Mr Montcrieff to his feet. Members of the press, who'd followed the sergeant's instructions to keep out of the search area, now poured on to the field to take photos of the weeping man. Other uniforms leapt into action, ordering them away. The police photographer took several snaps from different angles, and then a forensics officer dropped the white shoe into a bag, and pushed a marker into the ground. Nothing was being left to chance: the position of the clothes might prove to be significant.

Marek Gorski stood with the other volunteers, head bowed, watching the scene. He felt a heartbreaking rush of pity for Euna's father. This was the second kidnapping in a month. In the previous case, a child had been abducted, and her naked body abandoned with no attempt at concealment. That time also Marek had joined the volunteers, scouring the countryside for traces of her.

In his pocket was the photograph of Euna taken at the wedding. It showed a girl of eleven grinning into the camera. She had striking blue eyes, a pale complexion and long dark hair. The searchers had been handed this photo and instructed to familiarise themselves with the clothes, as the killer rapist's modus operandi after the first abduction had been to scatter them in a long trail across the fields. At first, the police had thought this was intended to lead them directly to the victim, but they were disappointed. They had to rake the nearby fields before they stumbled across the body.

The discovery of the shoe heralded the start of what Marek knew would be a certain outcome. The clothes would be found, flung into thick grass. But the searchers might also find a clue that would lead them to the killer. So far, however, clues had been sadly lacking. Still, they might be lucky today. Either way, it was now a matter of time before they found Euna.

Marek gazed into the blue bowl of the sky, marvelling at the unprecedented July heat, the consequences of global warming, if the experts were to be believed. At least it wasn't raining. In fact, he couldn't remember the last time they'd had so much as a shower. It was strange weather. First, the Beast from the East earlier in the year, and now this endless sunshine. He could hardly complain. The warmth leached into his bones, and the air was thick with the fragrance of hawthorn.

The sergeant signalled to them to continue. This was the part Marek dreaded and, judging by the slumped shoulders and general attitude of defeat, so did everyone else. Minutes later, another shoe was found, then the garland of flowers Euna had worn across her dress. He paused, his eyes closed, wondering if he could bring himself to continue.

There was a touch at his elbow. 'You okay?' It was a woman's voice.

'Yes,' he said wearily, trying a smile.

'I've seen you before. You were one of the searchers when wee Fiona was taken.'

'That's right.'

She gave him a sympathetic nod, and moved on.

He caught the eye of a man in a red T-shirt and shorts. Jamie Reid had been a photographer at the *Courier*, specialising in landscape photography, but had left to go freelance. Marek, who worked as an investigative journalist, had kept up with him, meeting him and his wife for the odd drink. When the call had gone out for volunteers, it was Jamie who'd suggested to Marek that he might want to join the search. That was when Fiona had disappeared. Mercifully, Marek hadn't been assigned to the group that had found the body.

Jamie caught him up. He was a cheerful Dundonian with lively brown eyes and a buzzcut. It had taken Marek a while to get used to his strong accent.

'How you doing, pal?' Jamie said. He had one of those soft voices you sometimes had to strain to hear.

'I've been better, to be honest.'

He nodded towards the sergeant. The man was holding up a white dress. The skirt, which billowed out in layers of chiffon, was crumpled and dusty. 'Not long now, I reckon,' Jamie murmured. 'She's around here somewhere.'

Marek felt his stomach churn. What he wanted now was for them to find Euna so he could go home.

They'd reached the boundary wall when the sergeant called a halt. There were two more fields to be searched, but they needed a break. He told everyone to come back in half an hour's time. Those people who still had an appetite drifted to the cars lining the street to eat their sandwiches.

'I think we could both use a wee dram,' Jamie said to Marek. 'I've got a bottle of Scotch in the van.'

'Thanks, but I'll fall asleep if I drink in this heat.'

With a sad smile, Jamie left to find his Hyundai Starex.

Marek was turning away when he glimpsed something in the woodland. It was a doocot, half hidden in the trees, with a single araucaria standing guard. It was in the style of a lectern, stone-built with a tiled roof and openings in the wall to let the pigeons fly in and out. String courses had been added to keep out the rats. A Gothic arch framed a heavy wooden door.

He approached the sergeant. 'Is it worth taking a look in there, do you think?'

The man, a round-faced giant with a thatch of ginger hair, peered into the trees. He was weighing up the chances of finding anything against tucking into his bacon sandwich and the flask of builder's tea.

'Aye, all right,' he said, with a sigh. 'But just a quick keek.'

That was all it would need, thought Marek. A quick keek and they'd soon know.

He wondered how he would feel if they found Euna inside. As a journalist, he'd seen his share of dead bodies, but they'd been adults, never an eleven-year-old girl. Mentally, he went through what he'd learnt from his detective sister, Dania, about what happens to a body after death. Euna had been taken in the afternoon of the previous day. So, less than twenty-four hours before. If she'd been killed an hour or so later, rigor would be well advanced. There was a two-to-three-day window before flesh flies appeared, so at least they'd be spared that.

They pushed through the trees to the doocot. The sergeant pulled at the door, but it wouldn't budge.

'Worth looking round the back?' Marek said hopefully. 'There might be another way in.'

The man rubbed his nose. 'Ach, we may as well, now we're here.'

The ground behind the doocot was thick with blackthorn, its powdered leaves wilting in the heat. The bushes were chest-high, and purplish-blue with tiny sloes. Marek saw that the sergeant was reluctant to wade in. He himself was prepared to risk it, despite the near certainty of getting scratched. He pulled down the sleeves of his shirt and buttoned them securely before tackling the bushes.

He was regretting his decision and thinking of turning back when he saw the window. It was grimy with age, and impossible to see anything through it.

'Can you pass me your water bottle?' he called to the sergeant.

A second later, a plastic bottle sailed towards him and hit his shoulder. Shielding his face from the thorns, he bent to pick it up.

'Thanks,' he murmured.

He dribbled water on to his handkerchief, and rubbed away at the dirt. Seconds later, the glass was as clear as it was going to be. He peered in but saw little in the gloom. His phone was in the back pocket of his jeans. He pulled it out and switched on the flashlight.

On the wall opposite were the pigeonholes, like huge hollow eyes. He played the beam over the floor, the light catching the calcified droppings, small stones, ragged plastic bags and other debris. It was as he was moving the beam into the corner that he saw something that nearly stopped his heart. There was a sudden rush of blood to his ears.

'Well? Can you see anything?' the sergeant called impatiently.

For a second, Marek was incapable of speaking. 'Yes,' he called back.

'Is it her?'

'I think you need to get in here and see for yourself.'

The sergeant muttered something under his breath. Marek heard him ploughing through the bushes, cursing as he tried to disentangle himself from the branches.

'Over there,' Marek said.

From where they were positioned, they couldn't direct the beam into the corner. What they did see was the bottom half of tattered trousers, ending in a pair of mouldy leather shoes. Whoever this was, thought Marek, as the chill spread through his chest, it wasn't Euna.

DI Dania Gorska was crouching over the figure, staring into what had once been a face. Although not an expert, she knew enough to realise that this child had been dead for years, possibly decades. The hair had disappeared, and all that remained of the soft tissue were patches of dried skin. There was a strong smell of mildew and mice.

She straightened, and stood back to let the photographer do her work.

'I don't suppose that's a school uniform,' DS Honor Randall said.

'Hard to tell. There's not much of it left. We'll get a better idea once we examine him.' Dania glanced around, dazzled by the harsh light from the arc lamp. Although it was cooler inside, she was sweating in her over-suit.

The photographer, a thin-faced woman with limp dark hair, took shots from different angles of the body and of the room. With a nod to the officers, she left the building. She would wait outside in case her services were needed again.

The two detectives approached the figure. Dania dropped to her knees and felt inside the pockets of the tattered jacket.

'Nothing,' she said.

She tried the breast and inside pockets, but only succeeded in pulling the material apart. Underneath the jacket were the remains of a shirt, chewed through in places. She imagined the rats crawling over the body, gnawing at the cotton in their attempts to get at the flesh. The material of the dark tie had rotted so much that it came away in her hand. She put her hands inside the trouser pockets, but all she could feel through the fabric were the thin leg bones. There was nothing to identify the body. The shoes looked like those a boy would wear, but that was all.

'How do you think he died, boss?' Honor said.

Dania motioned to the victim's arms. 'He was chained to the wall. So I'm guessing starvation.' She gazed at the faded paisley-patterned rag lying next to the figure. 'Whoever did this must have pushed the child's handkerchief into his mouth to keep him quiet. It would have fallen out during the stages of putrefaction.'

Honor shook her head. 'So no one heard the poor lad cry out.' She paused. 'Know what I'm thinking?'

'Tell me.'

'Why would you put chains in a doocot?'

'Maybe it wasn't always used as a doocot.'

'I'm betting that whoever brought him here attached those chains to the wall.'

'Planned it well in advance, you mean?' Dania studied the chains. They weren't the heavy-duty type found in agricultural equipment, but still strong enough to restrain an adult, never mind a child. 'I'm inclined to agree. Not only did he put them in, he found manacles that fitted securely round a child's wrist.'

'He was well prepared.'

'You know, Honor, when the call from the uniforms came in, my first thought was that we were going to find Euna Montcrieff.'

As soon as the notification that Euna was missing had come in to West Bell Street police station, the officers on duty had followed the UK's Child Rescue Alert protocol. Messages had immediately gone out on local radio and television.

'We need to get an ID,' Dania said, peering at the yellowing skull spotted with pigeon droppings. 'And also find out how long he's been here.'

'I guess this is one for CAHID.'

CAHID was Dundee University's world-famous Centre for Anatomy and Human Identification. As well as running student courses in anatomy and forensic anthropology, it aided the police in their investigations. Dania had used their services before and was well aware of how lucky West Bell Street was to have them on their doorstep.

'We can make a start looking through Missing Persons but, until we know the post-mortem interval, we may end up chasing our tail.' She got to her feet. 'I think we're finished here. We need to hand over to Forensics.'

Outside, they struggled out of their over-suits and slippers, watching the forensics officers file in to secure and catalogue the scene. Through the trees, Dania caught a glimpse of the blue-and-white police tape that cordoned off the area. The volunteers searching for Euna Montcrieff had long since dispersed and headed back down the A90 to Dundee, leaving the uniforms to continue the hunt. The sergeant had informed Dania that they'd found the clothes. They would be on their way to the lab to be tested for traces of the killer.

Since none had been detected on the clothes of the previous victim, Dania doubted any would be detected on Euna's. She didn't envy DI Owen McFadden, who'd been assigned by Jackie Ireland, the station's chief inspector and the senior investigating officer, to take the lead on the killer rapist investigation. Given the gravity of the case, almost everyone at the station was assisting him.

Honor leant against the araucaria. 'Looks quiet.'

'So does a graveyard.'

'Inchture. Been here before?'

'My first time.'

'It was in the papers earlier this year. Something about a new housing development. The locals didn't seem too keen. Do you think the owner will bill us?' Honor added, motioning to the broken door hanging on one hinge.

'I'm not sure there *is* an owner. Isn't this public land?'

'Something we'll have to check. I'll get on it as soon as we're back.'

'If there is an owner, there's one question I'd like to ask him.'

'Only one, boss?'

'For starters, anyway.'

Honor glanced at her. 'What is it?'

'We had to break that down,' Dania said, gazing at the door. 'But someone chained the lad up. And locked him in.' She turned away and stared into the distance to where the uniforms were sweeping the parched fields. 'So where's the key?'

CHAPTER 2

'What can you tell from the clothes, Kimmie?' Dania said impatiently. 'I know you were working on this yesterday evening. I was passing the building and saw your lights on.'

Kimmie, a dark-haired Australian, was the station's chief forensics officer. The two women had developed an excellent working relationship and consequently, as Kimmie herself was fond of saying, they were more than the sum of their parts. Despite her ridiculously high workload, she was always relentlessly cheerful.

'I've got Euna Montcrieff's clothes to look at,' she said, in a strong Australian accent. 'But I thought I'd get ahead with yours first.' She grinned. 'It's impossible to get bored shitless in this job.'

'Thanks for fitting me in. I appreciate it.'

'No worries. You caught me at a generous moment.' She looked enquiringly at Dania. 'Interesting that Euna's clothes were found close to where you found your chained lad. Do you think there's a connection?'

'I doubt it. Whoever chained that boy up did it years ago. It's not our killer rapist. He's been hunting for less than a month.'

'I wonder if the location's significant.'

'Do you know Inchture?'

'I drove through it once. I thought it would be one of those sleepy villages – you know the kind, full of newlyweds and

11

nearly-deads. But it's not like that. There are some lovely old houses. Maybe whoever owns the doocot lives in one of them.'

'We've started questioning the locals.' Dania turned her attention to the large plastic sheet on the table. 'So, what have you got for me?'

The chained boy's clothes were laid out as neatly as possible given their state: jacket, trousers and shirt above, and socks and pants below. The shoes and pieces of tie lay beside the paisley-patterned handkerchief. Everything was dirty and ragged, and the shoes and outer clothes were stained with grey pigeon droppings.

'First off,' Kimmie said, 'these are smart, good-quality clothes.'

'Navy-blue jacket and black trousers. Honor thought they might be a school uniform.'

'They look like the type of clothes that have been around for years, so I couldn't give you an estimate of when they were made. I'll write it up for you once I've had a chance to examine the fabric in detail.'

'The shoes look like they were expensive.'

'The word here is "were",' Kimmie said, fingering the mouldy, dried-out leather. 'The laces were so shredded, I'm afraid they fell apart. Not something a young boy would wear to meet his mates,' she added. 'So I'm with Honor here. My money's on a school uniform. But there's something that might help you pin it down.' She lifted the middle section of the tie, and carried it to the adjacent bench.

'This little beaut is my new stereomicroscope,' she said, laying the tie on the plate. 'As the name suggests, there are two different viewing angles. Means you get a three-D image.' She stood back. 'Have a look.'

Dania peered through the eyepieces.

'You may need to move the material around,' Kimmie said.

'No, I can see it. Could that be a shield?'

'I'm guessing it's a school crest. It's hard to get the detail because much of the stitching is missing. Can you see the shape of a cross in the centre?'

'Only because you've told me that's what it is.' Dania lifted her head. 'Can you magnify it?'

'Sure. And I can try different wavelengths of light. Why don't you leave it with me and I'll get photos for you?'

'When can you do that?'

Kimmie pulled a face. 'End of the day?'

'I owe you one.'

'You owe me a few, actually,' Kimmie said good-naturedly. 'Now come and take a gander at these,' she added, steering Dania towards the back of the room. 'It took us a while to get them off the wall – everything was rusted to extinction.'

On another table were four sets of chains and two manacles.

'These are lavatory chains,' Kimmie said. 'You don't see them now, except in old houses. They're not too sturdy, which is why whoever put this poor kid in there doubled them up. They were brazed to plates, which were attached to the stone wall in the usual way, by drilling holes and screwing them in. It was a pretty neat job.'

'What sort of equipment do you use to braze metal?'

'You're joining two metals together, so you need flux and a filler, which usually comes in the form of rods. And you need a high temperature to melt the filler.'

'A gas cylinder?'

'Yeah. And for a job as small as this, I'm guessing a hand-held torch.'

'And the manacles?'

'I think they were made especially for the boy. You don't need a key. You push this hinged bit down. If his arms hadn't been

13

forced so far apart, he'd have been able to get out of them easily. Again, it's a neat job.'

'I don't suppose you could get fingerprints off the manacles?'

'The thought crossed my mind. I did try, but there's nothing there.'

Dania played with the manacle, imagining the poor lad's frustration at not being able to reach it and free himself.

'So what are you thinking, Dania?'

'I'm wondering what kind of a man we're dealing with here.' She laid the chain on the sheet. 'Did he come back now and again, for example?'

Kimmie's eyes narrowed. 'Why would he?'

'To watch his victim slowly dying of hunger.'

As Dania entered the packed incident room, she caught sight of a prematurely balding, broad-shouldered man standing in front of the main touchscreen. Owen McFadden was gazing, thoughtful-eyed, at the photographs of the first abducted girl, taken when she was alive. Below were the photos taken after death. Her naked body and clothes had been abandoned in and around the woodland near Birkhill, out of sight of habitation. And nowhere near any CCTV or traffic cameras.

The file on Euna Montcrieff, the second abducted girl, had already been uploaded. Owen tapped the screen and images of her clothes appeared, along with a map of their location. Dania had to admit that, since the introduction of the touchscreens, their lives had been made considerably easier. The DIs now had desks in the newly enlarged incident room, which suited her greatly, as she could work more closely with Honor and Hamish Downie.

Honor had been her second-in-command since Dania's arrival in Dundee two years earlier, and was a highly popular officer at

West Bell Street. Her dark hair changed with the seasons, cut short one month, then left to grow wild, then cropped again. Currently, it was at that midway stage, neither short nor long. She was chewing toffee, because when she was at her desk she could rarely go five minutes without putting a piece into her mouth. Dania often marvelled at how the girl managed to maintain her slim figure.

'Where's Hamish?' Dania said, dropping her bag on her chair.

'Still out at Inchture, boss, questioning the locals about the doocot. I don't hold out much hope, myself.'

'Why not?'

'That lad has been in there for years. Assuming anyone knew anything then, they'll have moved away by now.'

Dania studied the girl. 'That's not my experience of rural communities. They tend to stay in the same location, they're close-knit, and everyone knows everyone's business. And they remember things that happened decades ago.'

'I can tell you listen to *The Archers*,' Honor said, smiling. 'Ah, here's our boy now.'

A solidly built man strode in and took the desk opposite. Born and bred in Dundee, Hamish Downie had returned the previous year from a stint in Glasgow where – as he put it – he'd shown those Weegies how it was done. He'd settled back into Dundee life as though he'd never left, speaking in an accent that was part Glaswegian, part Dundonian. Dania, who had difficulty with some Scottish accents, would occasionally take Honor aside and ask for a translation. As the muscle in the team, Hamish's contribution was particularly valued. What endeared him to Dania was that he was fiercely protective of the women in the squad, both in the office and in the field. The three of them worked well together, which gave Dania an immense sense of relief. At her previous post in London's Metropolitan Police, she'd been forced to listen to the endless childish squabbling, and watched how officers tried to undermine each other to win a promotion. Apart from an incident shortly after her arrival, nothing like that had happened in Dundee. She and Owen McFadden were the same rank, but they were constantly helping each other out.

Honor unwrapped another toffee. 'I was telling DI Gorska how you volunteered to be the one to traipse around Inchture,' she said to Hamish.

'Volunteered? Pish. You ordered me to do it,' he said, trying not to smile, and failing. 'I don't know why I always end up with the legwork.'

'You've got the best-looking legs.'

Hamish scrunched a piece of paper into a ball and threw it at her. She ducked and tossed him a toffee.

'So what did you learn at Inchture?' Dania said.

He picked up the toffee and examined it. 'I ken it had to be done, but it was a waste of time,' he said stiffly. 'No one could tell me anything. They were more interested in the search for Euna. Some of the locals are neighbours of the Montcrieffs and had been at the wedding.'

'Did anyone know who owns the doocot?'

'Half of them didn't even know there *was* a doocot. Aye, and of the ones who did, half thought it was a public building, and the other half thought someone owned it but they couldn't tell me who.' He paused. 'But no one could remember ever going inside.'

'And did they know of a boy who went missing years ago?'

He shook his head. 'On that point, they were quick to say they knew nothing.'

'Do you think they're closing ranks?'

'Hard to say, ma'am.'

'Once we get a firm ID, you can go back there.'

'Oh, joy.' He smiled. 'Although it beats sitting on my bahookie.'

'And you can take DS Randall with you.'

Honor nodded in resignation. 'By the way, boss, have you seen the DCI?' she said suddenly.

'Not this morning.'

'She's holding a press conference in a few minutes.'

Dania was glad it was her superior who was briefing the press. Since the killer rapist had risen to prominence, Dundee had fallen into a state of paralysis. With a second kidnapping, the fear level was such that girls were rarely allowed anywhere unsupervised. That a young girl had been abducted from a wedding reception, possibly in full view of other children, was a scenario that no one could have imagined. Which was why the killer had succeeded in getting away with it.

Honor was uploading images of the chained boy. 'Okay,' she said, getting to her feet, 'that's the lot.'

The touchscreen they were using for the chained-boy case was at the back of the room. Honor pressed a key on the hand-held and the screen burst into life. The photographic images from the doocot appeared, followed by those of the victim's clothes.

'Kimmie's promised us close-ups of the tie by end of play today,' Dania said. 'We think there's a school crest.'

'On it. I'll make a list of schools in the area.'

Dania smiled to herself. Honor was a great asset. She never said, 'Why?' She said, 'Why not?' It was an attitude that would ensure her rise up the ranks of the police force.

'Right, if anyone's looking for me, I'll be at CAHID,' Dania said.

Honor looked at her thoughtfully. 'Going to see Harry?'

'I'm here to see Professor Harry Lombard,' Dania said to the mousy-haired receptionist.

'Is he expecting you?'

'He is. DI Dania Gorska.'

'I'll let him know you've arrived,' she said, picking up the phone.

A minute later, Harry Lombard walked briskly down the corridor. He was in his short-sleeved blue tunic. Dania had worked with him on one of her major cases the year before. At the time, she'd been drawn to him romantically but nothing had come of it. Instead, he'd formed a liaison with Kimmie. Dania had often wondered how that was going but her hints to Kimmie were met with a glum silence, and she could only conclude that the affair had fizzled out.

'DI Gorska,' Harry said, pumping her hand. 'It's nice to see you again,' he added enthusiastically.

Heat rushed through her as she looked into the familiar warm brown eyes. 'Thanks for taking this on, Professor. I know you're busy.'

'Never too busy to help the police.' He smiled shyly. 'So, shall we make a start?'

'Please lead the way.'

He walked with her along the corridors, chatting about nothing in particular, until they reached what she recognised as the specimen room. He opened the door, and stood back politely to let her pass.

The low-ceilinged room held several trolleys, each with a large Anglepoise clamped to one end. On the nearest trolley, a skeleton had been carefully arranged, its hands rotated outwards, palms upwards and thumbs pointing away. Dania remembered this as the standard anatomical position. She was struck by how clean the bones were.

Harry must have guessed her thoughts. 'I've had my whole team on this. When news came in that someone had found a child's skeleton, people suddenly found time in their schedules.' He ran

18

a hand over his cropped dark hair. 'We're just a bunch of softies, you know.'

'I'm really grateful.'

He searched her face. 'I suspect these old cases must give you a headache.'

'All cases give me a headache.'

'Let me take you through what we've got so far.' His tone changed, as though he were speaking to one of his students. 'All his bones are present. As are his teeth.'

'It's definitely a boy?'

'Definitely.'

'How old would you say he was?'

'We examined the teeth and the growth lines in the enamel. That gave us his age accurately. He was nine when he died.' Harry paused. 'Where did you find him?'

'In a doocot. Chained to the wall.' She gazed at the skeleton. 'Nine years old. What an age to die.'

'Chained?' He gave his head a little shake. 'What a *way* to die.'

'Is there evidence of trauma? Broken bones? That sort of thing?'

'None. At first glance, he looked like a healthy lad.'

'He was chained up and locked in. Our suspicions are that he starved to death.'

Harry frowned. 'If he had no food or water, he'd have survived for about two to three weeks. Rapid starvation doesn't leave much evidence in the bones, I'm afraid. It's starvation after a prolonged period of malnutrition that leaves a signature.'

'I see.'

'There's one thing that may be of help to you. The lad had scoliosis.' He bent over the skeleton. 'You can see it here. The spine has a distinct curve, sideways and inwards. The X-rays on the wall show it more clearly.'

On the screen was a single image of a skeleton. Harry touched it, and the skeleton rotated jerkily. It was impossible not to see the twist in the spine.

'Would it have been painful?' Dania said.

'No. This isn't a severe case. But the condition would likely have deteriorated with age. There's more work we can do on the biological profile, but this may help you identify him quickly.'

She was conscious that Harry was trying to save them money. The more work done on behalf of the police, the more their coffers would empty. She threw him a grateful smile. 'It will certainly be quicker than looking through dental records. If he's in MisPers, there'll be a note of the spinal condition.'

'Assuming his parents decided to tell the police when they reported him missing.'

Dania stared at him. 'Why would they keep that to themselves?'

'They may not have thought it significant. And some people are ashamed to have children that are disfigured. Although I'd hardly call this a disfigurement.'

'But surely if it helped the police find him, they'd have mentioned it.'

'One would hope so.'

It was time for the million-dollar question. 'When would you say he died?'

'From the condition of the bones, and the fact that he wasn't buried, I'd say ten to fifteen years ago.'

She turned away so he wouldn't see her disappointment, although, from his answer, he would appreciate the scale of the task before her. Ten to fifteen years would narrow down the search, but such a long post-mortem interval would inevitably make their job extremely difficult.

'One last question, Professor. Is the scoliosis condition genetic?'

'We don't know. So I wouldn't assume he's related to anyone

else with it.' He straightened. 'When you're ready, let me know how you'd like us to proceed.'

She gazed at the skeleton, unable to see anything but the twist in the boy's spine. If they were lucky, the condition would help them ID him. But would it help them find his killer?

Yet the question that had been uppermost in her mind since she'd set eyes on his remains was: why would anyone do this to a young boy?

CHAPTER 3

Marek was sitting on one of the benches on Magdalen Green, a grassy area west of Discovery Point. It was a favourite spot, not just because of its stunning view over the Tay towards Fife, but because he had a weakness for places with atmosphere and this was Dundee's oldest park. Someone at work, who was research-ing churches, had told him there had once been a chapel dedicated to St Mary Magdalen here, but during the Reformation the lands of the Roman Catholic Church had been appropriated by the gentry, passing eventually to the town council. Behind him was Magdalen Yard Road, its four-storey houses bearing the full force of the wind that usually ripped in from the river. Not that there'd been any wind lately. Or cloud. The sunlight danced off the water, dazzling the strollers on the path along Riverside Drive.

One interesting snippet of information Marek had gleaned in his time in Dundee was that, during the war, Polish soldiers had trained at Magdalen Green. Now, the town's lads used it for the odd impromptu game of footie. But he himself came here for a completely different purpose – it was one of the places where he met his most valued informant.

He shook open the *Courier* and scanned the pages, although, as an employee of DC Thomson, he was familiar with the contents.

Minutes later, he became aware of someone sitting down next to him.

Without lifting his head from the newspaper, Marek said, 'You're late.'

'You say that every time,' came the wheezy voice.

'Because you're late every time.'

'Ach, no need to get all sooky lemon about it, son. You know I'm worth the wait.'

Marek had to agree that Gilie Wallace had a point. Their paths had first crossed when he was on an undercover mission researching illegal dogfighting in Templeton Woods. As he was secretly recording the proceedings with his bodycam, he saw a figure slip away from the crowd and creep towards the car park. Something about the way he was hunched over, trying to make as little noise as possible, had made Marek follow him. The man reached the car park and, without a moment's hesitation, made for one of the vehicles. He broke in quickly and silently, and removed the radio. Marek, hiding in the trees, captured this on the bodycam, continuing to record him as he made the rounds of the cars. Most were old enough not to be fitted with alarms, and the man knew which they were. When his rucksack was full, he sneaked out of the woods and down Templeton Road. After reaching the main road, he walked briskly towards Birkhill and straight into the inn on the corner.

Marek waited until he'd ordered a pint at the bar, then took the seat next to his. In a lowered voice, he told the man that he had the evidence he needed for the police to send him down. Gilie – as he introduced himself – seemed unfazed, a good sign since Marek was looking for someone who wasn't easily spooked. After a brief negotiation, he agreed to be Marek's eyes and ears. At fifty-five years old, he had his finger on the pulse of everything that went down in the city. Or was about to go down.

Consequently, Marek used his services more than those of his other informants. But, still, he didn't expect to be kept kicking his heels. He had standards, after all.

'What's your excuse this time, Gilie? Playing the ponies? No, wait, let me guess. Your alarm clock failed to go off this morning.'

Gilie snorted. 'How would I know? I was asleep.'

'What have you got for me?' Marek said, folding the newspaper.

'Straight in, just like that? No small-talk?'

'You want small-talk? We could discuss Brexit and how well the government is doing.'

Gilie pretended to fall off the bench. 'Anything but that, Marek. Okay, let's get down and dirty.' He glanced around, but at 9 a.m. the Green was deserted.

Marek gazed at the Victorian bandstand, waiting patiently. Gilie patted his pockets. He removed a pack of Superkings, shook out a cigarette and tapped it on the pack. Marek resisted the urge to grab the fags and chuck them away. Although Gilie always blew the smoke out of the side of his mouth, somehow the stink of the tobacco got into Marek's clothes. His short-sleeved shirt would have to go straight into the washing machine.

Gilie lowered his voice, unnecessary since they were alone. 'Someone's bringing in something illegal.' He clamped the cigarette between his lips and searched for his lighter.

'Illegal?' Marek said, frowning. 'You mean drugs?'

'Maybe. But whatever it is, it's big,' Gilie said, touching the tip of the cigarette with the flame.

'Bigger than heroin?'

'I don't know, son. But take it from me. This isn't big. It's huge.'

Marek stared at him. There was a fresh cut over his left eye, making Marek wonder whether he'd got it in the line of duty. With his grey hair gone and his broad lips drawn back over tobacco-stained teeth, Marek was forced to admit that, like the *Beano*, Gilie was made in Dundee.

'So is this something that interests you?' Gilie said, the cigarette in his mouth moving up and down as he spoke. 'When I used to be ambitious, I'd have offered that piece of intel to the highest bidder, right enough. Now, I save my best only for you.'

Marek knew he was lying. His journalist friends also used Gilie's services, and he wasn't sure the man didn't sell the same information to them all. But there was something about his edginess, the way he pulled furiously on the cigarette that made Marek conclude he was getting an exclusive. He wondered whether Gilie hadn't approached the others and they'd turned him down. It wouldn't surprise him. It had happened before. And it said something about the nature of the intel. Anyone who fell foul of the hard men bringing in the hard drugs was liable to end up in the Tay.

'Yes, it interests me,' Marek said. He was tempted to ask how Gilie had come by the information, but a good journalist never asks. And a good informant never tells. Not usually, anyway.

'Who's bringing it in?' Marek said, studying the man's flinty eyes.

Gilie shook his head slowly in a manner that suggested he had still to get that and he wasn't prepared to until he had his first payment.

Marek pulled a brown envelope out of his trouser pocket.

He was on the point of handing it over when Gilie said, 'I'm taking a bigger risk with this one, son. One wrong move and we buy ourselves a heap of shite.'

Marek threw him a glance, then took out his wallet and added two twenties to the cash in the envelope.

Gilie took it without a word.

They sat staring at the river, Gilie smoking quietly. He finished the cigarette and threw the fag end into the grass. 'So how about standing me breakfast?'

'I'll take a rain check.'

'It hasn't rained for ages.'

'I'll keep in touch with the Met Office.'

Gilie got to his feet, muttering under his breath, and loped off.

Dania had left CAHID and was walking down Miller's Wynd towards the Perth Road, named, like many streets in Scotland, for its eventual destination, when the call came through. Honor had been in touch with the Registers of Scotland. She was always assigned this task because she had built up a great rapport with one of the archivists.

'I've got news about that doocot, boss.'

'That was quick. How did you manage it?'

'Take a tip from the top. When you're working with archivists, flatter the pants off them.'

'I'll have to remember that.'

'I'm having this guy over to my apartment for dinner.'

'You call that pigsty you live in an apartment?'

'What do you mean? I washed the dishes only last month.'

'So what have you found?'

'Sean had to go right back to the early part of the Sasine Register to get copies of maps and stuff. You know, the sooner everything's digitised, the better, is all I can say. Anyway, the doocot and the land all around originally belonged to a Fraser Affleck. Now, it's owned by a Gregor Affleck, who I'm assuming is a descendant.'

'Good work,' Dania said warmly.

'It's nothing. Any genius could have done it.'

'And have you got Gregor Affleck's address?'

'I knew that would be your next question, so I checked him out. He lives in the Ferry. Hold on, let me find it.' A rustling of toffee papers. 'Okay, here it is.'

The Albany Road address was in Broughty Ferry, not to be confused, as Honor pointed out, with nearby Albany Drive or Albany Grove, and especially not with Albany Terrace north of Dudhope Park. 'Here's the postcode,' she added. 'That'll keep you straight.'

Dania glanced at her watch. Lunchtime. If she went now, she might catch someone at home.

'Want me to come with you, boss?'

'I'd rather you made a start on those school uniforms.'

'Which reminds me. Kimmie has been in touch. She's sent over images of the lad's tie. I've uploaded them.'

'The woman's a marvel. Can you forward them to my phone?'

'On it.'

Dania reached the squad car on Perth Road. She sat behind the wheel, waiting for the images to arrive. As she was about to scroll through, she caught sight of a tall, good-looking man with fair hair and an aristocratic appearance. He was usually dressed smartly in a jacket and pressed trousers, but the heat was such that he was in a short-sleeved shirt and pale-blue cotton chinos. She guessed he was heading for his flat on Union Place.

She rolled down the window. 'Marek!' she shouted across the street.

He stopped and, seeing her, smiled and waved. She beckoned to him, and he hurried over, dodging the lunchtime traffic.

'Danka,' he said, resting his elbows on the rolled-down window. He slipped into Polish. 'I'm on my way home to make lunch. Are you free to join me? It's mushroom soup,' he added, raising an eyebrow. 'We can eat it with *smalec*. I made it last night.'

Marek's mushroom soup was divine. It was the addition of sour

27

cream and lemon juice that did it. And he made the *smalec* – a type of pork fat – himself, adding *skwarki* or pork crackling to give it some crunch. Just the thought of it made her pile on the pounds but then, as her good friend Father Konrad Kliment had informed her, she was too thin for a Polish woman.

'I'd love to, Marek, but I'm on a call.' She remembered then that he was the one who'd found the remains in the doocot. She'd not had the opportunity to speak to him at Inchture, as the sergeant running the search had sent the civilians home. 'How are you keeping?' she said softly.

'I'm fine, Danka. Really.'

He hesitated, and she saw that he wanted to ask about the boy in the doocot. But he knew better. As did she. Neither pressed the other for details of the cases they were working.

'Why don't you come round for dinner?' she said suddenly. 'You've still not heard me play the Bechstein.'

The black Bechstein Concert 8 was a gift from Marek. He'd had the good fortune to earn a fat bonus from a client the year before, and had presented her with the upright. It meant she didn't have to rely on the baby grand in the Overgate for her piano practice, although on the odd occasion when she had spare time, she'd slip out of West Bell Street and down to the shopping centre. There was no comparison in sound quality, however. The Bechstein was unmatched in its tonal balance.

'How about later in the week, or the weekend?' Marek said.

'Great. Tell me what you'd like to cook, and I'll buy the ingredients.' He was the chef in the family, and she exploited it for all it was worth.

He laughed. 'Agreed. But I choose what you play, okay?'

She knew what it would be. His great love was Chopin. He was Polish, after all. 'I'll give you a call,' she said.

She watched his figure dwindle in the rear-view mirror, wishing she had his waved blond hair. Her own was streaked with brown and so thick that she could do little with it. She either wore it in a long bob, or tied it back off her face.

She wondered how he was coping. As twins, they were attuned to each other's feelings in a way other siblings weren't. They'd never been able to lie to each other but it didn't always stop them trying. There was something on his mind, and she guessed it had less to do with the skeletonised remains he'd found in the doocot, and more to do with the abducted girls. With luck, Kimmie's and Owen's investigations would move that case forward.

Dania scrolled through Kimmie's photos. The scientist had done a great job with different wavelengths of light, and had produced a composite image. The shield could be seen clearly now, the vertical bar crossed with four small horizontal lines, and the horizontal bar with vertical lines. It made the crest look fussy, but that was heraldry for you. There was also some detail around the shield, although it was impossible to make it out. But there was enough for Honor to work with. Perhaps by the time Dania returned to the station she'd have pinned down the school with this image on its ties.

The squad car was equipped with a super-efficient sat-nav, and Dania had no difficulty finding Albany Road. It was situated away from the urban sprawl of Dundee, and consisted of an orderly row of detached and semi-detached houses, partially obscured by trees. Gregor Affleck's house was at the eastern end, hidden behind a screen of horse chestnuts.

A pair of gates with finialled iron railings opened on to a magnificent garden awash with colour. The mingled sweet and woody scents filled Dania's nostrils as she walked up the raked gravel drive past an ancient fountain furred with moss, its three leaping dolphins smiling as water cascaded from their mouths. A palatial house of great architectural beauty was situated at the end of the driveway, the aspect spoilt by the large, ugly garage tacked on to its side. She reached the front door, a heavy wooden affair that wouldn't have looked out of place in a castle, and rang the bell, hearing it echo through the house.

A minute later, she heard the sound of bolts being drawn back. The door opened, and a woman wearing a pleated cotton dress in an unfashionable beige appeared. She was of middling height, with tight brown curls and an open, honest face. Her skin was soft and lined. Dania put her in her early fifties.

'Mrs Affleck?'

'I'm Mrs Spence. Mr Affleck's housekeeper.' The woman tilted her head quizzically. 'And you are?'

Dania opened out her warrant. 'DI Dania Gorska, from West Bell Street police station.'

The woman dropped her gaze to the card. She drew her brows together, and for a second Dania thought she was going to close the door in her face.

'Is Mr Affleck in?' she said, when the silence had gone on too long.

The woman looked directly at her. 'He is not.'

'Where may I find him?'

She paused, as if unsure whether to continue. 'He's digging,' she said finally.

'In the garden?'

'Today, he's off the Arbroath Road.'

'What is he digging for, may I ask?'

There was a note of warning in the voice. 'Best if he tells you that himself.'

'And do you know when he'll be back?'

'Not till teatime.' She hesitated, then seemed to make up her mind. 'If it's urgent, you'd maybe like to go there yourself. Aye, I can show you the spot.' She disappeared for a moment and returned with an Ordnance Survey Map. It was folded back to show an area of Dundee north of the A92. 'It's just here.' She ran a bony finger over the paper. 'You go up this road. Mr Affleck will be in the field on the right. His black Volkswagen Arteon will be parked on the road. You can't miss it. Or him. He's a big man.' She seemed suddenly to want Dania to find him.

'Thank you, Mrs Spence.'

She was turning away when the woman said, 'I'll have a pot of tea ready for you when you come back.'

The Volkswagen was where Mrs Spence had indicated, at the side of the road off the A92, which, in this part of Dundee, was dual carriageway. The area was a dreary sprawl of retail parks or open land ripe for development, with the odd straggle of bushes. Dania drew up behind the car.

In the yellowing grassland on her right, a man was bent over, thrusting a large spade into the soil. He seemed oblivious to her presence, giving her the opportunity to study him and his actions. He gave the impression of being well used to this kind of work, pushing the spade confidently in between the stones. Like most of Dundee, he was without a jacket. He had on a flannel shirt, open at the neck, well-worn denims and thick workmen's boots.

Dania left the car, slamming the door so that he'd hear her and not be taken by surprise. 'Excuse me,' she called. 'Are you Mr Gregor Affleck?'

He stopped and turned to look at her. He had heavy eyebrows and a hard, tight mouth. His dark, grey-flecked hair was combed back off his face, which was beaded with perspiration.

'Aye, I'm Gregor Affleck,' he said, in a deep voice. 'May I ask who you are?'

'Police,' Dania said, holding up her warrant. 'DI Dania Gorska. I wonder if I could have a word.' She glanced at the spade, buried deep in the soil. 'It's important.'

His expression changed, and for a second she thought she saw hope flickering in his eyes. But then it vanished, to be replaced with a look of helplessness. He shook out a red spotted handkerchief and wiped his face.

'In that case, we'd better go back to the house,' he said, working the spade out of the ground. 'I take it Mrs Spence directed you?'

'She said you'd be digging here today.'

He straightened, and gazed into the distance at the heavy traffic on the Arbroath Road. 'You'll know your way back, then.' It was a statement. Without waiting for a reply, he strode to the Volkswagen.

Dania watched him drive off before starting the ignition.

By the time Dania pulled in to the kerb at Albany Road, it was later than she'd intended. She'd been turning on to Fairfield Road when one of the warning lights on the car's dashboard had blinked on. It indicated she was low on petrol. How had that happened? She hadn't checked before she'd set off, that was how, she thought angrily. As she didn't want to risk arriving at the Afflecks' only to find herself stranded there, she decided to fuel up first. Fortunately, the sat-nav was able to give her the location of the nearest petrol station on the A92. Unfortunately, she'd had to wait behind a line of cars before she could fill the tank.

Now, back at the Affleck house, she hurried past the splashing fountain, hoping they wouldn't think she'd lost her way.

'Inspector,' Mrs Spence said, opening the door. 'Did you lose your way?'

'Something came up,' Dania said coldly.

The woman's lips twitched. She pulled the door wide.

Dania stepped into a large, marble-floored hall. The polished walnut panelling darkened the space, and had it not been for the side windows, she wouldn't have spotted the row of jackets and coats, and the neat line of shoes. To her right, an elegant mahogany cupboard was fixed to the wall above a matching table. High in the corner, a mounted eagle, its dusty black wings outstretched, fixed its glass eyes on her, and for an instant she had the uncomfortable sensation that it was about to launch itself into the air and rake her with its huge talons.

'I'll take you through to the living room,' Mrs Spence said, opening a door on the left. 'Please make yourself comfortable. The kettle's just boiled.'

'Has Mr Affleck arrived? I didn't see his car.'

'It's in the garage. He's upstairs, taking a shower. He won't be long.' She disappeared down a corridor.

The bright, airy living room was tastefully furnished with good-quality wooden pieces, and squashy sofas in a hyacinth blue. The tall windows looked out on to the front garden, and Dania would happily have watched the dolphins spewing water, had her attention not been drawn to the mounted leopard. It was pushing its head out of the wall, its fangs bared.

She was examining the framed photograph of a woman wearing a necklace of glittering green emeralds, their colour exactly matching her eyes, when the door opened. Gregor Affleck, his wet hair slicked back, entered carrying a tray laden with crockery and biscuits. He was wearing a lightweight, navy-blue jacket and black trousers.

'I managed to catch Mrs Spence on her way here, so I saved her the trouble.' He set the tray on the sideboard. 'It's a wee bit early for tea, but I thought you'd like some refreshment. And I could certainly do with a cup.' He clattered about, arranging the cups and saucers. 'Inspector Gorska, you said? You're Polish, I reckon.'

'Can you tell from my accent?'

'Not just from your accent. When I was a lad, we had a Polish gardener. He'd been stationed in Dundee for a radio mechanics course. When the war was over, he had the good sense not to try to return to Poland, and made a home here instead. He had a similar name to yours, but he pronounced it more like Goorski.'

'That's how it should be pronounced. There's an acute accent over the letter *o*, which gives it that sound. But after my parents came to Britain, somehow the accent got lost in the paperwork, and Górska became Gorska.'

'Hardly surprising. We Brits as a nation are bad at languages. My mother tried to learn Polish so she could have a blether with the gardener and make him feel less of an outlander, but she gave up when she saw the large number of consonants.'

He turned then. And that was when she saw it.

'Are you all right, Inspector?' he said slowly.

'That crest. On your tie.'

'Aye, that's the Affleck coat of arms. We have it on our ties, I and my sons.'

Dania dragged her gaze to his, but he turned and continued fussing over the tea. 'Milk and sugar?' he said.

'Just milk, please.' She glanced at his shoes. Black leather. With laces.

She waited until they'd taken their seats in the armchairs. 'How many sons do you have, Mr Affleck?'

'Two. Ross and Kenny. Why do you ask?'

'I understand you own land near Inchture. Is that right?'

'Aye, it is.' He frowned, deepening the net of wrinkles round his eyes.

'And the doocot?' she said, wondering how she could soften the uneasy truth of what she had to say.

'It's been in the family for generations,' he said, sipping. 'But I can't remember the last time anyone kept doos there.' He lowered the cup. 'Now it's my turn,' he said, a little harshly. 'What are these questions about? Why do you want to see me?'

'There's no good way to say this, Mr Affleck. Yesterday, the remains of a young boy were found in your doocot.'

Before she could continue, he said, in a faltering voice, 'How old was the boy?'

'Nine.'

'Oh, God,' he murmured. 'You've found him.'

'Found whom?' she said, leaning forward.

He was staring at a point beyond her shoulder. 'My son, Cameron.'

'Tell me about him,' she said, after a pause.

'He disappeared thirteen years ago.' He dropped the cup and, ignoring the tea spilling over his trousers, covered his face with his hands.

'I'm so sorry, Mr Affleck.'

He lifted his head. 'It's why I was digging. I've been digging in and around Dundee for thirteen years, right enough. Every so often, I get a tip-off that my wee lad might be buried somewhere, and I go out with my spade.' His voice broke. He pulled out the white handkerchief in his breast pocket, and wiped his eyes.

'Can you tell me about the last time you saw Cameron?' Dania said gently. 'I'm sure you went through this with the police at the time, but it would help me to hear it from you now.'

'I last saw him at the kirk. He and Davina – that's my wife – came back here. I went to work.' He ran a trembling hand over his brow. 'I got her frantic call and came straight over. We looked everywhere for him. In the end, we rang the police.'

'What do you think happened?'

'He must have slipped outside.' His gaze wandered to the window. 'Aye, he liked to play in the front garden.'

'Would he have run away, do you think? Was he that kind of boy?'

'Absolutely not,' Gregor said firmly. 'He was a good lad, always did as he was told.' He waved a hand dismissively. 'Almost always. He had his mischievous side, of course – what lad doesn't? – but he wouldn't have left the grounds. We'd drilled it into him that he could get run over if he went out of the gates. Aye, and why would he? He loved playing at the fountain.' A lost expression drifted into Gregor's eyes. 'He had a whole fleet of toy boats.'

'And what was he wearing? Can you remember?'

'It was a Sunday, so he was wearing a navy jacket, black trousers and black leather shoes. And the family tie, of course.'

She glanced at Gregor's clothes. He could have been describing what he was wearing now. 'Did he by any chance have a phone with him?'

'Of course not,' Gregor said emphatically. 'He was a bairn. Far too young to have a phone.' He seemed to relent. 'I know children have them now but they didn't then.'

'And the police found nothing here? No clues as to what had happened?'

'They searched around the grounds and in this area, but they couldn't find him. You'd think he'd be easy to spot. He had a slightly curved spine, you know.'

'Yes, our forensics expert told me,' Dania said quietly.

'Thirteen years,' Gregor said, bowing his head. 'In a doocot. I don't suppose he was . . . ?'

She knew he wanted to ask her about the state of the remains, but couldn't bring himself to.

'All this time,' he said, as if speaking to himself, 'I've hoped that he was alive, and that one day he'd walk through that door. Aye, every time I heard the bell ring, I'd feel my heart race. And then that crushing disappointment when I saw it wasn't him.'

'Who do you think took him, Mr Affleck?'

'Ach, if I knew that . . .' he said, letting the sentence hang.

'Can you think of anyone who might have wanted to do this to Cameron?' When there was no reply, she added, 'Do you have any enemies?'

'Enemies?' he said, with a harsh laugh. 'Everyone has enemies, Inspector. As for whether one of them would have gone to such lengths,' he frowned, 'that's hard to say.'

There would be a file on Cameron Affleck back at the station, so she'd be able to fill in the details. The senior investigating officer would have asked the questions that were on her own lips right now. But there was one he wouldn't have asked.

'Mr Affleck, Cameron was locked inside the doocot. Whoever put him in there must have had the key.'

Gregor stirred as if from a dream. 'The key? But he couldn't have.'

'Why is that?'

'Because that doocot is never locked.' He stared at her as if she were an imbecile. 'I may be wrong about that, Inspector, but the key is certainly never kept in the lock.'

'Then where *is* the key kept?'

He ran his fingers hard through his hair, scrubbing at the scalp. 'Here in the house. At least, I think it is. It'll be in the hall cupboard with the master keys. Davina and I always kept the keys where we could get at them easily.'

'Is your wife at home?'

'She passed away not long after Cameron disappeared, God rest her soul. You might say she died of grief. She blamed herself, you see. If she hadn't gone upstairs for a wee lie-down, she would always say, then Cameron would still be alive. It was heartbreaking to watch her waste away.' He pressed his handkerchief into the corner of each eye. 'She was such a bonnie lassie. When she smiled, it was like the sun coming up.' He squeezed his eyes shut, as if by this action he could squeeze away the pain.

'And you think Cameron went outside to play?'

'He was supposed to be reading in the living room. But Davina had a migraine and thought she could leave him, so she went upstairs. She had migraines regularly at that time – I always said she smoked too much. The rest of us never did. Anyway, Cameron probably thought she would be upstairs for a good while. He must have slipped out. We saw his boat in the fountain.'

'Why would a doocot need a key, Mr Affleck?'

He threw her a crooked smile. 'In the old days, pigeons were kept as food, as I'm sure you know. In fact, in winter they were the only source of fresh meat. An unlocked doocot would have been an invitation to thieves, and no mistake.'

'So shall we check if the doocot key is still there?'

He seemed surprised. 'Aye.' He got to his feet. 'Aye, I think we need to.'

In the hall, he motioned to the mahogany case. 'The keys are in here. We've always kept the masters in the house. Even for our properties elsewhere.'

'And how many of those properties do you have?'

'None now. We sold them off to a developer, and they were demolished. We just kept the land at Inchture. I lease it to the local farmer.' He took hold of the brass knob and pulled at the cupboard door. It opened smoothly to reveal rows of keys hanging from hooks. They were in all shapes and sizes, and the fact that many were rusting suggested they were rarely used. Under each key were a letter and a number.

'How do you know which is which?' she said.

He pulled the door wider. On the inside, in faded gold lettering, was a chart with the codes and the corresponding locations of the rooms or buildings.

He leant forward, squinting. 'The Inchture doocot is L two, according to this.' He ran his fingers down the keys, muttering 'L two, L two.' He had a butcher's hands, Dania noticed, large with square fingers.

'It's here,' she said, pointing.

The hook was empty.

Her initial reaction was to ask how many people had access to the cupboard, but the question was barely worth asking. The cupboard was in the hall, and had no lock. Even a casual visitor intent on stealing the key would be able to find a pretext for slipping out of the living room, opening the cupboard door quietly, and lifting the key. Provided, of course, he knew the keys were kept there.

Gregor was staring at the empty hook, his face dark with anger.

'Can you remember the last time you looked inside this cupboard, Mr Affleck?'

'No, Inspector.'

'And who knows of its contents?'

He transferred his gaze to her. 'Ross and Kenny. My housekeeper. Anyone who would have seen me remove the key that opens the summerhouse.' His voice softened. 'Aye, Davina used to hold some grand garden parties there.' His eyes took on a faraway look. He was seeing those events as though they were happening now.

'Mr Affleck?'

He gave his head a small shake.

'How big would the key to the doocot have been?'

He held up his hands, and moved the palms out. 'About this long, I reckon. Four inches.'

She glanced at the empty hook. It was on the bottom row. Easy to overlook if this wasn't the key you were after. And how observant are people in general? Even when you're looking for something and it's staring you in the face, you can't always see it.

'And is there only the one key?' she said.

'As far as I know. Why would anyone need two?'

After a pause, she said, 'Would you be prepared to give us a sample of your saliva? We can then be absolutely sure that the boy we found is Cameron.'

He nodded, his eyes clouding over.

'We can do it here or at the station. Whichever suits you. Someone will be in touch.'

'Aye, fine.' He took a card from the bowl on the table. 'You can reach me at these numbers, Inspector. I'm at your disposal.'

'And your sons, Ross and Kenny? I'll need their addresses.'

'They live here with me.' He must have seen her surprise because he added, shrugging, 'They've always lived here. It's a large house.'

'Are they married?'

'Ross is. Although he's not been married long. Less than a year.'

'To someone local?'

Gregor shook his head. 'A lass from London. She's settled in well, although the house is bigger than she's used to.'

'I think that's all for now, Mr Affleck.' Dania handed him her card. 'Do please contact me if you think of anything that's relevant.'

'And my wee lad's remains? When can I have them?'

'We may have further tests. I'm sure you'll understand that we need to keep Cameron for now.'

'Aye, of course,' he said, in an uncertain voice.

'I can assure you that we'll take the best care of him possible.'

He managed a tired smile. 'And his watch? Presumably I can get that back now?'

'We didn't find a watch.'

'Ah.' He seemed to shrink into himself. 'It's been taken, then.'

'Can you describe it?'

'It's been in the family for generations. Cameron loved it, so we let him wear it to the kirk.'

She couldn't bear the wounded expression in the man's eyes. There would be time later to get a description. She nodded, and made for the door.

A thought struck her. 'May I ask what you do for a living, Mr Affleck? You mentioned you were at work when Cameron disappeared. That was a Sunday. Do you normally work on a Sunday?'

'I own the Natural History Museum on Guthrie Street. Sunday is our best day for visitors. I occasionally look in then to make sure things are running smoothly.'

'You run a natural history museum?' she said, genuinely interested.

'We have a huge collection of mounted animals.' He looked up at the eagle, then down at her. 'I'm a taxidermist.'

CHAPTER 4

Gregor Affleck stood at the door, watching the Polish detective walk smartly down the drive. She was tall for a woman, which would make shopping for clothes difficult, but her light-grey trouser suit fitted her perfectly. He wondered idly what she wore when she wasn't on duty. Their conversation and the questions she'd asked left him in no doubt that if anyone could find Cameron's killer she could. Aye, she had a head on her shoulders, right enough. She stopped suddenly, pulled the phone out of her jacket and clamped it to her ear. A second later, she was running through the gates.

Gregor returned to the living room, only now aware of the dampness on his legs. Ach, tea stains were nothing. The advantage of black trousers. But he'd had a shock, and no mistake, learning what had become of his son. He imagined the wee lad locked in that accursed doocot, running around, calling for his mother, hammering at the door and crying to be let out. What kind of a man could do such a thing to a bairn? He felt a catch at his throat, and the tears started down his cheeks again. He'd have to tell Ross and Kenny. Kenny and Cameron had been close, with only three years between them. Ross had been born five years before Kenny, so his bond hadn't been as great. But he'd loved the lad, no question.

Gregor thought again about that fateful Sunday. He'd taken the two older boys to the Natural History Museum for a wee keek at the place because when they reached adulthood they'd be helping their father with the family business. Aye, Davina might well have blamed herself for having gone upstairs for a nap but he knew who was responsible. Had he not insisted that Ross and Kenny accompany him, they'd have been at home with Cameron. And Cameron would still be alive. He felt a sudden dull ache in his chest. He'd carried this guilt like an invisible weight. And he wasn't ready to put it down.

The boys wouldn't be home for another hour. He might as well go to the museum and make himself useful. There was work to be done. He hauled himself to his feet, catching sight of the framed photograph of Davina. Aye, she was bonnie, the envy of his male friends. And most of his friends were male. He'd seen one or two making overtures to her. But he knew she'd never stopped loving him. She'd loved him even more than he'd loved her – women were like that, capable of greater feelings than men. And she'd been steadfastly loyal, of that he was in no doubt whatsoever.

He gazed at the photo, at the soft green eyes and fluffy red-blonde hair. None of his children had inherited her colouring, although the shape of their faces and the way they laughed were pure Davina. After she'd passed on, he'd found himself talking to her, a habit that had never left him. Occasionally he'd glimpse her on the stairs, even smelling her cigarette smoke. When that happened, his heart would twist in his chest and he'd speak her name.

He shook his head. Ach, it was time to put it away. For now, at least.

In the hall, he called through to Mrs Spence that he was leaving. Then, with a final, thoughtful look at the key cupboard, he left the house.

★   ★   ★

Gregor parked the Volkswagen on one of the few stretches of Guthrie Street that wasn't marked with double yellow lines. He usually took the car into the museum's car park, but it was being resurfaced. The building's location among the converted mills wasn't ideal, although the tourists who came to this area west of the Marketgait to learn about the city's jute history stumbled across it. And its fame still drew a reasonable number. He hoped that, with the forthcoming opening of the V&A, those numbers would rise. Which reminded him that he needed to get some advertising sent over there.

Whenever he walked along Guthrie Street, he was reminded of how much Dundee's rise to prosperity was down to the jute industry. His grandfather had once told him that the first steam-powered mills were installed in this street. Yet it had been cotton, then flax for the linen industry, that was spun in the mills long before jute was imported. It wasn't until the late nineteenth century that his great-grandfather had started to ship jute from India, employing mainly women to weave it. Gregor could still hear the words of Mary Brooksbank's 'Jute Mill Song' about the 'shiftin' bobbins, coorse and fine'.

But the decline had begun with the building of the mills in Calcutta. Seeing the way the wind was blowing, his great-grandfather had decided to diversify. He'd bought one of the ailing jute mills for pennies, and converted it into a natural history museum. And then he'd learnt the business of taxidermy. He and his son had imported exotic animals in great quantities, which they'd mounted and displayed. The result was a museum the like of which was unknown anywhere else in Scotland.

In time Gregor, then his sons, apprenticed and joined the family business. Gregor's preference was for mounting birds, which he would shoot himself when the season allowed. When the import of animals dried up due to the increasing number and complexity of regulations, they'd found a welcome substitute by mounting pets that their owners wanted to memorialise. The odd hunter or fisherman would also get in touch, asking for their services. And the rabbits and hares that he and his sons shot were clothed and displayed in tableaux – a great hit, particularly with children. They turned nothing down, not even the road kill Kenny supplied from his roaming in the countryside around Dundee. He'd won a competition mounting a barn owl that had been struck by a motorist. Then there were the gulls killed because of oil spills. And once somebody had brought in a rare sea eagle that had flown into a power cable.

They even accepted animals killed by domestic cats. Kenny, who had a rare talent and could have been a painter, had branched out into a more artistic form of taxidermy, creating displays consisting of, for example, two birds or animals spliced together to form a composite mount. Aye, business was good. For now. But, as all good businessmen do, Gregor kept an eye to the future, and was constantly thinking of ways to grow.

He reached the museum but, instead of using the main door, walked round to the tradesmen's entrance at the back of the Victorian building. He punched in the keypad code that let him into the large workroom. A number of benches with half-finished mounts and dioramas were scattered around, but much of the space was taken up with the circular freeze-dry chambers, and the dry-ice chest freezers where the animals were kept ready for processing.

Ross and Kenny were at a nearby bench, putting the finishing touches to a commission from one of Gregor's friends. Anthropomorphic taxidermy, where mounts were dressed as humans, had soared in popularity. In this tableau, called *A Busted Flush*, half a dozen kittens dressed in evening clothes were seated round a table, playing poker. Gregor didn't ask where the kittens had come from, but since this friend owned a large number of cats, which seemed permanently in heat, he could hazard a guess.

His sons were deep in their work and barely glanced up as he entered. They had their father's looks: dark hair and eyes, and a thin, taut mouth. But while Kenny was softer in character, Ross had a cruel streak. Kenny would occasionally lose his temper, but Ross never did, which Gregor saw as an unhealthy sign. He'd often asked himself how this had come about. He'd raised the boys identically.

He hung up his jacket next to those of his sons. 'I need to talk to you both,' he said, his voice coming out in a growl.

The men stopped what they were doing, and looked up in surprise.

'What is it, Dad?' Kenny said, pulling off his apron.

Now that he had their attention, Gregor found he couldn't formulate the words. He sank into a chair and stared hard at the table. 'They've found Cameron's body,' he said, in a voice full of restrained emotion.

Kenny hurried over and took the chair next to his father's. 'Oh, Dad,' he breathed. 'Where?'

'The old doocot.'

Ross walked slowly towards the table, and stood with arms crossed. 'The one in Inchture?' he said, in a thick voice.

'Aye, son.'

No one spoke for a while, and then Kenny said, 'What was he doing there, eh? I mean, why was he in the doocot?'

'That's what the police are going to find out. I've had a visit from a detective.'

'Inchture is miles away. Why did Cameron go there?' Kenny said, letting the words drift.

Gregor balled his fists. 'The lad was locked in,' he snapped. 'Someone took him there.'

'Christ almighty,' Ross said, under his breath. 'Was he murdered, then? Did this detective tell you?'

'She didn't give me the details.'

'A woman?' he sneered. 'Couldn't they have found a man?'

Gregor eyed his son. 'I don't want to see that attitude from you, Ross. Not when she comes calling on you, which I've no doubt she will. Do you hear me?' When no answer was forthcoming, he slammed his fist on the desk. 'I said, do you hear me?'

Ross came to heel immediately. 'Yes, Dad.'

'Aye, and she'll be needing to question you too, Kenny. So I want complete cooperation from you both.' He paused. 'Now get out. And take Allie with you. We'll close up early. I have work to do and I want to do it in peace and quiet.'

The men grabbed their jackets and left without a word. They took the door into the corridor, which led through the display halls to the front desk, where Ross's wife, Allie, was working on the accounts.

Gregor sat for a while, staring into the distance, thinking through the details of his conversation with the Polish detective. She'd been quick to appreciate the importance of the missing key, right enough. Aye, whoever had it would surely be the bastard who'd taken his son. Yet who could it be? Had Mrs Spence left the front door open by accident, and someone had slipped into the house and lifted it? It was possible. But when had it happened? He felt his anger swell, but he had to tamp it down. Right now there were things that needed doing here, and he had to keep himself busy, or he'd go mad. He dragged himself to his feet, and pulled one of the clean aprons off the peg.

The task for this evening was to make a start on the Afghan Hound puppy. It was a pretty wee thing that had belonged to the wife of a friend, but it had died suddenly after a couple of years. The woman had been distraught and wanted the pup neither buried nor cremated, but kept in a condition where she could take him with her wherever she went. The husband had told Gregor he didn't care what it cost, he wanted the Afghan to look as life-like as possible and no mistake.

In the past, Gregor would have skinned and mounted the puppy, a procedure that would have taken about a week, but the method he used on small animals now was freeze-drying. As animal preservation went, it was a relatively new procedure, which, strictly speaking, wasn't taxidermy. Although it was simpler, it took longer: even for a kitten, the entire process could take up to six months. Gregor had discussed this with the couple, and impressed upon them that they would have to be patient.

The Afghan had been removed from the dry-ice storage com-partment that morning and would now be soft enough for the next stage. Gregor pulled on his gloves and lifted the animal out of the locker. He carried it to a plastic-topped workbench, and laid it on its back.

The first stage involved replacing the organs with artificial filler. He was so well practised at this, he could have done it blindfold. The trick was not to nick the intestines while removing them, which made an unbelievable mess and stink. After gauging by eye how much filler he'd need, he poked it through the incision and plumped up the puppy. It was important to get this process right as grieving owners were in the habit of cuddling their freeze-dried pets and would notice lumps or bumps.

He selected a colour of thread that was the best match, cut off a suitable length and threaded the long needle. His eyes were no longer what they used to be, right enough, and he needed a wee bit of help. The magnifying glass at the back of the drawer was the type that could be clamped to a bench. Once it was secured, he flattened the fur away from the incision and sewed up the skin with small, tidy stitches.

The next stage required inserting the glass eyes. It was a procedure that had to be done with precision since it was the eyes that gave the animal its lifelike appearance. The wrong placement and the effect was bizarre at best, laughable at worst. Over the course of time, the museum had acquired a large number of glass and acrylic eyes of all sizes and colours, and Gregor had been able to match the puppy's from recent colour photos. It was important to have the eyes looking forward and not sideways, a mistake inexperienced taxidermists often made.

When he was satisfied with the puppy's appearance, he set it on a tray and combed the hair thoroughly before straightening the ears. The final stage involved posing the animal in the way he'd agreed with the couple, which was a sleeping position, chin on paws, but with the eyes open.

He carried the tray to one of the large freezing vessels and laid it on the middle shelf. After fastening the door securely, he pressed the button that started the pump.

His work over, he stood unsure as to what to do next. And then the enormity of what the detective inspector had told him rushed at him. He felt the colour rise up his neck and into his face as anger surged through his body. Knowing there was no one to hear him, he threw back his head and roared. His rage slowly left him, to be replaced with an unnatural calm. He stood with his palms pressed to the wall and thought of his wee lad, and what he would do when the Polish detective caught his killer.

Ross pulled up on Albany Road and cut the engine.

'Not taking it into the garage, eh?' Kenny said, in surprise.

Ross's voice was sullen. 'We'll need the car later, remember?'

'Oh, aye, I'd forgotten.'

Allie was sitting in the back, where she always sat when Ross drove. She studied the nape of her husband's neck, wondering why they were coming home early. She'd been at the desk, working through the figures for last week's takings, when her husband and brother-in-law had thundered through the museum, which – luckily – was empty at that hour. Ross had ordered her to fetch her coat, but had offered no explanation.

They left the car and walked up the drive, Ross and Kenny in front, and Allie a respectful distance behind.

'That was some news about Cameron, right enough,' Kenny said.

'I'm glad they found him. I just wish we knew what had happened.'

Allie felt her body tense. Cameron. So that was it. Why they'd shut up shop early.

'I reckon it'll come out soon enough,' Kenny said. 'But will they find the wee shite who put him there?'

Ross snorted. 'A woman detective. What do *you* think?' he said viciously.

Mrs Spence must have been watching from the living-room window, because the front door opened as soon as they reached the steps. She stood back to let them in, then shut and bolted the door.

'We won't be staying for dinner,' Ross said. 'We'll have something quick in the kitchen.'

Mrs Spence nodded. 'As you wish, sir.'

'Come on,' he snapped at Allie.

Allie avoided Mrs Spence's gaze and followed her husband up the stairs. The bedroom, which they'd moved into after they'd returned from their honeymoon the year before, was on the first floor at the end of the corridor. Although it was a double room, it was smaller than the one Ross had used before he was married. But he'd insisted on taking it. It wasn't long before Allie discovered why – the room was away from the other bedrooms, and directly above a rarely used old scullery. It meant that no one could hear the sounds coming from it.

She hadn't known Ross much before their wedding. It had been the will of his father, Gregor, that his eldest son marry someone of Gregor's choosing. Otherwise the son wouldn't inherit the Natural History Museum and the associated taxidermy business on his father's death. Allie's own father was an old friend of Gregor's and had moved up to Dundee from Buckinghamshire years earlier. He'd urged her to consider the match seriously. The Afflecks were a well-established family and both sons would ensure the prosperity of the business. Love would come afterwards, he'd said. It had been the same with him. And – her mother had added, looking reassuringly at her husband – Allie and young Ross were a match made in Heaven. As someone with no real prospects of her own, Allie had eventually agreed to go along with it out of respect for her parents. It wasn't until later that she discovered why her mother and father were so keen on the match: they'd borrowed money from the Afflecks, which they could never hope to repay, and had been assured that the marriage would wipe out the debt.

It wasn't long before Allie understood what sort of a man she had married. At first, he'd been attentive, encouraging her to settle into the large family house. Then, gradually – so gradually that she would be hard-pressed to say when it had started – he began to choose what clothes she would wear, how she styled her hair, what make-up she would buy. Except that she no longer bought anything, having been forced shortly after they married to close her bank account. Ross had signed her up to a joint account, and arranged for her salary to be paid into it. Not that she earned much, working part-time. When she'd raised an objection that, without credit or debit cards she couldn't access her money, Ross had tried to set her mind at rest by pointing out that she no longer needed money: Mrs Spence dealt with the household expenses, and he was there to buy her whatever else she needed. He would take care of her, he'd added, stroking her hair off her face before gripping her throat. She didn't need to worry about anything. And wasn't she lucky to have such a caring husband?

Had this been all she had to contend with, Allie might have settled reluctantly into a state of bored domesticity. But one night, roughly a month after their honeymoon, everything had changed. She had phoned an old friend from pre-marriage days and asked her over. The two women had spent a merry afternoon in the living room, chatting and drinking wine. Allie sensed that Ross would disapprove and so had asked her friend to come straight after lunch, knowing that she'd be away well before 6 p.m. But Ross had come home early. He'd said nothing, just asked the visitor politely to leave. Then he'd grasped Allie's arm and marched her up the stairs to the bedroom.

It was the realisation that she bruised easily that had stopped him hitting her about the face. Instead, he'd directed his blows to her arms and body. He'd avoided the legs, whether it was because she wore skirts and the bruises would show, or because he might damage her so much that she'd end up limping, she didn't know. But that first time, when blood had gushed from her nose, revealed something about him that she hadn't expected. He blamed her for the abuse, stating that her behaviour had left him with no choice but to punish her, and that he was doing it because he loved her. On another occasion, after he'd told her to strip naked, he beat her badly with her own belt, finally stopping to examine the welts on her back. He urged her not to be so careless, or she might end up in Outpatients. Then he smeared antiseptic ointment on to the wounds, speaking to her with concern in his voice. That was followed by vigorous sex, made particularly painful because he insisted she lie on her back.

The physical abuse was soon followed by abuse of a different kind. When they went shopping, and he bought a dog's bowl, she wondered if this meant they would soon have a puppy, something he'd talked about and promised her for her birthday. If she behaved herself, that was. But when the day came and he brought her breakfast in bed, she was subjected to another form of humiliation – he emptied the contents of her plate into the bowl, then pulled her out of bed and made her go down on all fours and eat like a dog. After they'd had sex, he stroked her gently, repeating over and over in tender words how much he loved her. What frightened her more than anything was that she found herself starting to believe him.

Now, in their bedroom, she let him bend her face down over the back of the chair.

'You do know that I love you, Allie,' he murmured, as he unzipped himself.

As it wasn't a question, she decided it didn't merit an answer.

It was after the thrusts lessened and he moved off her that she began to formulate her escape plan.

CHAPTER 5

Dania had been walking down Gregor Affleck's drive when the call had come in that Euna Montcrieff's body had been found. She hurried into the incident room, pulling off her jacket.

Honor looked up startled. 'If you're looking for DI McFadden, boss, he's at the scene.'

'Where was she?' Dania said, throwing her bag on to the desk.

'On the opposite side of the A90. There's a thin belt of trees before the fields start. She was well hidden in the undergrowth.'

'And they're sure it's her?'

'Positive.'

'Has the father been notified?' Dania said, feeling her pulse quicken.

'Hamish offered to do it. He told me it would be better coming from a man. Something about men needing to cry but not wanting to do it in front of women.' She played with her pen. 'I'm glad it wasn't me. I haven't got your gentle touch when it comes to breaking bad news.'

Dania thought of Mr Montcrieff identifying Euna's body. The visit to the mortuary at Ninewells, the sheet being drawn back. His family would be devastated. All of them. No one at that wedding would ever be able to celebrate the anniversary because it would be overshadowed by the tragedy of Euna's death.

Honor glanced at the other officers. 'We've made a start looking at the traffic cams on the A90.'

'That'll be a wasted effort.'

'Why, boss?'

'Because he didn't take a car on to the A90. I think he left his
vehicle miles away and carried Euna's body over the fields.'

'Bit risky. He might have been spotted.'

'Not at three in the morning.'

'How do you know this?' Honor said, gazing at her without
blinking.

'I don't. But it's how I would do it. I imagine I'm the killer,
and go through the possibilities in my head.'

'I doubt he's as smart as you. He'll slip up,' Honor added
viciously. 'And then we'll bring him in and cut his balls off.' She
frowned. 'You do think we'll find him, don't you?'

'That's what they pay us for.'

'Now, about our chained boy, I've not been able to get anywhere with that school crest. I'll start looking at places outside
Dundee. Maybe he was a boarder.'

'There's no need.' Dania suddenly felt tired. 'It's a family crest.'

As briefly as she could, she told the girl about her meeting with
Gregor Affleck.

'The poor man,' Honor murmured. 'Digging up Dundee all this
time, looking for his son. I'd have gone crazy.'

Dania brought her chair over. 'We've got a bit of time, so let's
pull up Cameron's file.'

'Okay,' the girl replied, with renewed enthusiasm.

A short while later, having registered to search the archives, they
loaded up the file on Cameron Affleck. The first thing Dania saw
was that the case had been assigned to Detective Inspector Blair
Chirnside.

'Our old DI,' Honor said softly.

Dania remembered her first case at West Bell Street, and how supportive Chirnside had been, only to discover – after he'd died in a tragic accident – that he'd suppressed evidence in the case of two missing teenage girls. Detective Chief Inspector Jackie Ireland had given Dania his job a respectful time after his funeral.

'He was a rotten apple,' Honor was saying sadly.

'At least he's no longer in the barrel. Right, so here's Davina Affleck's statement.'

They scanned the text.

'It's like her husband said, boss. She and Cameron were back from the church service by eleven. She felt unwell and went upstairs, leaving Cameron to read Bible stories in the living room, something they did every Sunday. Chirnside reckoned Cameron must have slipped out of the room, opened the front door and gone into the garden to play. Davina states she was the only one in the house. That was June the twelfth.'

'She says she was asleep for about an hour and a half. When she woke, she went downstairs, found the front door open and Cameron gone.'

'Crikey! Is that where they live?' Honor said, leaning forward.

'I had the impression the house has been in the family for generations.'

'It looks more like a mansion than a house.' Honor folded her arms. 'I've said it before, and I'll say it again. Rich people are different from poor people.'

'Oh? In what way?'

There was a touch of envy in the girl's voice. 'They've got more money.'

Dania thought of the old Jewish saying her mother was fond of quoting: 'If you want to know what God thinks about money, look at the sort of people He's given it to.'

'What does this Gregor Affleck do for a living?' Honor said.

'He a taxidermist. And he runs a natural history museum.'

'And that pays enough to live in a house like this?'

'I wouldn't have thought so. He must have private means.'

'Old money,' Honor said, with a sneer.

'He mentioned he'd sold off his other properties. Perhaps he lives off the proceeds.'

'They won't last for ever. Could be he has an illegal enterprise going on the side.'

'Could be. But he didn't strike me as the type. What did strike me is the unusual set-up there. His other two sons are still living with him, and one of them, Ross, is married.'

'I take it we're interviewing them next?'

'Possibly not the wife. She and Ross haven't been married long. She was in London when Cameron was taken.'

'Do they have any servants?'

'I saw only the housekeeper, Mrs Spence.' Dania paused. 'Gregor dresses in the same formal clothes Cameron was wearing in the doocot, down to the black lace-ups. Maybe the other sons do, too.' She shook her head. 'That household seems to belong to another era.'

'Like I said. Old money.'

Dania nodded at the screen. 'Let's press on.'

Honor moved the mouse, and an image of a child appeared. 'Here he is. Cameron Affleck.'

Dania felt her heart constrict. The photo, taken from the waist up, was of a young boy with soft brown eyes and dark curly hair. His youthful bloom made her want to stroke his soft cheeks through the screen. He was smiling blissfully and holding up what could have been a school trophy, the watch on his left wrist catching the light. It had a maroon leather strap and looked huge on him, making Dania suspect this was the watch Gregor had told her about. It was impossible not to see that his left shoulder was significantly higher than the right.

'Look at the tie,' she said. 'His father wears one just like it. That's the family crest.'

'Do you think it's the identical same tie we found in the doocot?'

'When was the photo taken?'

'Says here it was April of the same year.'

'Then I'm guessing, yes, it's the same tie.'

'And the clothes. Navy jacket, white shirt and dark trousers.'

'His Sunday best. And maybe what he wore for formal occasions, like having his photo taken.'

'There's a mention of the twist in his spine. Although the photo says it all.'

Dania ran her hands through her hair. 'Right. What we've got so far is that between eleven and roughly twelve thirty on June the twelfth, Cameron goes missing. How did DI Chirnside proceed?'

'He did it by the book, according to this. The uniforms conducted an immediate search of the area. They interviewed the neighbours but no one had seen anything unusual.'

'And this is the list of interviewees,' Dania said, scrolling. 'It includes the housekeeper, Mhairi Spence. The DI also interviewed friends and acquaintances of the Afflecks. Every trail went cold.'

'And there was an appeal on local and national television.'

'No one would have thought to check out the doocot near Inchture. It's on the other side of Dundee. Okay, let's skip to the final report.'

There wasn't much to add. Dania sat back, pulling at her lip. Her recollection of Blair Chirnside was of a conscientious man who did his best under trying circumstances. The hurried way the report had been thrown together made her suspect he'd been swamped. She knew herself the difficulties of juggling cases, something all officers had to do. Police life was never as simple as having just the one case, despite what television shows suggested.

'Let's get back to the garden, and Cameron's abduction,' she said.

'Assuming that's where it happened.'

'How do you mean?'

'Sure, he went outside to play. But he could have wandered into the street, walked for miles in any direction, and been picked up.'

'His father says he wasn't the kind to wander off. And you're forgetting one thing.'

'Only one, boss?'

'Those chains. This was premeditated. He wasn't picked up on the street. Someone stole the key to the doocot well before June the twelfth.'

'To what end, though?'

'My money's on kidnap for ransom. The kidnapper could have spent days watching the house and waiting for the right moment. He'd have seen the lad playing by the fountain.'

'And seized his chance.'

'Now here's something to consider. The last known sighting of the boy was by his mother, who left him in the living room before going upstairs for a nap. She would have had to go into the hall to reach the stairs.'

'Okay,' Honor said, drawing out the word. 'And?'

'You didn't see that front door. There are bolts you have to draw back. I doubt that a nine-year-old boy could have done it, assuming he could reach up.'

'Maybe the door had been left open by accident.'

Dania shook her head. 'Think about it for a moment. A mother has left her young son in the living room and is about to go upstairs for a lie-down. Don't you think she'd have checked the front door was closed? Even locked it securely?'

'So what are you saying?'

'Someone was in the house. He could have slipped in earlier, perhaps after seeing Gregor leave with the two older boys.'

'Someone kidnapped Cameron from *inside* the house?'

'Yes, I think he did. And I think it was someone Cameron knew. Otherwise, he's unlikely to have gone outside without a fuss. He was taken in broad daylight, remember.'

Honor rubbed her forehead. 'There's nothing about this in the report. I wonder how the DI missed this.'

'It would be nice to be able to ask him.'

'Yep. It would.'

And not just about this. Dania had other questions she'd have liked to ask the DI. But Chirnside was in his grave, unavailable for comment.

Ross turned off the Coupar Angus Road and drove slowly into the Gardens. He cut the engine. The spot he'd chosen was well away from the streetlights but still gave him a good view of the high-rises. The entrance to the one he was interested in was on the other side of the building, but where he was parked was in shadow and therefore more suited to their needs. He counted up to the fifth floor. All the windows were dark. When the lights came on, they would spring into action. But softly, softly. They didn't want to attract unwelcome attention.

This stretch of the Coupar Angus Road was a strange one, and no mistake. All villas and leafy gardens, and then, bang!, there they were on the right-hand side: the cluster of high-rises. You couldn't miss them, even with those tall trees, which could never grow tall enough to block them out. Aye, he'd like to know which councillor had given permission for the construction, and how much had been in the brown envelope that had changed hands.

But he had other things to think about right now. The call had come in the day before. And he was well up for it. After sex, he was up for anything. Which reminded him, he'd have to call Allie later and see what she was up to. On the nights he had to leave the house, his main worry was that she would try to sneak out. But Mrs Spence would give him a full account of Allie's doings, and she wouldn't leave for the day until he returned. He'd given her a notebook. He'd insert the day's date, and she would fill in the rest. When he'd first instructed her to spy on his wife, she'd refused point blank. But he knew what her financial circumstances were, and how difficult it would be to find another job. The veiled hint that some of the more valuable objects in the house might go missing, and he'd arrange things so that the finger pointed at her was enough to make the woman do his bidding.

As well as watching Allie's movements, Mrs Spence was under instructions to prevent her from leaving the house, although he understood that would be difficult to enforce. There wasn't much the woman could do if Allie was determined. But she'd been determined only the once. Ross felt his lips twitch into a smile as he remembered the look on her face as she'd opened the bedroom door and found him waiting for her. Aye, and the stupid bitch had paid for it, right enough.

He glanced at Kenny. 'Okay, little brother?'

Kenny nodded, the motion almost imperceptible in the near dark.

Ross was glad his brother was with him. If things didn't turn out the way they intended, aye, well, two sets of fists were always better than one. Kenny was a good partner in these ventures, although if they had to wait too long, he didn't always keep the heid. An attack of nerves could scupper their plans. He himself had more patience. He was clear-minded and unflappable. And the more intelligent of the two.

His life had changed considerably for the better these past

couple of years. Until he'd joined the family business, he'd felt like a hamster on a wheel, with nothing to look forward to and nothing to look back on. Now, he was going places. And he had a wife, and would soon have bairns of his own. With luck they'd be boys. He'd need to keep an eye on Allie and make sure she did the right thing if she fell pregnant with a lass. No point having an extra unnecessary mouth to feed.

Aye, and it was high time Kenny settled down too, instead of visiting whores, something he'd tried to keep secret and failed. But Ross knew that Kenny preferred them younger. Much younger. He'd seen the way his brother looked at the schoolgirls who visited the museum. At least prostitutes kept him away from children. Although Ross had often wondered why Kenny disappeared for hours at a time without telling anyone where he was going.

A light suddenly blinked on in an upstairs window, causing Kenny to stir from what Ross had assumed was a wee nap. But the window was on the fourth floor. Kenny settled back.

Ross locked his fingers together, wondering how much longer they'd have to wait. After he'd left Allie whimpering on the bed, he'd taken a shower, and he and Kenny had grabbed a bite to eat in the kitchen. Mrs Spence always had something they could reheat, or eat cold. Tonight, it had been shepherd's pie. Somehow it tasted better microwaved.

Now, as they watched the window, his mind slipped back to the bombshell their father had dropped. Wee Cameron's body had finally been found. Except that, after all this time, it would be a skeleton, right enough. Ross had only vague memories of that doocot. There was a window, but it was too high for the lad to reach, and he never had been good at climbing on account of his affliction. Ross imagined the crumpled heap of bones under the window, the mouldy clothes. If only he'd stayed behind that Sunday. He could have persuaded his father if he'd tried. But once the decision to go to the museum had been made, he'd found he couldn't wait to see the place where he'd soon be starting work. Like a real man. How old had he been? Seventeen. And already beating the crap out of his school-mates. But in the years since, he'd always known he could have prevented his wee brother's disappearance. What had happened to Cameron was his fault. It was the stone in his shoe he could never remove.

He felt a nudge. 'He's home,' Kenny murmured.

Ross lifted the binoculars. A shadow passed across the window. Whoever it was returned and drew the blinds. But not before Ross had seen another figure behind him. 'He's got company. We'll have to bide our time.'

Aye, they wouldn't have to put their gloves on just yet.

CHAPTER 6

There was a hush in the crowded incident room as DCI Jackie Ireland strode in, her boots ringing on the floor. She always walked with her shoulders drawn back, which wasn't unusual for someone who'd spent much of her working life in the military. DI McFadden was holding a briefing meeting and she had decided to sit in, something she did on those occasions when she felt her presence could speed things along. It meant that she was unhappy with the glacier pace of the investigation, a situation everyone dreaded. Dania had come to realise that Jackie was one of those women who always wanted things done by yesterday. She'd thought this peculiar to the DCI, but had learnt on meeting other officers of the same rank that they all suffered from this condition.

Owen was shuffling his papers, and looking distinctly nervous. Having been a DI herself for just under a year, Dania knew how it felt when the brass breathed down your neck. And Owen was someone she had a great deal of respect for, having seen how he encouraged his team, and smoothed things over when they slipped up.

'Right then, let's sum up,' he said, facing the room. 'We now have two victims, both killed with the same MO, so in the absence of evidence to the contrary we'll assume we're dealing with the one killer.'

He turned to the touchscreen, where the faces of the two girls smiled out at them.

'The first victim is Fiona Ballie. Ten years old. Last seen on Friday, June the fifteenth. She was riding her bike near her home in Tealing. The last sighting we have is just after five p.m. when a neighbour sitting in her living room saw Fiona pass by the window. The parents raised the alarm when the lass failed to turn up later that evening.' He tapped the screen and a street plan of Tealing appeared.

Dania had had to look up Tealing, a village a few miles north of Dundee. To her astonishment, she'd learnt that, in May 1942, the Soviet People's Commissar for Foreign Affairs, Vyacheslav Molotov – the man who had brokered a non-aggression pact three years earlier with Germany's foreign minister, Joachim von Ribbentrop – had landed at Tealing. An aerodrome had been built during the war, and Molotov had arrived on a secret mission to meet Churchill. The arrival was kept so closely under wraps that the residents of Tealing had only learnt the identity of their esteemed visitor many years after the war had ended.

The purpose of Dania's own visit to the village was to interview the residents, including the neighbour who'd spotted Fiona. The woman could add nothing except to say that the lassie was a regular sight, riding her bike after school while her parents were out working on their poultry farm. And, aye, she was sure of the time, as the five o'clock news had just come on the radio. The village was quiet in the late afternoon, because the farmers were usually out and the Dundee commuters hadn't yet returned. As Hamish drove them to Tealing, Dania gazed at the unfolding country roads and the cut-up fields. Before they'd reached the outskirts and seen the spread-out houses, she'd known with a sick certainty that they were wasting their time.

'We questioned the entire village,' Owen was saying, 'including pupils at the local primary school, but the few people who were around at that time had seen nothing unusual.' He studied the map. 'We conducted a search of the buildings in and around the village, including the derelict structures in the airfield. With no result.'

'Remind me when you began the wider search,' Jackie Ireland said, her arms folded.

'The next day, we put out an appeal for volunteers. We were staggered by the response. This is where we searched.'

He touched the screen and a map of Dundee popped up. The centre of the city was encircled by the A90 to the north and the A85, morphing into the A92, to the south. The entire area to the east and west of Tealing was shaded red.

'It was when a tip-off came through on the Monday that a child's clothing had been found in the fields north of Birkhill that we realised we were way off the mark. Birkhill is some distance south-west of Tealing. Here,' he added, tapping the green dot, 'is where we found Fiona's clothes.' He moved his finger along. 'And Fiona's naked body was found at the foot of these trees.'

'So, not far from the clothes,' the DCI said. 'He carries her body to that spot, and scatters her clothes a short distance away. I wonder why he bothers.'

'And we haven't yet recovered the bicycle.'

They'd been careful not to mention this to the press. Owen had seen immediately that finding a missing bicycle might be their best chance of finding the killer. They'd urged the people of Tealing to keep its existence to themselves. And, so far, they had.

'Professor Slaughter at Ninewells has given us a full report on the post-mortem,' he continued. 'When we found the body, the smell of chlorine suggested it had been doused in bleach.'

He tapped the screen. Dania had already seen this image but was still shocked at the state of the girl's body. Had she not known otherwise, she'd have said Fiona had suffered third-degree burns. The corrosive effects of bleach on skin were well known, causing redness, swelling and blisters, but this was something even Milo Slaughter hadn't seen before. The girl's red hair, now several shades lighter, was a brittle, tangled frizz.

'Professor Slaughter's opinion is that the body had been completely immersed in concentrated sodium hypochlorite. Household bleach is normally up to ten per cent sodium hypo-chlorite, but this was industrial-strength stuff, which can be up to fifty per cent. However, it wasn't the bleach that killed her. Manual and ligature strangulation both cause discoloration of the skin, but it was impossible to tell in Fiona's case because of the caustic burns. The hyoid bone wasn't broken, as it's still flexible in chil-dren, but the internal damage to the neck tissue and other organs satisfied the professor that Fiona had been strangled. Whether by hand or with a cord, he couldn't say.'

'This was obviously before the bleach bath,' someone said.

'Again, there's no way of telling.'

Jackie Ireland waved an impatient hand. 'It's clear why the killer immersed the child in bleach. It was to destroy contact DNA. It defies common sense he'd do this before strangling her. So was there anything on the clothes?'

'No trace of him there either. So far, anyway. Forensics say there's more they can do.'

'And at the post-mortem did Professor Slaughter find any semen?'

Owen shook his head. 'He concluded the killer wore a condom.'

'He's forensically aware,' Dania said. 'Although, these days, that's not difficult.'

'And it makes our task that much harder,' Owen replied.

After a silence, Jackie Ireland said, 'And the second girl?'

'Euna Montcrieff. Abducted from her sister's wedding on Saturday, July the seventh. We found the clothes the following day, and Euna's body two days later. We're still at the start of our investigation on this one. The interviews aren't complete, and we're waiting on Forensics.'

'I'm assuming the condition of the girl's body is the same as that of the previous?' Jackie Ireland asked.

'Exactly the same MO. Death was by strangulation. She was immersed in bleach, so no point swabbing for DNA transfer. And, so far, nothing traceable on her clothes.' He paused. 'We've been careful to keep his use of bleach from the press. In each case, it was a uniform who found the body. They've been told to keep their traps shut.'

'What do these two girls have in common?' Dania said.

'We're still cross-referencing the reports,' Owen replied, in a tired voice, 'but as far as we can tell, absolutely nothing. They didn't know each other, they went to different schools, different play clubs, their parents have no mutual friends.' He gazed at the screen. 'But there must be something that draws the serial to them.'

'They were both young,' someone said unhelpfully.

'How does he find them?' Dania said. 'Perhaps if we knew that, we might have a chance.'

Jackie Ireland glanced at her. 'What's your current thinking? You've worked on cases like this in London.'

'He roams the streets, looking for a particular type of girl. When he sees one who fits the profile, he observes her movements and takes her when the time is right.' She paused for effect.

'Or he's an opportunist. Strikes with no prior planning. It's riskier, but many serials don't think about risk.'

'And which type is our serial?'

Dania studied the screen. 'Hard to say. The first girl was snatched off the street in broad daylight. It could be either opportunism or after careful monitoring. But Euna Montcrieff was taken at her sister's wedding. That's unlikely to be the result of planning.'

'Why?'

'Too much could go wrong. There were too many people. And Euna was playing with a group of children. I think the killer saw a chance and took it.'

'What did the children have to say?'

'One moment Euna was with them. Then they noticed she wasn't there. They were remarkably consistent in their accounts.'

'I bet none of them could agree on the moment she went missing, though,' Honor said.

'You're right. There was no agreement on that. Children are notoriously bad at timekeeping.' Dania studied the map of Inchture. 'Euna could have wandered off. Redwood Manor's grounds go on for ever.' She recalled the postcard-perfect setting. 'And there's woodland everywhere. The killer could have seen her wandering into the trees and followed her. But there's something else we need to consider. He finds them through social media. He could have arranged to meet both girls.'

'Fiona's phone was in her schoolbag, which she'd left at home,' Owen said. 'She had an Instagram account but there was nothing suspicious on it.'

'And Euna's phone?'

'She didn't bring it to the wedding. It's with Tech.'

'What about the dump sites?' Jackie Ireland said, after a pause. 'What's your view on those, Dania?'

'We shouldn't make too much of them. I know it's tempting to

69

assume we can trace the killer's whereabouts from a statistical analysis but there are only two victims.'

'Go on.'

'The trail of clothes didn't lead us directly to the victim's body. I think he's playing with us. He might even have been watching the searchers.'

'Do you think he chose the sites at random?'

'I don't know. Except that he chose sites well away from the cameras. We can keep scouring the traffic-cam footage on the arterial routes, but I'm convinced it'll tell us nothing. There are too many B-roads crisscrossing these areas, and none has cameras. My bet is he's using those roads.'

'Where does he take them?' Honor said. 'He must be a single man. Unless he's got a man cave at the bottom of the garden. But you'd think the neighbours would have seen something.'

Hamish had been quiet up to now. He was playing with the mouse mat. 'Not if he lives out in the boonies.'

'How do you think we should proceed?' the DCI said, addressing herself to Owen.

'I'm with DI Gorska on this one. We're going to have to approach this from another angle,' he said, skirting the question. 'But we're putting up posters, running an appeal on the media. The usual.'

'And the bleach?' someone asked. 'It's industrial strength.'

Owen gave a dismissive shrug. 'You can buy it online.'

'He'd need a huge amount, though. To immerse someone. Even a child.'

'What else is bleach used for?' Dania said.

'Cleaning mainly,' Owen replied.

'But it's a good point,' Jackie Ireland said. 'Our killer could have access to large quantities. That's worth checking.'

'What do we know about serials?' Hamish said. 'Apart from

operating in areas they know well. I mean, what would make them stop?'

'They stop for one of three reasons,' Jackie Ireland said. She counted off on her fingers. 'They die. They go to prison. Or they find a new hunting ground.'

The room fell silent. The ease with which these two children had been snatched from Dundee's rural hinterland suggested that the killer had no intention of moving base. And that was their greatest challenge.

It was the DCI who voiced their thoughts. 'Unless we find this bastard, we'll be hearing from him again.'

CHAPTER 7

Marek was sitting outside the Counting House, drinking coffee. The pub, which had once been a bank, was conveniently situated at the top of Reform Street, a short hop from the fine red-stone building where he worked. Consequently, whenever he needed inspiration, he would come here and contemplate the seated statue of Robert Burns gazing upwards, pen in hand. Behind it were the magnificent McManus Galleries, originally known as the Albert Institute, built as a memorial to the consort of Queen Victoria. The surrounding pedestrianised area was Albert Square, one of the many Albert Squares and Albert Streets that had sprung up across the UK after the prince's death.

Today, Marek wasn't in need of inspiration. He was in need of morning coffee. He took a sip, and opened the *Courier*, snapping the sheets flat. His gaze fell immediately on two large photographs. The first was of a man lying on rough ground. He was wearing shabby black denims, a ragged grey hoodie and dirty trainers. In his hand was a small orange container. The second showed him in close-up, his mouth open, drool trickling on to his chin. Sightless eyes stared out of a chalk-white face.

Marek skimmed the article. An officer from the Drugs Squad was telling the reporter about the street dealers who sold benzodiazepine as Valium. At a pound per tablet, it was within the reach of most users in the way heroin wasn't. But what the pills usually contained was etizolam, which was stronger. It also took longer to take effect, leading the user to think he needed more to get a high. The net result was an overdose, often fatal. The officer's bet was that the lab would find etizolam in the white capsules scattered across the grass. He concluded with a chilling warning. Benzos would soon be a thing of the past, as benzodiazepine was about to be overtaken by something more lethal, blowing in from the US. The latest designer drug, fentanyl, a synthetic opioid up to a hundred times stronger than morphine, and which used to be added to heroin, was now being added to cocaine. It was a worrying trend, he added, as cocaine is a party drug. Doing a line of it laced with fentanyl could kill you. His final comment was that Dundee – not Glasgow – was now the drugs-death capital of Europe, having taken over from that city the previous year.

Marek was turning to the editorial when a shadow fell across the page. He glanced up. A man was standing with his back to him, gazing at Burns's statue. Although he couldn't see the face, Marek recognised the slouch, and the back of the head with its grey tonsure. He waited until the man had moved off, then gulped his coffee, folded his paper and pushed his chair back.

He knew where Gilie Wallace was headed, and he took a different route. They met where they couldn't easily be seen, behind the statue of Queen Victoria on the other side of the Galleries. The place was deserted, except for a single car parked in front of the building.

'Let's cut to the chase, Gilie,' Marek said. 'What have you got for me?'

Gilie gave a little laugh. 'Always the same with you, son. No foreplay.'

Marek waited, folding and unfolding the newspaper. Gilie liked to keep him guessing, and he had no choice but to go along with it.

Gilie scratched behind his ear. 'It's the Lodge,' he said finally.

'Which Lodge?'

'The one on Guthrie Street.'

'There's a Masonic Lodge there?'

'Aye, son. And word is, they've got something nasty in their woodshed.'

'What's this got to do with the contraband?'

'Maybe nothing. Maybe everything.'

'You're talking in riddles.'

Gilie tapped him on the arm. 'I'm giving you the scoop of a lifetime, ken. And you're behaving like a numpty.'

Marek gazed at the double wooden doors, which opened automatically into the Galleries whenever anyone approached. He wondered if Gilie was trying to make a monkey out of him. But the man had always delivered in the past.

'That's all I can tell you, Marek. Except that there's an opening.' He glanced around but they were alone. 'The archivist buggered off suddenly, so there's a vacancy. If you get a move on, you'll be in with a good chance.'

'Don't you have to be a Freemason to work there?'

'Ach away. You're poking about in their library, nothing more. You don't even need to know the handshake.'

'How do you know there's a vacancy?'

He looked pointedly at Marek's newspaper. 'It's in today's *Courier*, son,' he said, with heavy irony. 'They're advertising for a replacement. Part-time, ken, so that should suit you.'

An archivist. Marek had been undercover as an archivist before, and knew enough about the job to blag his way in.

'This could be more than you're bargaining for,' Gilie said, studying him openly.

'I'm not bargaining.'

He leant forward and said softly, 'Watch yourself in there, Marek.'
He made the sign of the cross. 'Today is Friday the thirteenth.'

An hour later, Marek was on Guthrie Street, leaning against the
bell. He'd have missed the place, taking it for a slightly worn-out-
looking stone-built house, had he not seen the pillars topped with
globes, and the golden set square and compasses engraved on the
glass above the door. And the words '*SIT LUX ET LUX FUIT*'.
As he heard the bell jangle deep inside the building, he wondered
why there were thick bars on the ground-floor windows.

He'd had a quick discussion with his boss, who'd signed off on
the investigation, telling him to uncover whatever he could about
the Lodge, never mind the drugs or whatever it is, see if you can
find out about the rituals, and whether they do wear pinnies and
roll up their trouser legs. It amazed Marek that in this day and age
there was so much interest – no, downright fascination – with
Freemasonry. It was just a boys' club, wasn't it?

The door opened. A petite blonde in a long-sleeved dress pat-
terned in blues and greens peered at him over her owl-like glasses.
She frowned, dropping her gaze to his light-blue suit. He wished
now that he'd worn a tie instead of undoing the top button of
his shirt.

'Yes?' she said.

'I'm here about the archivist's position. My name's Franek
Filarski.' When she said nothing, he held up the *Courier*. 'It's
advertised in today's.'

She took off her glasses slowly. 'If you'd read that advert carefully, Mr—?'

'Filarski.'

'Filarski, you'd have seen that we ask applicants to send in a CV.'

He smiled ruefully. 'I did see that, but I thought that if I came along and you decided I was a suitable candidate, I could send it on afterwards.'

'Is that how you normally apply for jobs?'

'I don't normally apply for jobs.'

'So why are you applying for this one?'

He decided to appeal to her sense of decency. 'I need the money.'

Her expression softened. 'Would you like to come in?'

'Thank you,' he said gratefully.

He stepped into a hallway and then into a wide, brightly painted room. It was thickly carpeted in a deep grey, and dominated by a glittering glass-fronted case containing what looked like medals. Immediately to the right was a desk. Papers were spread across the surface in what he suspected was a precisely arranged system.

'I take it you have experience, Mr Filarski.'

'Please call me Franek. And you are?'

'Miss Ferguson.'

'It's nice to meet you,' he said, unable to tear his gaze from her face. She had huge eyes and the kind of flawless complexion women would kill for.

'Can you tell me about your most recent work as an archivist?'

'It was for the *Courier*,' he said, tapping the paper. He'd agreed the cover story with his boss. If anyone checked up, the office would be prepared.

'And how long were you there?'

'About two years.'

'And why aren't you working for them now?'

He'd rehearsed these answers at the office. 'It was a short-term contract. I finished setting up their new system, and then I left.'

He had her interest now. She gestured to one of the chairs. He waited until she'd taken her seat before sitting down himself.

'Tell me about this new system,' she said.

He ruffled his hair. 'It involved setting up a filing system. But my main task was to create a searchable online database.'

Her eyes widened. 'That's what we need here.' She thought for a while, drumming her manicured fingers on the table. 'Look, if you can give me the name and number of your boss there, I can give him a quick ring.'

'Of course,' he said, pulling a biro out of his jacket.

She pushed a piece of paper towards him. 'You understand that I can't take you on without a check.'

'Absolutely.' He decided on a gamble. 'If you feel you want to wait until I send in a CV, I will totally understand.'

'No, no,' she said quickly. 'Ideally, we'd like to have someone start right away.'

He scribbled down his boss's details.

She took the sheet, and then looked at the phone, biting her lip.

He guessed she wanted to have the conversation in privacy. 'I'll wait outside, shall I?' he said, getting to his feet.

She smiled for the first time. The effect was stunning. 'That won't be necessary, Mr Filarski.' She glanced towards the cabinet. 'Why don't you have a look at our jewels while I make the call?'

'Jewels?'

'Masonic medals. Masons call them jewels.'

'Oh, yes. Thank you.'

The cabinet was crammed full of what looked like war medals, some with ribbons, but on closer inspection were Masonic paraphernalia. There were rings, wristwatches, the familiar set square and compasses, stars, Templar crosses and a host of other regalia that meant nothing to him. The large number of items and their potential value might explain the bars on the windows and the serious-looking burglar alarm. He wondered idly if the Lodge was open to the public.

As he studied the jewels, he tried to hear what was being said. But Miss Ferguson kept her voice low, and all he caught was the question, 'Can I trust him to be discreet?'

'Yes, thank you,' she said finally. 'You've been most helpful.'

He pretended to be greatly interested in the display, and leant forward for a better look.

'Mr Filarski?'

He turned and hurried over.

Her radiant smile told him that the call had been successful. 'I'm delighted to be able to tell you that we can offer you employment.'

'That's marvellous.'

'I'll still need your CV for our files. Could you perhaps bring in a copy when you're next here?'

'Of course.'

'The hourly rate will be as advertised. You do know it's part-time?'

'Yes, I understand that.'

'I'll have the paperwork ready for next time you're here. Or someone else will. I work part-time, too. So when can you start?'

He puffed out his cheeks. 'Now?' he said hopefully.

'Excellent.' She got to her feet, smoothing down her skirt. 'Let me show you our archive.'

It was a good sign that she was prepared to trust him without a CV. But, then, he was trusting her to keep to her word and take him on without a contract.

She opened the door behind her.

The dark, wood-panelled room had that old-paper smell he remembered from his days poking about in library archives. The source was the large number of cardboard boxes crammed with ledgers and dusty papers. There were so many that boxes had been stacked on top of others, crushing the contents of those underneath. None of the boxes had been marked up so there was no way of telling what they contained.

He tried to keep the dismay out of his voice. 'Where do you wish me to start, Miss Ferguson?'

Her tone was brisk. 'We have several membership-roll books that we'd like to digitise. Our Lodge is relatively small with not many members, but the records go back a long way and there's much to be done. The roll books are from the nineteenth century, so there's no problem with data protection. The majority of entries are perfectly legible, but if you run into difficulties do come and fetch me. You need to set up a database, and enter the name and date of initiation. And age, address and occupation. And anything else that you feel should go in.'

'And I work there?' Marek said, nodding at the long table by the window. An open laptop lay on the surface.

'You'll be able to spread everything out. And the gloves are in that box on the floor. You should find a pair your size.' She studied him. 'You're not put off by the enormity of the task?'

'Not at all,' he said, with feigned enthusiasm.

'After you've completed the database, I'll go over what else we need. Basically, it's to set up a filing system for the letters and diaries. There are newspaper cuttings and periodicals too. And minutes of meetings.'

'And I file them where?'

'We've still to get round to storage. I'm thinking acid-free folders and boxes.'

'And I take it you want an electronic record of the letters and other papers, too? A database searchable by keyword?'

She smiled warmly. 'Exactly.' She paused. 'You've come in the nick of time. Murray, our archivist, failed to turn up on Wednesday. And then we got an email from him yesterday, saying he was leaving.' A shadow crossed her face as she surveyed the room. 'It's my responsibility to organise this,' she murmured, as though speaking to herself. 'And I *mustn't* fail.'

The slight note of panic in her voice didn't go unnoticed.

'You won't fail, Miss Ferguson. And I won't fail you,' he said, with determination. 'You know, I really should have sent in that CV.' He raised an eyebrow. 'I owe you an apology.'

She spoke with her head lowered. 'I don't need an apology. I need a gin and tonic.'

And so do I, he thought, gazing through the window at the bars.

Dania was at her desk, reading through Chirnside's report on Cameron Affleck in more detail when her phone rang.

'DI Gorska,' she said.

'Dania?'

She recognised the voice immediately. It was the Polish consul general, a serious, angular man with a close-trimmed beard. Since she'd met him a couple of years earlier, they had become firm friends.

'How are you, sir?' she said, speaking in Polish.

'I'm fine. And you?'

'Very well.' She was tempted to add, 'And very busy.' But he'd know that.

'I'm calling to ask you for a favour. You know that November the eleventh this year will be a special occasion.'

She smiled. 'Indeed, sir. Every Pole knows that.'

'I was wondering if we could book you for a concert here in Edinburgh. At the consulate. It will be for anyone who wishes to attend, but I expect the audience will consist mainly of Poles.'

She felt a warm glow. 'I'd be honoured. Is there anything in particular you'd like me to play?'

'Have a think about it and we can meet to discuss it. I'll be in touch again. Goodbye. Oh, and don't forget to bring Marek. He's always a great favourite with the ladies.' He rang off.

The room had fallen silent. She looked up to see them watching her. 'What?' she said.

'Didn't know you could speak Russian, ma'am,' Hamish said.

'I was speaking Polish.'

'Sounded like Russian to me.' He frowned. 'Was it a phone call from home? I hope everything's okay back there.'

'It was the Polish consul general. They want me to play at a concert on November the eleventh.'

'Armistice Day?' Honor said quizzically. 'What are you going to play? Chopin's Funeral March?'

'Actually, no. Poles celebrate rather than commemorate November the eleventh. Poland gained its independence on that date. In nineteen eighteen. So this year is the centenary.'

They were looking at her with interest. 'Independence?' Honor said. 'Who from?'

Dania was used to this reaction. 'For over a century, Poland was partitioned by the three empires, Russian, Prussian and Austro-Hungarian. When the Great War ended, it raised its head above the parapet again. Not for long, though,' she added ruefully.

'I guess a lot of vodka gets drunk,' Honor said, grinning.

'You have no idea.'

'So what will you play, ma'am?'

Dania exhaled noisily. 'Chopin. That goes without saying. Possibly his Grande Polonaise Brillante, Opus Twenty-two. It's better with an orchestral accompaniment, although it can be played solo. And maybe Liszt's Liebestraum Number Three. After all, Hungary got its independence back at the same time.'

They were nodding slowly, in apparent agreement.

'But I'll have to include some Paderewski. He became the prime minister.'

'As well as being a composer?' Honor said.

'And a renowned pianist.'

'Crikey. Our prime minister can't do any of those things.'

'Don't take this the wrong way,' Hamish said, 'but have you got the time to practise with everything that's on your plate just now?'

'Good point. But part of the secret of playing at concert level is having a good memory. Many pieces are so complicated that you can't keep looking at the sheet and then down at the keys the whole time. You have to memorise the notes. Fortunately, I can still remember most of the music I've played at concerts.'

'Aye, but that can't be the whole story.'

'No, obviously you do have to exercise the fingers greatly. I'll just have to ramp up.'

Hamish grinned. 'Piano practice in the wee hours of the morning, eh, ma'am? What'll the neighbours say?'

But Dania wasn't listening. She was thinking back to the last time she'd played at the consulate. Most of the Poles in Edinburgh would attend. And some Scottish dignitaries. She twisted a lock of hair nervously round a finger. November the eleventh. Four months away. Plenty of time.

'So where are we on the child found in the doocot?' Jackie Ireland said.

Dania was in the woman's office, giving her an update. Where the DCI was concerned, it was always best to get straight to the point. 'The doocot is owned by a Gregor Affleck,' she said.

'Gregor?'

'You know him, ma'am?'

'I've met him at the odd fundraiser. He's well connected.'

Dania waited, but when nothing more was forthcoming, she

continued, 'The remains are those of his son, Cameron. He went missing thirteen years ago.'

The DCI drew her brows together. 'I've met Ross and Kenny, but I had no idea there was a missing son,' she murmured. 'And you've a positive ID?'

'We confirmed it through DNA. Kimmie fast-tracked it. She asked CAHID for a sample of bone from the remains, and got it within the hour.' Dania smiled. 'I don't know where we'd be without her.'

'Australia's loss is our gain. So what have you uncovered?'

As succinctly as possible, Dania filled her superior in on what she knew about Cameron and how he had come to be missing.

Jackie Ireland folded her arms. 'What do you think the motive was?'

'We thought ransom, but I took a closer look at Cameron's file. No ransom note was ever received. DI Chirnside couldn't come up with a motive.'

'You think it was someone the Afflecks knew?'

'It must have been. Who else would have known where the key to the doocot was kept? But now that we have a firm ID, I can ramp up the investigation.'

'How do you intend to proceed?'

'I need to get a list of friends and acquaintances who may have visited the house.'

'It'll be a long list.'

'My gut instinct is that there's a better way to approach this, but until I know what it is, I have no choice but to start interviewing the Afflecks' friends. There's also the housekeeper, Mrs Spence.'

'Ah, yes, housekeepers can be a mine of information. What about Ross and Kenny? Have you talked to them?'

Dania shook her head. 'I've not got that far.'

'You'll catch them at the museum. They practically live there.'

'That's the one on Guthrie Street?'

'It's a family business.' She smiled enigmatically. 'You should get yourself over there and see what they get up to. It's a real eye-opener.'

'I'll take DC Randall. There may be some stuffed cats.'

Honor was crazy about cats. Although Dania had seen none in the girl's flat in Dundee, she happened to know that when Honor had worked in London, her apartment was full of them. She imagined them purring and weaving their bodies round her skinny legs.

'You know, Dania, before I met the Afflecks, I did wonder if they were that kind of family. You know the type. Stern patriarch, ruling over a dynasty. Sons doing what they're told.'

'And are they?' Dania said, when the woman seemed disinclined to continue.

'I can't make up my mind. Go and talk to them. Then *you* can tell *me*.'

CHAPTER 8

Dania drew up outside the house on Albany Road. She was debating with herself whether she shouldn't have joined Honor and Hamish, who were back at Inchture, showing Cameron's photo around. If they were lucky, someone would remember having seen the boy thirteen years before. If they were very lucky, they might even have seen him with someone. And if they were miraculously lucky, they might even know the name of this someone. But where murder cases were concerned, Dania didn't believe in either luck or miracles.

It was early afternoon, and the iron gates were standing wide, suggesting that the men were out. Which was exactly what she wanted. Her intention was to have a woman-to-woman chat with the housekeeper. And woman-to-woman chats were best done when there were no men around.

Dania made her way up the drive, breathing in the fragrant scents and marvelling at the variety and sheer number of plants. With no let-up in the weather, most were wilting in the heat, their petals curling, or dropping off altogether. Her own flat had no garden, just a view from the kitchen window on to an alley full of dustbins. She'd splashed out and bought cacti and spider plants, which she'd scattered around. But she didn't have Marek's green fingers, and they were slowly dying of boredom.

She strolled past the fountain with its smiling dolphins and took the steps up to the front door. Before she could ring the bell, she heard the bolts being drawn back. The door opened.

'Hello, Mrs Spence,' Dania said warmly. 'Do you remember me?'

'Aye, right enough. You're the Polish detective. I'm afraid the men are up at the museum.'

'Actually, it's you I've come to see. Could we have a chat?'

The woman's eyes widened. 'Me?' She ran her hands down her pleated cotton skirt. 'Whatever for?'

'You'll have heard by now that we found Cameron's remains at Inchture.'

She lowered her head and nodded.

'I know that you were interviewed when he disappeared, but it would help me greatly if you could go through it with me again. If you've time now,' Dania added hastily.

Mrs Spence looked hard at her. Then her expression cleared. 'Aye, of course. Come in.'

She bolted the door while Dania waited in the hall, fighting the urge to look at the hovering black eagle.

'Do you mind if we go into the kitchen?' Mrs Spence said brightly. 'I could make a cup of tea and we could have a blether while I do the ironing.'

'That would be kind of you.'

She led the way along a wide corridor and into a spacious, modern kitchen. Everything was spotless, which Dania guessed was down to the housekeeper, who seemed to be the only domestic the Afflecks employed. Something she needed to check.

The woman busied herself getting the kettle on and arranging crockery, giving Dania the opportunity to peer through the window. The back garden was smaller than the front, but still large enough to hold an army and a circus. Immediately outside, circular flowerbeds were planted with roses, their blooms falling apart. Behind them, a sprinkler threw rings of water on to the grass. In the distance, beyond the acres of lawn hemmed by privet hedges, was a large wooden structure. Gregor had referred to it as a summerhouse. Dania would have called it a pavilion. It was painted in pink and yellow, with long windows on all sides. An ideal place for summer parties. She imagined the fragrant Davina in a floating chiffon dress, serving champagne cocktails to her guests.

'Milk and sugar, Inspector?'

Dania glanced round. 'Just milk, please.'

'I'll put your tea here,' Mrs Spence said, indicating the wicker rocking chair. She set the cup and saucer on the table.

Dania sat in the chair, sipping carefully. The tea was hot and strong, exactly as she liked it.

The woman lifted a spectral-white shirt from the linen basket. 'So, what would you like to ask me, Inspector?'

'It's about the day of Cameron's disappearance. That was June the twelfth, a Sunday. The officer who interviewed you reported that you weren't here in the morning.' This was deliberately mis-represented, but it was a tactic that usually prompted people into talking. It worked with Mrs Spence.

'That's not strictly true. I was away all day.' She lifted the huge steaming iron and set it down on the shirt. 'My mother was ail-ing. She's since passed on, God rest her soul. Mr Gregor gave me the whole Sunday off.' She passed the iron over the shirt, with rapid, practised movements, sending up a faint cloud of steam. 'He's good that way.'

'What time did you leave for your mother's? Can you remember?'

'Aye, well, it was after my husband and I had walked back from early-morning church. I had to take the bus, so I reckon I would have left by eight.'

'And was there anyone else here during the day? Servants, perhaps?'

She stiffened. 'There *are* no servants, Inspector. I do everything. And I'm well capable for it.'

'I just wondered. This is a big house.'

'I do all the cooking and cleaning,' she said, with quiet dignity.

Dania took a gulp of tea. 'And who cooked that Sunday you were at your mother's?'

'I prepared a cold collation the evening before and left it in the fridge.'

'What was the routine here on a Sunday?'

Mrs Spence had moved on to the sleeves. 'They'd go to the kirk early. Then they'd spend the morning in quiet contemplation. I say "they", but it was sometimes only Mrs Affleck and the boys. On occasion, Mr Gregor would go straight to the museum because it's open on a Sunday. He'd stay only a wee while, though.' She set the iron on its stand and stared at the wall. 'But that Sunday, he was minded to take the older boys with him. He'd told everyone the night before that they were now old enough to see where they'd soon be working. I remember the wee rammy over dinner.'

Dania set down the teacup. 'They had an argument?'

'I was clearing the plates away. The older one, Ross, was whining that he didn't want to go. He wanted to play football with his mates. But there was no contest. When Mr Gregor decides something is going to happen' – she glanced at Dania – 'you can set your watch by it.'

'What are the boys like?'

Her mouth twisted. 'I'd give Ross a wide berth. He's a nasty piece of work, and no mistake.' She shook her head. 'I've no idea how he got like that. I've watched them since they were bairns. Aye, he's the cuckoo in the nest.'

'What about the other son, Kenny?'

'He's a wee bitty younger. He seemed willing enough to give up his time that Sunday. He loved the museum, and those animals. Aye, when he thought no one was looking, he'd be off to stroke that leopard in the living room. He'd fetch a chair and climb up.' She smiled fondly. 'He and Cameron were always getting up to no good together, despite the difference in years. I mind now that on one occasion, when Mr Gregor was away, they took a wee dook in the fountain.' She shook out another shirt and laid it on the ironing board. 'Cameron was such a happy bairn, despite his condition.'

'And Mrs Affleck didn't mind Ross and Kenny going that Sunday?'

'She always stood by her man, she did. Never contradicted him in front of the lads. They were very much in love, even after all those years of marriage,' she added wistfully.

Dania listened to the hypnotic hiss of the iron as it ran over the shirt. 'And did you return in the evening? From your mother's?'

'Aye, to wash up and generally get things ready for the following day. After that, I took the bus to my flat in Blackness.'

'You don't live here?'

'I don't, no.' She rearranged the shirt. 'When I got back here, of course, the polis were all over the place. Poor Mrs Affleck was in a right state.' She shook her head sadly. 'She never got over it. Passed away a few months later.' She gazed at the wall. 'That was a bad time for me, too. I had problems of my own to deal with.'

Dania was tempted to ask what they were but the finality in the woman's tone stopped her. It might well have been the death of her mother, and everything that followed. 'What do you think happened to Cameron, Mrs Spence?'

'I've thought about it many times. He wasn't the kind of lad to wander off. But he must have. There's no other explanation.'

'Do you think he opened that front door?'

'Or he went out the back.' She glanced at the kitchen door. It was solid wood, but with an ordinary lock and no bolts. And the key was in the lock.

'But the front door was found open.'

'Was it? I suppose Mrs Affleck must have left it like that when she arrived home with the boy.'

'If Cameron left the house on his own, how would he come to be locked in a doocot at the other end of Dundee?'

The woman clutched at the crucifix round her neck. 'It's a complete mystery.' She gazed at Dania with troubled eyes. 'You know, Inspector, I've often thought that, had I not gone to my mother's, I would have been here to prevent him leaving the house. I blame myself for what happened.'

'Can you think of anyone who might have put Cameron in that doocot?' Dania said gently. 'Anyone who had a grudge against Mr Gregor?'

'Aye, well, he knows a lot of people.'

'In the taxidermy business?'

'Not so much there. In fact, I don't think he knows any other taxidermists locally. No, I meant at the Lodge. He's a Freemason. So are his two sons. The younger one is an apprentice, mind.'

'A Freemason? How do you know? I thought they kept that sort of thing to themselves.'

Mrs Spence's mouth formed into a smile. 'There's not much that gets past a housekeeper, Inspector.'

Dania smiled back. 'I'm sure there isn't.'

'Housekeepers, at least the ones who've been around as long as I have, become invisible. I hear them blethering. And when they go to their meetings, they take their black briefcases with them. All their regalia is inside.' Her smile widened. 'The boys never put things away when they return from their Lodge dinners. They expect me to do it.'

'What sort of regalia?'

'Collars, cufflinks, white gloves. That sort of thing. And the apron, of course.'

'And is your husband a Freemason?'

'Sandy? Goodness, no.'

'He must miss you, with these long hours you keep.'

'Ach, he has his own work to keep him busy. He runs his own business,' she added, pride in her voice. 'Makes children's toys. Does a lot of work for the Lodge members. Aye, they keep him well occupied. Which is a good thing.'

'There's something I need to ask you, Mrs Spence. It's to do with the key.'

The woman paused in her ironing. 'Which key would that be?'

'The one to the doocot. Mr Affleck showed me the cupboard where the keys are kept. He said there was only the one key for the doocot. I'd like to know who had the opportunity to take it from that cupboard.'

She had the woman's attention now. Mrs Spence set down the iron. 'Apart from myself and the family, I couldn't say,' she said slowly.

'Mrs Affleck used to hold garden parties. Could her guests have seen her or Mr Affleck take the key for the summerhouse?'

'Aye, right enough, they could.' She paused. 'I mind the odd occasion when we were running late and guests had arrived, and the summerhouse was locked.' Her eyes narrowed. 'They would have seen Mrs Affleck take the key.'

'Would you be able to draw up a list? Of people who came to the house? It might be difficult after thirteen years, I'm afraid.'

Mrs Spence looked at her appreciatively. 'I used to write out the invitations. I still do. I have the names and addresses in my book. Leave me your details and I'll send the information over.'

'That would be really helpful.' Dania handed the woman her card. 'And now I should leave you to get on with your work.'

'This is my Friday-afternoon job,' she said, folding the ironed shirt. 'White shirts. The men wear them to work.' She nodded. 'And to Lodge meetings, of course.'

'Could I ask a favour?' Dania said suddenly. 'I'd like to look round the back garden, if I may.'

'Of course. Take as long as you like. Can I leave you to let yourself out afterwards? There's a side gate that takes you on to the front drive.'

'I'm sure I'll find it. And thank you for the tea.'

'I don't know if I've been of any use, Inspector.'

'You have. And if anything else comes to mind, anything at all, please get in touch.'

'Aye, I will,' the woman said. 'The back door's unlocked,' she added helpfully.

Dania let herself out, noting how easily – and quietly – the kitchen door opened and closed.

She guessed that Mrs Spence would be watching her, so she made a show of leaning over to smell the roses, and then sauntered past the sprinkler and down towards the summerhouse. She took the steps up to it, glad of the shade, and peeked in through the windows at the elegant furniture. From this distance, she could still see the back of the house. But the living room was at the front, so no one would spot an intruder creeping up the side of the garden in the shadow of the hedges and entering the house by the kitchen door.

Beyond the summerhouse was more lawn, which ended abruptly at a high stone wall. A large garden shed had been erected in front of it. It was made of dark, weathered wood, and was in good repair. The padlock was one of those heavy-duty types. It wouldn't have taken her long to pick it as she always had her tools with her, but it might be hard to explain what she was up to should Mrs Spence surprise her in the act. She peered through the grubby side window, noticing, among the gloves and tools, a petrol-operated lawn mower and an electrical hedge-trimmer. It seemed highly unlikely that Gregor or his sons would work in the grounds. They would employ several gardeners for the front and back, especially in summer and autumn. As she retraced her steps and slipped the latch on the side gate, Dania concluded that they'd need an odd-job man as well. After all, a gardener wouldn't oper-ate the brazing equipment tucked away in the corner of the shed.

CHAPTER 9

'Ach away, man,' Jamie said. 'You're never working in a Masonic Lodge.'

Marek spread his hands in a gesture of supplication. 'I tell you, it's absolutely true.'

They were in the Staropolska, a newly opened Polish bar and restaurant on the Perth Road. The interior was light and airy, decorated in the Polish colours of red and white, which set off the monochrome pre-war photographs of Poland lining the walls. The first time Marek and Danka had eaten there, they'd entertained themselves trying to work out where the photos had been taken. They'd managed all but one, which continued to defeat them. The proprietor, a well-upholstered man who was also the chef – never trust a thin chef, Marek had warned his sister – refused to enlighten them. Eventually, seeing them arguing, he took pity and informed them that it was the railway station in the magnificent city of Lwów. When Marek had pointed out that the city was no longer in Poland but had 'moved' to Ukraine and was now known as Lviv, a look of anger had crossed the man's face. Lwów, he'd said, *had* always been and *would* always be Polish. Not wanting to antagonise a chef, they'd wisely left it at that.

Marek usually met up with Jamie at the Dundee Contemporary Arts café but had decided it was time to introduce his friend to

the delights of Polish cuisine. He'd advised him to have no breakfast and only a light lunch.

'I take it you haven't jacked in the job at the *Courier*,' Jamie
said, lifting the glass of Scotch to his lips. 'This is you going in
undercover, right?'

'Right.'

'So which Lodge is this?'

'Guthrie Street.'

'I know the one. I was once asked over there to take photos
for their album.'

'And did you go into their main hall?'

'Aye, I did.' Jamie grinned. 'There wasn't much time to look
around. They were all lined up in their chains and aprons and
that, and I had to get on with it. Then I was escorted out pronto.'
He tapped the side of his nose. 'They were about to have a meeting.' He sipped his Scotch. 'What are you doing there?'

'I'm working as an archivist.'

'What are you expecting to find? The names of the good
citizens of Dundee who are also Masons?'

'Something else. But I'm keeping it under my hat, as the
Brits say.'

'I thought it might be that. I don't see you being into old
records, right enough.'

Marek shrugged. 'The correspondence is interesting. And the
papers have beautiful letterheads.'

'Square and compasses?'

'Temples with columns.' He held Jamie's gaze. 'By the way, it
goes without saying. Not a word about this to anyone, okay?'

'Scout's honour,' Jamie said, lifting his hand.

Marek smiled. He could rely on Jamie to keep his mouth
shut. They went back a long way and had worked on several
features together.

'There's a lady on the desk there,' Marek said.

'Ach, I know that expression on your face. I'm guessing she's a stunner, am I right?'

Marek threw him a crooked smile. 'Right. I've not met one who's as beautiful. She's got huge green eyes. The kind you could find yourself falling into.'

'Looks as if you're smitten. Is she married?'

'Unfortunately, yes.'

He looked at Marek with interest. 'What's she like, then? As a person.'

'Hard to say. She won't address me by my first name. Behaviour like that makes a man lose faith in himself. Anyway, I was surprised they employ women.'

'They won't let her into the main hall, you can put money on that.'

'Did you get a chance to peek into the other rooms?' Marek said guardedly.

'Unfortunately not. There's an upstairs. And a kitchen. For their Lodge dinners, I reckon. I think the building used to be a private house.'

'How do private houses become Masonic Lodges?'

'Beats me.' Jamie played with his glass. 'You met any of the Masons yet?'

Marek shook his head.

'They raised a small fortune a year or two back. Paid for that new hospital extension.'

'That was the Masons?'

'Aye, as Lodges go, this one's been particularly successful over the years.'

They lapsed into silence, and then Jamie said, 'Tell me if I'm out of order, pal, but something's bothering you. You're a wee bit jumpy.'

Marek stared into his beer. Jamie had always been able to see right through him. He was like Danka in that respect. 'I keep wondering if we're going to find another abducted girl.' He shook his head. 'Those poor parents. I don't know how you get over something like that.'

'You don't get over it, Marek. You adjust to it.'

'I can't get it out of my mind.'

Jamie frowned. 'Has there been another incident? I didn't catch the news.'

'No. Nothing.'

'Do you think the police are any closer to finding this man? Your sister must be working on the case.'

'We can't talk about it with her. You know the rules.'

'Aye, of course. But do you think they're trying to flush him out?'

'How do you mean?'

'Think about it. How does the killer find them?'

'He sees them. Follows them. Discovers where they live?'

'Possible, but a bit time-consuming, I reckon.'

'Maybe he knows them. He could be a teacher.' Marek paused. 'Or he gets them to come to him, like the Pied Piper.'

'Although, these days, he'd use social media.' Jamie snorted. 'Kids are never off it, are they? Maybe he's one of those people who pretends he's a girl and uses a chatroom to make contact. It's just an idea. Your sister might be working on that as a theory. Talking of which, what time did you say she was joining us?'

'It's not like her to be late on a Friday night. Something must have come up. Shall we have another drink while we wait?'

'Aye, go on, then.'

Marek was calling the waitress over when the door opened and Danka breezed in. She looked around and, seeing him, her face broke into a smile.

'Sorry I've kept you waiting,' she said, hurrying over.

'Danka,' Marek said, getting to his feet, 'this is my old friend, Jamie Reid. He and I used to work together at the *Courier*. Jamie, my sister, Dania Gorska. Detective Inspector Dania Gorska, I should say.'

There was more than a flicker of interest in Jamie's eyes. Marek smiled to himself. It happened every time. People either clammed up or showered her with questions. But Danka was used to that.

'It's a pleasure, Inspector,' Jamie said, smiling warmly.

'Please call me Dania. I'm no longer on duty.'

'Marek's told me a lot about you.'

'Oh?' she said, taking the chair Marek had brought over. 'And you're a journalist?'

'I'm a photographer. I work for myself now.' He grinned at Marek. 'But your brother and I haven't stopped being best pals.'

'And drinking buddies,' Marek said. 'What I can get you, Danka?'

'Żubrówka.'

'Of course. Why did I even ask?'

'I hear you're working on the case of the kidnapped girls,' Jamie said to her, adding quickly, 'I saw your name in the paper.'

'I was collared by a member of the press. Normally, I do my best to avoid them.'

'That must be an occupational hazard. I reckon they must lie in wait for you.'

'It's their job, I suppose.'

After a pause, he said, 'Marek told me about the remains found in that doocot.'

'It's been on the six o'clock news.' She looked at her watch. 'Which was fifteen minutes ago, so I can tell you both now. The remains are those of Cameron Affleck.'

'Affleck?' Marek said sharply. Just that afternoon, he'd been wading through a box of nineteenth-century ledgers full of records of Afflecks.

'The name is familiar?' she said.

He didn't want Danka to know where he was working. 'There's a museum by that name, isn't there?'

'Aye, that's right,' Jamie said. 'The Affleck Natural History Museum. It's on Guthrie Street.'

'Have you been there?' she said.

'There was a feature on the place last year. To do with a bear.'

'One they'd stuffed?'

'I was asked by a reporter to go along with him. There'd been the usual brouhaha about endangered species, and he reckoned it might make a good story. Turned out it was perfectly legit, and the Afflecks had the paperwork they needed to prove it.' He grinned. 'The reporter was sent away with a flea in his ear. But I was allowed to take photos of the displays for their publicity.'

'So where is this bear now?' Marek asked.

Jamie pulled a face. 'Ach, who knows? It was a private collector who brought it in. It's not on public display.'

'What did it look like?'

'Unbelievably lifelike. It was baring its fangs. I had nightmares for weeks afterwards,' he added, with feeling. 'I took a few photos of their workshop. It's full of strange-looking stuff.' He turned the glass in his hands, studying Danka. 'So this Cameron Affleck? Is he related to the museum people?'

'Gregor Affleck, the museum owner, is his father. He's been looking for his son for the past thirteen years. He's been digging all over Dundee, hoping to find him.'

'Hold on,' Jamie said slowly. 'Digging, you said? I think I saw him once. It was way up near Inveraldie.'

'When was this?'

'Now you're asking. Earlier this year. Aye, I was driving north.' He frowned. 'It was in the middle of nowhere. I mentioned it later to one of my mates. He told me the man is a common sight. No matter the weather, he goes out and digs and digs, looking for his lad. My mate didn't know his name but he'd seen him several times. It was pitiful to watch, he said. One time, he saw him stop and lean on his spade, crying like a bairn.' Jamie gazed into his

Scotch. 'And all these years, the lad was in the doocot.' He shook his head. 'Losing a child must be the worst thing.'

'Have you got any children?' Danka said gently.

'Me? No.' He shrugged. 'Pam and I haven't been married long enough.'

'Will she be joining us later?'

'She sends her apologies. She's just left the city.'

'Pam works as a wedding planner,' Marek said.

'That sounds interesting,' Danka said, smiling.

Jamie downed the rest of his whisky. 'It's how we met. I was doing a photoshoot.'

'So where is this event she's doing?'

'Ach, some swanky hotel up in the Highlands. She's making sure everything goes according to plan. I'm doing the photographs for this one, so I'll be taking the train there first thing tomorrow.'

'Jamie's always in great demand,' Marek said.

'I'll give you a special rate when you finally tie the matrimonial knot,' he said, laughing.

'Matrimonial knot? Matrimonial noose, you mean.'

'Don't be like that, pal. Marriage is great.'

'I'm joking. I fully intend to settle down one day and have a dozen children.'

'So, what do you think this lad was doing in that doocot?' Jamie said, turning to Danka. 'The Afflecks live at the other end of town from Inchture.'

'We're following various lines of investigation,' she said, which Marek recognised as her standard response when the public were asking questions they shouldn't. She looked at Jamie with curiosity. 'How do you know where the Afflecks live?'

'I did a photoshoot there years ago,' he said quickly. He seemed flustered. 'I mind it was for one of those homes-and-gardens magazines, I forget the name now.'

'It's certainly an impressive house.'

Marek took a gulp of beer. 'By the way, Danka, I had a call earlier from the consul general.'

'You, too?'

'So he's been in touch about the recital? He wants me to come along.'

'A recital?' Jamie said.

'My sister's a concert pianist. I mean, she could be, she plays so brilliantly.'

A look of awe appeared in Jamie's eyes. 'Aye, really? I've always wanted to play the piano, but never had the opportunity.' He gazed at Danka. 'If you could take one piece of music to a desert island, which would it be?'

'Chopin's Nocturne, Opus Twenty-seven, Number Two.' She smiled. 'There's no contest.'

He nodded. 'I'll check it out on YouTube.'

'If you do, find the recording by Rubinstein. No one plays it the way he does.'

At that point, a girl came over and told them in Polish that their table was ready.

'Shall we eat?' Marek said, glancing at the others.

'Aye,' Jamie replied. He stood up and stretched. 'It's a first for me. I've never eaten in a Polish restaurant.'

'We come here because of the *sernik*.'

'Which is what, when it's out?'

'A baked cheesecake. The one they serve here is heavenly.' Marek closed his eyes. 'It's made with sugared orange peel.'

'Please tell me we're eating a main course first,' Jamie said, looking from one to the other nervously.

Marek caught Danka's eye, and they both laughed.

CHAPTER 10

'You were right, boss,' Honor said, yawning. 'There was nothing unusual on the A90 traffic cams. Or on the cameras on the other major roads. If the killer rapist was on them, we've no way of knowing. DI McFadden's been notified.'

Dania crossed her arms. 'Is there any blood in your alcohol stream, Honor?'

The girl grinned sheepishly. 'It was Friday night last night. I was off shift.'

'So was I, but I didn't drink so much that I'm falling asleep.'

'Boss! I didn't have *that* much.'

'Aye, right,' Hamish chipped in. 'That's not how I remember it.'

'You were there too?' Dania said.

'Someone has to keep an eye on this lass when she goes for a heavy bevvy.'

'Except you never bought a single round,' Honor said, with just enough mockery in her voice. 'I don't know any man who stays as close to a pound coin as you.'

'Cheers,' he said sourly.

'All right, shall we do some work?' Dania said. 'How did you get on showing Cameron's photo around Inchture?'

Honor shook her head. 'In a word, we got zippo. We made sure to point out the twist in his spine. But no one recognised him.'

'And those people were at Inchture thirteen years ago?'

'Most of them.'

'Then we'll have to try another approach. No surprise there.'

'We've got a preliminary forensic report on the doocot, ma'am. It came in yesterday afternoon.'

'Anything useful?'

Honor screwed up her face. 'The scene was too old. Nothing but dirt, feathers, rat droppings and pigeon muck. And old bits of straw and leaves, presumably brought in by the pigeons.'

'Footprints in the dirt?'

The girl shook her head. 'And they swept everything up and sifted it, in case there were hairs.'

'No traces of food? Crumbs?'

'The rats would have had it.'

'I wonder what happened to Cameron's hair,' Dania said, remembering the dark curls in the photo.

'We asked them that, ma'am, and they reckoned the rats would have made off with it for their nests.'

'How did the rats get in?'

'There was a wee hole in one of the corners. The owners didn't keep up the fabric of the place.'

'It's the motive that defeats me. If we could get a handle on that, we'll have taken a step forward.'

'How did you get on with the housekeeper?' Honor said, after a silence.

'She more or less confirmed what Gregor told me. But if the boy did leave on his own, he's more likely to have gone out through the kitchen. He'd have turned the key in the back door without any difficulty and left through the side gate. My money would be on that, if it weren't for the open front door.' She thought back to her visit. 'There's one thing we need to pursue, though. There's a garden shed, which has all kinds of heavy machinery. Including welding equipment.'

'Aha,' Hamish said knowingly.

'My guess is they have an odd-job man whose services they call upon.'

His gaze sharpened. 'An odd-job man might well have been known to the lad.'

'I wonder how old that welding equipment is. It might not have been there thirteen years ago.'

'And did the housekeeper say anything else?' Honor asked.

'She's drawing up a list of friends of the Afflecks.'

'Didn't DI Chirnside interview them at the time?'

'He did, but he didn't ask about the doocot. That's where we need to concentrate our efforts. Someone may have known where the key was kept.'

'If they do, they're unlikely to admit it.'

'It depends on how we ask the question. And I learnt something else from Mrs Spence. The Affleck men are all Freemasons.'

'Get away,' Honor said, with a disdainful smile. 'I thought there weren't any left.'

'You're thinking of the Illuminati, lass,' Hamish said serenely.

'Which one of you is on duty on Monday?' Dania said.

'I am,' Honor said.

'Then you and I are paying a visit to the museum. With luck, the Affleck men will be there.'

From the look on the girl's face, Dania wasn't sure how she felt about it.

'Come on, Honor, let's live it up.'

'Yes, boss,' the girl said slowly.

Dania left West Bell Street and headed towards Dundee's newly refurbished railway station. She'd arranged to see the consul general and to try out the piano she'd be playing at the concert. It might seem like a waste of time, but each piano's sound gave the music a different colour, and until she heard the tone, she couldn't settle on a programme. She'd compiled a list of possible pieces she hoped the consul general would help her decide on because she was finding choosing the music an impossible task.

As she stepped inside the arc-shaped entrance, the first thing she noticed was the large arrivals and departures board. The second was that her train was delayed. No matter. It would give her a chance to look round the station, which had been renovated as part of the Dundee Waterfront Project. There should even be time for a coffee. And maybe a cake. But then she caught sight of a familiar figure. Jamie Reid was standing staring up at the board.

'Jamie?' she said, touching him lightly on the shoulder.

He wheeled round, a look of shock on his face. Seeing her, he relaxed visibly. 'Dania,' he said, relief in his voice. 'This is a surprise.'

'I'm guessing you're off to that wedding your wife is organising,' she said, glancing around the concourse. The railway station had been open for less than a week and had a clean, fresh feel that was unlikely to last. 'This is amazing. I'd never have recognised the place.'

'Aye, Dundee's marching to a different rhythm now. I got a sneak preview of the station before it opened.'

'Don't tell me you were asked to do a photoshoot,' she said, smiling.

'Listen, are you rushing off?'

The departures board told her she had forty-five minutes to kill. 'No, I've got plenty of time.'

'Then how about playing me that piece? You know, the one you said you'd take to a desert island?'

She turned and saw, near the main entrance, an alcove decorated with a brightly coloured mural. In it was an upright piano in a reddish-brown finish. It looked new.

'The piano was donated by a local man in memory of his wife,' Jamie was saying. 'So, will you play?'

Dania never needed to be asked twice. She drew out the stool. Chopin's haunting Nocturne, Op. 27, No. 2 in D flat major was six minutes long, a piece the composer had played during his visit to Scotland in 1848, something that might interest the Scots should anyone ask. She paused to fill her mind with the music, and then brought her hands down on the keys. By the time she was halfway through, she was already dissatisfied with her performance. It lacked the elegant simplicity of Rubinstein's but he, after all, was Chopin incarnate. As she finished the piece, she wished she could play it again with the left hand softer.

She got to her feet and turned to see people standing watching. One or two started to clap. Jamie's eyes were closed. He opened them in apparent surprise that the music had ended.

'Marek was right about your playing,' he said. 'If that was Chopin's music, it makes me want to be Polish.'

'You couldn't have paid me a greater compliment,' Dania said warmly. 'Look, if you've time, do you fancy a coffee?'

'My train leaves in less than fifteen minutes. Another time? I'll have to tell Pam. She'd love to hear you play.'

'Then you'll both have to come round to mine.'

'Done,' he said eagerly. He glanced at his watch. 'I have to run. And thanks.'

She watched him hurry towards the escalators, dragging his small wheelie case after him. There was something she had wanted to ask, something to do with their conversation at the Polish restaurant. But when Chopin's music had filled her head, the memory of what had been bothering her had vanished. It was as she was boarding the train to Edinburgh that she remembered: she'd wanted to ask Jamie what year he'd gone to the Affleck house for the photoshoot. And did he remember a little boy with dark curls and a wide smile?

CHAPTER 11

'Why are we heading in this direction, boss? Guthrie Street is on the opposite side of the nick. And why are you carrying flowers?'

'We're taking a detour. To the Howff.'

'Ah.'

The ancient burial ground in the centre of Dundee was no longer used for interments but was a handy location for the odd stroller who didn't want to venture far from the city centre. The area was crisscrossed with paths, and such trees as there were provided little shade. The headstones were covered with green lichen, and some were misshapen or broken. It was tripping over one of these broken stones in pursuit of a drug dealer that had caused DC Laurence Whyte to lose his life. That had been just over a year ago, and West Bell Street still felt the loss keenly. Hamish especially. He'd been there when it had happened. Whenever she had time on a Sunday, Dania visited the spot and laid flowers, offering up a silent prayer for her former colleague. But she'd been in Edinburgh this weekend, staying the Saturday night at the consulate, and returning to Dundee late on Sunday evening. Her time with the consul general had been well spent, though. Between them, they'd compiled the programme for the Independence Day concert.

She and Honor entered the graveyard via the railed iron gate on Meadowside.

'Do you think he can see us?' Honor said.

'Who?'

'Laurence.'

'I'm not sure about that. But whenever I come here, I can see *him*.'

They found the stone, still at the same angle and still easy to trip over. On it were the withered remains of the bouquet of lilies she'd laid the last time she'd been there. She placed the pink and white carnations next to it.

They left the Howff and headed west along Ward Road, reaching the Marketgait minutes later. Directly opposite was the entrance to Guthrie Street, with the road closed off except to pedestrians. The Monday-morning traffic was heavy and they crossed with some difficulty.

The area was a mix of modern flats, boarded-up shops and graffiti-covered walls. They met no one as they walked along the street.

'Not my favourite part of Dundee,' Honor said.

'I wonder what it was like when the mills were going.'

'Steam and dust everywhere. It got into the workers' lungs and they'd cough up jute balls when they got home. Nice. Hamish was telling me about it. It was mainly women who worked the mills. There were so many that Dundee became known as a "she town".'

'I read that some of these old buildings are being bought up and converted into hotels and restaurants.'

'Not before time,' Honor said, with feeling.

'You don't think they should be left as monuments to the city's history? There's a real atmosphere here.'

'Monuments to misery and exploitation is more like it.'

'Do you miss London?' Dania said, after a while.

'Like an aching tooth. The men are much more welcoming

here in Scotland. And I don't get all that mansplaining I used to at the Met.'

'Okay, this is the place,' Dania said, stopping suddenly.

The museum was a three-storey Victorian building no different from its surroundings, yet there was something about it that made it seem grander than its neighbours. And more forbidding. The words 'Affleck Natural History Museum' were displayed in unnecessarily large letters above the door.

'Cripes, boss, that's some pile.'

'Strange place to put a natural history museum. In the middle of a mill town.'

Honor smoothed her jacket. 'Do I look all right? I dug this outfit out of the back of the wardrobe. I haven't worn it for years.'

Dania eyed the girl's clothes. The jacket was too large and the trousers too tight. She failed to imagine what Honor had looked like when the clothes fitted her. But she knew her well enough to try a joke. 'What do you want me to be, Honor? Diplomatic or truthful?'

'Boss!' Honor said, pretending to be scandalised.

'At least you're wearing something approaching a suit.'

'Have I gone a little too far with the shirt?'

Dania studied the red, pink and orange zigzags. Anyone with a lesser constitution would come down with a migraine. 'I wouldn't say that, no.'

Honor nodded, apparently satisfied. 'So how do we approach this?'

'It's the sons I want to speak with. If the father's there, I'll have to be straight with him.'

'Why would having the father there be a problem?'

'Sons don't always speak freely when their fathers are around.'

The girl chewed her lip. 'I've never met a Freemason.'

'Try not to look so nervous. They're only men.'

'I've heard all sorts of things about them.'

'And all probably untrue.'

'I don't know about you, but I could do with a drink.'

'A drink? Another one? Do you want it in a glass or a funnel?'

Honor ignored the jibe and, straightening her shoulders, marched into the building.

A young man with straggly hair was sitting at the reception desk, sorting through a pile of leaflets. He glanced up as they approached. He had a pale complexion and vacant eyes.

'Two tickets, ladies?' he said listlessly. 'That will be twenty pounds. Unless you'd like to buy an annual pass?'

'We're not here to look round the museum.' Dania held up her warrant. 'I'm DI Gorska and this is DS Randall.'

The man's eyes widened. 'Police?' he murmured.

'We'd like to speak with Mr Ross Affleck.'

'He's through in the workshop. His brother Kenny is with him.'

'And Mr Gregor Affleck?'

'He's not here today.'

'So how do we find the workshop?'

'It's straightforward enough. You go right through the halls until you come to a door marked "No Entry". It takes you into the workshop. Shall I phone Ross and Kenny and let them know you're coming?'

'If you would,' Dania said.

'The first hall is right there,' he said, indicating the doors behind them. 'The rooms are numbered, so you can't get lost. Just follow the arrows.' He peeled a couple of leaflets off the pile. 'A plan of the place. And some general information.'

'Thank you.'

They pushed open the swing doors.

'Whoa,' Honor said, under her breath.

Had it not been for the glass cases, they could have walked into a jungle. They moved slowly past the displays, seeing elephants with their trunks raised, curly-tailed monkeys climbing trees, and leopards baring their teeth. The animals had been posed in some form of arrested motion, in dioramas intended to mimic their natural habitats. The result was that the place had that strange feeling of timelessness.

But, on closer inspection, it was evident that some of the older specimens had been inexpertly mounted and were so old that their hides were in need of restoration. Although the display cases had been sealed to prevent insects finding their way in and laying eggs in the fur, the powdery moths lying near the animals suggested that the seals had long since given way. Dania thought of her grandmother's old mink coat, and the trouble the woman had had with it.

She was glad to skip the tarantulas and scorpions and enter the cold polar world of penguins and walruses. The final room on the ground floor transported them to the African savannah. This was by far the largest display, showcasing spotted hyenas, elephants drinking at the riverside, big cats, rodents neither she nor Honor could identify, giraffes, zebras and even a white rhino.

'Come on,' Dania said. 'We'll take a closer look on the way out.'

Honor dragged herself away from the diorama of a cheetah bringing down an impala. Perhaps she was wondering how a domestic cat would fare under similar circumstances.

They reached the lit 'No Entry' sign. Dania pushed open the door on to what might once have been the mill's storeroom. About a dozen large tables took up much of the space, and along the walls were rows of huge metal cylinders with complicated-looking dials and gauges. They hummed gently, the frequency and amplitude making her wonder how anyone managed to stay awake.

Two men were working at the nearest table. They were wearing identical dark trousers and white shirts with the sleeves rolled up. And spotless aprons. Scattered over the surface were tiny creatures dressed in brightly coloured old-fashioned clothes. The men were fixing them to a long wooden tray, and were so engrossed in their work that they didn't notice the women come in.

'Good God, are those rats?' Honor shrieked.

The men's heads shot up.

'What are you doing here?' the taller one said. 'The public aren't allowed in the workshop. There's a "No Entry" sign above the door. Can't you read?'

The receptionist had obviously not phoned ahead. Perhaps he'd thought they'd still be oohing and aahing over the exhibits. Dania pulled out her warrant card. 'We're police.' She returned the man's gaze. 'Detective Inspector Dania Gorska.'

'Let me see that,' he muttered, snatching it out of her hand. He frowned. Then his expression shifted slightly. 'You're the woman who's investigating Cameron,' he said, handing back the card.

'And this is my colleague, Detective Sergeant Randall. You're Ross Affleck, I take it.'

'Aye.' He jerked his head at the other man. 'My brother, Kenny.'

Looking from one to the other, Dania could see the resemblance. And the resemblance to their father. But where interest gleamed in Kenny's eyes, Ross was more wary. He stared at Dania without hiding his suspicion.

'I've got it,' Honor said suddenly. 'It's *The Twelve Days of Christmas*.'

'Aye, that's right,' Kenny said, his face breaking into a smile. For a second, he looked like Cameron. 'We're trying to get it ready for one of the hotels. But the rats keep falling over.'

Ross shot him a glance, as if to say, 'Keep your trap shut.' He turned to Dania. 'If you've come to ask us questions, you're wasting your time. We don't know anything that'll help you.'

'Let me be the judge of that.'

'All right, then, Miss Detective,' he said more calmly. 'Fire away.'

'You'll know by now that we found Cameron in a doocot. He was locked in. I want to hear your theory as to why.' She kept her tone and body language non-confrontational. 'I'm sure you've given it some thought.'

'We've thought about nothing else.' A perplexed look came into his eyes. 'It must have been a psycho.'

'Do you know of anyone who would have a reason to do it?'

'Kill a bairn? No, I don't know anyone like that,' he added, with contempt. His expression suggested that by asking this question she'd somehow insulted him.

Kenny had been shifting his weight, as if he wanted to speak but no one would give him the cue. 'It could have been some lads doing it for a lark,' he blurted finally.

'Cameron was locked in,' Dania said. 'Whoever did that took the key from your house.'

The shock on their faces told her this was news to them. So, Gregor had decided to keep that snippet of information to himself.

'You're saying the key is kept in the house?' Ross said mechanically.

'Didn't you know that's where it was?'

'But it would have been left in the doocot door, eh?' Kenny said. He sounded uncertain, glancing at his brother.

'You numpty,' Ross said. 'Leaving a key in a door? Someone would have stolen it long before now.' He frowned at Dania. 'Bill might ken something about it.'

'Bill?'

'Aye, Bill Baxter. He's been with the family for years. Does work round the house.'

'What sort of work?'

113

'Building work. He put our new sash windows in a year or two back. He can turn his hand to anything.'

'And was he employed by your father thirteen years ago?'

Ross's eyes blazed. He took a menacing step forward. 'Let me give you a word of advice, Detective. Before you go accusing people, you'd better have the facts to back it up.'

'We started out nice and friendly, Mr Affleck, so let's try and keep it that way. In case you haven't noticed, I'm not accusing anyone of anything. I'm simply gathering those facts you talk about.'

He seemed to consider this. 'Aye, Bill was working for us thirteen years ago. He started working for the family long before then.'

'And have you got his contact details?'

'You'll need to ask Mrs Spence. She runs the house.'

'I'll do that.' Dania looked squarely at him, not wanting to miss his reaction. 'Your father told us you used to do a lot of entertaining.'

'We still do. What of it?'

'The key to the doocot was kept in a cupboard in the hall. And the cupboard isn't locked.'

He seemed to realise where this was going. 'And you think one of the guests took it.'

'*Someone* took it.'

He shook his head slowly. 'You're wrong, Detective. None of the guests would have stolen that key.'

'How do you know?' Dania said, making her tone confrontational now.

'Because most of them are members of our Lodge.' His eyes gleamed. 'They're Freemasons,' he added, as if that explained everything.

Mrs Spence had told her that the Affleck men were Freemasons, but Dania hadn't realised, although perhaps she should

114

have, that that extended to many of their friends. She was tempted to ask Ross why he thought being a Freemason ruled out being a murderer but doubted that line of questioning would be productive.

'Which Lodge are you a member of, Mr Affleck?'

'The one down the road,' he replied promptly. 'Aye, and I need to take myself over there. We're organising a fundraiser for one of the city's charities.' He pulled off his apron and threw it on to the table. 'My brother will see you out.' He snatched the jacket off the back of the chair and strode out of the room.

Dania turned to Kenny, who was scribbling on a pad. 'What are you fundraising for?' she said.

He glanced up. 'Dundee has a drug problem. We're trying to help solve it.'

'I didn't know that's the sort of thing Freemasons do.'

He smiled as he continued to scribble. 'We don't really tell people what we do.'

'What are those things for?' Honor said suddenly.

'Those?' he said, following the direction of her gaze. 'They're our freeze-drying vessels.' He put the pad down. 'We use them to freeze-dry the smaller animals.'

'And what about the larger ones? The ones that won't fit inside.'

'We skin them and mount the skin over a form. Our polar bears, which are nearly a hundred years old, were mounted using that method.'

'Must be messy. All that skinning and stuff.'

He seemed to consider this. 'My dad's grandfather, Mungo, tried embalming.'

'What, like with Egyptian mummies?'

'Aye, but he didn't get very far. He gave up in the end.'

Dania was keen to leave. 'Thank you for your time, Mr Affleck, but we have to be on our way.' She handed him her card. 'Do

115

please get in touch if you think of anything that'll help us find Cameron's killer.'

He nodded, pocketing the card without looking at it.

'We'll see ourselves out.'

They were almost in the corridor, when he said, 'Hold on, I nearly forgot.' He tore off a sheet from the writing pad on the table. 'This is for you,' he said, handing it to Honor.

While Dania and Ross had been having their conversation, Kenny had been secretly sketching Honor. The pencil drawing was spot on, showing everything that made Honor Honor: the over-large jacket and skinny trousers, her wild hair and upturned nose, the way she lolled on one leg with her hands clasped behind her back. But what he'd captured perfectly in a way that demonstrated his skill as an artist was the girl's uncompromising look of disdain.

CHAPTER 12

'Mr Filarski,' Miss Ferguson said. 'I thought that, after your mammoth session on Friday, you'd abandoned me.'

'Never that,' Marek said, smiling. Seeing her strawberry-red dress and matching scarf, he was glad now that he'd worn a smart jacket and tie.

'Have you brought your CV?'

He laid the folder on the desk. 'I've put everything in here, including the testimonials.'

'Excellent.' She handed him a form. 'No need to fill it in this minute. As long as you let me have it before you leave.' She glanced at his suit. 'You might want to take your jacket and tie off. It can get hot in the archives. Murray used to work in T-shirt and shorts.'

'In a Lodge?' Marek said, raising an eyebrow.

She threw him a dazzling smile. 'I won't tell if you won't. Anyway, the Brotherhood rarely go into the archives.'

'I'll make a start, then.'

'I'll be out here if you need anything. I'll bring in a cup of coffee at about eleven. How do you take it?'

'Milk. No sugar.' He patted his stomach. 'Cutting down.'

She held his gaze slightly longer than was necessary, then turned her attention to her laptop.

He set to work in the archives, soon shedding his jacket and tie, and rolling up his sleeves. The previous Friday, he'd created the database with the required fields and entered the records from the first roll book. It had given him a fair idea of the scale of the task. The script was the copperplate he was familiar with from nineteenth-century records and, once he'd deciphered the individual letters, he'd been able to make good progress.

Today, however, as he started on another roll book, he found that the handwriting was significantly different. For a start, the capitals G and J were indistinguishable and it was only by reading the rest of the word that Marek was able to hazard a guess. But that took him only so far. After an hour in which he felt a headache forming, he knew he would have to seek help. Fortunately, he wasn't one of those male drivers who never ask for directions.

Miss Ferguson was frowning into her screen. She glanced up as he approached.

'I'm afraid I need assistance,' he said, smiling.

She straightened, dropping her gaze to the open ledger in his hands.

'May I show you?' he said.

'Of course.' She brushed aside her papers and moved the screen back to make room.

He set down the ledger.

'What seems to be the problem?'

He pulled up a chair. 'I can't decipher some of the letters.'

'Only some?' she murmured, bringing her face close to the page.

'This one here. It could be a *t* or it could be an *f*.'

'I see what you mean.' She sat back, running her fingers over her mouth. 'All right, here's what I suggest. Let's find a word where we're sure of those letters. So, for example, here we've got "St John". And now we know what the letter *t* looks like.' She studied him. 'Would it help if I digitised the page and you could enlarge it on the laptop?' She opened the desk drawer. 'You might also need this.' It was a magnifying glass, the brass handle engraved with a set square and compasses.

'Thank you so much,' he said gratefully.

She opened the door next to the archives. The small storage room doubled as a kitchen. Boxes of stationery were piled along one wall, and under the window there was a sink, and a working surface with a kettle and white mugs stamped with the familiar set square and compasses motif.

A large scanner copier stood behind the door. 'This is an old model,' Miss Ferguson said, switching it on. 'It takes a while to warm up. We may as well have our coffee while we wait. I'm afraid it's only instant.'

'That's fine.'

'I take it from your name and accent, Mr Filarski, that you're Polish,' she said, busying herself with the kettle and coffee powder.

'That's right.'

'Were you born there?'

'In Warsaw. Our parents moved to the UK when we were children.'

She smiled over her shoulder. 'And how did they cope?'

'They struggled with English. Someone once stopped my mother in the street and asked where he could spend a penny, and she replied, "What do you want to buy?"'

Miss Ferguson laughed lightly. 'That's a good one.'

'How long have you worked here?' he said, after a while.

'Me? Ages. Too long.'

'What attracted you to this place?'

She opened the door to the small fridge and took out a carton of milk. 'Attracted? Nothing. It's a job, that's all.'

'Do you have much to do with the members?'

'Not really. Although I've met most of them.'

119

'What are they like?'

'Surprisingly normal, actually. Some are very sweet to me. But I don't see them often. My dealings are mainly with the Master.' She looked steadily at Marek. 'Did you apply for this job because you want to become a Mason?'

'Good heavens, no. I'm a Roman Catholic. I doubt I'd be eligible.' He smiled. 'And I'm sure I'd have to get a dispensation from the Pope.'

'It's why Murray came to work here. He confessed to me once that he'd always dreamt of being one of the Brothers.'

'And did he become one?'

She poured the milk. 'I'm afraid not,' she said, handing Marek a mug. 'He suspected it was because they found out he was gay.'

'Surely, in this day and age, that shouldn't make a difference.'

'I'm sure you're right. But who knows what ancient rules they have? It's a closed book.'

Marek sipped cautiously, afraid of burning his tongue. 'Have you ever seen a Masonic ceremony?' he said, trying not to sound too interested.

'They wouldn't let a non-member in. Especially one who's a woman.'

'I take it you need a large room if the whole Lodge attends.'

'That door across the hall leads into the meeting room. It's also where they initiate new members.'

'And what's it like inside?'

'No idea. It's always kept locked.'

He blew on his coffee. 'Don't you have the keys?'

'I haven't got that one. No, it's the Master of the Lodge who guards the key. I think he goes to bed with it round his neck.'

Marek smiled. 'You sound as though you'd like to see inside.'

'Wouldn't you?'

'Now that you've told me it's always kept locked, yes, I would. If the door was unlocked, I wouldn't be at all interested.'

'My sentiments exactly, Mr Filarski.'

'Please, you must call me Franek. So who is the Master?'

'Niall Affleck.'

'Affleck?' Marek wondered. 'Is he related to Gregor Affleck?'

'They're brothers.'

'What is Niall Affleck like?'

She pulled a face. 'He oozes charm. I'm always suspicious of men like that. I've heard the other members talk about him. The room next door to the meeting place is where they get dressed, and the door's always open.' She smiled enigmatically. 'Voices carry.'

He saw that she was willing to tell him more, but he didn't want to seem too keen.

'What sorts of things are you working on at the moment?' he said.

'It's mainly this new fundraising initiative, Niall Affleck's baby. There's lots he needs me to do. Letters and letters.' She gestured at the packs of A4. 'And more letters.'

'What are the Masons fundraising for?'

'They're trying to alleviate the city's drug problem.'

'A worthy endeavour. And what does Niall Affleck do for a living? Do you know?'

'He a writer.'

'A journalist?' Marek ventured.

'Oh, no, they're the lowest of the low. No, he writes fiction.'

Marek was about to reply, when they heard a banging. It seemed to be coming from the front door.

'Strange,' she said, frowning. 'I'm not expecting anyone.' She set her mug down and walked past him into the hall.

He heard the door being opened.

'Yes, can I help you?' came Miss Ferguson's voice.

'I've come about Murray.'

'He's not here.'

'I *know* that.'

There was enough suppressed anger in the voice to make Marek ditch his mug in the sink and hurry out.

'I think you'd better come in,' Miss Ferguson said.

'Thank you.'

The man paused as he caught sight of Marek. He was a big brute with restless eyes and slicked-back fair hair. 'My name's Blackie,' he said, looking from Marek to Miss Ferguson. 'I'm Murray's friend.'

They waited.

'I'm wondering if he left a forwarding address.'

'I'm afraid he didn't,' Miss Ferguson said.

'He can't have given up his job just like that.'

'I'm afraid he did. He didn't show on Wednesday, and then we got an email from him on Thursday saying he was leaving Dundee.'

'It's my fault,' Blackie said, in a wail. 'We had an argument. He told me he never wanted to see me again.'

'When was that?' Marek said.

'Tuesday night. He threw me out.' Blackie chewed his thumbnail. 'I went back on Wednesday evening when I knew he'd be at home but there was no reply when I knocked.' He gazed at Marek. 'Why would he do that? He always let me in after we'd had a row.'

'I'm so sorry,' Miss Ferguson said automatically.

'Did he talk to you about leaving Dundee?' Blackie said. He was starting to sound desperate.

She threw him a sympathetic smile. 'On the contrary. He gave me the impression he was happy here.'

It was the wrong thing to say. Blackie's face grew dark with anger. 'You're telling me it's my fault he left, then. Is that it?'

'No, *you* said that.'

He paced the hall, his hand pressed to his forehead. Suddenly he stopped and stared at her. 'Look, I'll give you my number. If he comes back, will you call me?'

'Well—'

'Please! I'm begging you!'

'All right.'

'If you give me yours, I can text you mine,' he said, pulling out his phone.

'I've lost my mobile, I'm afraid, and I haven't had time to get a new one.' She took a pen and notepad from her desk. 'Here, write your number down.'

He scribbled the number, tore off the sheet and pressed it into her hand, curling her fingers round it. 'Promise you'll get in touch.'

She looked into his eyes. 'I will.'

He gripped her arm. 'Promise!'

She cried out in pain.

Marek stepped forward and slapped his hand away. 'Right, that's enough,' he said firmly. He shoved Blackie hard and put himself in front of Miss Ferguson. 'The lady said she'll ring you. I think you'd better leave now.'

Blackie lifted his hands in a show of surrender. 'Okay, okay, I'm going.' He threw Miss Ferguson a final glance and shambled out of the building.

Marek turned to her. Her face was white with shock, and she was shaking. 'Hey, come on,' he murmured, putting an arm round her shoulders and squeezing gently. 'It's all right. He's gone.'

She buried her face in his chest, then quickly got a grip on herself. She pulled away, rubbing her arm. 'I'm sorry, Mr Filarski.'

'What for?' he said softly.

She collapsed into the chair. Her colour was returning. 'What a brute. Manhandling me like that.'

Marek raised an eyebrow. 'Love does that to people sometimes.'

'Does it? I wouldn't know.'

But the exchange had piqued his interest. 'This Murray, was he the type to quit suddenly?'

'That's just it. He'd spent absolutely ages sorting the ledgers in those boxes. When I had a spare moment, I'd give him a hand. Mind you, the dust was awful – he had to tie back his red hair, which was always all over the place. He told me he couldn't wait to finish so he could make a start on the digitising.' She looked up at Marek. 'Why would you leave a job you enjoyed so much after a lovers' tiff?'

'It does seem rather extreme. There must have been another reason.'

'It doesn't make sense. Unless—'

He took the chair next to her. 'Unless what?' he said slowly.

She stiffened. 'Nothing,' she said, smoothing her dress over her knees. 'Except that he's not the first to disappear. This place has a reputation.' She lowered her voice. 'I've heard the men talking.'

'While they were getting changed?'

She shook her head. 'At the end, when they were about to go home. Two of them stayed behind. They were standing there,' she added, pointing at a spot in front of her. 'They didn't know I was in the storage room. They were talking about old Mr Affleck.'

'The father of the child who went missing years ago?'

'Yes, I heard about that,' she said vaguely. 'No, this was Gregor's grandfather, Mungo. He was Master of the Lodge. And a taxidermist. He owned the museum down the road.'

'And what did they say about him?' Marek said, when she seemed reluctant to continue.

'Just that he had a particular way of dealing with his enemies.' She gazed into Marek's eyes. 'He made them disappear.'

CHAPTER 13

'Have you been in touch with your parents, Dania?'

Dania was sitting in Father Konrad Kliment's tiny living room at St Joseph's, drinking coffee. This was something she did regularly, having promised her parents she would stay in contact with him. The two of them were so at ease in each other's company that they often lapsed into silence without feeling the need to keep the conversation going.

Dania had been mulling over the events of the morning. After she and Honor had left the museum, they'd continued a short way down the street, stumbling upon the elegant stone building with its Masonic symbol over the entrance. A strange place to build a Lodge. Had the mill owners been Masons? Perhaps it was a requirement if you wanted to get on in business. Her thoughts returned then to her encounter with the Affleck brothers. The older had been unnecessarily unpleasant, which Honor had picked up on and talked about afterwards, declaring that she wouldn't give him the olive out of her cocktail. Dania was reflecting on the brothers' different personalities when the priest spoke, so his question caught her by surprise.

'I have to confess, Father, that I've been too busy to write to my parents.' She dropped her gaze. 'It's usually Marek who does that. He passes their news on to me.'

Konrad nodded, saying nothing. He normally stood slightly stooped because, although he was over six feet tall, he was constantly having to bend forward to deliver Communion. In his armchair, however, he sat ramrod straight, his thoughtful eyes huge behind his black-framed glasses. He was usually wreathed in smiles, especially when in the company of children, and a frequent visitor at their hospital at Ninewells.

'Marek tells me they're well,' she said. 'Retirement seems to suit them.'

She knew from his expression that Konrad was thinking back to the 1980s, when her parents' and his own participation in Solidarity had landed the three of them with prison sentences. Konrad had been a young man straight out of the seminary when a strike at the Lenin Shipyards in Gdańsk, in what became known as the Polish August, had started a movement that, nine years later, had ended in the fall of Communism. When Poland joined the EU in 2004, all three had moved to Scotland but, unlike her parents who eventually returned, Konrad had stayed and made a life here. And, like her parents, he spoke little about those times when Solidarity had been the only hope in Poland.

What he *had* spoken about during one of their more talkative evenings was his own father's wartime exploits. The man had escaped to France during the invasion of Poland, then escaped again after France's capitulation, reaching Great Britain. After a course of training in Scotland, he was sworn in as a member of the Home Army, joining the group known as the Cichociemni, or Silent Unseen. These covert special operatives of the Polish Army in Exile were secretly dropped into occupied Poland to work with the underground. In 1941, Konrad's father had parachuted into Warsaw, where he had spent most of his time forging new identification documents for the Jews in the ghetto, and then for the Poles, until the Uprising in 1944.

In the ensuing chaos, as Warsaw was being systematically razed to the ground, he had escaped to the West, eventually making his way back to Britain. His sweetheart, a girl he'd met in St Andrews, had waited faithfully for him. But, unable to bear not living in Poland, he had returned with her to Warsaw and took an active part in the post-war reconstruction of the city. Yet he told no one about his role in the Cichociemni, and continued to remain silent and unseen as he watched the authorities in the People's Republic arrest and execute those Cichociemni reckless enough to tell people who they were and what they'd done. It wasn't until after 1989, when the Soviets left, that the remaining members were able to speak freely about their wartime activities.

'And will you be going to Warsaw for August the first?' Konrad said.

'I hope to go next year,' she said brightly. 'For the seventy-fifth anniversary.'

He brushed his fine silver hair off his forehead. 'I expect the commemorations will be even livelier. I may go myself.'

Like all Poles, he knew it was unnecessary to name the event: 1 August meant only one thing – the anniversary of the Uprising. Every year, at 5 p.m., sirens sound across the city and the population gets to its feet to observe a minute's silence. Cars stop, and the inhabitants leave their vehicles and stand in the road. As with other similar events, it was only after 1989 that the people of Warsaw had been able to commemorate the part they'd played in the liberation of their city.

'More coffee, Dania?'

'Thank you, but I won't sleep if I have any more.'

'I have no difficulty where that's concerned.' He poured himself another cup, adding three heaped teaspoons of sugar. 'And how is work going?' He nodded at the pile of unread newspapers on the sofa. 'When I have time, I'll catch up with what is happening in Dundee.' He stirred the coffee. 'Tell me that the police have caught the man who took that little girl.'

'We haven't.' Dania looked at her hands. 'And now he's taken another. We found her body a week ago.'

A cloud seemed to pass across Konrad's face. He put the cup down and ran a trembling hand over his forehead. 'Perhaps it's a good thing that I don't have time to read the news. Will he kill again?' he added, in an anguished voice.

'He may not know it yet but he will.'

Konrad's eyes flared. 'And these poor people who take drugs. And ruin their lives. There seem to be more and more of them with every passing year.'

She stared at him in helpless astonishment. This was the first time she'd seen his anger. He was usually the oasis of calm she sought out when the pressure of work threatened to overwhelm her. She felt suddenly ashamed that she and her colleagues had been unable to do more to solve that particular problem. Yet what could she tell him? That it wasn't the drug takers who were at fault, but the drug dealers. And, as time passed, they became better at smuggling in the goods. Hamish had started an initiative whereby he and Honor visited schools to warn against the dangers of substance misuse. But, as he had reported back, in many cases it was a wasted effort. The glazed eyes and hopeless expressions told them better than words that they were too late.

Konrad was gazing pleadingly at her. She turned her head away, unable to bear the reproach in his eyes.

'This man who killed the girls,' he said, back on the subject, 'what will happen when he is caught?'

'He'll be tried and sentenced. And then imprisoned, hopefully for life.'

'And after he dies, the innermost ring of Dante's inferno will be waiting for him.'

She was tempted to tell the priest that Hell would be waiting for the man here on earth. There was a code in prison that saw rough justice meted out to certain categories of criminal. Child rapists were among them. She didn't rate the man's chances of survival too highly.

'I'd better go, Father,' she said, getting to her feet. 'I've stayed too long.'

'I'll pray that you find this killer, my child.' He walked her to the door. 'And do remember me to your parents.' He paused eloquently. 'When you write to them.' He looked at her over the top of his glasses in a way that made it abundantly clear that he expected her to do it. And to do it soon.

After the door had closed, Konrad took a seat on the creaky sofa, thinking through his conversation with Dania. He realised suddenly that he'd failed to raise what had been on his mind for some time, which was to engage her in a small project he was planning. One of the children in the hospital was a gifted pianist but hadn't played since her admission to the ward some months before. He'd told her he knew a concert pianist and, when the wide-eyed girl had asked if she could hear her play, hit upon the idea of a masterclass. There was an old piano somewhere in the building, which could be wheeled into the ward so the other children could watch the proceedings. Dania wouldn't refuse him this: the child had less than a year to live. But it had slipped his mind. No matter, he would get in touch with her.

Mentally, he went through what had to be done in the coming week, starting with the repair of the organ. Somehow he had to raise the necessary funds, an impossible task, given the state of the economy. And yet the parishioners had rallied round, assuring him that they would find the money. He had come to realise the truth of what his father had told him, which was that the Scots, far from being the miserly nation their cousins south of the border depicted them to be, were generous and warm-hearted. Ah, and Dania could throw a series of fundraising concerts. But would she have the time? Catching this killer was surely her number-one priority. He felt his mouth form into a smile as he remembered the last time he'd heard her play in the Overgate. She'd run through the Military Polonaise without the sheet music in front of her. And played it without a single mistake! *Mirabile dictu.* Yes, he thought triumphantly, he would ask her. And she would say yes.

His glance fell on the growing pile of newspapers. These days, he had little time to read. Before he threw them out, he should at least skim the most recent and find out what was going on in Dundee. Otherwise, he'd have nothing to discuss with his parish-ioners. As long as it wasn't about Brexit.

He picked up the *Evening Telegraph* and scanned the front page. As he'd expected, it was Brexit. There'd been resignations from the cabinet over something called the Chequers plan, whatever that was. He really should keep up with events. He turned the page. There was a large photograph of a young boy holding some sort of prize. He was smartly dressed in his school uniform. That was unusual, these days. Konrad gazed into the soft brown eyes, feel-ing his heart melt.

He was about to turn to the puzzles section with the sudoku and crossword when something caught his eye. It was Dania's name, although they should learn to spell it properly with the accent over the letter *o*. He started to read the article. And as the words leapt out of the page, he felt himself grow cold with fear.

The sheets dropped from his trembling fingers, and he collapsed back against the sofa. He stared at the Styrofoam tiles on the ceil-ing, dazzled by the glowing corona from the unshaded lightbulb. His breathing grew shallow. And then, without wanting it, his memory dragged him back to that day thirteen years before when, through the fine mesh of the musty-smelling confessional, he'd heard the words that would stay with him until his last day on earth.

'Bless me, Father, for I have sinned . . .'

CHAPTER 14

'And that's the complete list, boss?' Honor said incredulously. 'There's no way Chirnside interviewed all these.'

When Dania had seen the large number of names and addresses of Gregor Affleck's friends her reaction had also been one of dismay. 'You'll need to get their work addresses. Mrs Spence couldn't help there.' She smiled bravely. 'We'll have to divide it up, or we'll be at it into next year.'

'Dividing up the telephone directory would be quicker.'

Hamish was scratching his neck. 'And this son – Ross – said the family friends are Freemasons?'

'We'll have to be careful how we approach that. Stress that we're talking to them because they're family friends, not because they might be Masons.'

'Do we mention the key?' Honor said.

'I see no point in keeping quiet about it. Gregor may have told them.' She paused. 'But bring it up as though it's an afterthought. Or they'll think we're accusing them of something. See if you can get some of the other officers on this, too.'

Hamish shook his head. 'I reckon they're too busy on the killer rapist case, ma'am.'

'Can I take one of the uniforms?' Honor said.

'Tell you what, you and Hamish go together. See how you get

on. My own first port of call is the Master. I'm hoping to find him at home. If he's not there, I'll try the Lodge.'

Honor looked uncertain. 'The Lodge? And you're going alone?'

'Masons may have a reputation for being gods among men.' She smiled. 'But they're just men, nothing more. I won't be genu-flecting. I only do that in church.'

She caught the look between Honor and Hamish as they left the room.

Niall Affleck lived in Broughty Ferry, towards the east end of Reres Road. En route to Niall's, Dania had called in at Gregor Affleck's, intending to make enquiries about Bill Baxter, but there'd been no answer to her knock. She didn't expect the men to be in and was hoping for another chat with Mrs Spence but, then, even housekeepers aren't always home to keep house.

The woman who answered Dania's ring at Reres Road informed her that she was the cleaner, but she had no idea where Mr Affleck was, hen, but he was likely to be at the Lodge, that was the Lodge on Guthrie Street, as that was where he spent most of his time these days when he wasn't in the conservatory writ-ing, because he's a novelist, did you ken that, lass?

Dania resisted the urge to back away slowly and thanked the woman before hurrying to the car. She reset the sat-nav and started the engine, casting a final glance at the fine sandstone house capped with a steep tiled roof. Given its size and condition, she put it at three-quarters of a million. Or more. When it came to money, being a detective was a bad choice. She made a men-tal note to seek out the man's novels.

She decided to leave the car at the station and walk to the Lodge rather than negotiate the narrow roads in search of a section with-out double yellow lines. Her gym membership had lapsed and she needed the exercise. And the tall buildings provided shade from the sunlight that poured down from the blue-white sky.

It took her only minutes to reach the Lodge. No sooner had she taken her hand off the bell than she heard a voice shouting, 'I'll get it,' followed by rapid, heavy footsteps.

A powerfully built man in a lightweight tailored suit opened the door. He stared at her with blank blue eyes. 'May I help you?'

She held up her warrant. 'DI Dania Gorska. West Bell Street police station. I'm here to see Mr Niall Affleck. Is he in?'

'I'm Niall Affleck,' he said, with a well-groomed smile. 'May I ask what this is about?'

'It's in connection with the murder of Cameron Affleck.'

'Aye, of course. You'd better come in.'

He took her through a carpeted hallway into an airy reception room with doors leading off. Her attention was immediately drawn to the glittering objects in the glass-fronted case.

He glanced towards the empty desk. 'Our receptionist isn't in today, so there's just myself and the archivist. We'll use the office. It's this way.' He ushered her along the corridor on the left and opened the door at the end.

The centrepiece of the room was an oval mahogany table, suggesting that the 'office' doubled as a dining room. The walls were plastered in a tasteful grey, several shades lighter than the thick-pile carpet. On a small scallop-edged table under the window, four mounted squirrels were dressed in frilly tutus and feather tiaras. They had been posed in the dance of the little swans from *Swan Lake*, heads bent, arms joined, and one leg crossed over the other.

The surface of the dining table was scattered with papers. Niall swept them to one side. 'I'm sorry about the guddle, Inspector. I'm working on a fundraiser at the moment. Please take a seat.'

Dania was tempted to ask if this was how the Masons funded themselves but the question might lead to a long discussion and, besides, Kenny had already indicated that the money the Lodge was raising was for charity.

'Can I offer you a coffee, Inspector? Mr Filarski's just made some, so the kettle's boiled.'

'That's kind of you, but no, thank you.'

'So, you've been put in charge of the case,' Niall said, relaxing his expression.

'That's right.' She pulled out her notebook. 'Perhaps I could start by asking whether you're related to Gregor Affleck.'

'He's my brother.'

'Are you close?'

He smoothed down his sandy hair. It had a natural wave and sprang straight back. 'Aye, well, as close as brothers can be. We have a lot in common.'

'Do you have anything to do with his taxidermy business?'

'Good heavens, no,' he said, with a light laugh. 'I can't stand having those dead animals around.'

She glanced at the diorama.

He must have caught the movement because he said dismissively, 'Not my taste, I'm afraid. It's Gregor's. He owns the building.'

'He owns a Lodge?'

'He's a Freemason, Inspector,' he said, in the tone of a teacher admonishing a pupil for her stupidity. 'Our chapter rents this building from him.' His lips curved into a sanctimonious smile. 'You'll be wondering what goes on here. I can tell you in one short sentence: we seek to lead men to the light.'

'Only men?'

'We don't need to admit women. Men have been put on this earth to guide them.'

Dania was glad Honor wasn't with her. She could imagine the girl's reaction. She glanced towards the window. 'And did you have those bars put in? Or were they there when you set up the Lodge?'

His smile faded. 'One of our ancestors put them in. But we're glad he did. We have antique jewels on display in the hall.'

'Jewels?'

'Masonic regalia. They've been gifted by the families of deceased Brothers.'

Dania turned a page in her notebook. 'Let's talk now about Cameron and his abduction. When did you first hear about it? Can you remember?'

'Aye, how could I forget? I loved that lad.' Niall rested his clasped hands on the table. 'It was the day following his disappearance. The Monday. We were due to have a Ceremony of Initiation for the First Degree, and Gregor was to officiate. When he didn't show, I rang him at home. He was in a bad way. The doctor was there. He'd sedated poor Davina. She never recovered from her experience,' he added, in a changed voice.

'And what was your initial reaction?'

He gazed at her. 'Bewilderment. Then deep, deep sorrow.'

'And what was your initial reaction when you learnt that Cameron's remains had been found in a doocot?'

'Shock, of course. But also amazement.'

'Why amazement?'

'Why?' he said harshly. 'Because I thought that whoever had kidnapped him had taken him far away from here. Gregor has been searching for him all these years. There's never been the slightest trace of the lad.' He shook his head. 'And then we learnt that he'd been found in a doocot right here in Dundee. Aye, and after all this time. Wouldn't that amaze *you*, Inspector?'

'Cameron was locked in,' she said, watching his reaction.

'He must have been, right enough. Otherwise, he'd have got out and called for help.'

'The doocot belongs to Gregor. The key – the *only* key – was kept in his house.'

136

She waited for this to sink in. It didn't take long.

'So whoever took Cameron must also have taken the key,' Niall said, in a faltering voice.

'And he must also have known where it was kept.'

'Gregor keeps the keys in a cupboard in the hall. Everyone knows that.'

'Everyone?'

'By that I mean everyone here.'

'How do they know?'

'He has a spare set of keys to the rooms in this Lodge. It's his building, after all. If a key is lost, it means we can get a replacement made.' He smiled wryly. 'It happens from time to time.'

'I understand that Gregor was always entertaining at his house.'

'I see where you're going with this, Inspector,' Niall said slowly. 'You think one of the Lodge members took the key.'

'At this stage in the investigation, I merely want to establish who had the opportunity.'

'And how do you expect to do that? Can you get the names of everyone who passed through Gregor's house thirteen years ago?' he said, disbelief in his voice.

'We've already got them. Gregor's housekeeper has drawn up the list. We're casting a wide net.' She paused for effect. 'Housekeepers have excellent memories, I find.'

For an instant, a look came into his eyes that told her better than words that she had somehow overstepped the mark. His hands clenched, the knuckles whitening. 'You're wasting your time, Inspector.'

'Why do you say that?'

'Whoever took the key won't be on the list.'

'Unless you know who took it, how can you say that?'

'As Master of this Lodge, I forbid you to seek out those people.'

'*Forbid* me?' she said incredulously.

He seemed to realise what he'd said. 'Ach, I meant that I'm sure there's a better way of approaching this.' He must have understood how patronising he sounded, because he added, 'I'm sorry. I didn't mean to be disrespectful. You're the detective, of course, and I shouldn't tell you how to do your job.'

'Let's talk about motive, then. Why do *you* think Cameron was locked in that doocot?'

'I've no idea. And that's the truth of it.'

'And where were you between the hours of eleven and twelve thirty on the morning of June the twelfth, two thousand and five?'

He stared hard at her. 'Are you seriously suggesting I took that lad? My own nephew?' The clenched fists again.

'I'm not suggesting. I'm merely asking. You must understand that this is a question we're asking everyone.'

He took a deep breath. 'I was at home.

'Alone?'

'Alone.'

'Is there anything else you'd like to tell me?' she said, after a silence.

'Nothing,' he replied, with seeming indifference.

She laid her card on the table. 'Thank you for your time, Mr Affleck. If you do think of anything that might be pertinent, will you call me?'

'Aye, that goes without saying.' He gazed at the card, and then glanced up. 'I take it you're Polish.'

'That's right.'

'Then before you leave you must meet our archivist.' He got to his feet. 'I'm sure he'd like to meet you.'

Back in the hall, he opened one of the doors and poked his head inside. 'Mr Filarski, come and meet a fellow countryman.'

Dania heard a chair being scraped back. Then faint footsteps, and a man appeared.

She was aware that her expression – and his – could be seen by Niall. But the man was practised in the art of keeping his composure. And so was she.

'This is Mr Franek Filarski,' Niall was saying. 'Mr Filarski, Inspector Gorska. She's Polish too.'

Marek played the part to perfection. He held out his hand, and she put hers into his.

'It's a pleasure to meet you,' he said, in Polish. He lifted her hand and brushed it lightly with his lips, his eyes never leaving hers.

'The pleasure is mine, Mr Filarski,' she simpered.

Niall was watching the display with amusement. 'Wonderful,' he murmured. 'Now why don't the British do it that way?'

'Goodbye, gentlemen,' Dania said, as she made for the door.

As Dania left the building, she heard Niall Affleck say, 'Is that you finished for the day, Mr Filarski? Don't forget your jacket. I think you left it behind the last time you were here.'

She walked smartly towards the Marketgait, and stopped at the intersection with Brown Street. She slipped into the street and waited out of sight, sneaking a quick peek back now and again.

The Lodge door opened and Marek appeared. He glanced up and down the road as though searching for someone, pulled out his phone, then thought better of it and put it away. He swung his jacket over his shoulder and strode purposefully in her direction, head bent.

He passed the spot where she was hiding and continued down the street, apparently deep in thought. She followed him, trying to keep her footsteps quiet.

He was nearing the Marketgait when she called out to him. 'Marek!'

He wheeled round. 'Danka,' he said, in a gasp.

She caught him up. 'So you're an archivist now?' she said, in Polish.

He grinned. 'I'm working undercover.'

'I'd guessed as much. I don't suppose you can tell me anything.'

'I'm after a story.'

'About the Freemasons?'

'Partly that,' he said, looking at his feet.

She decided not to press him. It would be unlikely to have anything to do with her investigation. 'I'm making enquiries about Cameron Affleck,' she said.

'The lad in the doocot?'

'His father's a Freemason, and so are many of the family friends. We've started interviewing them.' Even to her own ears, her voice sounded strained. 'The problem is that there are so many.'

'Why do you think they can help you with your investigation?'

She saw no reason to keep it from him, as she'd discussed it with both Gregor and Niall. Briefly, she told her brother about the key to the doocot, and her suspicion that one of Gregor's friends had taken it.

He stared at her in amazement. 'But why would they?'

'That's what we don't know. The motive is the hardest thing about all this.' She leant against the wall. 'We've no leads.'

'Listen, Danka, I'll keep my ears open. If I hear anything, I'll be in touch. Okay?'

'Thanks,' she said gratefully. 'But don't get yourself into trouble on my account.'

He smiled in the way that always sent women crazy. 'I never get into trouble. Anyway, I'm a big boy and I can take care of myself.'

'How many times have I heard that? And then had to come to your rescue?'

He tried to look shocked and failed. 'Listen, we need to get that dinner organised. How about inviting Jamie and his wife?'

'Sounds like a plan.'

He squeezed her arm. 'I'll give you a call.'

She watched him weave through the traffic, taking his life in his hands. Why he couldn't cross at the lights like a sensible person was beyond her.

She walked along the Marketgait, debating with herself whether having someone inside the Lodge would benefit her investigation, and decided it wouldn't. She wondered what Marek was up to. Doubtless she'd find out when she read his article in the *Courier*. But for the first time in a long time, she found herself seriously questioning how they were going about the Cameron Affleck investigation. They were having to do it by the book, and she was sure that in this case it wouldn't work. But, until she came up with something better, she had no option but to continue. It didn't help that patience wasn't one of her virtues.

She'd arranged to meet Honor and Hamish for a quick debrief in Jock's café. The tearoom, opposite the Sheriff Court House, was reached through an archway, and sold some of the best cakes in town. The owner was a jovial Scotsman who said little but knew Dania so well that he had her pot of builder's tea ready before she'd reached the counter. The reek of hot fat, which greeted customers who came for the full Scottish breakfast, was absent so late in the day.

'Cake, lass?' Jock said, as she closed the door. He drew his heavy brows together. 'Aye, you look like you could use one.'

'Go on, then.'

'I've got a nice gingerbread.'

'With butter?'

'Need you ask?'

'Just a small piece.'

He grinned, then cut her a huge slice. She took it and the tea

141

to the corner table. There was one other customer, but he was out of earshot.

Minutes later, Honor and Hamish arrived. One look at their faces told Dania what she needed to know. 'Can you put theirs on my bill, Jock?' she called to him.

'Aye, okay, lass.'

'Thanks, boss,' Honor said, with a smile.

Hamish nodded. 'Ma'am.'

They huddled in the corner, drinking tea and eating ginger-bread.

'So how did it go?' Honor said. 'You've got your sad face on, so I can guess.'

'You first,' Dania said wearily.

Honor wiped her fingers. 'Right, well, it wasn't our finest hour. We talked to three people on the list. They remembered being questioned at the time Cameron disappeared, and seemed annoyed we'd singled them out to interview them again. They stressed they had nothing to add. It didn't help that they were at work and busy, busy, busy.'

Dania could imagine how the interviews had gone: business-men working to pressing timetables wouldn't appreciate being disturbed when they'd already given their statements.

'We told them we weren't singling them out, and added that we'd reopened the case now that Cameron's remains had been found, and hadn't they read about it in the paper? They calmed down after that.'

'But there was something else,' Hamish said, glancing at Honor.

'That's right. I asked one of them, a solicitor, about the Lodge and how long it had been running. I was trying to ease into the more difficult questions. Well, he started to natter on about a Mungo Affleck.'

'Mungo. Didn't Kenny mention him?' Dania said. 'So he was a Mason as well as a taxidermist? Like Gregor?'

'The solicitor's father was in the room, they work in the same practice, and I caught the look he gave his son. He was warning him to keep his trap shut.'

'About Mungo?'

'Must have been.'

'Anyway, at our next port of call, we decided to bring up Mungo's name,' Hamish said. 'Same reaction. The shutters came down faster than a hoor's drawers.' He coloured slightly. 'Sorry, ma'am, that just came out.'

'This Mungo was Gregor's grandfather, according to Kenny,' Honor said. 'He'll be long dead, even thirteen years ago, so I don't know what all the fuss is about.' She took a gulp of tea. 'So how did you do, boss?'

As quickly as she could, Dania recounted her interview with Niall Affleck, describing how he'd ordered her not to seek out the people on Gregor's list.

'Too late,' Honor said. 'We've already started.'

'Know what I reckon?' Hamish said, playing with the packets of sugar. 'Those Masons have got something to hide.' He glanced up. 'And we may have taken the lid off a can of worms.'

'Or it could simply be that a secret society likes to be secretive about everything,' Dania said.

They nodded. But they didn't look convinced.

'Has something come up, Niall?' Gregor said, closing the front door. An evening visit from the Master was a rare occurrence, so he wasted no time in getting to the point. And the man was looking a wee bit grey, as though he'd had a shock.

'Your boys at home?' Niall said.

'They're both out.'

'And the housekeeper?'

'In the kitchen. And my daughter-in-law's upstairs.'

'Braw. We won't be overheard.' He followed Gregor into the living room.

Gregor gestured to the sofas by the fireplace. 'Glenmorangie?' he said, striding across to the sideboard.

'Thank you.'

Their drinks poured, the men settled themselves.

'Look, I'm sorry to bother you so late,' Niall said.

'Nine o'clock is hardly late. I take it this isn't about the fundraiser.'

'It's more serious than that. I had a visit today from a Polish detective.'

'That would be about Cameron. She's investigating the murder,' he added, pausing before speaking the word. Although all these years he'd known in his heart that that was what must have happened to the lad, now that the word 'murder' was on everyone's lips, he almost couldn't bring himself to say it.

Niall swilled the liquid round the glass. 'She's got it into her head that it must have been someone you know.'

'Aye, I can well understand why she's come to that conclusion. The officer who ran the case at the time thought the same.'

'The thing is, I've had a stream of complaints from the Brothers. This detective and her team of plods are going around interviewing them. Your housekeeper gave the detective a list of names.' He made a gesture of distaste. 'Ach, no point looking at me like that. It's not her fault.'

'I wonder how far back the list goes.'

'That's not the point.'

'Give it to me straight, man. What's worrying you?'

'She may turn her attention to the Lodge itself. One of the

144

Brothers warned me that the woman detective showed more than usual interest in the place.'

'Why would she do that?'

'I don't know. I don't know how detectives' minds work. I don't know how *women's* minds work.' Niall looked squarely at him. 'But I'm telling you, if that Polish woman comes poking her nose into corners she shouldn't, we'll have to do something about it, won't we? And that would turn out to be disastrous.' He paused eloquently. 'For her, that is.'

'She's police, Niall. That makes her untouchable.'

Niall said nothing. He knocked back the whisky. Gregor noticed his hands were shaking.

'Another drink?' he said.

'I'm driving. While I'm here, we need to discuss the date of the next Lodge meeting. I've drawn up the minutes. The business of the Craft will be short: we have two applications for admitting new members. The other item is the conferring of the degree of Fellowcraft on Kenny. I'm wondering about Friday, July the twenty-seventh.'

'A Friday's always a good night, right enough. I'll have word sent out.'

'And I'll see about getting the dinner organised.' Niall got to his feet. 'Have your boys been interviewed by the police?'

'Aye, early on. We all were.' Gregor held the other man's gaze. 'They know what's at stake, Niall. You can rely on them.'

Niall nodded thoughtfully. 'No need to get up. I'll let myself out.'

After he'd heard the front door close, Gregor poured himself another Scotch. Although he'd tried not to show it, the Master's visit had unnerved him. Aye, and to the extent that he might spend the evening polishing off the rest of the Glenmorangie. He cast his mind back to his conversation with the Polish detective. She'd looked the type to hold a bone in a vice-like grip once she'd picked it up. That was good news for the investigation into Cameron's murder. But the other matter? It would be disastrous if she stumbled across the Lodge's secrets. All of them . . .

He gazed at the photograph of Davina. Those wide green eyes and that red hair. She'd always given him inspiration when he'd most needed it. But she was failing him now. He would have to hope to God that the Polish detective confined her investigation to his wee lad's murder. And that his brother didn't take matters into his own hands.

CHAPTER 15

'Mrs Spence?' Dania said, as the door opened.

'Inspector.' The woman threw Dania an embarrassed smile. 'I'm afraid I've forgotten your surname.'

'Gorska.'

'Aye, Inspector Gorska.'

'May I come in? I'd like to talk to you about something.' She glanced at the woman's red-stained apron. 'If you're not too busy.'

'Surely. Please come in.'

Dania followed her into the kitchen. The room was full of the smell of hot fruit, which she traced to the large preserving pan on the hob.

'I'm making rhubarb-and-strawberry jam,' the woman said. 'I'm at the potting stage. You don't mind if I do the last few while we talk?'

'Not at all,' Dania said, lowering herself into the rocking chair.

'Do you make jam, Inspector?'

'I don't, but my mother does.'

'Does she bide in Scotland?

'Warsaw.'

The woman glanced at her. 'What kind of jam does she make, then?'

'All kinds, but mainly rosehip. She goes out into the country and picks the fruit. We used to help her when we were children.'

'Would you like a jar of mine?'

Dania thought of Marek and his sweet tooth. 'I'd love one.'

Mrs Spence took one of the jars from the working surface. 'This one's cooled.'

'Thank you,' Dania said gratefully.

She watched as the woman ladled the last of the jam into two pots, then twisted the lids on firmly.

'What did you want to talk about, Inspector?' Mrs Spence said, washing her hands at the sink.

'I've come about Bill Baxter.'

The woman turned. 'Bill? What about him?'

'Do you happen to know where I could find him?'

'He lives out Lundie way.' There was a defensive note in her voice. 'Why do you ask?'

Dania had half expected the same closing of ranks she'd experienced at the museum and was ready with the script.

'It's routine, Mrs Spence. We're talking to everyone who knew Cameron.' She smiled reassuringly. 'I'm trying to build up a picture of what he was like.'

The woman wiped her hands on a towel, studying her. 'Aye, right enough, Bill would surely be able to tell you. He knew the boy well.' She put the towel down. 'Maybe you'd like to see his bedroom. It's been unchanged all these years.'

'Cameron's?'

'I go in to dust now and again but, apart from that, it's exactly as it was the last time he used it. Even the sheets haven't been changed.' She smiled sadly. 'Mrs Affleck gave strict instructions that nothing was to be touched. She would go in from time to time, lie on the bed and stroke his pillow. Ach, it wasn't healthy. But who was I to tell her?'

148

'Did the police examine the room when Cameron was reported missing?'

'I think they swabbed for prints, or whatever the term is. That fingerprint dust got everywhere. After they were done, I gave the place a good clean.'

'I'd very much like to see it.'

Mrs Spence smiled and pulled off her apron.

They climbed the oak staircase to the first floor, giving Dania a close-up view of the mounted eagle. From this distance, it looked even dustier. And even more determined to fly at her.

A number of doors led off the red-carpeted corridor to left and right. Mrs Spence opened the one directly opposite. 'This is Cameron's,' she said unnecessarily.

The room was large and bright, made brighter by the insertion of a picture window, which took up most of the wall and gave a breathtaking view of the back garden. It was sparsely furnished with a bed, wardrobe, and a low table and chairs in wax-crayon colours. The scuffed laminate floor was bare of rugs because they would impede the motion of the various toy vehicles scattered around.

Mrs Spence must have followed the direction of her gaze. 'Aye, he fair liked his wee cars, did the lad.'

'May I look inside the wardrobe?'

'Go ahead, Inspector.'

The double wardrobe opened to show an assortment of clothes a boy of nine would wear, mainly jeans, T-shirts and jumpers. There was also a fine kilt and velvet jacket. Hanging at the back were a couple of pairs of black trousers and a tiny navy-blue jacket. A white handkerchief had been neatly folded into the breast pocket. Dania fingered the jacket, remembering that Cameron had been wearing one like it, albeit larger, when his

149

remains were found. The bottom of the wardrobe was a clutter of shoes, mostly trainers, with some black leather lace-ups.

Mrs Spence must have seen her touching the jacket. 'The Affleck men wear those clothes for formal occasions,' she said. 'The ties are hanging up inside the wardrobe door.'

There were half a dozen, all with the Affleck crest. Dania closed the wardrobe.

High above the table there was a wall clock in the shape of a smiling elephant and, below it, a single long shelf loaded with picture books. The rest of the walls were covered with a child's drawings.

'Cameron loved to draw,' Mrs Spence said wistfully. 'He did these ones here when he was a wee bairn, but those at the end were later. They're watercolours.'

One of the paintings was of the Affleck house from the front gates. The driveway up to the mossy fountain with its three dolphins was unmistakable.

'He was always pestering Bill to show him his tricks,' Mrs Spence went on.

'Bill Baxter?'

'Aye, he was something of a painter himself. Never made enough to live on, ken, although he tried hard. It must be sad when you can't follow your dream.' She nodded behind the door. 'Those are Bill's. They're a good likeness of the lad.'

The pencil sketches were of Cameron at different stages of childhood and had been executed when the boy's attention was elsewhere. In one, he was sitting cross-legged, playing with a toy train, his curly hair flopping into his eyes. In another, he was caught in profile at the edge of the fountain, reaching down to pick up a paper boat. The sketches were signed 'W. Baxter' in the bottom right-hand corner.

'Bill wanted to sell those and make a bit of money but Mr Affleck would have none of it.'

'Mr Gregor Affleck?'

'Aye. He told Bill in no uncertain terms that he'd take him to court if he tried. I remember there was a wee bit of a stooshie. That was shortly before the lad went missing.'

'I'm not sure he could have done that. Taken him to court, I mean.'

'But Bill didn't know, did he?' She shook her head. 'It was a bad time for him, and no mistake. He confessed to me that he was afraid he'd be evicted – he'd missed his rent two months running. Even asked if Sandy and I could give him a wee loan. But what could we do? Neither of us earns much.' She gazed through the window, an expression of sadness on her face.

'So what happened?' Dania prompted.

'We were afraid Bill would do something daft. He'd already had a stint in prison.' She stopped as though she'd said too much.

'He went to prison? On what charge?'

'Mr Affleck doesn't know, so I'd be grateful if you didn't tell him. I reckon Bill will lose his job otherwise.'

'Is he a good worker?'

'Aye. He's the best handyman in the area.'

'You've never employed anyone else?'

'Why would we?'

'What did Bill do that got him sent to prison?'

Mrs Spence lowered her voice, as though Gregor could hear. 'He stole the lead off a kirk roof. He and a pal came as workmen and did it over several days. A cleaner noticed daylight coming through the ceiling and that was how they discovered it. His pal clyped on him. The wee shite – pardon my language – got away with it. But Bill was sent down for a spell,' she added bitterly.

'And Mr Affleck took these drawings away from him?'

'As you can see.' She peered myopically at the wall. 'There's one missing, though. I can't mind now which it is. But Bill did six pencil sketches. And there are only five here.'

'Did he manage to find a way to pay his rent?'

'He must have. He's still in that cottage in Lundie.'

'Could you give me his address? I'd like to talk to him.'

She laid a hand on Dania's arm. 'Watch yourself, lass. He has a temper on him.'

Hamish scowled through the windscreen. 'It's all well and good having sat-navs, ma'am, but they're about as useful as a chocolate coffee pot if you don't have the postcode.'

Dania had decided that, as Bill Baxter lived out in the sticks and had a temper on him, it would be advisable to bring along backup. And DC Hamish Downie was the best kind of backup police money could buy. She'd rung ahead before setting off for Lundie and scooped him up from the nick.

The address Mrs Spence had given was Sidlaw Cottage just before you come into Lundie, you can't miss it as it's at the junction of two roads and you can see the Sidlaw Hills in the background, Inspector. She'd shown Dania the exact spot on her Ordnance Survey map. At the time, Dania had been confident she'd find it but now, as the parched fields stretched endlessly on either side, flanked by ditches and hedgerows and the odd tree, she was less sure.

'We could always stop and ask someone,' she said. 'It must be around here somewhere.'

'That would be a good idea, but we haven't seen anyone since we left Muirhead. We haven't even seen a house.'

She was considering ringing the nick for directions when she saw it. 'Look, there's a cottage. Pull up, and I'll ask them.'

'As you wish, ma'am,' he said stiffly, bringing the car to a halt.

'You needn't come with me. I won't be long.'

'I'll leave the engine running, in that case.'

The white cottage on the corner was barely visible through the straggle of hedges. It was a single-storey building with a shallow-pitched roof and broken guttering. To call the cottage white was something of an overstatement: pieces of harling had fallen away and greenish-black mould was spreading up from the ground. Behind the rusted chain-link fence, a scrap of shrivelled lawn was bisected by a slabbed path. There were windows on either side of the door, and both sets of curtains were drawn.

After knocking and getting no response, Dania tried the handle. The door was unlocked.

'Hello?' she called into the room. 'Is anyone at home?'

When there was no reply, she pushed the door wide.

'Who the hell are you?' came a no-nonsense voice from inside.

She froze. 'I'm sorry, I didn't mean to intrude. I'm looking for Sidlaw Cottage.'

'Aye, so you've found it. What do you want?'

She toyed with the idea of calling Hamish but didn't think it would go down well with the voice's owner. 'I'm looking for Bill Baxter.'

There was a scraping noise and, in the gloom, a dark figure lumbered to its feet. 'I'm Bill Baxter.' He stank of sweat and diesel oil.

'I'd put that shotgun away if I were you,' she said, with a bravado she didn't feel.

'It's not loaded. I use it to scare away thieves. And, anyway, the firing mechanism's broken.'

A glance around the room told Dania that if a would-be thief came calling he'd be leaving empty-handed. There was little to steal – a scarred table, a few rickety chairs and a dresser with nothing on it but pieces of chipped china.

'I take it you've got a licence for that thing,' she said, indicating the shotgun.

'Aye, of course.'

He was looking at her in a strange way, as though he'd seen her before and was trying to remember where. With his untidy brown hair and thick sideburns, which were fashionable once but hadn't been for decades, she put him in his late forties or early fifties. His face was puffy, and she'd have guessed she'd woken him from his bed had she not seen the half-empty whisky bottle and the half-full glass on the table. He was wearing oversized denim jeans, which had seen better days, and a stained green sweatshirt.

'Well, what do you want?' he growled. 'I'm not going to keep asking you.'

She pulled out her warrant card. 'I'm DI Gorska. West Bell Street police station. I'd like a few words.'

Shock registered on his face. He lifted the shotgun but, before she could react, she heard rapid heavy footsteps and she was pushed aside. With a movement that looked born of practice, Hamish knocked the weapon away and slammed his fist into the man's face. Baxter reeled backwards, loosening the grip on the shotgun and giving Hamish the opportunity to snatch it out of his hands.

He was readying himself for another swipe when she gripped his arm. 'That's enough,' she ordered.

Baxter crashed into the table, knocking the bottle over. He tried to grab it but was too late. It rolled off and fell on to the floor, leaving a thin trail of liquid in the dust. He seemed to be more anguished by the loss of the whisky than the blood running from his nose.

'Shall I cuff him, ma'am?' Hamish said, opening the shotgun and peering into the barrels.

'Is it loaded?'

'It isn't. I had no way of knowing,' he added. He closed the shotgun and leant it against the wall.

Baxter wiped his nose with the back of his hand, his attention on Hamish now.

'All right, Mr Baxter,' Dania said. 'Please sit down. We'd like to ask you some questions.' She could barely see his face, it was so dark. 'I think we need more light in here.' With sharp movements, she threw open the curtains. The afternoon sunshine flooded into the room, specks of dust floating in its beams.

She was turning away when she saw the pencil sketch on the wall. It was an unmistakable likeness of Cameron sitting cross-legged in the grass and holding up a toy aeroplane. Behind him was a stone building with a tiled roof. A Gothic arch framed the heavy wooden door.

She pulled out her notebook. 'We're investigating a murder,' she said, watching Baxter. 'Cameron Affleck's.'

His gaze flew to the sketch, and then back to her. 'Aye? And?' he said softly.

'I believe you knew him.'

'I've worked for the Afflecks on and off for over twenty years. Of course I knew him.'

'What was your relationship with him?'

His nostrils flared. 'Are you saying I'm a paedo?'

'I'm asking a simple question. It's one I'm asking everyone.'

He relaxed, running a hand over his mouth. 'Aye, I knew the wee lad. We'd do the odd bit of painting together.'

'I saw those in his bedroom.'

'You've been in there, then.' He made it sound like a challenge.

'I'm running a murder inquiry, Mr Baxter, so, yes, I've been in

155

there.' She glanced around the room. 'What sort of work do you do for the Afflecks?'

'This and that.'

'Can you be more specific?'

'General handyman.'

'What skills do you have?'

'Where's this going?'

'Just answer the question, man,' Hamish growled.

'I've done plumbing, carpentry. That sort of thing.' He thought for a moment. 'And welding. A lot of that. I've got a qualification. SVQ, level six,' he added, with a hint of pride.

'Where's your equipment?'

'In the shed. Why do you want to know?'

'Can you show us?'

He shrugged. 'Ach, all right.' He hauled himself to his feet. 'There's no back door so we have to go out the front.'

He led them out and round the side of the cottage.

The back garden, if it could be called that, was in a worse state than the front. It could best be described as a rectangle of earth with a sycamore in the corner. The tree was resting its lower branches on the roof of a dilapidated shed.

He opened the door and stood aside. The shed was crammed full of different kinds of gardening tools in such a way that it would have to be emptied to get to the stuff at the back. But near the front was a set of brazing rods and a gas cylinder.

'And you use this when you work at the Afflecks' place?' Dania said, indicating the equipment.

'I don't need to. They have everything I need. And their stuff is much better quality than this,' he added, with a shrug.

'Have you got a key to their shed?' she asked, remembering the heavy-duty padlock.

'Mrs Spence unlocks it for me.'

'Tell me something, Mr Baxter. What do you think happened to Cameron?'

'Someone took him and left him in that doocot, according to the *Tele*.'

'It's the same doocot that's in your sketch. The one at Inchture.'

'Aye, I ken that.'

'What were you doing there with the boy?'

'I can't mind now – it was too long ago. I gave my statement at the time. It'll all be there.'

She caught Hamish's glance. They'd checked the statements in Chirnside's report. There was none from Bill Baxter.

'Did you go inside that doocot?' she said.

'Why would I?'

'Weren't you curious? Or wasn't Cameron? Surely a young lad would want to have a peek inside.'

'But it was locked.'

'Do you know where the key is?'

'As far as I ken, it's missing. Has been for years. Decades maybe.'

'Yet someone locked Cameron inside.'

His face clouded. 'Aye, right enough,' he said, half to himself. He shook his head. 'When I read about it in the *Tele*, I couldn't believe it. I saw that photo of the wee lad, and it was like he was there in front of me. He had that smile no one could resist. We had some braw times, him and me.' His voice became strained. 'He was always asking me to help him with his painting. I wasn't so good with the watercolours, to be honest, I was better with a pencil, but I did my best.' He looked into the distance. 'I've always blamed myself for his disappearance.'

'Why is that?'

'I took him out of the garden once or twice so he could draw the house from the road. The day he vanished, he must have wandered out with his paints and that.' He lowered his head. 'And

157

some bastard took him. But I'm the one to blame. I've thought about it all these years.' He lifted a hand and let it drop. 'I gave up trying to get it out of my mind. The drink didn't help me forget. Still doesn't.' His voice tailed off.

Dania glanced at Hamish. He shook his head.

'I think we've got everything we came for, Mr Baxter,' she said, closing her notebook. 'We'll see ourselves out.'

They left him staring at the ground.

'What do you reckon, ma'am?' Hamish said, as he started the engine.

'I think he's telling the truth.'

'Aye, he didn't deny anything. He even told us he's a welder.'

'And he said he'd been with Cameron at Inchture. If he'd locked him in the doocot, I doubt he'd have kept that sketch on the wall for everyone to see.'

Hamish turned on to the A923. 'I did wonder about motive. You said he'd had an argument with Gregor Affleck?'

'Harbouring a grudge is one thing, but chaining up a child and leaving him to starve is something else.'

'I'm inclined to agree, ma'am.'

'But there's one thing that puzzles me. And we'll have to check it out.'

'Why isn't there a record of his statement on file? I'll get on to that as soon as we're back.'

But Dania was only half listening. She was thinking about Bill Baxter standing staring at the ground and, like everyone else, blaming himself for Cameron's disappearance.

CHAPTER 16

It was Friday before Marek was back at the Lodge.

'Why aren't you in shorts, Mr Filarski?' Miss Ferguson demanded, her gaze running over his cream suit.

He raised an eyebrow. 'I'm not sure the ladies of Dundee are ready for the sight of my legs yet.'

Her laughter filled the hall. She was wearing a bluebell-coloured trouser suit and white blouse, all made of silk, which explained why she looked so cool. He himself was starting to sweat. The Lodge suffered from having no air conditioning. Then again, how many buildings in Scotland had air conditioning? Central heating was more common.

'I'm about to put the kettle on,' she said. 'Would you like to have a coffee before you start?'

He was tempted to say he'd prefer to take her out for a beer, but she'd already walked into the kitchen-cum-storage room.

'Is there another kitchen in the building?' he said, as she filled the kettle. 'For a house this size, this little room doesn't seem adequate. And there's no oven.'

'Actually, there *is* another kitchen. It's along that corridor to the left when you come in. Opposite what used to be the dining room but is now the Master's office.' She plugged in the kettle and switched it on. 'This isn't a purpose-built Lodge so the rooms

159

aren't terribly big. The two largest were knocked together and converted into the meeting hall.'

'And who cooks when the members have their Lodge dinner?'

'They get someone in to do the catering.' She smiled over her shoulder. 'You always know when they've had a dinner. You can still smell the food the next day. Murray was always poking about the kitchen looking for leftovers. But we haven't had a dinner for a while. Summer's never a good time, as so many people are away.'

Her mention of Murray reminded Marek of their last conversation. His investigator's instinct told him that, if his informant Gilie was right and something illegal was going on, then Murray was involved. And his disappearance – innocent or not – had something to do with it. His plan for today was to make a start on getting to the bottom of it. His challenge was not knowing if he should take Miss Ferguson into his confidence.

He pulled the carton of milk out of the fridge. 'How long had Murray been working here?'

'A few weeks. Why do you ask?'

'It's like you said before. It seems odd that he left so suddenly.' He paused. 'It would be nice to know why.'

She turned and looked at him strangely, as though trying to make up her mind about something. 'I think there was more to him than met the eye.'

'In what way?'

'I'm convinced he had another reason for coming to work here.'

'You did say he wanted to be a Mason.'

'No, something other than that.' She busied herself making coffee.

'What do you think it was?' he said, breaking the silence.

'I don't know.' She handed him a mug. 'I'd occasionally hear him talking to one of the Brothers. They'd stop as soon as I walked in.'

Marek blew on his coffee. 'Could it have been about the records? Are they confidential?'

'I doubt it. I can look through those records whenever I want.' She sipped slowly. 'No, it was something else.'

He felt his skin prickle. Could this be the lead he was looking for? 'Did you ever ask him?'

'He was good at changing the subject, was Murray. And something about his manner made me stop questioning him.'

'He didn't threaten you, did he?'

'Oh, no, nothing like that. He didn't tell me to mind my own business, or anything. He simply became ultra-polite and gave me monosyllabic answers.' She gazed into her mug. 'I did wonder if he was up to something illegal.' She drew out the word.

'What could he have been doing that was illegal?'

'I don't know. Trying to steal something?'

'What is there to steal? The Masonic jewels, perhaps?'

'Oh, those old things. I don't think they're worth that much.'

'They might be to a collector,' Marek ventured.

'I suppose.' She frowned. 'But he never showed the slightest interest in that cabinet.'

'Is there anything else in this building that's valuable?'

'There may be in the meeting room. But if there is, I don't know what because I've never been in. Anyway, we won't know now what Murray was up to, will we? He's gone. Which reminds me: I need to decide what to do about the money we owe him. It's not much but it belongs to him.'

Marek smiled. 'Maybe he'll come back.'

She looked at him in a way that suggested she'd like to believe him but couldn't find a reason to.

After a minute, he said, 'I notice you're married.' He gestured to her wedding finger. 'What does your husband think about your working in a Masonic Lodge?'

She stiffened. 'I'm a widow.'

'I'm sorry. I didn't realise.'

She waved a dismissive hand. 'No matter.'

'And you've kept your maiden name?'

'I worked here before I was married, so everyone was used to calling me Miss Ferguson. I saw no point in changing it.' She looked at the floor. 'When my husband died, it broke my heart for a while. It mended, but it was never quite the same heart again.' She lifted her head and gazed into his eyes. 'I fill my life with clerical work and trips to the cinema. But nothing can take the place of a man.' She sounded suddenly at the edge of tears. 'Except another man.'

He was surprised at the strength of emotion behind her words. For once, he was at a loss as to how to reply.

'Well, I'd better crack on,' she said, in a small voice. 'I'll be upstairs if you want me for anything. We have our old tax records there, and I need to dig them out.'

He followed her out of the room. She headed for the stairs.

When he heard her feet on the floor above, he closed the door to the archives and crept along the corridor. He had no specific plan but guessed that, if something was being imported, a rarely used kitchen was an ideal place to stash it. Where better to hide something than in plain sight? And the more he thought about it, the more he was convinced it was drugs that were coming in. At first, he'd assumed it was heroin, but then he remembered Gilie's words: *Take it from me. This isn't big. It's huge.* Yet what could be bigger than heroin? There was only one candidate: fentanyl. He'd seen the documentaries from the States, the blue lips and foaming mouths, the interviews with distraught mothers. And hadn't he read in the *Courier* last week about fentanyl coming into the UK? If he found the slightest trace of the drug, he'd be straight on the phone to Danka. This wasn't something he would keep to himself in the hope of getting a scoop.

At the end of the corridor, he tried the door on the right, but it was locked. The one opposite, however, opened into a large kitchen. The walls were covered with ancient cream-coloured plaster, spidered with cracks. There were the things you'd expect in an old kitchen: glass-fronted wooden cabinets, a sixties-style Formica-topped table and a red four-door Aga. But there was also a huge two-door American-style fridge, complete with ice dispenser. Given the unrelenting heat, he was sorely tempted to get it running.

He closed the door behind him and sat at the table. What form would the fentanyl take? Probably either powder or pills. He pretended the room was his. So where would he hide drugs? The obvious place was in the cupboards, although that would be risky. He imagined the caterers looking for flour with which to thicken their soup and adding fentanyl by mistake. On the other hand, Miss Ferguson had said they hadn't had caterers in for a while.

He went through the top cupboards slowly and systematically. They contained crockery and empty containers. One shelf held small spice jars. He removed the lids and sniffed cautiously. Unless the drug was heavily disguised as cinnamon or turmeric, he was wasting his time.

He tried the bottom cupboards. Buckets, brushes, cleaning materials. More cleaning materials. He considered testing the contents of the huge bleach bottles, then decided against it.

As he was closing the last cupboard door, his gaze fell on the Aga. Somehow, it seemed too obvious. Then, again . . .

He opened one of the doors and peered inside. It looked clean enough, although there was a faint smell of grease. He put his hand in, feeling around with his fingers.

'You know, I caught Murray in here, doing the exact same thing.'

He wheeled round.

Miss Ferguson was watching him, frowning. He straightened slowly. He should have realised he'd never have heard her light footsteps on the thick-pile carpet.

She closed the door and leant against it.

'May I ask what you're doing, Mr Filarski?' She crossed her arms. 'And why you had your hand inside the Aga? Did you find anything?'

'Nothing.'

'Not even a dead body? No? So what were you doing?'

His heart was thumping wildly. A number of possible excuses chased themselves round his head, but something made him say, 'I'm an investigator working undercover.'

Her wide eyes widened further.

When she said nothing, he added, 'I had a tip-off that drugs are being brought into the Lodge.' He shrugged. 'Possibly.'

'And you're looking for them here? In the kitchen?' She made it sound as though she were taking him seriously.

He threw her a crooked smile. 'It's where I would hide them.'

'I think there might be better places.' There was calculation in her eyes. 'I think you need to get your jacket.'

'Are you firing me?'

'Good heavens, no,' she said, alarm in her voice. 'I'm letting you take me out for morning coffee.'

'I discovered this place not long after I started working here,' Miss Ferguson said. 'The Lodge keeps a tab because the members sometimes drop in. Jock makes the most divine scones, but it seems he's out of them today. I can't say I'm surprised.'

'Not a place I know,' Marek said, glancing around the café. The general impression was that of a small, family-run concern with the usual mix of home baking and homemade sandwiches.

She bit into a brioche topped with sugar crystals. 'The police station is across the road.'

'I take it you're not going to turn me in?'

'Now why would I do that, Mr Filarski?'

'I'm working under false pretences as an archivist.'

'But you *are* working as an archivist. I've seen what you've done with that database.'

He studied her over the rim of his cup, wondering where this was going.

'The thing is,' she was saying, 'whatever it is you're looking for, Murray was looking for it, too.'

Marek chose his words carefully. 'And the fact that he's disappeared might have something to do with it?'

'I'm sure of it,' she said firmly.

He sipped his cappuccino, pondering the coincidence of two professional investigators working undercover on the same job. Then he dismissed the thought: Murray had come to the Lodge to work on their records and had simply stumbled across whatever was going on.

Miss Ferguson wiped her fingers on the napkin. 'I suppose we'd better get back.'

'So I'm not getting the sack?'

'You're not. I need you to help me find Murray.'

'Ah.'

'And, in the process, you may also find what you're looking for.'

They left the café and walked the short distance to the Lodge.

'You know, Mr Filarski, I've often wondered what this area must have been like when the jute mills were in operation, with all that steam and the smuts. Very different from now, don't you think?'

They'd stopped at the Lodge door. 'I do wish you'd call me Franek. And I still don't know your first name.'

'Only my friends call me by my first name.' She hesitated. 'It might be best if you went home now. I'll see you on Monday.' She inserted the key into the lock.

He recognised when he was being dismissed.

He'd walked just a few paces when he heard her call him.

'Mr Filarski.'

He turned. 'Yes?'

She looked steadily at him. 'My name's Allie,' she said finally.

CHAPTER 17

Allie let herself into the Lodge, deep in thought. So Franek Filarski was an undercover investigator. Working for whom, though? It hardly mattered. Except that whoever was employing him might be after the same thing as Murray. And perhaps whatever had happened to Murray might also happen to him. She thought of Franek's magnetic blue eyes and devastating smile. He was the polar opposite of her husband, Ross. Which reminded her that she needed to finish her emails and hurry down to the museum. Having two part-time jobs, even when the buildings were close to one another, was less than ideal. She wouldn't mind so much except that her earnings now no longer went into a joint account but straight into Ross's, to which he denied her access. Although, if it came to it, she could always pawn her engagement ring. He must have suspected she'd entertained that idea, because he always checked her hand as soon as they arrived home. As if that weren't enough, he phoned the Lodge and the museum several times a day when he wasn't there and she was.

She fired off the emails, expecting the same negative response as she'd received to date. Fundraising for anything to do with drugs didn't have the same appeal as raising money for a new hospital. When she'd shown Niall the replies, his jaw muscles had tightened and his eyes had bored into hers. As though this were somehow her fault. Idiot man.

She powered down the laptop, picked up her bag and left the building.

A few minutes later, she was at the museum, taking over from Dougie, the part-time student with moony eyes and lank hair. He looked happy to leave. Maybe Ross had been giving him a hard time over something trivial, which he liked to do as it reinforced his sense of himself.

She was running through the previous week's takings for the second time, wondering if she had made a mistake or whether the software had, when Ross marched in.

'Leave that, and go in and help Kenny,' he snapped. 'I have to go out.'

She kept her eyes on the spreadsheet. 'I just need to—'

He slammed his hand on the desk, making her jump. 'Pay attention when a man talks to you.'

She stared at him. She knew that look, and realised that if she didn't behave in a suitably submissive manner she would pay for it later. 'I'm sorry.' She lowered her head. 'What does he want me to do?'

'The jaguar. It needs two people.'

'What about the reception desk?'

'We'll close early. The taxidermy's more important.'

She was about to say that he could have asked Dougie to stay on. He'd have said yes, as he needed the money. But that was Ross. He rarely thought ahead.

'Lock up after me and put the sign on the door.'

'Yes, Ross.'

After she'd locked the building, she walked slowly through the display halls, wondering when they'd see the end of the jaguar. In one of his rare moments of humour, Gregor had recounted the story of its acquisition. He'd seen the animal when it was live, as it had been a gift from a Mason friend to his wife. Rumour had it that this man had asked her what she wanted for her birthday. When she replied, 'A beautiful jaguar,' he'd assumed she meant the big cat. What she'd had in mind, however, was the car. Gregor had to admit that the animal was impressive. It was kept on a chain, and the wife would escort it on walks round the garden. It was said to be tame, although Gregor had looked into its eyes – from a comfortable distance – and wouldn't have put money on it. Like Allie, he fell into the category of those who believe that no wild animal can truly be tamed, and it was just a matter of time before it turned on its owner. It had therefore come as something of a surprise to learn that the animal had died. The vet had assumed it was a tragic case of inadvertently eating poisoned rodents. Gregor confided to Allie that he suspected the husband had had a hand in it.

The museum had been charged with creating a taxidermy mount that could be displayed in the hall of the couple's palatial home. Gregor had seen the space at the bottom of the curving staircase and deemed it eminently suitable.

He had made the measurements a few months earlier and Kenny, who was better with his hands than his brother, had used them to carve the polyurethane form over which the skin would be stretched. They'd been working on this for ages now, and Allie hoped the messy process of skinning was over. She'd had the mis-fortune to be present when Ross had skinned a leopard. It was supposed to be done without opening the body cavity, but he'd made a complete hash of it by slicing through the intestines. The stench had been appalling and had hung around the workshop for so long that she still felt sick whenever she thought about it.

Kenny was working at the tables near the sink. 'You're late,' he barked, seeing her come through the door.

169

He didn't usually speak like that, but with her he always tried to sound like Ross. She had learnt the hard way that neither brother had much time for women. Except when they were hungry for sex. Which seemed most of the time.

She was relieved to see that the jaguar's skin was lying splayed on a table, ready for mounting. She sashayed over to the pegs, aware that Kenny was watching her. An apron was necessary for this stage of the process, and she always went through a little ritual when she was alone with him. She tied the straps securely, and then smoothed the material, slowly running her fingers over her breasts and down her body. His gaze sharpened, but he said nothing. She pulled on a pair of gloves and strolled over to where he was working.

The jaguar's form had been placed on a movable Perspex platform. Kenny had already added the glass eyes, which gave the structure the appearance of a giant white cat. The mouth was closed which meant they'd save themselves time by not having to bother with the tongue or teeth.

Kenny took up a pot and brush and quickly added a thin layer of slow-drying glue to the polyurethane. He picked up the skin and laid it over the form. Allie knew what she had to do but he always felt the need to tell her.

'Pull it at the back and hold the stretch while I get the head done, eh.'

She did as she was ordered, gripping the skin while he tugged and smoothed. When he was satisfied, he pulled the edges of the hide together, adding upholstery pins as he went.

'Hold this bit underneath,' he said, with a glance at her.

What he wanted her to do required them to work in close proximity to one another. She crouched half under the form, holding the skin under the belly while he pinned the hide behind the front legs, constantly smoothing and pulling with his

170

long-fingered hands. She inched towards the back as he dealt with the underside, kneeling so close to her that she could feel his hot breath on her face. As he paused to wipe his forehead with his apron, she caught a glimpse of the bulge in his trousers. But she knew she had nothing to fear from Kenny. Ross would have killed him had he made a move.

She used to wonder what Kenny was like in bed, whether he was considerate towards his partner, or whether, like his brother, he satisfied his sexual urges in the way an animal does. She'd overheard a conversation between Kenny and Mrs Spence, and learnt that he regularly visited a sexcam girl in her student flat. What he paid for her services covered the rent. Allie had no idea how this conversation had started, since she'd come in partway, but it ended with Mrs Spence's gently but firmly remonstrating with Kenny, and his telling her to mind the house and not his business. Allie amused herself by imagining a scene in which she told Niall Affleck what was going on. But he'd probably conclude that paying the student's rent was an act that discharged Kenny's obligation to contribute to charity, as all Masons are required to do. That the student had to open her legs to facilitate Kenny's moral responsibility Niall would almost certainly view as an unimportant detail.

After a few months of marriage, Allie's own appetite for sex had fizzled out. Although when Franek Filarski smiled at her, she felt the heat rise in her blood. He'd be the perfect gentleman, putting her needs before his, of that she was sure. She imagined lying under him, her legs scissored round his waist. But nothing could come of it. She couldn't risk her life – or his – by encouraging him. It would complicate matters and might derail what she had in mind for him.

Kenny had finished pinning the hide. He sat back, surveying his work, which to Allie looked as though the big cat were having a course of acupuncture. With a frown and a shake of the head, he went back to the beginning and gave the mount a final firm smooth-down.

'Do you need me for the rest?' she said, knowing the answer but trying anyway.

'Aye, get the needles threaded.' He jerked his head towards the table. 'Everything's laid out on the tray.'

Despite herself, Allie found this part of the procedure fascinating. Using what he'd once explained was an upholsterer's stitch, Kenny would sew the ends of the hide together, removing the pins as he went. She'd seen him do this with a red fox. He wasn't fast, but he was accurate, keeping the hair out of the way of the thread.

On the tray were several identical needles, and pre-cut lengths of thread of the right colour. Kenny had at least prepared well. Prior planning, he would often say to his brother, who was more inclined to do everything at the last minute and consequently had to be rescued.

Allie's task was to keep the needles threaded, and hand them and the scissors to Kenny at the right moment, like an assistant to a surgeon. The work was slow and laborious, and she found herself thinking again about Franek. An investigator working undercover. And he'd mentioned drugs. Which meant that he was totally on the wrong track.

'Right, that's the body done,' Kenny said, tying off the knot.

He'd already added the lining to the ears and tail. But there was one final task, and he'd left it to the end so he could do it with Allie, although he could have done it by himself.

He got to his feet, his knees cracking. 'Fetch the foam and the clay.' He took up a crouching position at the back of the form. 'I'm waiting,' he said, looking squarely at her.

She did as he'd commanded, and brought over the tube of stiff foam and the packet of red clay. He marked off a length of foam and handed it to her.

She inserted it into the skin that had covered the jaguar's penis, pushing it in as far as it would go.

'Check it's in all the way,' Kenny said thickly.

'I think that's it,' she said, trying to sound bored.

'Now the balls.' He handed her two lumps of clay.

She pushed them into the scrotum, moving them around.

'Aye, I bet that feels good,' he murmured. 'Does Ross let you do that?'

She said nothing, not wanting to indulge his fantasies.

He sewed up the holes. 'Just the feet now, and we're done, eh.'

'Do you need me for that?' she said. 'I'd like to finish checking the takings before we go home.'

He was like one of his freeze-dried rats: that same look of surprise, mingled with indignation. She thought he'd insist she stay, but he said, 'Ach, all right. You can go.'

As she threw the apron into the bin, her gaze fell on one of the dioramas he and Ross had been working on. Several mice were sitting at a long table. There was something familiar about the composition, the way the rodents were placed in groups of three, with a lone mouse in the centre, his arms outstretched. With a sudden jolt, she recognised it as a recreation of Leonardo da Vinci's *The Last Supper*.

He must have seen her staring. 'You ken what we're doing with that, eh?'

'No. Enlighten me.'

'Entering it into a national competition. The winner's going to be announced in December.' Something shifted in his expression. 'Aye, and we'll all be going down to London for the ceremony.'

Allie smiled to herself as she left the room. *Oh, no, not me. I'll be long gone.*

CHAPTER 18

Saturday morning saw Dania taking a shortcut through the Overgate. She had a rare half-day off and needed to stock up. She'd bought food at the Polski Sklep on Dura Street, but since her coffee-maker had died in a cloud of smoke, she'd had to sustain herself with what they served in the police canteen, and she'd finally decided enough was enough. She was on her way to Debenhams.

In front of the curved windows on the Overgate's ground floor, not far from Costa Coffee, was the white lacquered baby grand. It was the Steinway she'd played regularly until Marek had bought her the upright. Seeing the lid open and no one playing, she found she couldn't resist. She set down her shopping bags and pulled out the seat. She was considering what to play when she noticed a hardback book someone had left on the piano. It was a coffee-table edition entitled *The Art of Florence*, with Michelangelo's David in all his full-frontal glory on the cover.

There was only one piece she could play now. She brought her hands down on the keys and ran through Scott Joplin's 'Fig Leaf Rag'. She much preferred his slow, melancholy rags to the faster, livelier ones, and made it last four and a half minutes, which she guessed was about the right tempo. She was getting to her feet when a boy, who looked no older than six, sidled up to the piano. He had soft brown eyes and scruffy hair.

'Can I play something with you?' he asked.

'Of course,' she said warmly. She shuffled over to make room. 'What would you like to play?'

'"The Blue Danube Waltz". I'm still learning it and I just know the right hand. And I have to play that with both hands.'

'That's perfectly okay. I can play the left hand. So what key do you know it in?'

'It's in C.'

'Right. How about I play an intro and then you come in?'

'How will I know when?' he said anxiously.

'You'll know. And if you don't, I'll give you a signal.'

'Is that how they do it with orchestras?'

'It's exactly how they do it. The conductor catches the eye of the performer.' She smiled at him. 'Are you ready?'

He glanced around. People were standing watching. 'Shouldn't we tell the audience what we're playing?' he said brightly.

'I think everyone knows "The Blue Danube". And if they don't know it now, they'll know it by the end.'

He nodded, apparently satisfied.

'Ready?'

He nodded again.

The intro required her to play a number of high notes. Rather than lean across the boy, she put her right arm behind him and played while giving him a cuddle.

As she slowed in anticipation of his entry, she put her lips to his ear and said, 'Now.'

His timing was impeccable. And he was finger-perfect, moving effortlessly between the staccato and legato passages. She played more quietly than she would normally so that his music could be heard above hers. He finished with a flourish.

People were standing applauding wildly. Even the customers at Costa Coffee were on their feet.

'You're supposed to take a bow,' she said, nudging him gently.

To the sound of cheers and whistles, he got to his feet and bowed awkwardly.

His face broke into a toothy grin. 'Will you be here again next Saturday?' he said eagerly.

'I'm not sure.'

'If you are, will you play with me?'

'Of course. My name's Dania, by the way.'

'Mine's Duncan.' His eyes were glowing. 'Do you think I'll be able to play like you when I'm your age?'

'Well before, I should think.'

'And can we get ourselves on to YouTube?'

'I don't know about that,' she said, laughing.

A woman pushed through the crowd. 'Duncan!' she shouted. 'What have I told you about running off? I've been looking everywhere for you!'

'Sorry, Mum,' he said, in a small voice.

'Seems like I caught you just in time. You were going to play that piano and embarrass yourself, weren't you, eh?' She took his arm and dragged him through the crowd. He had time to throw Dania a quick thumbs-up before disappearing.

She was picking up her bags when she saw a familiar figure. Owen McFadden was climbing the steps up from Costa.

'So, this is what you do when you're not being a detective,' he said, smiling.

'It's not often I have the opportunity to play duets with children.'

'Is it better than playing with adults?'

'Playing anything with children is better than playing with adults. Children are less self-conscious, for one thing.' She glanced towards Costa. 'Are you on your own?'

'Aye, I needed a coffee, so I snuck out. What they serve in the canteen is hardly worthy of the name.'

She wanted to ask how his investigation was going, but the Overgate was too public. 'Look, do you fancy some lunch? I've been so busy that I've not seen you.'

He threw her a tired smile. 'I'd appreciate talking over the case. Shall we get a couple of sandwiches and find a quiet bench? Or do you want to go back to the nick?'

'It's too hot to stay indoors. Let's go down to the waterfront.'

They bought sandwiches at Costa, and left the Overgate, crossing the High Street towards Union Street. Dania had been pleasantly surprised when she first came to Dundee to discover that you can't get lost in the city centre because the streets slope down to the river. They continued past the railway station until they reached the waterfront. Ahead was the new V&A, separated from the three-masted RRS *Discovery* by a pool of still water. They sat down on one of the granite seats.

'Okay, what do we know so far?' Dania said, unwrapping her tuna-and-cucumber sandwich. 'Tech have checked Fiona's phone and there's nothing suspicious on it. So did they find anything on Euna's?'

Owen shook his head. 'Only the usual nonsense kids put on their mobiles. We've cross-checked with everyone on her Contacts list, and it's all in order.' He bit into his prawn sandwich.

'So, no predator masquerading as an eleven-year-old girl?'

'Not that we could find,' he said, chewing. 'We've also cross-referenced the interviews and gone over them again in case we missed something vital. Same result.'

'And has anyone responded to the posters, or appeals for information?'

'We've had the usual eejits wanting our attention,' he said, with a disdainful smile.

It was par for the course. Every investigation had its share of people who seemed to think it was a lark to waste police time.

'And the bleach?' she said.

'We've been in touch with the wholesalers. No one has ordered bleach in large quantities. And we were careful how we made the enquiries. The press still haven't caught on to that part of the story.'

'It's our best hope. If the killer believes we don't know he used bleach, he may become careless. Although how he could think that is beyond me. It would come up at the post-mortems.' She played with her sandwich. 'Do you think he planned all this ages ago and bought the bleach then?'

'We thought of that, too. The thing is that bleach doesn't keep. It'll last several months, a bit longer if you store it in a cool place. But eventually the oxygen goes and you're left with common or garden salt water.'

'Then you only need to look back over a few months' worth of shop records. Although he could have bought a bottle in each of a number of shops.'

'Making it impossible to find a correlation.'

'And what did Kimmie say about Euna's clothes?'

'Nothing that helps us.'

'It's just that I worked on a case in London where we caught the perp through a particular type of pollen on his victims' clothes.'

Owen looked at her with interest. 'Is pollen unique?'

'Unique to a particular species. It turned out that the killer had a rare plant in his garden. I forget the name of it now, but he'd left the victims' bodies there until he was ready to dump them. I know it was circumstantial but it eventually led us to him, and we were able to find the evidence we needed to nail him.'

This had been one of Dania's earliest cases at the Met. Five young men had been kidnapped, and their bodies found in Beddington Park a few days later. Their faces had been sliced off in what the police assumed was a crude attempt at identity concealment. Pollen on the front of their clothing indicated that they'd been lying face down in a garden where that particular plant grew in profusion. The fact that it was a rare plant had worked in their favour.

'What do you make of the dates the girls went missing?' Owen was saying. 'We have Fiona taken on Friday, June the fifteenth, and Euna on Saturday, July the seventh. Roughly three weeks apart. It's July the twenty-first today,' he added ominously. 'If the timing is significant, we have a week left to catch him before he kills again.'

'I don't know that serials work to such a rigid timetable. But the fact that he waited so long between Fiona and Euna is significant. Given the opportunity, he would have taken more.' She turned to him. 'And it's that lack of opportunity that's our way in. We need to know why he waited three weeks before taking Euna.'

'He might have been waiting for the furore to die down.'

'Unlikely.'

'You don't think he's gone to ground?'

'I think something's stopping him kidnapping again.'

'Maybe he's gone on holiday,' Owen said, in a voice tinged with irony. 'Anyway, what about you? How are you getting on with your chained boy?'

'I've been concentrating on opportunity. And I've been getting nowhere. It's time to think about motive.'

'What motive could there possibly be? A young boy left to starve in a doocot? What kind of psycho does that?'

'I did think at first that it *was* a psycho. And he'd go back from time to time to watch the lad slowly dying. We had a case like that in London. A husband did it to his wife.'

179

'But?'

'I'm not sure, now.'

And Bill Baxter, their only lead, had led nowhere. Hamish had double-checked the archives and found that the man's statement had been misfiled. Baxter had been questioned by Chirnside, and made no secret of the fact that, in the school holidays, he and Cameron would sometimes go out into the countryside, painting and drawing. Mrs Affleck accompanied them, bringing a picnic basket. Chirnside had added that, on the Sunday in question, Baxter had a cast-iron alibi: he'd been in Dumfries visiting his cousin and her family.

'Cold cases are the worst,' Owen was saying. 'Aye, whatever difficulties I'm having, I still wouldn't want to swap with you.' He smiled. 'Thanks for giving up your free time to talk this over. Are you at work tomorrow?'

'All day. I don't know when I'll find time to go to Mass. It'll have to be the six a.m. service in English. I usually go in the evening to the Polish Mass.'

He looked at her sadly. 'Hasn't being a detective, and seeing what one human being can do to another, made you lose your faith?'

'Strangely, no.'

'I'd better get back. I'll see you tomorrow.'

She watched him go, aware that, as someone with young daughters of his own, he was finding this case particularly distressing. Jackie Ireland would have known that before she assigned it. Maybe she thought being a young father was a strength. Or maybe she didn't think like that at all.

Dania was reaching for her bags when her phone buzzed.

'Hi, Marek,' she said.

'Danka, I'm glad I caught you. I'm having Jamie and Pam over to dinner tonight. You wouldn't be free to join us, by any chance?'

'Tonight? Yes. But I'm on duty until six. And that's if nothing comes up.'

'I won't serve until seven, in that case.'

'I'll call if I can't make it. And I'll bring dessert,' she added, glad now that she'd been to the Polski Sklep. 'But don't wait for me.'

She was about to ask him what he was going to cook, but he'd disconnected. No matter. Whatever he made was always worth the wait. Pity the same couldn't be said for her, she thought, as she fingered the remains of her sandwich. A seagull landed not far from the bench and sidestepped towards her. She threw what was left on to the ground and, in a single fluid movement, the bird took off, swooped down to scoop up the bread and flew away.

Her thoughts harked back to little Cameron Affleck, his dark curls and melting smile. Hard as she tried, she couldn't escape the image of the skeleton chained in the lonely doocot. It was there when she awoke, and it was there at night when she drifted off to sleep. Had he still been alive when the rats came for him? Anger bubbled inside her, threatening to boil over. When that happened, she found it difficult to contain her rage. She vowed silently that, whatever it took, she would find his killer. And bring him to justice.

CHAPTER 19

'Aye, right enough,' Jamie was saying. 'That was even better than the blowout we had at the Staropolska.'

They'd finished their *gołąbki*, which Marek made in the traditional way, wrapping pieces of lightly boiled cabbage round a mixture of rice, minced beef and onions, and baking them.

'Is it typically Polish?' Pam said. She was a pale-skinned woman with long brown hair piled untidily on top of her head.

'It's hard to find anything more Polish.' Dania looked questioningly at Marek. '*Pierogi*?'

'We could argue about it all evening,' he said, getting to his feet. 'Everyone has their favourite typical Polish dish.'

'Hold on, Marek, I'll help you clear,' Dania said.

Jamie pushed his chair back. 'No, you ladies stay where you are. We'll do it.'

The men took the dishes into the kitchen.

'It's so nice to finally meet you,' Pam said. 'Jamie told me he heard you play at the railway station. And you've got a concert on in Edinburgh later this year?'

'I was on my way to the consulate to sort out the programme when we ran into each other.'

'And have you sorted it?'

'There are some new pieces I have to learn. It's finding the time.'

Pam shook her head. 'Aye, there's never enough time for everything we want to do, is there?' She studied Dania. 'So why did you become a detective and not a concert pianist? I reckon you'd have made more money.'

'I like solving problems. That's it, really.'

'It must be satisfying when you close a case.'

Dania thought of what closing a case meant for detectives working in the Murder Squad. Yes, there was elation when the investigation came to an end, but it was always tempered by a feeling of sadness, and the realisation that the lives of the families caught up in the case had been destroyed.

Marek and Jamie had monopolised the conversation with tales of life at the *Courier*, and the sorts of scrapes they'd got into, and got out of. Now, with the men in the kitchen, Dania had her opportunity. 'Tell me about your work as a wedding planner,' she said.

Pam played with her glass. 'It's enormously creative. But also incredibly tiring. You have to design something you think will work in the setting the clients have chosen, but also listen to what they want.'

'I bet their ideas don't always chime with yours.'

'Aye, you've got that right. And their ideas keep coming long after the time when you need to start putting stakes into the ground. The music is the hardest thing. There's never any agreement.'

'What do you have? String quartets?'

'Sometimes. What the clients seem to prefer is romantic piano music.' She looked pointedly at Dania. 'You wouldn't be interested, would you?'

'Me?'

'Most of the weddings are at the weekends.'

'I'm flattered to be asked but, like all police officers, I have weekend shifts. And, even when we get leave, it can be cancelled.'

'Must wreak havoc with your private life.'

'Private life? What's that?' Dania took a sip of wine. 'Have you ever had a client pull out at the last minute?'

'Ach, I make them sign on the dotted line before I commit my finances. But I once had a bride jilted at the altar. Would you believe her parents wanted their money back?'

'Did they get it?'

'Aye, right.' Pam smiled wryly. 'When the dust had settled, I referred them to the small print on the contract. And the fact that they'd gone ahead with the wedding breakfast anyway.'

'Jamie told us he sometimes takes the official photographs at your weddings.'

'He helps me when I can't get my usual man. But I try not to ask him too often as he has his own business. And his mother died earlier this year. Any spare time he has is spent clearing her house. Landscape photography is what he concentrates on, although he does other kinds from time to time. Have you seen his work?'

'I have to confess I haven't.'

'He has his own website, which showcases it,' she said enthusiastically. 'Enter his name and "landscape photography" and you'll find it.' She opened her bag. 'Here's my card, by the way. In case you change your mind about playing at my weddings,' she added, pushing it across.

The men returned, bringing dessert and coffee.

'So what's this?' Pam said.

'*Makowiec*,' Marek said. 'Courtesy of my sister.'

'I confess that I didn't make it,' Dania said. 'I bought it in the Polish shop.'

'How would you describe it, Danka?'

'Like a Swiss roll with poppy seeds.'

'And after coffee, we'll have *wiśniówka*. It's a vodka flavoured with cherries.' He frowned at Jamie. 'You're not driving, are you?'

'You told us not to.'

'Good man.'

As Marek cut the *makowiec*, Dania said, 'There's something I wanted to ask you, Jamie.'

'If it's about a photoshoot, the answer's yes.' He grinned. 'I think it's well time the *Courier* did a feature on you,' he added, glancing at Marek for confirmation. 'I reckon not many police stations have a detective who's a concert pianist.'

'It wasn't that, no. I wanted to ask you about that photoshoot you did at the Affleck house.'

He stared vacantly, as if trying to remember.

'You said it was for a homes-and-gardens magazine. Can you remember when?'

'To be honest, no, I can't. It was years ago. Why do you ask?' he added softly.

'I wondered if you remembered Cameron Affleck.'

'The lad in the doocot?' He shook his head emphatically. 'He wasn't there. The first time I laid eyes on him was that photo in the papers. I didn't even know Cameron existed until then.'

'Was it only Gregor Affleck in your photos?'

'And the two older boys.'

Dania gazed at him without blinking. He sounded cagey, as though he had something to hide. But maybe he genuinely couldn't remember, and simply didn't want to appear vague.

She was about to press him further, but Marek was looking at her in the way he did when she was going too far with her questioning.

She gestured to the bottle with its brightly coloured label. 'Shall we have the vodka with the *makowiec*?'

'Now *that's* what I call a plan,' Jamie said, with a thin smile.

Once the *wiśniówka* started to flow, the evening soon degenerated. But as midnight approached and the Reids said their goodbyes, leaving to find a taxi to their home in Newport-on-Tay, Dania was regretting not having persisted with Jamie. She might have learnt more about him and what he'd really photographed at the Affleck house. Because, for no reason she could fathom, she couldn't rid herself of the feeling that Jamie was indeed hiding something. And the opportunity to uncover what it was had been lost. She would therefore need to find another.

'You're welcome to stay the night, Danka,' Marek said, as they carried the glasses into the kitchen. 'That goes without saying.'

'Thanks, but I have an early shift tomorrow, so I should get going.'

'I'll walk with you in that case.'

Dania knew better than to argue. Marek would never let a woman walk home alone. Especially so late at night.

Darkness was settling on Dundee as they made their way along the Nethergate. The advantage of living so far north was that the nights were short close to the summer solstice and, although the sky darkened, it never became inky black in the way it did in winter. But the deep blue, with its sprinkling of stars, suited Dania − and the police − better. Crimes were less likely to be committed if the perpetrators were more easily visible.

'Did I tell you that I ran into Father Kliment a couple of days ago?' Marek said. 'He wasn't his usual cheery self. I'm worried about him. Will you be seeing him tomorrow?'

'I doubt it. I'll have to go to early Mass, and it will be someone else.'

'Can you drop in on him later?'

'If I have time. Do you know what's troubling him?'

'I didn't ask. But I've never seen him like that. He looked like a man twice his age. You know, Danka, when a priest has something on his mind, it often ends badly for the rest of us. Actually, it nearly ended badly for him. He crossed the street without looking where he was going. If I hadn't pulled him back, he would have been under a car.'

They reached the Marketgait and turned left. Lights were burning in an upstairs window in the police station.

'Someone on the late shift?' Marek said, smiling.

'Or someone forgot to switch the lights off.'

'By the way, did you know there's a great little café here on the left?' He peered into the shadows.

'I often bring the team their coffee from there.' She hesitated. 'Marek, can I ask you something?'

'Ask away.'

'How well do you know Jamie?'

'How well do you know anyone?'

'That's not an answer.'

'Okay, so he joined the *Courier* about six years ago. We worked pretty closely for a while. Then he left to go freelance.'

'And you've remained good friends?'

'The best.' There was a note of irritation in his voice. 'And now you can tell me why you're asking me these questions.'

Dania was good at thinking on her feet. 'I'm curious as to why someone would give up a well-paid, secure job to go freelance.'

'And what conclusion have you come to?'

'I'm assuming his wife earns the big money.'

'You may be right. He left the *Courier* shortly after they were married.'

'Do you trust him?'

187

Marek stopped. 'Now what kind of a question is that?' he said angrily.

She was conscious she'd crossed a line. 'Ignore me. I'm always like that with new people I meet. Being a detective makes you question everyone and everything.'

He said nothing, which meant he was angry but didn't want to take it further in case he said something he'd wish he hadn't. They walked the rest of the way in silence.

As they said their goodnights, Dania was deeply regretting the clumsy way she'd phrased the question. Because Marek was now unlikely to want to assist her. And there were further questions she wished to put to him. And they were all about Jamie Reid.

CHAPTER 20

Allie poked her head into the archives room. 'Franek,' she said, 'shall we have a little tête-à-tête?'

Marek looked up from the records book. 'Is now a good time?'

'Now is a very good time. Mr Affleck has left. We can go into the office. It's more comfortable there.'

She picked up the embroidered shoulder bag on her desk and led him along the corridor. As she reached the room opposite the kitchen, she lifted the flap of the bag and drew out a bunch of keys.

'This door is normally kept locked,' she said, opening it.

The room was decorated in the same shade of grey as the hall. With the oval table and matching chairs, it looked more like a dining room than an office. Only the neat pile of papers on the table suggested that something other than eating went on here.

'Good heavens, what's that?' he said.

She followed the direction of his gaze. 'The swans from *Swan Lake*.'

'But they're squirrels.'

'Yes, well, there's no accounting for taste.'

They took seats at the dining table. After a glance at Marek, Allie stared at her hands as though unsure whether to continue. In such circumstances, he always found it better to wait.

189

'I want to talk to you about Murray,' she said finally. 'If that's all right.'

'Of course.'

She ran a nail lightly down the table. 'I haven't been totally honest with you. You see, some weeks after Murray started work, he took me into his confidence.'

'About the drugs?'

'He knew he needed my help if he was to have a chance of finding them. So we decided to partner up.'

Marek ran a hand over his hair. 'You're saying he thought they were hidden here in the Lodge?'

'He'd overheard Niall Affleck talking to someone on his mobile.' She smiled. 'Murray always worked quietly in the archives room and, anyway, archivists are invisible.'

'And were you here at the time?'

'He told me all this afterwards.'

'What exactly did he overhear?'

'From Niall's side of the conversation, he deduced that there was a shipment coming in. Niall agreed to keep the package, whatever it was, safely in the Lodge. He didn't say where. It was clear, though, that whatever was coming in was illegal. And worth a bomb.'

Marek's mind was racing. So he was right, and the fentanyl was somewhere in the building. Or had been. In his experience, drugs rarely stayed in one place for long. Then again, maybe shipments were coming in regularly, and fentanyl was hidden here right now.

'It seems the Master isn't quite the saint he makes himself out to be,' he said, with a sneer. Niall's supercilious attitude had irritated him from the start. He treated Marek as though he were the office boy. He could still hear his olive-oil voice: *Perhaps tomorrow you could arrange to get yourself here on time, Mr Filarski. Those records won't enter themselves into the computer, you know.*

190

'He's a novelist,' Allie said dismissively. 'Novelists are capable of anything. Bringing in drugs must be a nice little earner. And I think he needs every penny. He's divorced and has to make regular payments to his ex-wife.'

'Where would he hide the shipment? Where's the best place?'

'I'll cut to the chase, Franek. We thought the package would be in the office safe.'

'Which is where?'

'Behind you.' She looked at the wall. 'Or, to be specific, behind that painting.'

He turned, seeing a landscape of Eilean Donan at sunset, with the castle and mountains in the background.

'If you take that frame off the wall, there's a safe behind it. It's got one of those keypad things.'

He looked at her with admiration. 'How do you know this?'

'I was leaving the kitchen and saw the door to this room was open. Niall was keying in a number. He opened the safe and put something inside. Then he closed it and put the picture frame back.' She held up a hand. 'And before you ask, no, I didn't see what number he entered. I was too far away.'

'How many people know the combination?'

'I haven't the faintest.' She clasped her hands together. 'Here's what we decided to do. Murray offered to try to crack the safe.'

'Without knowing the code?'

'He said people often use their date of birth. I happened to know the Master's.'

'I'm guessing that didn't work.'

'I wasn't here that day. That was the Tuesday, July the tenth. But I got an email from him later the same evening telling me what had happened. He'd heard the front door open and close, which meant that the Master had left, so he'd decided it was okay to have a go. He was so busy trying various combinations that he didn't hear the Master return.' She smiled faintly. 'You know yourself how thick the carpet in the corridor is.'

'So what happened?'

'Niall threatened him with the police unless he told him what he was up to. Murray confessed to overhearing the conversation about the shipment.' She looked away. 'But he didn't give up my name.'

'And then?' Marek said, when she fell silent.

'He was sacked. On the spot.'

'And did he say anything else in the email?'

'Just that he'd be in touch again once he'd figured out what to do. Anyway, the next day I was back here working. I tried emailing Murray but got no reply.'

'Didn't you phone him?'

'I haven't got a phone. I mean, I've lost it.'

'He said he was *trying* to open the safe. That suggests he didn't succeed.'

'That's what I assumed. And then the day after, which was the Thursday, I received a last email from him saying he was leaving Dundee. It was very formal, the kind you send when it's final, I suppose. But it was sent to the Lodge email address, not mine.'

'Didn't you find that strange?'

'It wasn't like him at all.'

'What conclusion did you come to?'

She played with her fingers. 'It crossed my mind that he'd opened the safe and found the package. And scarpered with it.'

'And that stuff about being surprised by the Master, and sacked?'

'Was just a load of guff.'

'Did you ask Niall about Murray? Whether he did actually sack him?'

'I didn't dare. You don't know the man like I do.' She frowned.

'When he saw you working here, he asked who you were, and I told him that Murray had left Dundee, and I'd taken you on to replace him.'

'What was his reaction?'

'He didn't look particularly surprised. But that could mean anything.'

'If he *had* sacked him, surely he'd have told you. You had things to do, like stop his salary and so on.'

'That's what I thought,' she said triumphantly. 'So Murray must have succeeded in opening that safe.'

And, if the package had been inside, and Murray had known what it contained, he'd have had a ready market in Dundee, the drugs capital of Europe.

'Allie, have you considered he may still be in Dundee?'

'I did think that, yes. He lives up in the Dryburgh area. He might still be in his flat, for all I know.'

'Would you be willing to give me his address?' Marek said softly.

The gleam in her eyes gave him his answer.

Marek pulled up outside one of the multi-storey blocks in Lansdowne Gardens. This wasn't an area he knew well, as his investigations usually took him to the south and east of the city, but he glimpsed the high-rises through the trees whenever he took the Coupar Angus Road north.

He sat in the Audi, surveying the tenement block. It was in three sections with balconies at the corners. He wondered what the difference in price would be for a corner flat.

He left the car and strolled into the reception area, ready with his story in case he was accosted by the caretaker. But the office was deserted. The block was one of those with two lifts: one for odd- and one for even-numbered floors. He rode the lift up to the fifth.

The door opened on to a wide corridor. He turned left, counting off the doors until he found Murray's. He knocked loudly, waited, then knocked again, more loudly.

The door to the left opened, and a young woman with long dark hair and slightly slanted brown eyes appeared. Her complexion was that of a twenty-a-day smoker, and Marek would have put her in her forties had it not been for her figure, which was of a woman half that age. She was wearing a tight red T-shirt and no bra, and even tighter jeans. He was having difficulty keeping his eyes on her face.

'You looking for Murray?' she said, in a cracked voice.

'I am. My name's Franek Filarski.'

'Polish?'

'That's right. And you are?'

'Lorraine Barrie. *Miss* Lorraine Barrie.' She smoothed her hair, pulling it over her left shoulder. 'You a detective?'

He smiled. 'I'm an investigator.'

The smile did the trick, as he'd hoped it would.

'I haven't seen Murray for nearly a fortnight.' A look of suspicion crept into her eyes. 'What are you investigating him for?'

'We think he's been defrauding the Inland Revenue. I wanted to ask him a few questions.'

A knowing grin spread across her face. 'It's the income from his extra-curricular activities that he's not been declaring, eh?' She nodded. 'I hear everything through the walls.'

'And which activities would those be?'

She glanced up and down the corridor. 'You'd better come in.'

Marek followed her into a low-ceilinged lounge. The main features were a drab three-piece suite in a faded blue, an enormous television, and an IKEA-type sideboard cluttered with framed photos.

'We'll need to keep our voices down,' she said, brushing magazines off one of the armchairs. 'The bairn's asleep next door.'

'I understand.' He lowered himself on to the sofa. 'So, what can you tell me about Murray?'

'I ken he was a record-keeper in some library, but when he wasn't doing that he had clients in and out the place the whole time.'

Murray dispensed the drugs from his flat? Convenient, but risky.

'And how long had this been going on?'

'Ever since he moved into the building.' She screwed up her face, as though trying to remember. 'That would have been about a year past.'

Something didn't add up. Murray had been working at the Lodge for only a few weeks. If he'd been dealing drugs for nearly a year, where was he getting them?

'Did you ever see him do it?'

'Excuse me?'

'Did you ever see him with a client?'

'Are you accusing me of being a Peeping Tom?' she said, a note of mild outrage in her voice.

'I'm not accusing you of anything, Miss Barrie. I'm just wondering if you witnessed the transaction.'

'That sort of transaction, as you so delicately put it, would never be done in a public place.'

'In my experience, it's usually done in a public place. But in such a way that no one sees.'

Her jaw dropped. 'What the hell are you talking about?'

'I'm talking about drug dealing.'

She blinked in astonishment. Then her cackles echoed through the room. She must have remembered the sleeping baby because she stopped suddenly and threw a glance at the door.

'Miss Barrie, what are *you* talking about?'

'You wee daftie. Murray was a sex worker! I heard everything through that wall,' she said, gesturing behind him. 'Sometimes I'd be wheeling the pram to the lift and I'd pass one of them coming out. They were all fair gantin' for it.'

Marek stared at her. He had a strong desire to laugh. 'Seems we've been at cross purposes.'

'I'll tell you something, though. If he paid his taxes on what he earned on his hands and knees, Scotland would solve its budget-deficit problem.' She frowned. 'What made you think he was a drug dealer, eh?'

'I'm acting on a tip-off.'

'Aye, well, I suppose he might have been dealing drugs on the side. Lots of them do.'

Marek was starting to wonder how many sides Murray had when she said, 'Have you tried getting in touch with him?'

'He doesn't reply to our letters.'

'I've heard nothing through those walls for a fortnight. Maybe he's moved his sex business elsewhere.'

'Then it looks as though he really has gone missing,' Marek said, half to himself.

'Missing?' She smirked. 'Missing in action, more like it.' She studied him, her gaze running down his pale-blue suit. 'Do you want a keek round his flat, eh? I've got a spare key.'

Before he could reply, she jumped to her feet and left the room, returning seconds later.

'Murray and I exchanged spares in case we ever locked ourselves out,' she said, handing him the key. 'The caretaker's never around when you need him.'

Marek couldn't believe his luck. 'Thank you. You've been most helpful,' he added, getting to his feet.

He'd hoped the finality in his tone would make it clear he intended to search Murray's place alone, but Miss Barrie followed him into the corridor.

'Are you looking for evidence he was a sex worker? I reckon it would have been cash in hand, don't you?'

'There might be something written down, a diary perhaps.'

'Don't folk put that on their phones now?'

'He could have scribbled something on a paper diary.'

'Aye, I do that. I've got a calendar on the kitchen wall.'

He waited, turning the key over in his hands.

She took the hint. 'When you've finished, knock on my door, eh.'

'I'll do that,' he said, smiling.

She watched him insert the key in the lock, then turned and disappeared.

Murray's flat was so similar in décor to Miss Barrie's that Marek suspected the same landlord owned both properties. Unlike Miss Barrie's, however, it was surprisingly tidy. He pulled on a pair of latex gloves and set to work checking inside the sideboard. There was little there other than an old-fashioned china set and half a dozen dusty glasses. The drawers were empty, except for one containing old bills. He glanced through them. Nothing out of the ordinary.

The bedroom was dominated by a double bed, which occupied much of the room. The duvet was pulled back, revealing a crumpled sheet and squashed pillows. Murray obviously wasn't a great one for tidying up in the morning. Marek could hardly criticise. He himself was no better. A lamp and a wind-up alarm clock stood on the bedside cabinet. The drawers were empty.

Inside the mirror-doored wardrobe, a dozen shirts and T-shirts in various colours hung from the rack, along with several pairs of jeans and a couple of pairs of shorts. A good-quality dark suit was squeezed in among them. Trainers and a single pair of black leather shoes were arranged neatly on the wardrobe floor next to a plastic box containing folded underwear and socks. And right at the back, in the shadows where he might have missed it, was a black wheelie case. He pulled it out and opened it. Inside was a passport. Murray Johnson, a serious-looking man with impossibly curly red hair, gazed out at him.

Marek sat on the bed, his thoughts swirling. If Murray had done a bunk with the shipment of drugs, he'd obviously not bothered to take his belongings with him. Understandable, if he knew he was about to make a fortune from selling fentanyl. But his passport? Why would he leave that behind? Was he about to take on a new identity? If so, surely he'd want to erase the old one. And erase it completely. It made little sense.

The second bedroom, smaller than the first, contained a single bed and an astonishing assortment of sex toys laid out neatly on a purple velour rug. Marek guessed that Murray would entertain Blackie in the double bed, and the single bed in the spare room was for his clients.

The bathroom was tiny but modern, with an electric shower over the bath. The cabinet above the washbasin was empty but for a packet of ibuprofen, a pair of nail clippers and a cordless electric razor. Soap, a toothbrush and a tube of toothpaste – squeezed from the middle – lay abandoned in the basin.

The kitchen had been kitted out with a microwave and small fridge. The washing machine would be in a shared utility room. The food cupboards stored an assortment of tins and dried goods, and the fridge contained a half-used carton of milk, a tub of margarine and packets of ham and hot-smoked salmon. A dried loaf of bread surrounded by crumbs and the odd mouse dropping lay on the fold-up table.

Nowhere was there a single trace of drugs in any form. Unless Murray had a hiding place behind the walls or under the floorboards. Which was possible. Yet wouldn't his clients have wanted to get high before sex? If he had legged it in a hurry, Marek would have expected to see the remains of a line, or a spoon or syringe. But there was nothing.

His time was up. Miss Barrie would be wondering what he was doing.

He left the flat, locking it behind him. As he was shoving the gloves into his pocket, the door to Miss Barrie's opened.

'Did you find what you were looking for?' she said, as he handed back the key.

'Unfortunately, no.' He smiled encouragingly. 'Can you remember the last time you saw Murray? Which day exactly?' He raised an eyebrow. 'Or heard him through the wall?'

'I can't mind now which day it was. But in the evening, his boyfriend showed up. He'd usually drop round late.' She snorted. 'I'm surprised Murray had the energy, but they'd go at it as soon as he was through the door. That night, though, they had a row.'

'What did this boyfriend look like?'

'A big beast. Blond hair, back off his forehead. Had something of an attitude. I don't ken his name.'

She'd described Blackie to a T.

'Maybe this man had something to do with his disappearance,' she added, in a helpful tone.

Marek doubted it. He recalled Blackie's anguish on learning that Murray had disappeared.

Her eyes were unnaturally bright. 'That's a sexy accent you've got, Mr Filarski. You wouldn't like to go to bed, eh?' She moved closer, giving him a view of her wrinkled mouth and grey skin. 'I can be very creative,' she added, putting her face close to his.

He tried not to inhale the stench of stale tobacco. 'It's a tempting offer, Miss Barrie, but I'm afraid I have to go.'

'You're not from the Revenue, are you?'

Before he could reply, the sound of a wailing baby came from inside. Miss Barrie closed her eyes and mouthed something silently before hurrying back into the flat. She left the door open, a clear indication that she intended to return.

He took the opportunity to make good his escape, reaching the lift before she reappeared.

As he stepped out on the ground floor, he noticed a middle-aged man moving stiffly towards the reception office. The man turned and nodded in a kindly way.

'Good afternoon,' Marek said, keeping his expression friendly. 'Are you the caretaker?'

'Aye. And who might you be?'

'Franek Filarski from the Inland Revenue. I was looking for a Murray Johnson. But he doesn't appear to be in.'

'A few of his friends have been looking for him these past couple of weeks, right enough.'

'Can you remember when you last saw him?'

'It was the day they got those lads out of the cave in Thailand.'

'The ones in the junior football team, you mean?'

'Aye, that's it.'

'And was Mr Johnson leaving the building?'

'He was. It was very late and I was about to go off shift.'

'We've been trying to find him. He didn't happen to tell you where he was going?'

'He didn't stop for a blether. He was with a couple of men.'

'Oh?'

'I couldn't tell you who they were. Except that he seemed none too pleased to be going with them, like he wanted to get away, ken. I thought they were polis, they had that look about them. You know, smart clothes, the way the polis walk.' He studied Marek. 'Aye, that's where you might make your enquiries. At the station.'

Marek looked up at the cameras.

'Ach, well,' the man said, seeing the direction of his glance. 'We've been waiting to get them fixed for several weeks, now.'

'What did these men look like? So I know I've got the right officers,' he added hastily.

The caretaker pursed his lips. 'I couldn't see their faces. It was too dark.' He thought for a while. 'But from their general appearance, ken, and the way they were walking, I'd say they were brothers.'

Lorraine Barrie stood by the open window, softly shoogling her whimpering bairn as she watched the Pole hurrying towards his car. Pity he'd had to rush off like that. He looked as if he'd be red-hot in bed. But those questions he'd been asking about Murray? She was half tempted to leave it at that, except he could have caught the caretaker on the way out and learnt that Murray hadn't been alone when he'd left the building. She had no idea who else might have seen him with those two men, but she couldn't take the risk. Her instructions had been clear – she was to call a number if anyone came asking. And the money she'd been given would cover the rent for the next twelve months. Aye, and there'd been the promise of more.

She carried the sleeping bairn back to the bedroom and laid him in the cot. Her phone was on the sideboard. She called a number she'd stored in Contacts.

'This is Lorraine,' she said.

'Aye?' came the thick, deep voice.

'You told me I was to phone if anyone came calling on Murray. Well, someone was here just now.' She squinted at the scrap of paper where she'd scribbled the Pole's name. 'He gave his name as Franek Filarski. Said he was from the Revenue.'

A pause. 'Franek Filarski, you said?'

'He's Polish.'

'Did he say why he wanted Murray?'

'He said he was defrauding the Revenue, and he wanted to ask him some questions.'

'You did the right thing telling us, lass. What did he look like?'

'He was a bonnie lad. Fair hair. And well built.'

A pause. 'Anyone else comes, you be sure to ring us.'

'Aye, I will.'

He hung up.

She stared into the phone, wondering what would happen to Franek Filarski now. Perhaps the same that had happened to Murray, whatever that was. But she'd learnt something today. Murray had been into drugs, and drugs were what had taken her man and left her a widow. Finding him with that needle in his groin had changed her. Hardened her. Murray deserved whatever had happened to him, and if this Pole was in the same racket – she didn't believe for one minute he was a government man – he deserved whatever happened to him, too. Aye, two drug dealers taken out of circulation were better than one.

She put the phone back on the sideboard. Her conscience was clear. After all, when you dance with the deil, he's the one who always calls the tune. And although she had no idea who she'd spoken with on the phone, he sounded just like the deil.

CHAPTER 21

'How are those reports coming on?' Dania said, setting down the Styrofoam tray. Honor and Hamish had spent much of the previous week traipsing round Gregor's associates, and were in the process of entering and cross-referencing their findings.

'We're getting there,' Honor said, as Dania handed her one of Jock's coffees. 'What, no gingerbread?' she added, with a grin.

Dania set Hamish's coffee on his desk. He mouthed a quick 'Thank you.'

His mobile rang. She recognised the ringtone as 'Up Wi' The Bonnets' played on an accordion. It was – so Marek had informed her – the anthem of Dundee FC.

'Here we go,' Honor murmured to Dania. 'It's his latest squeeze.'

'Who is it?'

'No idea.' She raised her voice. 'Tell her you love her so we can all get back to work.'

Hamish grinned, said something they couldn't hear, and ended the call.

'This is what I'm talking about, boss. He's so smitten, he hasn't time to take me drinking.'

'I'm a big boy,' he said, peering at the screen and typing slowly. 'I'm allowed to play with girls.'

'Are you going to let a girl come between us after all we've been through?'

'What girl are you talking about?'

'Is there more than one?'

He smiled secretively. 'You need to find yourself someone, lass.'

'If you're enquiring about my love life, I'm in between men.'

'What about the guy who drew that?' he said, nodding at Kenny Affleck's sketch.

'Not sure he's my type.'

'Wasn't he good-looking?'

'He was, in a brutish sort of way,' she said, in a noncommittal voice.

Dania was about to make a comment when the call came through. Owen was out, and she was the senior officer in the room. She listened to the message carefully, scribbling the details down.

'We need to go,' she said, grabbing her bag.

'What is it, boss?'

'Morag Pinkerton went for a sleepover last night. She was supposed to return home this morning.'

It was Dania's use of the word 'supposed' that made Honor and Hamish spring to their feet and hurry after her.

The Pinkertons lived on Brackens Road, one of many roads leading off Strathmartine, the long route that led north to the Sidlaws. And, as Honor had pointed out gloomily, it was yet another road that had no CCTV.

They pulled up outside a two-up two-down semi with a low stone wall and a neatly trimmed privet hedge. Their arrival must have been anticipated because the front door was thrown wide before they'd even opened the garden gate. A woman with unnaturally bright eyes and long brown hair scooped up in a bun stared at them.

'Are you polis?' she said, in a hoarse voice.

Dania held up her warrant. 'DI Gorska. This is DS Randall, and DC Downie.'

'Thank God.' She closed her eyes briefly. 'Now we'll find her.'

'You're Mrs Pinkerton?'

She nodded and disappeared into the house.

They followed her into a small but tidy living room with a well-worn three-piece suite, and a coal-effect fire. An upright piano stood against the wall, the lid open and the seat pulled out, as though someone had just finished playing. The sweet smell of lilac, which Dania traced to the sprigs in the Chinese vase on the windowsill, filled the room.

Mrs Pinkerton collapsed on to the sofa, clutching her phone.

Dania sat down next to her. 'Mrs Pinkerton, when did you last see Morag?' she said, opening her notebook.

'Yesterday evening, at seven o'clock.'

'Exactly?'

'*The Archers* had just come on. She left the house to go to her friend's. It's only a wee walk from here.' The woman's eyes clouded and she added, in a rush, 'Oh, God, I should have gone with her, I should have – why didn't I? Why didn't I?'

'Where does this friend live?'

She continued to gabble to herself.

'Can you write down the address, Mrs Pinkerton?' Dania said, putting the pen and notebook on the woman's lap, and gripping her wrist.

The unexpected touch seemed to bring the woman to herself. 'It's in Laird Street,' she murmured, scribbling. 'Five minutes away.'

Dania tore off the sheet and handed it to Hamish. 'You know what to do. And can you arrange for a family liaison officer?'

'Got it, ma'am,' he said promptly.

'What time was Morag due home this morning?' Dania said.

'This morning?' the woman said, in a stricken voice. 'We didn't set a time but it was to be straight after breakfast. She's due at the dentist's for a check-up.' Her hands flew to her cheeks. 'I never called him. He'll be expecting her.'

'Don't worry about that now,' Dania said gently.

'If she misses it, we won't get another appointment for ages.'

'Honor, can you find the kitchen and make Mrs Pinkerton a cup of tea?'

'On it.' The girl jumped to her feet.

Tears were streaming down Mrs Pinkerton's cheeks. Dania squeezed her hand. 'Did you call Morag's friend to see whether she'd left?'

'They said she never arrived. They got a text saying she'd cancelled.'

'A text from Morag?' Dania said sharply.

'Aye, she must have sent it after she left here.'

'Can you give me the number of Morag's mobile?'

The woman reeled off the figures.

Dania felt something twist inside her. Up until now, there'd been a chance that Morag might have wandered off while walking back home. And might still be alive. But cancelling the sleepover *after* leaving the house meant only one thing – she'd been abducted, and the kidnapper had forced her to send the message. Or sent it himself. It was intended to buy him some time because Morag wouldn't be missed until the following morning.

Honor arrived with a mug. 'Here we go,' she said cheerfully. She sat on Mrs Pinkerton's other side, and held out the mug, not letting go until the woman had wrapped both hands round it. 'Thank you, lass,' she murmured.

'Can you tell me what Morag was wearing?' Dania said.

206

The woman seemed to rally. 'Aye, you'll need to know, if you're to find her.'

Dania caught Honor's eye. They were both thinking the same – if the other two abductions were anything to go by, they'd find the clothes before they found Morag.

'She had dark brown jeans, and her favourite green T-shirt,' Mrs Pinkerton said.

'Trainers?'

'Let me think, let me think.' Her expression cleared. 'That's right, they were black. With green soles.'

'No jacket?'

'It was too hot. We'd been out earlier and didn't take jackets then either.'

'Where did you go?'

'To the Wildlife Centre in Camperdown Park.' She took a sip. 'It's a place we often take Morag, because she's mad keen on animals. She wants to be a vet. We've started saving up for her college.'

The Wildlife Centre in Camperdown Park. This might work for them.

'And what time did you leave for the park?' Dania said.

'It was after lunch.'

'About two o'clock?'

'A wee bit earlier.'

'Do they issue tickets?' Honor said. 'I can't remember.'

'They don't, no.'

'How did you pay?' Dania said. 'By credit card?'

The woman frowned. 'Aye, I think we did.'

'Have you got the slip?'

'It'll be in my purse,' she said, nodding at the brown canvas shoulder bag on the chair.

'Could I have a look?'

'Go ahead.'

'And you took your car?' Dania said, unzipping the bag.

'We always do.' She looked at them in bewilderment. 'Why are you asking me these questions?'

'We're trying to build up a picture of Morag's movements,' Dania said quickly. 'Knowing the times and places she went could be useful. The credit-card slip will tell us more precisely.'

'And did you pay for parking?' Honor said.

'Parking is free there. We came home and I started to make the tea. Morag was up in her room, getting her things together.'

'For the sleepover?'

'She put everything in the little backpack.'

The woman was shaking. Honor lifted the mug out of her hands and took it to the kitchen.

'What does the backpack look like, Mrs Pinkerton?'

'It's black with animal pictures all over it.'

'And her pyjamas?'

'Beige and black. They're really just wee shorts and a sleeveless top.' She was rocking now.

'Where is your husband?' Dania said, slipping an arm round her. 'We'd like to talk to him.'

'He's out looking for Morag. He took the car.'

'Could you call him?'

'His phone's in the kitchen. He left in such a hurry that he forgot to take it.'

Honor had returned. She sat in the armchair, her gaze wandering round the room.

'Have you got a recent photo of Morag?' Dania said. She wanted to add, 'We'll need one if we're to find her.' But she couldn't bring herself to say it. Why raise the woman's hopes to have them crash down again when the news came in that her daughter's bleached body had been found?

'Aye, well, the most recent is the one I took at the Wildlife Centre. It's on my phone.' She raised her hollow-eyed face to Dania. 'Will that do?'

'It'll do fine.'

'I took a few. Morag's in them all.' After scrolling through, she handed the phone over.

Dania had visited Camperdown Wildlife Centre with Marek the year she'd moved up from London. That summer had been wet and windy. They'd driven along an avenue of trees, their branches bent over in tall arcs, showering the car with droplets. In Camperdown itself, huge horse chestnuts shaded the paths, giving the place more of a park-like atmosphere. The animal enclosures sprawled over a wide area, unlike zoos she remembered as a child, where the animals were crammed into cages. She'd been impressed by the range of wildlife on display, which included a white stork, its nest like a crown, the only one she'd seen outside Poland. Although the bird had room enough to fly around its enclosure, the roof of wire netting made escape impossible.

The girl in the photos had long blonde hair and sky-blue eyes. Her mother had captured her in a variety of daft poses. In one, she was standing to attention in front of a low-walled, sandy enclosure, adopting the same rigidly alert posture as the meerkats perched on the tree stumps. In another, she was making her hands into claws and growling, the brown bear behind her watching with silent interest. Then there was the African elephant sculpture made from recycled steel, said to be from boats that had sailed the Tay. Morag had curved her arm in front of her face to make a trunk. The photos had been taken from such a distance that there were other people in the shot. They were mostly children but some were adults.

'I'd like to make copies of these, Mrs Pinkerton.'

The woman waved a resigned hand. 'Take whatever you need.'

'What was Morag like?' Dania said, sending the images to her phone.

'How do you mean?'

'Was she the sort to wander off?'

'I can't think why she would.'

'Had she ever gone to this friend's house on Laird Street without telling you, for example?'

The woman shook her head slowly. 'She was a good lassie that way. And when she visited her friends, she came home when she said she would. If she was held up, she always phoned me. Or the parents did.'

'And have you got any other children?'

She took deep, gulping sobs. 'Only Morag.'

There was a knock at the door. Honor left the room, returning with the family liaison officer, a young woman with fluffy brown hair. Dania had worked with her before and knew she was one of the best.

'This is Police Constable Bridget Walsh,' she said to Mrs Pinkerton. 'She'll stay with you for as long as you need her.' She hesitated. 'There's one final question I have to ask you. Did Morag know either Fiona Ballie or Euna Montcrieff?'

From the sudden look of panic on the woman's face, Dania knew that the truth of what must have happened to her daughter had finally sunk in. 'What are you saying?' Mrs Pinkerton cried, her eyes wide with fright. 'That Morag's been taken?'

'It's a possibility we have to consider.'

'But she hasn't been. She's missing, that's all – she just decided not to go to the sleepover. Calum will find her! They'll come through the door any minute and—'

After a silence, Dania said, 'We may need to talk to you again.' She squeezed the woman's arm. Mrs Pinkerton was staring straight ahead, her face white and pinched.

'Will you call the station when her husband gets home?' Dania murmured to Bridget.

The girl nodded. 'Aye, I'll do that.'

With a final look at Mrs Pinkerton, Dania left the house with Honor.

'Call Hamish,' she said, as soon as they were on the pavement.

'He's here, boss.'

Hamish was sprinting towards them. He always looked ready to burst out of his suit, especially when he was running.

'I've been to Laird Street and spoken with the Hamiltons,' he said, in between breaths. 'They told me Mr Pinkerton rang them this morning asking if Morag was there. They were fair surprised, as the lass had texted yesterday evening to cancel the sleepover. And a wee bitty miffed that she'd waited till the last minute before doing it,' he added. 'They'd made something extra-special for tea.'

'We've got Morag's number,' Honor said. 'We can find out where the message was sent from.'

'Then let's get back to the nick,' Dania said. 'DI McFadden should be there by now.'

'He won't exactly be happy as Hogmanay to hear this news, ma'am.'

'That must be the understatement of the year,' Honor said, with a grim smile.

As they headed south on the Strathmartine Road, Dania made a mental list of the things they needed to do. But by the time they'd reached the town centre, two thoughts remained uppermost in her mind. The first was that Morag Pinkerton was already dead and had been when the call came into West Bell Street. The second was that the place to start looking for her killer was the Wildlife Centre in Camperdown Park.

★　★　★

211

The incident room was buzzing with activity. Dania had phoned ahead so they could hit the ground running as soon as they arrived.

Jackie Ireland was waiting with Owen McFadden and the team. 'Can you fill us in, DI Gorska?' she said briskly.

While Honor transferred the photos from Camperdown to the main screen, Dania gave an account of her conversation with Mrs Pinkerton. Owen listened, frowning.

'How old was Morag?' Jackie Ireland asked.

Dania was about to confess that she hadn't asked this question when Hamish said, 'Eleven, ma'am.'

Owen touched the screen and brought up the area north of the A90. 'Okay, let's have a look at the map.'

'The Pinkertons live on this part of Brackens Road,' Dania said, indicating the section.

'And Laird Street is south of Brackens,' Hamish said. 'To get to the Hamiltons', Morag could take one of two routes.' He traced with his finger. 'She could go west, turn down Kingsmuir Park and on to Laird Street. Or she could go east, then along Strathmartine and reach Laird Street that way.'

'Bit of a no-brainer,' someone said. 'Both families' houses are close to Strathmartine.'

'Aye, that's my bet. She went via the main road. It's such a short walk and there are houses all along there, so Mrs Pinkerton must have thought it safe to let her go.'

'I suppose, at that time of evening, people were indoors having their tea,' the DCI said. 'Are there traffic cameras on that stretch of Strathmartine?'

'No, ma'am. And none on Brackens Road or Laird Street, either.'

Jackie mouthed something that could have been a swear word. 'All right, you all know what to do. We need to start house-to-house on that stretch of Strathmartine as a matter of urgency.

We've got photos of the girl dressed in the clothes she wore when she vanished. That's a big plus. Someone may remember her.' She caught Dania's eye. 'DI Gorska?'

'We should also check at the Wildlife Centre in Camperdown Park. Morag was there earlier in the day.'

'You think the man who snatched her saw her there?'

'I do.'

Jackie crossed her arms. 'Why?'

'A gut feeling, that's all.'

She nodded. 'We'll get out an appeal on the media, asking for anyone who was at the park to come forward.' She studied the photos of Morag. 'Someone may remember a young girl larking about like that.' She glanced round the room. They were avoiding her eyes. 'And we need to get the search for Morag's body organised.'

CHAPTER 22

Owen wasted no time in arranging the search for Morag. The appeal went out over the lunchtime news, and by late afternoon a huge number of volunteers had gathered in various locations in Dundee's hinterland.

While the hunt continued until it was too dark to see, Dania and the other officers swung into action. Bridget, the family liaison officer, had rung earlier in the afternoon to say that Mr Pinkerton had returned. His dashcam told the police where he'd been in his search for Morag, although given this was a good eighteen hours after the girl had gone missing, it was a case of horse and stable door. The man was in a worse state than his wife but, with Bridget's gentle prodding, they'd managed to draw up a list of Morag's friends. Dania and Honor split the names between them, while Hamish joined those on house-to-house in and around the Brackens-Strathmartine area.

By late evening, exhausted and demoralised, they were forced to admit defeat. None of the residents could remember seeing anything unusual that evening, and Morag's friends could tell them nothing. But one positive result – if it could be called that – was that none of these friends knew Fiona Ballie or Euna Montcrieff, and were adamant that Morag didn't know them either. The girl's parents, once they felt able to be questioned further, confirmed this. Morag's friends were a close-knit group who shared everything. And, no, the girls said, she never talked about new 'friends' she'd made on social media: they'd been warned at school about the perils of chatting to strangers online, they never uploaded pictures of themselves, well, only one or two and nothing they'd be ashamed of and, no, they couldn't think of anyone who would want to harm Morag.

Tech had pulled out the stops and confirmed that the last message sent from Morag's mobile was at 7.16 p.m. from the Brackens-Strathmartine area. The phone had then gone offline. But Morag had left the house when *The Archers* started, which was just after seven. As Dania hurried back to the incident room, she thought through the implications. To send a message at 7.16 p.m. cancelling the sleep date meant that the kidnapper had been quick off the mark. He must have seen the phone in Morag's hand, which was where it was likely to have been if her school friends were anything to go by, and somehow persuaded her to send the message to the Hamiltons. Possibly from inside his vehicle. It was hard to tell from the text-speak whether Morag or someone else had sent it. That was the problem with SMS language, Dania thought gloomily. The Agatha Christie days of analysing the style of a handwritten letter, and identifying who had penned it, were over.

Honor and Hamish were the only ones in the room, typing up their reports.

'We're in luck, boss,' Honor said, glancing up. 'We're getting in loads of videos from visitors to Camperdown Park. With luck, we might see Morag there. And with even more luck, we'll see someone showing her more than usual attention.'

'That's something, at least,' Dania said. She felt drained. It was approaching midnight, and the following day she would be up before the sun. As would everyone.

'Hope you don't mind, but your phone buzzed and I answered it. I thought it might be important.'

'No, of course I don't mind. Who was it?'

'It was a priest. He started speaking in Polish, and then realised I wasn't you.'

'That'll be Father Kliment.'

'He's asking you to ring him as a matter of urgency.'

'Did he say what it was about?'

The girl shook her head.

Dania guessed it would be the series of summer concerts he'd been telling her about. It was now late in the season to organise them, and he must be getting anxious. She felt a sudden prickle of annoyance. Surely he must realise how much she had on her plate with this latest abduction. And, if he didn't, he'd soon be reading about it in the *Evening Telegraph*.

'Did you tell him I'd call him back?'

'Nope. Just that I'd deliver the message.'

She nodded in satisfaction. When she next had a breathing space, she'd get in touch. But as no promise of an immediate call-back had been made, her conscience was clear.

Dania's alarm went off. It was one of those wind-up affairs whose ear-splitting ring could have woken the dead. For a moment, she couldn't remember why she'd set it, and was half thinking of curling up under the duvet hoping to drift off when her memory returned. She pushed back the duvet and swung her legs out of bed.

Swaying from the effort of staying awake, she dragged on her clothes. A shower would have to wait. There was time only for breakfast, which was a giant cheese sandwich she'd made the night before. She wasn't hungry, but she knew enough about what she would be doing to force it down. She grabbed a bottle of water and hurried out of the flat.

The sun was turning the sky a blue shade of grey as she reached Claverhouse Road. The muster point was off the roundabout leading on to Old Glamis Road. Although Dania had the morning off, she'd decided to join the search for Morag. The uniform in charge was reading out the list of areas to be covered, and taking names and contact details of volunteers. Anyone under eighteen was sent away. Everyone else was allocated a place on a team led by a uniform, and the rules were explained in detail before the party split up.

Dania had been assigned to a field north of Claverhouse. She set off with the others, glad that she'd had the foresight to put out her walking boots the night before.

'Dania? Is that you?'

She turned to see Jamie Reid hurrying to catch her up.

'I didn't recognise you with your hair up,' he said.

'Hello, Jamie.'

He looked around. 'Marek not with you?'

'I haven't seen him. They're searching all across Dundee, so he could be anywhere.'

Jamie fell into step with her. 'I didn't reckon this is something DIs do,' he said cheerfully. 'I thought it was left to their underlings.'

'They don't usually, but I've got some time off, so I decided to pitch in.'

'That's decent of you.'

They walked for a while, and then Dania said, 'Is Pam also taking part in the search?'

'She's away. Another wedding. This one's way up near Stonehaven. Would you believe there are people who want to hold the wedding in Dunnottar Castle?'

'It's a ruin, isn't it?'

'And the guests have to dress as Jacobites.' He grinned. 'It's the *Outlander* effect, I reckon.'

'What about the bride and groom? Are they in Jacobite garb, too?'

'No idea. But Pam said it's been a nightmare setting everything up. The wedding itself will be outdoors but the reception is in the vault.'

'Isn't that where they imprisoned the Covenanters?'

'Aye. A strange place for a wedding breakfast, and no mistake. And there are a couple of dozen pipers, according to Pam. If they play indoors, they'll deafen everyone.'

'So who are the bride and groom?'

'Americans. *Outlander*'s big over there.'

'You've not been asked to take photographs?'

'The groom's brother is doing that.'

'I have to admit it's a stunning location on that spit of land.' He glanced at her. 'Poland must have loads of castles on its coastlines.'

'The only coastline is the Baltic Sea. The best-known castle is probably Malbork.'

'Worth a visit?'

'Definitely. They do medieval battle reconstructions. At least, they used to. Teutonic Knights. That sort of stuff. Marek and I went when we were children. That's when he announced he wanted to be a knight when he grew up. In a way, I suppose he is.'

'Teutonic Knights? Weren't they Germans?'

'You have to remember that who owned what in that part of Europe was constantly changing.'

They reached the field. The uniform called a halt and waited until everyone had caught up. He was a plump, round-faced man with a shiny scalp that glistened in the heat.

'Right,' he said, studying the map on his hand-held. 'We're

218

searching beyond that low wall.' He surveyed them with a serious expression. 'Now, side by side, mind, and arm-lengths apart. Those of you with sticks, use them. Go slowly. And if you find anything, call me. Don't touch it,' he added, eyeing Dania.

She felt like saluting, but she just nodded.

'Okay. Let's do this.'

They followed him into the field and took up position, walking slowly and silently, parting the stalks with their canes. Dania wasn't sure what sort of crops were grown here but the stalks came up to mid-calf and, given the green and brown shades, would camouflage Morag's clothes perfectly.

The light changed rapidly as they scoured the area. They reached the wall and paused briefly before tackling the adjacent field. It was sown with spring barley and looked ready for harvesting.

Jamie took a gulp of water from the bottle at his waist. 'You think we'll find this lassie today?' he said, looking away.

'Hard to tell.'

He wiped his mouth with the back of his hand. 'You must be up to your ears in work.'

'We all are, although it's one of my colleagues who's taking the lead on the missing girls.' She met his gaze. 'My principle investigation is centred on Cameron Affleck.'

'Aye, you mentioned that before.'

'It doesn't help that he was such a quiet child,' she added, with a sad smile. 'Everyone we've spoken to said they could hardly get a word out of him. I feel I don't know him, and that's not good for the investigation.' She tried to make it sound like a throwaway comment.

It worked almost every time – if you said something that was blatantly untrue, people were often quick to tell you you were wrong. But Jamie didn't rise to the bait. 'I wouldn't know, Inspector,' he said slowly. 'As I said before, I never met the lad.'

The uniform was shouting to them to crack on when his phone rang. He listened carefully, then called them over. 'They've found something way up off Emmock Road,' he said. He looked at them as though wanting to let them down lightly. 'You can all get away home. We'll take it from here.' He added, as an after-thought, 'Thank you for your time.'

'What is it?' someone said. 'Morag?'

'Clothes.'

'Oh, Jesus,' Jamie murmured.

The group started to disperse, everyone talking at once.

'Can I give you a lift?' he said to Dania. 'My Hyundai's back near the meeting place.'

'I'll have to stay here.'

'Aye, of course.' He nodded, and then moved away.

She showed her warrant card to the uniform, who was speaking into his mobile. His eyes widened as he realised who she was. 'Where is it?' she said.

He ended the call. 'The car's coming, Inspector.'

As Dania climbed out of the squad car, she saw a group of uniforms standing at the side of the road. They were talking to a boy who looked not much older than ten. He had tangled brown hair, and a head that seemed too big for his slight frame. He was distinctly nervous, as though he knew he'd done something wrong and was about to get it in the neck from the high heid yins. In his hands was a UAV controller with a mobile phone attached. One of the uniforms was examining a four-rotor red-and-black drone, turning it over in his hands.

Dania flashed her warrant. 'DI Dania Gorska.'

'We've found Morag's clothes, Inspector,' one of the uniforms said. 'To be precise, it was this lad's drone that did it. His name's Angus. He had the good sense to call us straight away.'

Dania smiled at the lad. 'Good work, Angus.'

He tried a grin, which came out lopsided.

'Did you come out looking for Morag?' she said.

'Aye, I heard it on the news. I thought I'd be able to help.'

'That's great,' she said warmly. 'Can you show me what you've got?'

'Okay.' He detached the phone. 'This is a recording. That means it's not live,' he added, glancing at her as if to check she understood.

The video, which was of surprisingly high quality, showed the edge of a field shadowed by woodland. The camera was skimming the ground, giving them a good view of what was in the grass.

'I'll need to move it on a wee bit,' Angus said. 'Aye, here it is. See that?'

'Can you freeze it? And zoom in?'

The flickering image was unmistakable: a black backpack covered with animal pictures.

'There's more,' he said. He moved the video on a few frames, then stopped it and magnified the image. It would have been hard to identify against the background had Dania not known it was a green T-shirt.

'We'll need to get a copy of that recording, Angus.'

'I can forward it to you.' He saw her hesitate. 'Or do you want to borrow the phone?' he added, looking unhappy.

'Tell you what, why don't we take you down to the station, and we can make a copy in your presence? How does that sound?'

His eyes lit up. 'I've never been inside a polis station.'

'Glad to hear it, son,' one of the uniforms said, his lips twitching.

'Can I see the rest of the video?'

He played the recording through to the end. One by one, Morag's clothes appeared, including the shorts and sleeveless top she wore in bed. Everything was well enough camouflaged and half hidden in the fringes of the long grass that it might have escaped an initial sweep by a search party.

'Do we know where this area is?' Dania said to the uniforms.

'The lad showed us. It's right at the edge, almost in the woodland.' The man scratched his cheek. 'Not like with the other two lassies. Their clothes were left in the middle of fields.'

'I take it Forensics are on their way?'

'Aye.'

'Can you let me see it again, Angus? From the beginning. And can you slow it down?'

The lad played with the mobile. 'Here, Inspector,' he said, with an air of importance.

She watched the unfolding scene – the backpack, jeans, T-shirt, knickers, socks, trainers and pyjamas.

'Hold on, can you go back a bit? There. Stop!'

He didn't need to be told to magnify it.

She stared at the white skull mask. It was baring its long teeth, grinning obscenely.

'Any joy?' Dania said.

Owen shook his head. 'We've secured the scene, and Forensics have finished. But there's no sign of Morag. I don't understand it.' He looked tired, and seemed to be struggling to get the words out. 'With the other two lassies, we found the body not long after we found the clothes.'

'We'll find her.'

'But that lad did well this morning,' he added.

'We gave him a certificate.' She smiled. 'He was thrilled.'

Before taking Angus to West Bell Street, Dania had phoned ahead and tasked Honor with having it ready by the time they arrived. The girl had excelled herself in creating a certificate that said all the right things about the police being grateful to Angus Nairne for the sterling work he'd done in helping them with their investigation. At the top was the blue Police Scotland thistle-and-crown logo with the motto: 'SEMPER VIGILO'. Angus's face had broken out in a smile that could have lit up Dundee. Under his watchful eye, they'd made a copy of the video, and a uniform had taken him home.

'This one's not like the others,' Owen said. 'I mean, what's with the mask? Was he wearing it in case he was seen when he scattered those clothes?' He stared at the stills from Angus's recording. 'Do you think he wore it when he was with Fiona and Euna? And we've just got lucky that he dropped it by accident?'

'I think we were meant to find it.'

'Kimmie is giving it priority. We might get his DNA.'

'Somehow I doubt he ever wore it.' Dania massaged her face wearily. 'He's toying with us. He's doing it differently this time. Morag's clothes were well hidden, whereas in the other two cases they were found easily. And the mask is something new.'

'So why is he doing it differently?'

'Because he can. To throw us off the scent. Or for another reason we haven't yet thought of.'

'A change in MO.' Owen closed his eyes. 'Aye, that's all we need.'

'We've found the clothes. It's a matter of time before we find the body.'

'It could be he's still got her.'

'Or she's better hidden this time.' Dania studied the incident board. 'Like the clothes.'

CHAPTER 23

It was Thursday before Marek saw Allie again. He was let into the Lodge by Niall Affleck, whose vacant blue-eyed gaze followed him into the archives room. He waited until Marek had sat down before saying, 'Mr Filarski. A word, please?'

Marek returned to the corridor. The hum of the photocopier through the wall suggested that Allie was in the kitchen-cum-storage room.

'I didn't see you here yesterday,' Affleck said tonelessly. 'I hope you didn't take advantage of our receptionist's absence to have a day off, thinking no one would notice. I do come to the Lodge from time to time, you know, and I'm well aware of your comings and goings.'

Marek suppressed the urge to hit him. 'I joined the search for Morag Pinkerton.' He made no attempt to keep the dislike from his eyes. 'By all means dock my wages if you want to.'

'Ah, well, that of course explains things. And did you find the lass? There's been nothing on the news.'

'They found only her clothes.'

Affleck lowered his gaze. 'I see.' After a respectful pause, he nodded towards the archives room. 'Please carry on.'

Cossack, Marek thought, as he watched the man leave the building.

As soon as the front door had closed, he hurried into the kitchen.

Allie wheeled round. 'Franek. You gave me such a fright.'

'I'm sorry. I didn't mean to.'

'Has the Master gone? I can never hear when this thing is going at full speed.'

'Yes, he's away.' Marek watched the sheets churning off the machine. 'What are you copying?'

'The Brothers are having a meeting. I need to get these papers ready.'

He studied her face. There were deep creases in her forehead and she looked paler than usual. Perhaps the news of Morag Pinkerton was affecting her in the way it was affecting him. 'I haven't seen you since Monday, Allie. I was wondering if something had happened to you.'

'I've got a second job,' she said, shoving blank sheets into the empty tray. 'I have to divide my time, I'm afraid.' She glanced up, and her expression changed as though she'd suddenly remembered. 'Did you go to Murray's?'

As quickly as he could, he told her about his search and what he'd found. Or, rather, not found. She listened, wide-eyed.

'Here's the thing, though,' he said. 'On the way out, I ran into the caretaker. He told me that Murray was taken away by two men. That was on Tuesday, July the tenth.'

'That Tuesday was the day Niall caught him at the safe and sacked him.' She thrust her hands into her pockets. 'All right, let's go through what we know.'

Marek leant against the wall, feeling suddenly tired. 'First of all, the last time anyone saw Murray was the evening of Tuesday, July the tenth. Blackie called round to his flat. And then he left.'

'And Murray sent me an email that same evening saying he'd been sacked.'

'But there was no reply to Blackie's knock when he went back on Wednesday night.'

'And if the caretaker saw Murray being frogmarched away by two men on the *Tuesday* night, it would explain why.' She bit her lip, frowning. 'It's because he never returned to his flat.'

'And the email Murray sent to the Lodge address on *Thursday*, saying he was leaving Dundee, may not actually have been sent by him. You did say it didn't sound like him. And it was odd he didn't send it directly to you.'

She searched his face. 'Something bad's happened to him, hasn't it? Who do you think those men were?'

'There's a number of possibilities. The obvious one is that they're drug dealers. Murray was muscling in on their patch so they got rid of him.'

She stared at Marek in horror.

'Drug dealers are protective of their areas, Allie. They show no mercy to anyone who encroaches on them. And Murray strikes me as something of an amateur.'

'And you don't believe the package is still in his flat?' she said nervously.

Marek picked up the photocopies that had fallen on to the floor. 'I've been thinking about that. Murray's been missing for over two weeks now, and his flat hasn't been touched. If a drug dealer came round intending to make him disappear, he'd have turned the place upside down, either then or later, looking for drugs. Which is why I'm inclined to disregard that theory.' He tidied the sheets neatly and laid them on the machine. 'The other reason is: why would a drug dealer either force Murray to send a message to the Lodge saying he was resigning his post, or make him give up his email address and do it himself? Why would he bother? Why would he even know where Murray was working? No, I think something else is—' He straightened.

Why would he even know where Murray was working?

'I've just realised. It's obvious.' He stared at her. 'The Master sent those men there.'

'Niall Affleck?'

'Think about it, Allie. Let's suppose everything Murray said was true. He gets caught trying to open the safe. The Master is furious, interrogates him, learns what Murray is looking for and sacks him immediately. But after Murray's gone, he realises he can't let him live. He may not have found the drugs, but he knows too much. He'd overheard the phone conversation, after all. So the Master sends a couple of heavies round.'

'Good heavens. He did that?'

Marek threw her a crooked smile. 'Didn't you say novelists are capable of anything?'

'So Murray has been made to disappear,' she said, half to herself.

'And I think the drugs are still here. In the safe, perhaps, or hidden somewhere in the building.'

'Murray and I looked in all the rooms. But we couldn't find anything.'

'You looked everywhere?'

'We turned the building upside down. I gave him the front-door key and he sneaked in at night.'

'Did you search the meeting room?'

'Especially there.'

'I thought you said you didn't have the key to that room,' Marek said, keeping his voice level.

She switched off the copier. 'I haven't been totally honest about that either,' she said, avoiding his gaze. 'The Master left the key lying on the table in the office. So I pinched it. It was a while before he noticed he didn't have it and by that time he'd forgotten where he'd left it.' She shrugged. 'He must have had another one

227

made because, a week or so later, I saw him unlock the meeting-room door.'

'Why did you take the key?' Marek said softly.

'Oh, I don't know. To make life difficult for him, I suppose.' She put another batch of papers into the tray and restarted the copier. 'I can't stand the man.'

'Why?'

'It's the way he looks at me. He sort of undresses me with his voice. And his eyes.'

'I can completely understand why,' he said, without thinking. Her sudden silence made him immediately regret his remark. 'All right, so where do we go from here?'

'There's no point searching the rooms again. It would be a waste of time and effort. Murray and I did it extremely thoroughly.' She gazed through the window bars. 'I'm beginning to wonder whether the Master really would keep the package in the building.'

'I'm sure of it. It's far too risky keeping it at his house. For that matter, it's too risky keeping it in the office safe, now I think about it. If the police raided those places and the drugs were found, the man would be facing a long jail sentence. But if they're hidden somewhere in the building, he could point the finger at any of the Masons. Or at you. Or even me.' He crossed his arms, studying her. 'Allie, did it ever occur to you that they might all be in on it?'

'The Brothers?'

'I know it seems far-fetched. But who would suspect a Freemason of importing drugs? And raising funds to solve the city's drug problem would be the perfect cover.'

She looked intently into his eyes. 'You know, Franek, you might be on to something.' Her glance fell on the newly printed copies gathering in the tray. 'The Masons are meeting tomorrow night.' She handed him a copy. 'This is the final agenda.'

He scanned the sheet. 'Applications for membership?'

'And they're conferring the degree of Fellowcraft on one of the members.'

'I see there's the usual AOCB item. What might that be? Brexit?'

'Good Lord, no. The meetings are non-political. No political or religious discussions are allowed.'

'How do you know all this?'

'I occasionally hear the Brothers chatting. The question is,' she added, drawing out the word, 'will they discuss things you could never explicitly put down on an agenda?' She looked at him meaningfully.

'It's a pity I can't be a fly on the wall and see what's going on.'

'Or even hear what's going on.'

And, as soon as she'd spoken the words, he knew how they could do it.

'Franek Filarski?' Gregor said. 'She's sure that's his name?'

Ross was sprawled lazily on the sofa. 'She's sure. She wrote it down so she wouldn't forget it.'

'And he was asking about Murray?'

'He said he was from the Revenue.'

'You don't believe him?'

Ross took a gulp of whisky. 'She thinks he's a drug dealer. Like Murray.'

Gregor strode over to the sideboard and poured himself another Scotch, trying not to show his alarm. When Niall had told him about the visit from the Polish detective, he'd played it down. The detective was trying to find Cameron's killer, and knew nothing about their other business. But this archivist, Murray Johnson, was an entirely different matter. Somehow he'd got wind of what they were up to. Aye, and now this Filarski was looking for him.

He returned to the armchair. 'Did she give a description of the man?'

'Tall, blond and handsome.'

'Could be anyone.' He glared at his son. 'And how have you tried to find him?'

Ross gazed into his whisky. 'We've done all the usual things. But there's no record of him.'

'Did you check with our man in West Bell Street?'

'He confirmed he's not in the database.'

'What about your other contacts?'

'I told them to ask around. There's one I've still to hear back from.'

'If Filarski's a dealer, he may not be the only one looking for Murray. This thing may start to grow arms and legs.'

'Aye, Dad, I'm aware of that.'

'Have you spoken to Niall?'

Ross looked up in surprise. 'Why would I?'

'He's been a wee bit anxious lately. Best to keep quiet about Filarski for now. It'll just be between the three of us.'

'Aye, all right.'

'Talking of which, where's Kenny?'

'He's out following a lead.' Ross smiled slyly. 'We may get our hands on Filarski sooner than we think.'

'And you'll know how to deal with him when you do.'

It wasn't a question, so warranted no reply.

'Okay, Dad, I'm turning in.'

'Aye, best not to keep your wife waiting.'

After Ross had gone up, Gregor sat for a long time, thinking through their conversation. Things had taken a turn for the worse. But he had to keep his nerve. God knows, he'd had plenty of practice. And he could count on Ross, who would make sure Kenny was kept in line. No, it was Niall who was likely to cave in under pressure. He'd need to keep a close watch on the man. He glanced at the photograph of Davina, seeing her smiling at him with a slight admonishment in her emerald-green eyes. And for the first time since he'd heard the news about his wee lad, he realised with a jolt that his murder was no longer uppermost in his mind. And that was not a good thing.

Despite the best efforts of the volunteers, Morag's body remained undiscovered. The nearby fields had been searched and searched again with the same negative result. Dania knew that they were simply going through the motions: the clothes were being examined, as was Morag's phone, which they'd found in the pocket of her jeans, and the skull mask was being swabbed for DNA. All this had to be done, but Dania was convinced they needed to find another way. Which was why she and Honor were driving up Emmock Road.

As the narrow road meandered on, taking them north of the city centre, the foliage grew denser and the trees taller. The sun was past its best, but it was still warm enough to make them shed their jackets.

'What have you done to your hair?' Dania said. 'It looks different.'

'I'm having an ugly day, boss.' Honor changed down before the bend in the road. 'Remind me again why we're doing this?'

'I'm convinced Morag's here somewhere. Somewhere that's not obvious.'

'The uniforms searched the area thoroughly. Could be our man hasn't dumped the body yet. Maybe we'll catch a break and see him doing it.'

'He's too clever for that.'

'You know something, Strathmartine is just a few hundred metres west of Emmock,' Honor said, nodding at the sat-nav. 'They're connected by Harestane Road.'

'Let me guess. There's no CCTV there either.'

'We're still doing house-to-house. Tempting to think he cut across from there to here. But my guess is he drove somewhere miles away in the opposite direction, and then doubled back in a huge circle.'

'Don't forget he needs a safe place to kill her, and then bleach the body.'

'I can't get that image out of my head,' Honor muttered.

They drove in silence for a while. Through the trees, they caught glimpses of fields stretching into the wooded distance. Dania thought of the countryside outside Warsaw, not greatly dissimilar, but the trees were different varieties and she couldn't remember many low stone walls. Perhaps the Communists had removed them after they'd appropriated the farms in an attempt to demonstrate that all men are created equal, and private owner-ship was to be abolished. But whatever the similarities in landscape, she doubted she'd find the ditches between the trees where the Germans had buried the bodies of their Polish victims.

'Okay, Honor, let's stop.'

'Why here?'

'It's around here that Angus was playing with his drone.'

They pulled up and left the car. The news of the discovery of Morag's clothes had rippled across Dundee, and bunches of flowers were starting to appear along the wall, some with messages of condolence. It had fallen to Owen to inform the Pinkertons that they'd found their daughter's effects. He'd returned with a determined expression, and set everyone humming with renewed enthusiasm. The mood hadn't lasted long as, one by one, they'd hit dead ends.

'Got your stick?' Dania said.

'Yep. So where do we start?'

'Morag's clothes were found at the edge of this field. But see that bit of woodland? That's where we're going.'

'Didn't the volunteers search in there?'

'Something tells me they missed something vital. Or looked in the wrong place.'

Honor was gazing at her in the way she did when she thought her boss was havering, but she was too polite to say. 'How did you come to that conclusion, may I ask?'

'I was doing my piano practice late last night. The piece I was playing is a great workout for both hands. "*Frühlingsrauschen*" – Rustle of Spring – by Sinding. Do you know it?'

'Can't say that I do.'

'The right hand goes manic while the melody is developed by the left. I was making a total mess of it and had to stop. My brain must have been in overdrive because it suddenly came to me that Morag's body is definitely here somewhere. So we're going to search again.' She tapped at the screen on her mobile. 'This app will tell us where we are. And how much of the area we've covered.'

Honor looked unconvinced. It said something about her loyalty and/or her belief in her boss that she was prepared to go along with it. She followed Dania over the wall and into the wood.

They moved through the trees, watching where they were treading. Under the carpet of leaves were deep holes and tree roots that could trip up a careless stroller and send her crashing. Honor kept her attention on the ground, poking her stick into the deeper drifts.

233

'Boss, do you think there's any significance in the days the three girls were taken?'

'How do you mean?'

'Fiona was taken on a Friday evening and Euna disappeared mid-afternoon on a Saturday. But Morag wasn't kidnapped at the weekend. She was taken on a Monday.'

'It's possible there's a significance. But I don't know what.'

'Or it could be nothing. By the way, I've been looking again through the home movies we got from the Camperdown Park visitors.'

'And?'

'Morag appears in some but not many.'

'Anyone acting suspiciously?'

'Hard to tell. They were mainly close-ups of children. Now and again you see someone in the background but they're looking at the animals, and have their heads turned away.'

'Any videos taken in the car parks?'

The girl shook her head.

'What about CCTV?'

'I went up there with Hamish and had a butcher's at the place. There's not much. The home movies are more informative. Okay, so why are you looking into the trees?'

'I thought Morag might be up there.'

'Wouldn't you expect to see loads of crows?'

'Perhaps the bleach puts them off.'

'Depends on when he gave her the bath. It would evaporate off eventually.'

'Right, let's stop for a bit. We've covered about half this wood.'

'Do you think the midges are rising?' Honor said, slapping her neck. 'I'm not an outdoor person.'

'Do you get midges in woodland?'

'Well, *something's* biting me.'

234

Dania peered up into the meshed branches. 'When I was a child, I once saw a huge wasps' nest in the trees.'

'Get away,' Honor said, her eyes wide.

'Marek thought it would be fun to throw stones at it. He knocked it right off the branch.'

'What happened?'

'We both got badly stung. He told me he'd confessed his sin and the priest had given him a highly unpleasant penance. But through the grille he could hear the man trying not to laugh.'

'What was the penance?'

'I can't remember now. That particular priest had a habit of making the punishment fit the crime.'

Honor grinned. 'Was it a crime against you, or a crime against the wasps?'

'Both.' She ran her stick over the ground. 'We need to get on or it'll be dark before we finish.'

They continued through the wood. The ground was matted with undergrowth, making the going slow. The story about the priest had reminded Dania that she still hadn't contacted Father Kliment. But she knew what the outcome would be: endless meetings about endless concerts. She'd have to do it soon, as her conscience had suddenly started to bother her.

After another fruitless half-hour, she decided it was time to admit defeat.

Honor had the good grace not to rub it in. She nodded at Dania's mobile. 'What's the quickest way out?'

'That way on the left will take us on to the road. Then it's a short walk to the car.'

'Sounds good.'

The trees grew so dense in this part of the woodland that they had to push through the low-hanging branches. They reached the wall and were about to step over when Dania said, 'Wait a minute, what's that there?'

Honor pulled away a branch. 'Judging by the sheds and all the muck, I'd say it's a farmyard.'

'No, not there.' Dania made her way back through the cluster of trees. She peered up into the branches. They were so intertwined that their leaves formed a thick canopy. The twisted trunks made climbing ideal. 'Up here,' she said.

'I think it's a treehouse, boss. Or something close to it. Hard to tell.'

'I'm going up.'

'Let me do it.'

'Rank has its privileges. Anyway, someone has to stay down here and make a report when I fall and break my neck.'

She took hold of a branch and hauled herself up, realising with dismay that what had seemed a straightforward climb was anything but. The footholds were too widely spaced and there were precious few handholds. She wondered if she should abandon the idea, but she wasn't someone who quit easily. After pressing on, she found that halfway up the climbing became easier, but the treehouse, a dilapidated wooden structure, remained stubbornly out of reach. '*Cholera jasna*,' she muttered. Perhaps if she could grab one of the slats . . .

'Careful!' Honor shouted. 'You know, I think it might be easier from the other side.'

'No, wait! I can see how to do it.' She grasped a branch firmly, steadied herself, and then half jumped, half swung on to the adjacent trunk. Shock surged through her. She risked a glance down. Honor was standing with a hand over her mouth.

The treehouse was now only a couple of metres away. It was so old that it had fallen victim to nature, and offshoots from the trees had forced their way through the slats and up into the roof.

There was a platform with a low wooden rail and the remains of what might have been a rope ladder. Given the difficulty of reaching the building, it seemed an unlikely hiding place. But she had to check. She'd come this far.

She studied the approach to the platform. The trick was to keep a grip on a branch before shifting her weight. And her movements would have to be slow and deliberate. But, as she stepped cautiously on to what she thought was a firm piece of branch, it gave way and, in panic, she grabbed at whatever was within reach, which happened to be the railing. A wave of fear coursed through her as it came away in her hand, taking some of the platform with it.

She snatched at the nearest branch, which miraculously held her weight, and had just managed to find another foothold when, with a sickening creak, the rest of the platform collapsed. Her heart lurched as she watched the wall and then the roof fall apart. They plunged crashing to the ground, leaving a silence that seemed to reverberate through the air.

When her breathing had steadied, she peered down.

Honor had had the foresight to jump out of the way. She was standing beside the wreckage of branches and rotten wood. But she wasn't staring at the broken slats. Her attention was fixed on the red and swollen body of a young girl, her limbs outspread and her long blonde hair in a wiry, tangled mess.

As quickly as she could without risking falling, Dania climbed down, her heart pounding. She gazed into the opaque white eyes of the spread-eagled figure, and then at Honor. Neither woman spoke. They'd found what they'd been looking for.

The man who'd been watching the women's passage through the wood crept away from the thicket, chuckling to himself. That was a close call for the detective, right enough. It was brave, if a wee bit reckless, of her to climb into those trees, but then he supposed that was what detectives were paid to do. When he'd scoped the place out, he'd come to the conclusion that he wouldn't be climbing into those branches carrying a lassie's body. Attaching an old rope ladder had done the trick, but it had given way as he was coming down.

He hurried out of the wood, trying not to make too much noise. The police would be arriving soon with their little helpers. Aye, and he'd have to be well away before they saw him.

He remembered his first. Fiona. With the red hair. He'd seen her riding her bicycle on the deserted street. She'd been easy to entice into his vehicle. The first one was always a piece of piss. The ones that followed were harder, because their mothers kept them at their sides, as mothers should. Although taking Euna had been a dream. She'd run into the woodland, chasing a butterfly. Daft lassie. Those blue eyes and that dark hair, though. They were irresistible. And when he'd undressed her and seen her little cupped breasts, he knew he'd never be able to stop.

Morag hadn't been too hard, either. He'd spotted her at Camperdown Park earlier that day, and heard her mother call her by her name and say something about a sleepover. Pure dead brilliant. He'd followed the family to their car and then to the house. The hardest part was waiting for the lass to leave. Addressing her by her name, and telling her he remembered her from school, had almost clinched it. But seeing her initial reluctance, he'd decided it might be wise to leave it. He'd made this decision at the outset, realising that one wrong move could prove fatal: a lass who'd been pressed too hard would tell her parents. And give the police a description. He was driving off when she called him back. Sweet. He didn't find it easy to kill, but the circumstances demanded it – they'd all seen his face.

As he reached the layby where he'd left his vehicle, he was already thinking about Girl No. 4. She would require more attention, a more detailed plan. And a new hunting ground.

The noise of the sirens grew louder. He started the engine and eased the van on to the road.

CHAPTER 24

'And Professor Slaughter is doing the autopsy on Morag Pinkerton today,' Owen said. 'Although from an initial examination, it looks as though it's the same MO as with Fiona and Euna,' he added, concluding the briefing.

He looked shattered. At his request, Dania had accompanied him the evening before to Brackens Road. In a voice close to tears, he'd told the Pinkertons that the body of a girl they believed was Morag had been found. Jackie Ireland had reminded him not to go into too much detail until the shock had worn off, and on no account mention the bleach. He'd nodded unhappily, and Dania knew he would have preferred someone else to break the news. But as the DI running the case, it fell to him. Mrs Pinkerton had listened stoically. It was her husband who'd collapsed.

'What made you go back to that area, DI Gorska?' Jackie said. 'Don't get me wrong, we're all glad you did. I'm just curious.'

Dania shrugged. 'It was a hunch, nothing more.' She avoided Honor's gaze. The explanation that she'd had her epiphany moment trying to play Sinding sounded lame now.

The DCI turned to the others. 'We carry on as usual. DI McFadden and I are briefing the press in fifteen minutes.'

Dania watched them leave. She jerked her head at Honor.

The women sat at Dania's desk.

'We've got a bit of a breathing space,' Dania said, 'so I want to run something by you. It's to do with Cameron Affleck.'

Honor puffed out her cheeks. 'I'd almost forgotten we're working that case too.'

Dania described her conversations with Jamie Reid, leaving nothing out, especially what he'd said about Cameron.

Honor was frowning. 'You're telling me he emphatically denied having seen the lad at the photoshoot.'

'That's it. And he said it on two occasions.'

'And you don't believe him?'

'I can't see how he could have missed the boy.'

'Maybe now that the case is all over the news, he doesn't want to be linked to it.'

'Then why did he tell Marek and me about the photoshoot? Cameron's name was already in the papers.'

'Do you think he had something to do with the boy being chained up in that doocot?'

'I don't know. But he's hiding something, I'm sure of it. And if we can find out what it is, it may give us a lead.'

The girl grinned. 'Your hunches have been spot on so far, boss.'

'I'd normally ask you to hunt down the magazine article with those photos, but with everything that's going on, I can't justify your time. I don't even know which year he did the photoshoot.'

'What are you expecting to find? Apart from photos of the boy.'

'I'll know that when I see it.'

Honor looked at her appreciatively.

'We're fighting the clock with Cameron Affleck,' Dania said. 'You know how difficult it is with cold cases.'

'Yep. The longer it takes, the less likely we are to get a result.'

'I don't intend to leave a single stone unturned, Honor. I think constantly about that little boy, alone, and starving to death. He's the first one I think about when I wake up in the morning, not those three girls.'

'I know,' Honor said sadly. 'I can see it in your face.'

'Hello, Mrs Spence,' Dania said, as soon as the door had opened. 'Are you busy? I'd like a quick word, if that's okay.'

The woman hesitated for so long that Dania thought she'd make an excuse and put her off. But she smiled suddenly and stepped back. 'Please come in, Inspector.'

'Is Mr Gregor Affleck at home?'

'The Affleck men are at work. It's just me and Sandy here.'

'Sandy? Your husband?'

'Aye, perhaps you'd like to meet him.'

Dania followed the woman through the hall and into the kitchen.

A bulky man with his head drooping on to his chest was sitting in the rocking chair. As the women entered, he lifted his head and gazed at Dania with wine-washed eyes. He started to drag himself to his feet, but it seemed such an effort that she said, 'Please don't get up, Mr Spence.'

He stared at her in surprise, then sank back heavily.

'Sandy, this is Detective Inspector Gorska,' Mrs Spence said.

He seemed suddenly ill at ease, and his unfocused eyes grew dark with suspicion. It was a reaction Dania had seen many times when people were introduced to the police, and knew it meant nothing. He seemed to remember his manners, and mumbled what might have been a greeting.

'Sandy's taking a wee break. He's joined me for morning coffee. Would you like some, Inspector?'

Dania glanced at the full wine glass in front of Sandy. 'No, thank you.'

'Do please take a seat,' Mrs Spence said, after a silence. 'How can I help you?'

'I wondered if you'd remembered a photoshoot here some years ago,' Dania said, watching Sandy extend a trembling hand towards the glass.

'Here? When would this have been?'

'I can't give you a date, I'm afraid. But it would have been when Cameron was alive.'

'Aye, now it's coming back to me. Oh, Sandy! How could you be so careless! You've spilt wine all over your shirt.' She hurried to the sink and returned with a wet rag. Muttering to herself, she sponged down her husband's denim shirt, getting most of the red stain off. 'That'll have to do. But it's going in the washing machine later.' She seemed to remember Dania and threw her a quick smile. 'So, the photoshoot,' she said, returning to her seat. 'Now, let me have a wee think. We've had a few of those from time to time. But when the lad was alive? I'm not sure I can recall any.'

'The photos were published in a homes-and-gardens magazine.'

Her expression brightened. 'Aye, I've kept all those. They're here somewhere.'

Dania held her breath. This was more than she could have hoped for.

Mrs Spence went over to the fine wooden dresser, the only old piece in the modern kitchen, and returned with a pile of magazines. She took the chair next to Dania. Sandy seemed no longer interested in what was going on. His empty wine glass had fallen on to his lap, and his eyelids were starting to flicker.

Mrs Spence fumbled in her apron pocket for a pair of reading glasses. 'We were featured in the *People's Friend* a few months back,' she said proudly, handing Dania the magazine.

The colourful cover showed a red-and-white-striped lighthouse and the words 'Pilgrimage to Plymouth'. Dania turned the pages, making a show of being interested.

'You said Cameron was alive when the photos were taken, Inspector.' She looked at Dania over the top of her glasses. 'Can you remind me when he disappeared?'

'June the twelfth, two thousand and five.'

She riffled through the magazines. 'Right, here we are.' She squinted at the date. 'May the twenty-eighth. Two thousand and five. Now, I seem to mind we had a huge spread somewhere.' She turned the pages. 'So where is it?' she muttered. 'Maybe it wasn't this edition.'

Dania resisted the temptation to snatch the magazine out of the woman's hands. *Look at the index*, she felt like saying.

'I reckon I need to look at the index. Aye, here we are.'

She turned to the appropriate page and spread out the magazine. The article was about the Affleck house, and featured photographs of the interior as well as the gardens and summerhouse.

'Have a look, Inspector, while I see to Sandy.' She pushed the magazine across and got to her feet. She reached her husband just as he was falling forward and caught him before his head hit the table. 'Come on, Sandy, dear,' she murmured, helping him up. 'Let's get you outside for a wee while.' She steered him to the back door.

Dania turned her attention to the photographs. In one, a strawberry blonde with lightly curled hair was sitting at the edge of the stone fountain, watching a little boy. The photographer had captured the boy's delight perfectly. Dania felt her heart clench. Little Cameron, dressed in a kilt and silver-buttoned jacket, was clutching a toy boat and smiling into the camera, his eyes screwed up against the sun. In another, the entire Affleck family stood stiffly at the front steps, Gregor and Davina in the middle, and the two older boys at the flanks. Ross must have been told to smile but had managed to look as though someone had stolen his parking spot. Kenny was grinning like a baboon, as if to make up for his brother's scowl. Cameron stood in front of his mother, who had laid protective hands on his shoulders, unwittingly drawing attention to their unevenness. The men were in red-and-green kilts, which Dania guessed must be one of the Affleck tartans.

The interior shots had been taken with and without family members. But in all the photos where one or more Afflecks was present, Cameron was there too. In the less formal pictures, he was beaming at the cameraman as though they were sharing a private joke. One photo, taken from inside the summerhouse, showed him cheekily peeping from behind the door.

Dania turned to the end of the article and squinted at the acknowledgement. The photographs were copyrighted to Jamie Reid.

He wasn't there. The first time I laid eyes on him was that photo in the papers. I didn't even know Cameron existed until then.

Mrs Spence returned. 'He's better outside in this weather, Inspector,' she said, without a trace of embarrassment. 'I've settled him in the garden seat.'

Dania kept her tone friendly. 'You said your husband makes children's toys.'

'Aye, he's a carpenter. He's always been good with his hands. We're lucky he can work from home.'

'You live in Blackness, don't you?'

'Well remembered.' She smiled wearily. 'He's not been the same since he had his wee accident.'

'I'm sorry to hear that.'

'It was a nasty fall. We're on the top floor, and there's no lift. He took a tumble down the stairs. He was in a coma for five months.'

'But he's all right now?'

'It's left him depressed. Ach, it comes and goes,' she said, sinking into her chair. She glanced at the wine glass. 'And he likes the drink. He never used to.'

After a pause, Dania said, 'May I borrow this magazine? I'll return it to you.'

'Of course. Was it a help?'

'I need to look at it more closely.'

'The photographer took many more photos than you see there. I suppose they have to do that for their editors. I don't know what he did with them. But a week later, that magazine came out.' She rested her gaze on Dania. 'And how are things going with those poor lassies?' She gripped the crucifix at her throat. 'I can't begin to think what their mothers are going through. There's no coming back from the death of a child.'

A sudden noise from outside made the woman spring to her feet. She hurried to the window. 'Oh, my word, he's fallen off the bench,' she murmured. 'He's all right, though.'

'I'd better leave you to get on, Mrs Spence. I'll let myself out.'

'Before you go, let me give you some more rhubarb-and-strawberry jam.' She opened one of the cupboard doors. 'You must have finished the one I gave you.'

'No, there's some left,' Dania said, thinking of the unopened jar in her kitchen.

'Aye, here we are.' She put the jar into Dania's hands, closing her fingers round it. 'Nothing like a bit of sugar for getting those brain cells firing, my nan used to say.'

And mine, thought Dania, as she turned to leave.

Dania was at her desk, ignoring the hubbub around her. She was thinking about the evening at Marek's, and what Pam Reid had said about her husband's website: *Enter his name and 'landscape photography' and you'll find it.*

She launched Google. A second or two later, she was browsing through Jamie Reid's site. The home page carried a photo of a younger Jamie with a shock of brown hair in place of the buzz-cut. He was dressed casually in a yellow T-shirt, and was gazing out with a roguish smile. She was surprised to see that he'd won a number of awards but, then, Mrs Spence's magazine was the first time she'd viewed his work. There were links to various themed collections. She glanced through a few at random, recognising Loch Rannoch, a snow-covered Schiehallion and the area around Killiecrankie. There was a collection entitled 'Beast from the East' that consisted, unsurprisingly, of black-and-white snowy windy landscapes taken from unconventional angles. At the end were the usual contact details, instructions on how to purchase copies, and a section where you could leave a review. Given the quality of the work, she could have predicted the positive comments and the five-star ratings.

But what she was looking for were photos taken in and around Dundee. A bit of searching and she was scrolling through the city's green spaces, including ones she hadn't visited, like Stobsmuir and Clatto Country Parks. In Templeton Woods, captured in winter, snow coated the branches of the trees, and a thin white shroud lay over the ground, stealing the colour from the landscape. A few photos had been taken in the early morning. A mild haze lay over the fields, stretching into the wooded distance.

She flicked through the collection of ancient churches, one said to be founded by St Boniface in AD 710. There was a large number of images from the Affleck Natural History Museum. They were all there: the jungle animals she and Honor had gawped at, the scorpions and the tarantulas, the seals and the penguins. Even the brown bear Jamie had told them about. The last few had been taken in the workshop and showed Ross and Kenny bent over their dioramas. In one display, a group of mice were dressed as DC Thomson characters in their typical poses: Dennis the Menace, Beryl the Peril and Desperate Dan. In another, more elaborate, diorama, tuxedo-wearing robins were sitting on bar stools, drinking brightly coloured cocktails from tiny glasses. Her favourite had to be the squirrels standing round a table, playing snooker.

She continued to browse the pages. And then, suddenly, she was staring at it – the doocot at Inchture. With its lectern-style structure, string courses and Gothic archway, it was unmistakable. Jamie had captured the building and its surroundings from different angles and at different times of year. In one photo, the tiled roof was speckled with snow; in another, taken from a distance, trees were dropping their russet-coloured leaves, barely concealing the doocot behind them.

He had helpfully inserted the dates on which he'd taken the photographs. The ones of the doocot were from late 2004 through to early 2005. She glanced at the date on the homes-and-gardens magazine: 28 May 2005. Cameron had last been seen alive on 12 June of the same year. In other words, two weeks after the magazine had come out, which, according to Mrs Spence, was a week after the photoshoot.

Dania sat back, running her hands over her face. Leaving aside Jamie's clumsy lie about not having photographed Cameron, two facts were uppermost in her mind. The first was that the doocot had interested Jamie sufficiently that he'd taken several photos, returning repeatedly to capture it changing with the seasons. He might well have been interested enough to make enquiries as to who owned it, and therefore who had the key to the door.

The second was that Jamie was at the Afflecks' house in May 2005 for a photoshoot, and one of the places he'd photographed was the inside of the summerhouse, which was normally kept locked. What had Gregor said when she'd asked who knew where the doocot key was kept? *Anyone who would have seen me remove the key that opens the summerhouse.*

Could Jamie have seen Gregor open the cupboard in the hall, and realised that the key to the doocot was kept there also? And, in all the comings and goings at the photoshoot, could he have slipped back into the house unseen and lifted it? And then, having appreciated the level of wealth in the Affleck house, could he have befriended little Cameron, returned three weeks later and enticed the lad outside and into his Hyundai Starex?

CHAPTER 25

'And you're sure it's safe to go in?'

'As sure as I can be, Franek. The Master told me he wouldn't be back for at least an hour. Possibly longer.'

Marek frowned. Given what was at stake, it would be catastrophic if Niall Affleck walked in on them. 'Did he say where he was going?'

'He said he had an appointment with his agent. That's all I know.' Allie met his gaze. 'If we're going to do it, we need to do it now.'

He was impressed by her resolve. He himself was starting to doubt the wisdom of their plan. But it was too late to back out now. And the last thing he wanted was for her to think him a wimp. 'Have you got the key?' he said.

A smile crept on to her lips. She slipped her hand into the pocket of her white trousers and produced a Yale key. She held it up.

'So, what are we waiting for?' he said.

She moved past him into the hall. She was inserting the key into the lock in the meeting-room door when the phone rang.

'Shall I get that?' Marek said.

'No! I'll do it!' she said, in a voice edging towards hysteria.

He watched, astonished, as she ran to the phone and grabbed it.

'Yes?'

He heard only her side of the conversation.

'Yes, I'm here . . . No, I've not been out.' A pause. 'I've been at my desk all day. I give you my word.' Another pause. 'I'm getting things ready for the meeting. There's a lot to do.' She took a deep breath. 'Yes, the archivist's here.' A glance at Marek. 'He's helping me get everything ready.' She closed her eyes. 'All right,' she said, in a subdued tone. She disconnected.

'Is everything okay?' Marek said. 'Was that the Master checking up on you?'

'No one thinks I'm competent to run things in this place,' she muttered, looking at the floor.

He was overcome with a desire to put his arms round her. '*I* think you're competent,' he said.

She lifted her head. 'That's because you're a decent man. There aren't many of those around.' She smoothed her hair. 'Come on, let's do this.'

She unlocked the meeting-room door and switched on the light. He followed her in, instinctively closing the door behind them.

She raised her arms and turned round in a circle. 'This, Franek, is a Temple of the Great Architect of the Universe.'

At the end of the windowless room, opposite the door, there was a short flight of three steps. It led to a platform with an elaborately carved wooden chair. Above the chair was a painting of an interleaved circle and triangle, with an eye in the centre. Part of the wooden floor had been re-tiled in black-and-white squares, and on them was a mahogany pedestal with kneelers on each side. Tall electric candles stood like sentinels at three corners of the pedestal.

Two neat rows of chairs lined the walls to left and right of the platform. A quick count told Marek that forty Brothers in total could be admitted. Although he hadn't seen the list of members, from something he'd heard Allie say to the Master he understood that the current membership stood at just under twenty.

The ceiling was a marvel. It was a deep blue and studded with tiny stars. In the centre was a larger star, its golden light radiating in all directions. The walls were covered with pictures, which on close inspection were on canvas, framed in wood. One was of a Masonic hall, recognisable from the chequerboard floor, platforms and pedestal with candles. Another showed a closed coffin painted with symbols, the four points of the compass stamped in gold letters on the frame. In a painting of what might have been Jacob's ladder, a robed figure was stepping on to the lowest rung. The entire room glittered with Masonic emblems – on the walls, the ceiling and the floor. Some, like the set square and compasses, with the G in the centre, he recognised. Others were a mystery. There was even what looked like Hebrew script.

'I've never seen a room like it,' he said.

'Everything here is symbolic. See those platforms round the place? The number of steps leading up has some sort of meaning, but I don't know what.' She pointed to the picture above the carved wooden chair. 'That's the All-seeing Eye. And I'm guessing the Master sits below it.'

'And is this a Bible?' Marek said, peering at the open book on the pedestal.

'I think it's called the Volume of Sacred Law, or something like that.'

He turned the pages. 'But it *is* a Bible.'

'I think we need to get on, Franek. Tell me how it all works.'

He held up a small device. 'This is a smart camera. It communicates with the laptop in the archives room.' He'd brought his own machine, a more powerful and sophisticated model than the one he'd been using to set up the records database. 'Now, according to the agenda, the meeting starts at eight this evening.'

'That's right. The Brothers have their dinner at six thirty, get togged up, then have the meeting while the caterers take everything away.'

'I'll programme the camera to start sending the video stream at five minutes to eight, regardless of the light level, and stop when the light level drops below a certain value.' He raised an eyebrow. 'I'm assuming someone switches the lights off after the meeting is over.'

'The camera can do all that?' she said, wide-eyed.

'You'd be amazed what toys undercover investigators have, these days.'

'What about the laptop? Does it stay on?'

'After a certain time when no video reaches it, it will stop recording.'

'We'd better lock the archives room in case one of the Brothers decides to peek inside.'

'We could put the laptop somewhere else.'

She shook her head. 'The archives room is as good a place as any.'

'What I need to do is test it works, and that we get good-quality images.'

'How long will that take?'

'Five minutes.'

He set to work. The test required him to point the camera at something, start up the software on the laptop, and check that the timing worked, particularly the switch-off mechanism when he plunged the room into darkness. Fifteen minutes later, he confirmed the test a success.

'So where do we put the camera?' Allie said, excitement in her voice.

He glanced around. He was in a position to record a Masonic meeting and see things that only Freemasons saw. It was no longer just about the shipment of fentanyl. 'I'm guessing the action takes place at this pedestal. So ideally we want the camera pointing more or less at it.'

They turned and looked at the Master's throne. Above it was the All-seeing Eye.

Marek laughed softly. It couldn't have been better . . .

There was standing room only in the incident room. Owen took them through the latest reports. Morag's autopsy had thrown up no new information: in his summary, Milo Slaughter had high-lighted the evidence of sexual assault and prolonged immersion in bleach. Which was what they'd expected. Kimmie had conducted a number of tests on the skull mask and come to the conclusion that it had never been worn. This produced groans from the room. DNA evidence, which was missing from both the girl's body and clothes, would have given them a badly needed boost. And the phone in the pocket of Morag's jeans revealed nothing suspicious. All the numbers in her Contacts list had been checked.

They were watching Owen, waiting to see how he'd react. Dania could have predicted it.

'We're no further forward, I'm afraid,' he said. 'Therefore we've no choice but to go back and work the cases again. Different people will conduct the interviews, as per usual.' It was a tactic that occasionally worked. Someone new might spot something or ask a different question that led to a breakthrough. 'I've drawn up the roster,' he added.

Honor caught Dania's eye. 'What do you reckon, boss? Will this work?'

'It has to. We've got nothing else.'

254

Her thoughts were constantly slipping back to Jamie Reid.
She'd shared her suspicions with Honor and Hamish, who had
done her the courtesy of taking them seriously. Hamish's suggestion that a second person might have been involved, who'd
actually locked the boy in, was worth pursuing. That was if they
could figure out how to go about it. Getting a list of Jamie's
friends was the place to start. Marek could help with that, but the
thought of involving her brother didn't leave Dania with much
hope of success.

She was thinking this over when Owen called to the room that
the preliminary list was up. He was starting with Euna. She was
their best bet: with all those guests at the Montcrieff wedding,
someone had to have seen something.

Dania picked up her bag, nodding to Honor and Hamish. 'Let's
go,' she said.

They didn't seem ultra-keen. Like her, they didn't rate their
chances of success.

The guests at the wedding of Euna Montcrieff's sister lived across
Dundee and Fife, but Dania had been assigned the addresses of
those in Inchture. Her hope was that the locals who'd attended
the nuptials were more likely to have seen something and that,
with the passage of time, what they'd seen would start to appear
relevant.

'Seems like only yesterday we were looking inside that doocot,'
Honor said, as she took the turning off the A90.

'Only yesterday?' Dania said. 'To me it feels like a million
years ago.'

Hamish was staring through the window. 'This is a lovely village, ma'am. All that waving grass. And those trees in leaf.'

'Nice to have one romantic in the team,' Honor said. 'So where shall I pull up?'

'Try that car park down from the church. We can meet back there when we're done.'

'This place is a bit on the sprawly side. Hope we don't get lost.'

'Look into the sky for those spires and you'll find the church. We'll go somewhere afterwards and have a late supper.'

'Most of the villagers will be having theirs now,' Honor said glumly. 'And they won't be best pleased at being interrupted.'

'It can't be helped.'

They pulled up in the car park and left the vehicle.

'Good hunting,' Honor said. She and Hamish strode off down the main street.

There was no reply at the first two addresses on Dania's list. But she had luck with the third.

An elderly man with red-rimmed eyes and wispy white hair opened the door. He wiped his mouth with his napkin. 'Yes?' he said politely.

'Mr Montcrieff?'

'Aye, that's me.'

She held up her warrant. 'I'm DI Gorska from West Bell Street. I know it's an inconvenient time, but could I ask you some questions? It's about the murder of Euna Montcrieff.'

His friendly expression vanished, and he exhaled loudly. 'I've already been asked about that.'

'I understand, but I wondered if you wouldn't mind being questioned again. I promise I won't take up too much of your time.'

'You're certainly more polite than the officer who came the first time. You'd better come in.'

'Thank you,' Dania said, wondering who that officer was.

He led the way through the hall into a cluttered living room. The main feature was the large window, which gave a view of a modern housing estate.

He indicated the sofa. 'Please take a seat,' he said, easing himself into the armchair.

She took out her notebook. 'Are you related to Euna, Mr Montcrieff?'

The answer would be in the file at the station, but it was a good opener.

'Her grandfather is a third cousin of mine. You'll find quite a few Montcrieffs round here.'

'And you were one of the guests at the wedding on July the seventh.'

'Aye.'

'Can I ask you to think back to that day and tell me what you remember? I'm after anything unusual. However insignificant it seems.'

He rubbed his chin. 'It was the first time I'd been to that place. Redwood Manor. It hadn't been open long.'

She smiled encouragingly.

'You see, no one thought anything could happen to the children. After that first lass – what was her name?'

'Fiona.'

'Fiona. After Fiona was taken, everyone was more careful. They kept the children in sight the whole time.' A look of bewilderment crept into his eyes. 'But this was a wedding, ken. A happy occasion. And there were so many people. Who would have thought the wee lass would be taken?'

'I understand she was playing outside when it happened. Did anything strike you about the hotel grounds?'

'The grounds?'

'The garden at the hotel.'

'Aye. That garden was huge. I mind there were many kinds of shrubs . . . But there was woodland further on. We thought she'd slipped away into the trees, which was why we searched there as soon as the flag went up.'

'Can you remember what time that would have been?'

Before leaving the station, Dania and the team had picked through the interviews. There were the usual discrepancies in the guests' accounts, especially when it came to timings, so she was surprised when Mr Montcrieff said, 'It was four p.m. I ken the time fine well because that was when the married couple were to leave, and I'd arranged a horse and carriage to arrive at precisely then. The driver had just clip-clopped into the yard, and I was looking for the photographer who was supposed to capture the moment when my daughter, Wilma, came running in. She'd gone to fetch the children for the photo. Aye, especially those wee bridesmaids. There were eight of them.' He ran a hand across his chest. 'They had a string of white flowers here.' His eyes misted over. 'But Wilma could only find seven.'

'And then?' Dania said, when he lapsed into silence.

'Everyone was running around demented. I organised them into groups. We searched everywhere. The driver lent a hand. We went all over, even into the fields.'

'It's helpful to have this time of four o'clock, Mr Montcrieff. But do you remember the last time you actually saw Euna?'

'Now let me think. It would have been about half an hour before. Folk had finished eating, and we were about to start the speeches and toasts. The children were getting restless – ach, you know how they are, throwing things around and raising a rumpus. They had their own tables at the door. Euna had started to sing.' His expression softened. 'She has a lovely voice, the wee lassie. Anyway, someone must have decided they could go out and play.'

'And no one went with them?'

'Why would they? We could see the garden from the dining room. Well, most of it. It disappears round the side.'

'How many children were there?'

'About twenty, I'd say. Afterwards, when we asked them about Euna, well, they'd all been doing different things. They'd split up into groups.'

Dania understood how easily it could have happened. She'd read the children's accounts, defensive and apologetic, although, God knows, they couldn't be held responsible. None of them had seen anything out of the ordinary. And none could remember the last time they'd seen Euna.

'Did you know all the guests, Mr Montcrieff?'

'On my side of the family, I did. Why do you ask?'

'Please don't take this the wrong way, but can you remember if anyone was missing from the room? I mean when the speeches were being made?'

'It's possible. One or two folk left earlier for a wee fag break.' He looked thoughtful. 'The other detective didn't ask me that. Do you reckon the man who took Euna was at the reception?'

'We have to consider everything.'

'Aye, I ken that. What I can't say is whether the smokers returned. There were over a hundred folk spread across several tables. And from where I was sitting, I couldn't see them all.'

'Presumably the official photographer was there for the speeches. He'd have photographed the entire room.'

'He must have. But I'm afraid I haven't seen the photos.' He lowered his head. 'Ach, I'm not sure the bride and groom would want them after what happened.' He looked up and smiled sadly. 'Hardly a day to remember, is it?'

She returned the smile. 'Is there anything else you'd like to tell me?'

'I can't think of anything.'

She closed the notebook. 'I'll be going then, Mr Montcrieff. Please don't get up, I'll see myself out. And thank you for your time.'

She left the house but, instead of trying the next address on her list, she headed in the direction of Redwood Manor. The magnificent rose-stone building was a short walk away, and not far from the famous avenue of giant redwoods. Although the plan of the hotel, complete with photographs, was up on the incident board, she wanted to see the place for herself.

The gravel driveway led her to the steps up to the open front door. She peered through the windows on the left, seeing a yellow-walled room with elegant lighting and plaster horns of fruit on the ceiling. Round tables laid with spotless cloths glittered with silver cutlery. She walked past the steps and looked through the windows on the other side. Behind the bar was an impressive array of malt whiskies. There were the usual bar stools, and tables and chairs. The room was empty.

In front of the hotel, a large garden had been lovingly laid out with flowerbeds and scented bushes. It continued round three sides of the building, and was soon out of view of anyone watching from the dining room. A glance upwards confirmed the absence of CCTV cameras.

Dania strolled across the garden and into the woodland. The trees grew so thickly that, after a minute or two of walking, the hotel was no longer visible. She pressed on, hearing the noise of the traffic on the A90. Had the kidnapper waited for Euna in those trees, out of sight of the building? It seemed the obvious place. But his car would have had to be nearby. So where had he left it?

She retraced her steps to the garden, and followed it round towards the back of the building. The grass and flowerbeds disappeared suddenly, and she realised she was standing on asphalt. The garden had morphed into the hotel's car park.

'And that's what I think happened,' Dania said, her mouth full.

Honor had taken the bacon out of her sandwich and was pulling off the rind. 'So you reckon he was a guest.'

'He *may* have been a guest.'

'Saw a chance and grabbed it?' Hamish said.

'Or he wasn't a guest, but he heard about the wedding and knew there'd be lots of children. Either way, he left his car in the car park. He took Euna – willingly or unwillingly – through the woodland and into his car.'

'Didn't you once think he'd parked his car miles away?' Honor said. 'And come over the fields?'

'That was later when he returned with her body. No, I'm talking about the abduction itself. Let's go through the possibilities.'

'If it was a guest, ma'am, I reckon he'd have to have been operating on his own. But the people who came alone checked out, from what I remember.'

'We should take another gander at their statements,' Honor said, abandoning the bacon. She picked up Hamish's cheese sandwich and tucked in.

'But we now know something we didn't before,' Dania said, wiping her fingers on a napkin.

They looked at her expectantly.

'Thanks to Mr Montcrieff, we have a more accurate estimate of the time Euna went missing. It's between three thirty and four p.m.'

'But we checked the ANPR,' Honor said. 'We know which guests brought cars. There weren't that many, actually. Most came by taxi so they could have a drink. But none of them was on that main road at that time in the afternoon.'

'Forget the ANPR, Honor. He didn't use the A90.' She brought up Google Maps on her phone. 'There's a road that leads south from Inchture. You turn west and follow the coastline through Kingoodie. I bet there's no CCTV there.'

Honor sneered. 'I bet there's no tarmac either.'

'And the road will take you right into the centre of Dundee.'

'It was never this hard in London. There were cameras everywhere.'

'The timing is something new, though. We need to start with that. One thing that might work in our favour is that some of the guests left for a cigarette break. If our man was one of them and slipped away to abduct Euna, he won't have returned. If we can get the photos from the dining room, we may be able to pin him down.'

'Aye,' Hamish said. 'Someone I interviewed said the photographer was running around all over the place. He'll have loads of snaps. Now that photography has gone digital, they take many more than they actually use.'

'You know, boss, I have a feeling that DI McFadden went over all this. He and his team looked at the photos, the ones the guests took as well as the photographer's.'

'We need to look at them again,' Dania said. 'But this time check the time-stamps. We have to establish who wasn't in the dining room between three thirty and four.'

'And if we can't, ma'am? Where does this leave us?'

'Right back at square one.'

'I'll get on to those photos as soon as we're back, then,' Honor said.

The girl seemed to have found a new lease of life. She'd left half of Hamish's sandwich uneaten.

CHAPTER 26

It was Monday before Marek returned to the Lodge. An excited Allie was waiting for him. She put her finger to her lips, which he took as the sign that they weren't alone. As quietly as she could, she unlocked the door to the archives room, and he slipped inside. His laptop was on the desk in sleep mode. He checked it quickly. The size of the video file on the desktop suggested all had gone according to plan.

Allie was watching nervously from the door. He nodded, giving her the thumbs-up. She rewarded him with a smile that made his heart stir.

'Miss Ferguson?' Niall Affleck's voice came from the hall.

'Yes?'

'These are the minutes of Friday's meeting. Will you please have them typed up by tomorrow?'

'Of course.'

'I'll be out for the rest of the morning, in case anyone wants me.'

After Marek had heard the front door close, he hurried into the hall. 'I need to remove the camera ASAP, Allie. Someone may find it when they clean the place.'

'Good point.'

263

After a glance towards the front, she unlocked the meeting-room door and switched on the lights. As far as Marek could tell, the room looked identical to the way it had on Friday. There was nothing to indicate that anything had taken place there.

Allie stood on guard, while he climbed on to the Master's chair and carefully prised the camera from the pupil of the All-seeing Eye. The heavy-duty double-sided tape had done the trick. And the camera's anti-reflective coating had ensured that it hadn't been noticed by a Brother throwing a casual glance in that direction. He slipped the device into his pocket and jumped down.

She gripped his arm. 'I don't think it's safe to watch the video here. I'll shut up shop and we can go somewhere else.'

He was about to suggest his flat when she added, 'Let's go to Jock's. It'll be deserted this time in the morning. I'll make sure Jock leaves us alone.'

'If you like.'

A few minutes later, they were sitting at the back of the café, two large coffees in front of them. A quiet word from Allie, and Jock had disappeared into the kitchen.

Marek started the video. The quality was surprisingly good for such a small camera, but given what he'd paid, it damn well ought to be.

The meeting room was empty, although the lights were on. Nothing happened for several minutes, and Marek was beginning to wonder if there'd been a change of plan when the door opened and Niall Affleck entered. He was dressed in a black suit and bow tie, and wore a brightly coloured apron. A glittering chain hung from his neck. He walked towards the camera, climbed the three steps to the platform and disappeared from view, presumably either to take his seat or stand in front of it. The Masons filed in silently, each raising a hand to the Master in salute. They moved to the chairs at the sides and stood staring straight ahead, apart from two who walked solemnly to chairs on either side of the Master.

The Mason to Niall's left strode across to the pedestal and placed a book on the lectern.

'Most holy and glorious Lord God,' he read, 'the Great Architect of the Universe, the giver of all good gifts and graces, Thou hast promised that where two or three are gathered together in Thy Name, Thou wilt be in the midst of them and bless them.'

'So they start with a prayer,' Marek murmured.

The man finished with an 'Amen', which was greeted with 'So mote it be.' He disappeared from view, and the assembled Masons took their seats.

The Master spoke a few words of greeting and opened the meeting to the sound of a gavel coming down.

Another Mason distributed a sheaf of papers. After everyone had been issued with a set, he read out the agenda. Marek had already seen the contents: minutes of the last meeting, applications for membership, AOCB and, finally, the conferring of the degree of Fellowcraft on one Kenny Affleck, whom Marek assumed must be Niall Affleck's son.

The minutes were concerned mainly with an item discussed at the meeting of two months earlier. The roof was leaking, and the decision as to how it would be repaired was under consideration. Everything proceeded according to protocol: anyone who wanted to speak raised a hand, and then – presumably at a signal from the Master – stood and said their bit, addressing the chair as 'Worshipful Master'. It was politely done and extremely efficient with no time wasted on nonsense. There was no talking among the Masons, and no one pulled out a mobile phone, something that Marek had rarely seen in a business meeting. Then again, this was no ordinary business meeting.

'Pity the lot at Westminster can't see this,' Allie said, glancing at Marek.

'So who's this?' he asked, watching a man with greying hair. He was going through the list of quotes from local roofers.

'Gregor Affleck.'

'The one who owns the Lodge.' And whose young son had been walled up in a doocot . . .

'Looks as if he's going to foot the bill himself. But, then, it's his building.'

The fundraiser was discussed next. The Master spoke, describing the negative response to the campaign. There were several suggestions for how this could be taken forward.

The gavel was brought down again, signalling the end of the discussion. The next item was applications for membership. To Marek's great surprise, the applicant was a journalist friend of his. The two backers putting forward the name spoke at length about his merits, assuring the assembly that he had no criminal convictions, and had declared his belief in a supreme being, in his case, the Christian God. A ballot followed, at the end of which he was admitted. Everything zipped along, suggesting the men were well practised. The next item was AOCB. With luck, they were about to find out where that packet of fentanyl was hidden.

Marek paused the video. 'Another?' he said, pointing to Allie's empty mug.

'Go on, then.'

At the counter, he called through to Jock who was sitting in the kitchen reading the paper. He got to his feet hurriedly and made two more coffees.

Marek returned with the mugs. 'Ready?'

Her eyes were gleaming. He pressed play, and then sat back, sipping.

But, to his disappointment, the single item of AOCB was a

proposed educational presentation by a Masonic scholar from another Lodge in Scotland. He glanced at Allie. She was staring at the screen with a thoughtful expression.

'We may as well watch it to the end,' she said. 'Kenny's about to get the second degree.'

'You know him?'

'I know all the Afflecks.'

A Mason at the back of the room made a show of leaving and closing the door behind him. They heard the door being locked.

'He's locked them in?' Marek said.

'That's the duty of the Tyler. He checks that only Masons come in, and makes sure the room is sealed to outsiders.'

'What if someone comes late? Does he let them in?'

'No idea, but I expect he does. Mind you, I have a feeling that conferring a degree isn't something you interrupt. Look, it's about to start.'

They heard the sound of the gavel coming down, followed by Niall Affleck's voice.

'Officers, take your respective stations and places. Brethren, assist me to open the Lodge in the Second Degree.'

They watched in amazement, their coffees growing cold, as the ritual unfolded.

Dania and Hamish were studying the incident board. Everyone else was out interviewing, something she and the team should have been doing, but Honor was keen to show them the fruits of her labours.

'Right,' the girl said. 'I've tagged all the photos taken in the dining room between three thirty and four. To be on the safe side, I went back to three o'clock. And here's the seating plan. I've added the names of the guests.'

'Ah, so seating wasn't unrestricted?' Dania said.

Honor grinned. 'We're in luck there.'

The photos had been taken from every angle and were mostly of the top table with the bride and groom and their special guests. But there were some close-ups of the other guests, their heads together, holding up glasses, or caught unawares, their mouths open and forks raised. Dania tried to see which chairs were vacant, but it proved impossible.

'Here's an interesting one,' Honor said. 'The children at the back of the room.'

'Looks as if they're about to go mental, right enough,' Hamish said.

'I think once they've eaten their bodyweight, they get bored. But this was taken at three twelve, according to the time-stamp. And, look, in this one they're getting up.'

'That's at three sixteen,' Dania said. 'Good work, Honor.'

'Does it get us any further forward?'

'I can't tell if anyone's left the room, can you? So, no, I'm afraid it doesn't.'

It was a null result. At least they could tick it off and turn their attention elsewhere. Dania was used to disappointments, but Honor had put in some late hours and looked crushed.

'I checked DI McFadden's report,' Honor said. 'He states that the guest list tallies with the list of names taken by the police after they arrived for the interviews. It's why he reckoned it had to be someone from outside. Watching from the woodland.'

'Mistakes can still be made,' Dania said. 'It's why we're revisiting this. Did you double-check the lists yourself?'

'It took me a while to find them. But nope. No one was missing.'

Hamish was scrolling back through the images. 'Am I the only one who doesn't think these photos look particularly professional?'

He glanced at Honor. 'Do you know which were taken by the official photographer?'

'In the dining room? As far as I remember, he took none.' Her expression changed. 'Hold on, that can't be right. He must have taken *some*.'

'Who was the official photographer?' Dania said.

The girl looked at her blankly.

'He would have been interviewed,' Dania pressed. 'He's the first person DI McFadden would have sought out, in case he inadvertently caught the killer on camera.'

'Aye,' Hamish said. 'He'll be on the list of interviewees.'

Honor returned to her desk. 'Here are the transcripts of the interviews, all cross-referenced.' She ran her finger down the screen. 'Whoa.'

'What it is?' Dania said. 'You've found his name?'

It was some moments before Honor spoke. 'Jamie Reid.' She looked up. 'His name's Jamie Reid.'

The silence in the room was absolute. The three detectives stared at one another. Dania had the oddest sensation that each was thinking something entirely different. She herself had only one thought: why had Jamie not mentioned that he was the photographer at Euna's sister's wedding? At the Staropolska, he'd brought the subject up himself. She could still hear his soft voice: *I hear you're working on the case of the kidnapped girls.*

'Boss,' Honor began.

Dania raised her hand. 'Don't say anything. I'm trying to think.' A moment later, she said, 'Right. Pull up all the photos he took that day.'

They went through them slowly. There were the informal ones of the bride leaving her house in Inchture, her proud father at the door, clasping her hand. Then the guests were arriving at the church, which Dania recognised as the rose-stone building opposite the car park. As for the eight flower girls, Jamie had taken several photos, evidently unable to get the giggling children to keep still. None inside the church, which didn't surprise her as she doubted the Church of Scotland would allow it, but Jamie had made up for it by taking a large number as the bride and groom were leaving the building. The paired-up flower girls followed, still giggling. The photos were in high resolution and had the stamp of professionalism that was absent from the snaps taken by the guests.

'Okay, here are the ones from Redwood Manor,' Honor said. 'He's caught the wedding party arriving.'

There were endless images of various groups in different parts of the garden: women only, men in kilts, the flower girls again. There were even one or two of the newlyweds in the woodland. They were standing under a canopy of branches and gazing into each other's eyes.

'What's the time-stamp of the last outdoor shot?' Dania said.

'One fifty.'

'Now they're going in for the wedding breakfast,' Hamish said.

'And this is the wedding party at the high table,' Honor said. 'I must admit, that's a lovely dress.'

'Time-stamp?' Dania asked.

'Two ten.'

'Let's see the rest.'

'That's it.'

'That's the last photo Jamie took in the dining room?'

'The last photo Jamie took full stop.' Honor looked at her. 'There are no more.'

'So, his last photo was at ten past two.'

'Where did he go after that?' Hamish said. 'Do photographers stay and eat with the guests?'

'I doubt it. My bet is he grabbed something at the bar. But he'd be back for the toasts and speeches. Or, at least, he should have been.' She gazed at the plan of the dining room. 'Show me the layout of the entire ground floor.'

Honor swiped and pinched until the image filled the screen.

'I checked out the Redwood's yesterday,' Dania said. 'From the bar's windows, you can see the steps into the building. If he bought a sandwich in the bar, he could have eaten it at the window.'

Honor said it for her. 'And there's no way he'd have missed a group of noisy children leaving. That would have been shortly after three sixteen. He could have sneaked out of the hotel unnoticed and gone straight into the woodland.'

Dania traced the path with her finger. 'After taking Euna, he'd have continued through the wood straight to the car park.'

In the growing silence, her thoughts drifted to the few times she'd met Jamie. Apart from lying to her about photographing Cameron, he'd come across as an ordinary happily married man. And someone Marek had known for years and would vouch for. She felt a sudden prickle of uncertainty. Surely it couldn't be Jamie. But she had to do what all detectives do – examine the possibilities, however unpalatable.

'What time was Jamie Reid interviewed?' she said.

'Five fifty-five, boss.'

'At the hotel?'

'At the hotel.'

She pulled out her notebook. 'This is part of the statement given by Mr Montcrieff yesterday: *The driver had just clip-clopped into the yard, and I was looking for the photographer who was supposed to capture the moment.'* She looked up slowly. 'The driver arrived at four p.m.'

'But Jamie didn't,' Honor said.

After an awkward pause, Hamish said, 'I reckon we're all thinking the same thing, aren't we? Three sixteen to five fifty-five is – what? Over two and a half hours. He could easily have driven to Dundee across those back roads, returned the same way and slipped through the woodland into the hotel grounds. Everyone would have been rushing around in a panic, and the police cordons wouldn't have been up yet.'

'It's all circumstantial,' Honor said, chewing her thumb. 'There might be a perfectly good explanation for his disappearance.'

Dania nodded at the screen. 'What did he say at his interview?'

A second later, the text appeared. It was Owen himself who'd questioned Jamie. They read the report in silence. The gist was that Jamie had sat in the bar while the guests were at the wedding breakfast. When he'd seen everyone spilling out of the hotel, he'd left the building, as he'd been asked to take photos of the married couple leaving. But then someone started yelling that a girl had gone missing. He immediately joined the search in the woodland, which widened out to include the entire town. The police arrived, and he'd hung around, waiting to be interviewed.

'Sounds plausible, ma'am.'

'Too plausible.'

'He gives his address as Newport-on-Tay, just across the bridge,' Honor said. 'And just as easy to get to quickly as the centre of Dundee.'

'What about the bar staff? Could they corroborate his account?'

Thanks to the cross-referencing, they were able to pull up the reports without difficulty. After serving Mr Reid, the bar staff had been called to help with the wedding breakfast. The bar had been left unattended.

'Bring your chairs round,' Dania said, sitting down at her desk. She tapped at the keyboard. 'This is Jamie Reid's website. It showcases all or most of his photography.'

'He's a good-looking feller,' Honor said appreciatively.

'What are we searching for, ma'am?'

'Evidence that he came into contact with the other two girls.' She scrolled down the list of Jamie's collections, wondering where to start.

'Hey, isn't that the Natural History Museum?' Honor said.

'Yes, he was commissioned to take a large number of photographs.' She moved the mouse. 'It's this landscape collection here that made me think he had something to do with Cameron Affleck's murder. See the doocot?'

'He doesn't say where it is, but it's unmistakable.'

'Any pictures of Inchture itself, ma'am?'

'Here's the church,' Dania said, scrolling until she found it. 'He's got a huge number of churches in his collection. He must have visited every one in and around Dundee.'

Honor leant forward. 'Hold on. Can you go back a bit? There. Stop!'

'This one?'

The caption read: 'St Boniface. Built in AD 710'.

'I've seen that church,' Honor said, excitement in her voice. 'I passed it when we were interviewing.'

Dania zoomed in on the small print. The church was in Tealing. Tealing. Where the first girl, Fiona, had been abducted . . .

'It says the photos were taken in June of this year,' Honor added. 'Fiona went missing that month. On the fifteenth.'

So, Jamie had visited Tealing around the time Fiona had disappeared. Dania stared at the screen, hardly daring to breathe.

'Would it be worth trying for a warrant, ma'am? If the

273

time-stamp on those photos puts him there on the fifteenth, I think we could pull him in for questioning.'

'The problem is getting the warrant,' Dania said. 'We need reasonable cause.'

Honor had enlarged the image of St Boniface's. 'Our case would be strengthened if we could also find photographs that link him to Morag. They live on Brackens Road, off Strathmartine.'

'Is there anything worth photographing there?'

'Nope. It's a road.'

'Wait a minute,' Dania said, running her hands through her hair. 'He may not have seen Morag on Strathmartine Road. She was at Camperdown the day she was taken. When was it?'

'July the twenty-third.'

'Right, let's see if he was there that day.'

The Dundee Parks collection was larger than Jamie's others, and it was a while before they found Camperdown. Like Templeton Woods, it had been photographed through the seasons. But there were no photos taken in July.

'Bummer,' Honor said. 'I thought we'd get lucky.'

'Maybe he hasn't put them up yet,' Hamish suggested.

Dania picked at her lip. 'Or it's possible they're in a collection on their own. It was the Wildlife Centre that Morag visited.' She entered 'Camperdown Wildlife' as a search term. A second later, images flooded the screen.

Jamie had been careful not to capture the faces of members of the public. Given that this was the height of the holiday season, it would have been something of a challenge. He must have photographed every animal and bird, making Dania wonder if this had been a special commission. The heading read: 'Camperdown Wildlife Centre, July 2018'.

July 2018. He'd been there in July. And maybe even on the twenty-third. She closed her eyes, trying to contain her anger. If she hadn't been so fixated on looking for evidence that Jamie had kidnapped Cameron, she might have spotted this connection earlier.

It was Hamish who spoke first. 'Where do we go from here, ma'am?'

'I don't know. It could all be a coincidence. But we need to follow it up. I'm just not sure how to do it.'

What she meant was that she didn't *want* to do it. She didn't want to believe that a good friend of her brother's was a killer rapist. She'd felt bad enough when she'd suspected Jamie of Cameron's murder – and that had given her plenty of sleepless nights, and he might still be implicated, and she would have to investigate that – but this was something else. Although she dreaded Marek's reaction, she knew she had to pursue this to the end.

'What do we know about Jamie Reid?' Hamish said, breaking into her thoughts. 'Is he married?'

'He is,' Dania said. 'To a wedding planner. Her name's Pam.'

'A wedding planner,' Honor said. 'Did she plan the one at Inchture?'

'That's a good question, but I doubt it. I'm sure she would have told me.'

And yet Jamie hadn't told her he was the photographer at that wedding. Maybe Pam also had a reason for keeping her participation quiet.

'She'll have a website, boss.'

Honor was always quicker at these things. Dania surrendered the mouse without a murmur.

'Nothing under Pam Reid,' Honor muttered.

'She was a wedding planner before she was married. She may be operating under her maiden name.'

'Which is?'

'She gave me her card.' Dania hunted in her purse. 'Here it is. McSween. Pam McSween. No, it's Pamela McSween.'

As Honor searched, Dania thought back to that dinner at Marek's, where she'd had her only conversation with the woman. What was it she'd said about Jamie? She had a feeling it was something significant. Yet she couldn't get her mind to close on it.

Honor interrupted her thoughts. 'Yep. "Pamela McSween, Wedding Planner". Wow. Lovely photos.'

'I don't suppose she gives dates or anything?'

'There's a calendar with her availability.'

'Euna's sister's wedding was Saturday, July the seventh.'

'And according to this, Pam was unavailable from Friday the sixth through to Sunday the eighth. Could that be the Inchture wedding?'

'I'd say not. Why would she need three days? The wedding was local. And, anyway, I think it was arranged by the bride's family. Mr Montcrieff told me he himself had booked a horse and carriage to take the married couple away. No, I think those three-day stints are further afield, when she stays away overnight.' Dania closed her eyes and pressed her fingers into her temples. 'I'm trying to remember what she told me.' She opened her eyes. 'No. It's gone.'

They were looking at her strangely.

'I know what will help your memory return, ma'am,' Hamish said. 'I'll be back in a tick.'

'Wow,' Marek murmured, after the video had come to an end. 'What on earth was that?'

Allie stared at the screen. Her eyes were glazed. 'All those times the gavel came down. I wonder how anyone can remember what to say, and when to say it. No one used notes. And the number of times they said "So mote it be."'

'What was that stuff about north and south, and so on?'

'I think the meeting room is supposed to be lined up east to west, so everyone sits at one of the points of the compass.'

'And that was Kenny Affleck they brought in? Is he the Master's son?'

'Gregor Affleck's.'

'Gregor had two sons?'

'Three. There's also Ross.'

'Was he there?'

'He was.'

'It's true then, about the blindfolding and rolling up the trouser leg. I understood from what was said that it's the right knee that's bared for this ceremony. I wonder if it's the left knee when you get the first degree.'

'And that bit where he had to kneel on one knee, and have the other knee out at an angle, and his arms doing something else. I thought he was going to fall over.'

Marek powered down the laptop. 'But no mention of anything to do with a shipment. If all the Masons are in on it, this would have been an ideal time to discuss it. I'm beginning to think it's only the Master.'

'And his brother Gregor, and Gregor's two sons.'

'A family business, you mean?'

'Exactly.'

'So, what do we do now?'

'We can't talk about it here.' She glanced towards the door. A shaggy-haired man in a kilt had shambled in. 'People are coming for morning coffee and Jock's scones. And we need to get back before we're missed,' she added nervously.

They left the café and made their way to the Lodge. Allie was deep in thought. He was out of ideas.

He waited in the hall while she checked that the office was empty.

'It's fine,' she said. 'Niall's still out.' She hesitated. 'What now?'

'We're right back where we started. But if Niall Affleck is in this racket, either on his own or with anyone else, he'll have hidden the drugs in this Lodge. I'm sure of it.'

She seemed suddenly to make up her mind about something. 'It's not drugs, Franek, it's jewels.'

He glanced at the cabinet. 'Masonic regalia?'

'No. Jewels, proper jewels. Gemstones.'

'You mean diamonds?' he said, stunned.

'Emeralds. Colombian emeralds, to be precise.'

Colombian emeralds. He felt his heart race.

'Murray said they were of exceptionally high quality. The purest you can get. I don't know how he found that out, but he did.'

Marek knew little about gemstones except that high-quality emeralds sold for more than diamonds. So this was what Gilie was hinting at. *This isn't big. It's huge.*

'Emeralds are being smuggled into the Lodge?' He stared at her, mystified. 'Why did you tell me the package contained drugs?'

'I didn't. *You* said you thought it *might* contain drugs. And I went along with it. I thought that if whoever you're working for is after drugs, you'd lose interest if you found out it was emeralds.'

Although the emeralds would be worth far more than the fentanyl. That was if they were as pure as Murray had said.

'I'm sorry I led you astray,' she said, lowering her gaze.

'It hardly matters in the grand scheme of things. Drugs. Emeralds.' He studied her. 'Think hard, Allie. Is there *anywhere* you and Murray didn't search?'

She lifted her head. 'There is one place.' She glanced towards the stairs. 'That door to the left. It leads to the cellar.'

'Did you search there?'

'We've been told not to go in. The ceiling's falling down and it's not safe.'

'Then that's the obvious place.'

'There's one problem. I haven't got the key.'

'Ah.'

'And this time, Franek, I'm telling you the truth.'

CHAPTER 27

Dania licked the jam off her fingers. Jock's scones might not have brought her memory back, but they'd lifted everyone's spirits. As had his extra-strong cappuccinos.

Hamish drained his cup. 'So, ma'am? Any joy?'

'The only thing I can remember is that Pam told me she asks Jamie to help her out when she can't get her usual photographer.'

'Then sometimes he's away when she is.'

'That's right.' Dania gazed at Hamish. 'That's given me an idea. If Jamie is our killer rapist, he's more likely to operate when his wife is away. Agreed?'

'Agreed.'

'Let's draw up a chart with the dates the girls were taken. We have Fiona abducted on June the fifteenth and found on the eighteenth. That was Friday to Monday.' She watched Honor enter the information. 'Then Euna was abducted on July the seventh and found on the tenth. Saturday to Tuesday.'

'Another weekend, boss.'

'Morag was taken on July the twenty-third.'

'And you found her in the trees on July the twenty-seventh. Monday to Friday, so during the week this time.'

'Now, was Pam away on those dates? Start with the weekend of June the fifteenth to the eighteenth.'

'Yep,' Honor said. 'The calendar shows she was unavailable.'

'And July the seventh to the tenth? Saturday to Tuesday?'

'She was away from Friday the sixth to Sunday the eighth.'

Dania could feel her heart bumping. 'And the last set of dates? July the twenty-third to the twenty-seventh? That's the Monday to Friday.'

'According to the calendar, Pam was unavailable from Sunday the twenty-second to Wednesday the twenty-fifth.'

'Aye, and what about the rest of June and July?' Hamish said. 'Was she away?'

Honor ran the cursor down the calendar. 'Nope,' she said triumphantly. 'She had no events on then.'

'And if she was here in Dundee,' Dania said, feeling the excitement mount, 'Jamie would be unlikely to go hunting.'

She remembered her conversation with Owen outside the V&A, in which she'd aired the theory that something was stopping the killer taking another girl. The presence of his wife was a good candidate.

'Wait! Bummer! I've missed one.' There was a note of disappointment in Honor's voice. 'Pam was *also* away from Friday, July the thirteenth to Sunday, July the fifteenth.'

'*That's* what I was trying to remember,' Dania said. 'On Saturday the fourteenth, I ran into Jamie at the railway station. I was on my way to Edinburgh, to the consulate, and he was about to catch a train and join his wife in the Highlands.'

'So they were *both* away that weekend.'

Hamish was frowning. 'Okay, *Pam* was away when the girls were snatched. But do we know whether *Jamie* was here in Dundee?'

That would be harder to establish. 'He was in the same group of volunteers as I was when we were out searching for Morag.'

'He was in the search party?' Honor said, looking uncertain.

'A good way of throwing the police off the scent, don't you

281

think? Join the group looking for your victim's body. Maybe he joined the searches for Fiona and Euna too.'

Marek might know if Jamie had volunteered. But the uniforms had taken the names of the searchers. They could easily check.

'From what you know of him,' Honor said, 'do you think he could have done it?'

Dania thought back to similar cases at the Met. When the perpetrators had been apprehended, many turned out to be mild-mannered, honest-looking, happily married men. Charming, even. Like Jamie Reid. A profiler might be able to spot a child rapist, but she couldn't. She shook her head. 'It's time I talked this over with DI McFadden. This is his case.'

She tried to imagine Owen's reaction. He'd ask her how she'd come to suspect Jamie in the first place. Her reply, that Jamie hadn't mentioned he was the photographer at the wedding, might cause him to raise his eyebrows. And everything that followed – the time he'd taken his photographs, the absence of photos of the dining room after the children left, the fact that he could have snatched Euna and returned in time to be questioned – was purely circumstantial.

They were looking at her.

'We've talked about this before, boss, but if we could find where he takes the girls, we might have him. What is his house in Newport-on-Tay like?'

'Let's look on Google.'

The girl pulled up the map. 'Here it is, on Kirk Road.'

She moved the cursor over the pleasant-looking, semi-detached stone building. There was a tiny greenhouse in the garden, and not much else.

'Somehow I don't think he'd be taking them there, ma'am.'

'I agree. It's far too crowded.'

'Empty during the day, though. Newport-on-Tay is a commuter town.'

Dania folded her arms. 'He'll need somewhere he can keep the bleach. Professor Slaughter said the girls had been immersed in it, so there'd have to be a bath or large container.'

'In the old days, photographers had workshops where they developed their photographs,' Honor said. 'I saw it done on telly once. But it's all digital now.'

'Maybe he has access to an old warehouse,' Hamish said. 'Or a friend's house. Someone who's away for six months.'

A friend's house . . .

And then, without warning, Pam's words flew into her head.

His mother died earlier this year. Any spare time he has is spent clearing her house.

She sat up sharply. 'That's it. His mother's house! He's emptying it.'

'His mother's!' Honor stared at her. 'Do we know where it is?'

'No idea. But she died a few months ago. See if you can find a lady with the surname "Reid" in the register.'

It took Honor less than a minute to come up with an Isla Reid, who'd passed away on 9 January 2018.

'Last-known address?' Dania said, unable to contain her impatience.

'Harestane Road.'

'Where have I heard of Harestane Road?'

'Google Maps.'

And there it was: Strathmartine and Emmock – where the drone had found Morag's clothes – were linked by Harestane Road.

'This has to be our man,' Hamish said fiercely. 'It *has* to be.'

Yes, Brackens Road, where Morag lived, was off Strathmartine. Jamie, driving over to continue the clearing of his mother's house,

283

could have seen the girl walking to her sleepover that fateful evening.

'Can we pull him in now?' Honor was chewing her thumb. 'Please say yes.'

But before Dania could reply, a uniform came running in.

'We've just had the call,' he said, in a stricken voice. 'Another girl's been taken!'

Dania scribbled down the details, her heart thumping. Katie Macalister was one of a group of children who'd volunteered to clear rubbish from the beach at Tentsmuir in Fife. After they'd finished, they'd made for the nearby car park. It was as they were boarding the minibus that the adult in charge noticed Katie was missing. She called the Dundee police straight away.

'This is over to you,' Dania said, looking earnestly at Honor. 'Put out a Child Rescue Alert, then get yourself to Tentsmuir. DI McFadden is interviewing way up in Forfar, and you'll get to Fife faster than he will. Call him, give him the details and start the investigation.'

'What about you, boss?'

'I'm taking a gamble that it's Jamie, and he's on his way to Harestane Road with Katie. There's no time to lose if we want to save her. Hamish, you're with me. There may be some action.'

'Right, ma'am.'

They left the station running. There was only one squad car in the car park.

'You take it, Honor,' Hamish said. 'DI Gorska and I can go in mine.'

'On it.' She scrambled into the car, revved the engine and sped off.

They climbed into Hamish's blue Ford Fiesta. He drove quickly but carefully, and minutes later they crossed the A90, reaching Harestane Road a short while after.

'It's that one there,' Dania said, indicating the harled house with the red-tiled roof. And the double garage with its doors open. 'Pull up a little way down.'

'What's the plan, ma'am?'

'I haven't got one. But I'm not suggesting we ring the bell.'

'Do you reckon he's still on his way here?'

'I think he's arrived. He's got a Hyundai, and I'm guessing that's it in the garage.'

'Aye, in that case, we have to move.'

They left the Fiesta and approached the house from the garage side. Dania had decided that, even if it meant disciplinary action for breaking in without a warrant, she would do it, no question. The alternative, which might mean a child losing her life, wasn't something she was prepared to consider.

'We need to go softly, softly, Hamish,' she murmured, as they reached the driveway.

He said nothing, but the determination on his face showed that he was ready for action. She was relieved he was with her.

She was hoping the garage had a door directly into the house, but their luck was out. There was, however, one at the back. She nudged Hamish, who followed the direction of her gaze, and nodded.

They crept through the garage. Dania indicated by pulling out and holding up her gloves that he should put his on.

She listened at the door. Nothing. She gripped the handle and pushed.

The door opened on to a small stone-paved garden. Weeds grew between the slabs, and a few wooden tubs of dead or dying plants stood dotted around. Thick bushes, which had been allowed to grow tall and wild shaded the area from the neighbours' prying eyes.

Immediately to the right was a slatted garden shed. The door was slightly ajar.

Dania had pulled it open only a little way when she was hit by the smell. Instinctively, she drew her head back. It was the unmistakable stench of chlorine.

'Look, ma'am,' Hamish whispered.

A row of identical plastic containers lined the wall. She didn't need to read the labels to know that they contained industrial-strength bleach. Other than the rusting garden implements, the only item in the shed was an ancient enamel bath, its surface dull and chipped. A heavy-duty plastic sheet lay crumpled inside it.

'We've got the wee shite,' Hamish murmured.

Dania gripped his arm. 'See that, there in the bushes? That's a child's bicycle.'

'Fiona's,' he said grimly.

'He must have forgotten about it. Come on, we need to move.'

The unlocked back door let them into a medium-sized kitchen in need of modernisation. There was room for a table and chairs but everything that could be lifted had been removed. The surfaces were bare and the fridge was unplugged, its door open.

They crept across the curling floor tiles into the corridor. Hamish was about to speak, but Dania lifted her hand for silence. Faint sounds were coming from upstairs. She pointed upwards, and then put her finger to her lips.

They stole up the carpeted stairs as silently as they could. To Dania's immense relief, there were no creaks.

She stopped on the landing. A child's laugh came from the room at the end.

Without pausing to think, she rushed along the corridor and

slammed into the door. She'd expected it to be locked but it opened easily, and she almost fell inside.

A girl with wavy brown hair and hazel eyes was sitting on the double bed, her legs crossed and her arms resting behind her on the duvet. She jumped up in surprise as the detectives came crashing into the room. Her expression changed from astonishment to alarm.

Jamie was standing behind a tripod, adjusting what looked like a video camera. He straightened and stared open-mouthed at Dania, then at Hamish. A look of understanding crossed his face. 'Dania,' he said angrily. 'What the hell are you doing here?'

She pulled out her handcuffs. 'James Reid, I am arresting you for the murder of—'

Before she could finish, the girl hurled herself at her, shouting something incomprehensible, kicking at her legs and beating her fists against her arms. Dania dropped the handcuffs. As Hamish stepped forward to grab the girl, Jamie rushed past him into the corridor.

'Go after him!' Dania yelled. She gripped the girl's wrists. 'Katie. Katie! Calm down!'

The girl continued to fight and kick. Suddenly, she stopped and glared at Dania.

Sounds of a struggle came from the corridor. Holding Katie firmly, Dania put her head round the door. Jamie was lying on the floor groaning, clutching his groin, while a red-faced Hamish delivered a few well-placed kicks to his ribs.

'That's enough!' Dania said. 'Pick him up.' She turned to Katie.

The girl's eyes were filling with tears. 'He said he was going to take photos of me and put them online,' she said, in a small voice. 'And in magazines.'

Dania put her face close to the girl's. 'Did he tell you who he is?'

'A famous photographer. He said he takes picture of models.' She started to whimper. 'He was going to make me a celebrity.'

'Oh, Katie,' Dania said sadly. She picked up the handcuffs. 'Can you stay here for a second?'

The girl nodded unhappily.

Jamie was doubled over, gasping. Dania pulled his arms behind his back, and snapped on the cuffs, speaking the words of arrest.

'Why didn't you let me kill him, ma'am?' Hamish said, panting.

'Because the law has this romantic notion that you're innocent until proven guilty.' She pushed Jamie towards Hamish. 'Take him to the station and book him. I'll wait here for DI McFadden.'

'What about Katie?'

'Phone the nick and get a uniform to come out for her. If there are no squad cars, it'll have to be a cab.'

'Aye.'

She watched them go, Hamish guiding a handcuffed Jamie down the steps.

In the bedroom, Katie was sitting on the duvet, her nose bubbling. Tears were sliding down her cheeks. Dania sat down and put an arm round her.

'Katie, a policewoman is coming to take you to the station.'

The girl looked at her, her eyes huge. 'Did I do a bad thing?'

'No, of course not,' Dania said, squeezing her shoulders. 'But running off like that with a stranger isn't a good idea. Promise me you'll never do that again. Ever.'

She nodded silently.

'Come on, then,' Dania said, pulling her gently to her feet.

Downstairs, they waited in the hall for the uniform to arrive. Katie remained subdued and, although she let Dania put an arm round her shoulders, she avoided eye contact. Fortunately, it wasn't long before they heard a car pulling up.

Dania opened the front door.

A young policewoman with brown eyes and a wide smile was getting out of the squad car. Dania recognised her immediately.

'Katie, this is PC Tanner. She'll be looking after you at the station.'

Katie glanced up at her. The woman's expression softened and she held out her hand.

As the two of them were leaving, Dania touched her colleague's arm. 'Remember that we need to wait until her parents arrive before anyone questions her.'

'Understood, ma'am.'

After the door had closed, Dania returned to the bedroom. The camcorder was still on the tripod. She lifted it off and, sitting on the bed, played with the controls.

Fiona Ballie's face suddenly appeared, smiling, puzzled, anxious, and then frightened. The image was blotted out for a second by someone in a red T-shirt. Unable to watch, Dania stared at the carpet. And, as she listened to the girl's terrified, muffled screams, feeling her heart ripped to shreds, she knew that they'd finally come to the end of their search.

CHAPTER 28

Franek had just left for the day when the phone rang.

Allie snatched it up, but before she could speak, she heard Ross's thick voice. 'We're on our way so make sure you're ready at the door.' He rang off.

His tone had been unmistakable. Something had angered him. She felt sick with anxiety as she realised he might have tried to phone her while she was at Jock's. There was a number of ways in which he could inflict punishment on her, and they'd all be confined to the bedroom. The last time, he'd thrashed her backside so hard that she couldn't sit properly but had to perch on the edge of her chair. God knows what it would be tonight. Then she instantly blocked the thought. She picked up her bag and left the building, locking the door behind her.

The Affleck brothers were at the end of the street, walking briskly towards her. Kenny was rabbiting on, animated about something, probably that diorama of *The Last Supper*. Ross was staring straight ahead, swinging his briefcase and giving no indication that he was listening. They reached the Lodge and, ignoring Allie, made for the Volkswagen parked a short distance away. She fell into step behind them.

Not a word was spoken as they drove to Broughty Ferry, with Kenny expertly negotiating the rush-hour traffic. There was a time when Allie would have worked herself into a nervous rag wondering what Ross was going to do. But she'd set wheels in motion and knew that, with Franek's help, she would soon escape the hell she was living. The knowledge that her life there was strictly time-limited was what got her through the ordeals.

They reached Albany Road in record time, due largely to Kenny's jumping the lights at every opportunity. She wondered why he was in such high spirits. He'd probably taken a break that afternoon to go and visit his sexcam student.

Mrs Spence was waiting in the hall. 'Your father's home,' she said, lowering her eyes under Ross's steely gaze. 'When you're ready, he wishes to talk to you.'

Ross nodded, then jerked his head at Allie, indicating that they were to go upstairs.

She followed him up, and into the bedroom. He closed the door quietly.

'Where were you this morning?' he said, smiling.

She never could come to terms with the wax and wane of his moods. Sometimes he began in a friendly enough fashion, and at others he lashed out the instant the door was closed.

She was formulating her reply when he said, more firmly, 'You can't have heard me, so I'll say it again. Where were you this morning?'

'I was working at the Lodge.'

'Don't lie to me. I rang the Lodge several times, and there was no reply. I won't ask you again.'

'You must have caught me when I was in the loo,' she said, desperately trying to keep the fear out of her voice.

'I told you not to lie to me.'

'All right then,' she said, displaying a rare, bitter flash of hatred. 'I went over to Jock's café. I needed a break.'

'Did you go alone?' he said softly.

'Of course. There was no one else in the building.'

She realised her mistake as soon as the words were out.

'The archivist was there, Allie,' he crooned. 'I've checked his schedule.'

Now was not the time to keep lying. 'Yes, of course he was there,' she said contritely. 'I'd forgotten.'

'You'd forgotten?'

She stared at the vicious eyes and the thin slit of a mouth, and was overcome with a sudden loathing.

'Did he also go to Jock's?' The softness in the voice was gone. 'Was he there with you?'

She didn't dare reply.

'Answer me, you bitch!'

She knew he could always check with Jock, although the man was likely to have one of his famous bouts of amnesia.

Ross strode over and, gripping her arm, ripped the sleeve of her green silk dress. 'I've got a wee surprise for you,' he said, opening his briefcase. 'Something new.'

He drew out a heavy-looking black device, flicked a switch and then held the thing against her wrist.

Pain shot up her arm and through her body. It was as though red-hot needles had been jabbed into her skin. She cried out in agony, and fell back, struggling to keep her balance. Her initial reaction was amazement that such a small instrument could cause such excruciating pain.

From his expression, it was clear that this was the first time Ross had seen the device in action. He applied it again, further up the arm where her bare skin was visible through the tear. This time, he held it there for longer. Her entire body felt on fire. Almost as bad as the lacerating pain was the complete lack of control, both physical and psychological. As soon as he pulled the thing away, she dropped on to the floor, gasping for breath, her face close to the carpet.

'Change your clothes,' he ordered. 'You look a mess. And be quick about it. It's nearly time for dinner.'

He dropped the device on the bed and marched out of the room.

Allie lay in bed, watching the sky change colour from murky grey to deep blue. Ross couldn't sleep in the dark, so the curtains were always left open. She turned her head slowly, hearing the gentle rise and fall of his breathing, punctuated by the odd soft snore. As quietly as she could, she slipped out of bed and padded over to his side. His mobile was where he'd left it on the bedside cabinet. She memorised its position so she could replace it exactly.

She could have put on her clothes – Ross insisted she sleep naked – but she didn't dare waste precious time looking for her dressing-gown. She crept across to the door and opened it gently. With a last glance at the bed, she tiptoed into the corridor, and closed the door behind her.

She knew where the creaks were in the floorboards and took care to avoid them. The stairs also needed attention as most of them groaned under even her slight weight, but with constant experimentation she'd discovered that, if she hugged the wall, she could glide downstairs without making a sound.

She reached the hall and paused to listen. The quiet weight of the house seemed to press in on her, but this wasn't the time to lose her nerve. She hurried across the marble floor to the wall cupboard and felt around for the brass knob. The door opened silently, something else she'd had the foresight to check. She held the phone up to the faint light from the window, found the right button, and directed the phone's flashlight towards the cupboard. Inside the door, in faded gold lettering, was the chart with the codes for the rooms. What she was looking for was near the bottom, where the keys to Gregor's other properties were kept. A spot of eavesdropping on one of Mrs Spence's chats with her husband had informed Allie that the Lodge had originally been called Angus House. And there it was – Angus House: M5.

She slipped the key off the hook. It was unlikely she'd get the chance to return it but, if her luck continued to hold, she wouldn't need to. As she turned, the light from the phone caught the dusty black eagle in its beam. The bird stared at her with its piercing glass eyes. She switched off the torch and hurriedly retraced her steps to the bedroom.

She stole over to Ross's side and replaced the phone, moving it around until she was satisfied it was as he'd left it. Back in bed, she felt under the sheet for the edge of the mattress. Some months before, she'd used one of Ross's razor blades to make an invisible cut in the upholstery. Concealed inside were the things she didn't want her husband to see. She pushed the key in and drew the sheet back over the mattress. She smiled as she realised she was a step closer to freedom. The key would stay hidden until the time came.

CHAPTER 29

'Let's start with the first missing girl,' Owen said.

He and Dania were in the main interview room, facing Jamie, who'd waived his right to a solicitor. In a way, this was a formality since, the day before, he'd admitted everything to Hamish on the way back to West Bell Street. Once he'd started he couldn't stop babbling.

Jamie was sitting folded in on himself. He was a changed man. Even his voice, usually so soft, was strident, as though he'd had an operation on his throat and was testing whether he could speak. 'What do you want to know?' he said.

Owen opened the file and laid a photograph on the table. 'The suspect is being shown a photograph. Have you seen this girl before?'

'Aye.'

'When did you first see her?'

'I can't remember the date.'

'All right. *Where* did you first see her?'

'In Tealing. I was taking photographs there.'

'Of what?'

'There's an old doocot. And an earth-house. Oh, and an ancient church and graveyard. If you look on my computer, you'll find them.' He smiled knowingly. 'If you haven't already. You can get the date from that.'

'What was Fiona doing when you saw her?' Dania said.

'Riding her bicycle. I was getting into the Hyundai when she cycled past. I shouted to her to stop. In a friendly way, of course. She saw my camera.' He shook his head. 'That's what did it every time. The camera. They can't resist it, the idea of having their photos taken professionally, and getting their pictures everywhere.'

'And then?' Owen said.

'Something happened to me, right enough. I don't know what. I'd never done anything like that before. Maybe it was her red hair. But I saw a chance, so I told her I photographed models for a living.' He laughed softly. 'You should have seen the look in her eyes. As though I'd shown her a million pounds. "I'll take some photos of you now, if you like," I said. She didn't need much persuading. She was the first, so no one had warned her there was a bad man about.'

They'd found those photos on Jamie's computer, exactly as he'd described them. And the time-stamp put him in Tealing at the time, and on the date, that Fiona had been abducted.

'I told her I'd need to drive her to my studio to take better photos. I bamboozled her with techno-stuff about lighting, and so on.' He looked at his hands. 'She got into the Hyundai without any further persuading. I shoved her bike into the back.'

'Where did you take her?' Dania said.

'To my mother's house on Harestane Road.' He lifted his head and glared at her. 'Where you and that ape found me.'

'Why there?' Owen said.

'I've been clearing it. It was an ideal place to take the girls.'

'Especially when your wife was away,' Dania said, her voice level.

'Aye, it couldn't have been better. An empty house with a sheltered garden, and a way in at the back of the garage.' He chuckled. 'And the lassies came willingly.' His expression changed. 'But that first one, Fiona, screamed so much that I did consider killing her first, and then raping her.'

Dania was conscious of Owen's balled fists under the table. 'Tell me about the clothes, Jamie,' she said. 'Why did you scatter them across the fields?'

'Ach, it was so that I could join the search. I had this idea that suspicion would be unlikely to fall on me if I did that. And also because I know fine well that there are these whizzo computer programs that work out things about killers, and where they're based. I thought I'd make it difficult for you by introducing a wee bit of complexity.'

'And what did you do after you'd killed Fiona?'

'I took her down to the shed. The bathroom is getting a makeover before I sell the house, so it's been stripped out. The old enamel bath was ideal.' He scratched his throat. 'I saw one of those CSI programmes where someone used bleach to destroy traces of themselves.' He frowned. 'Looks as if it can't have worked that well, otherwise how else did you find me?'

'When did you do this?' Owen said. 'The bleach.'

'When it was dark, I took her body downstairs. I left her in the bleach for a couple of days, while I looked for somewhere I could dump her without being picked up on the traffic cams. Not difficult. I know the Dundee countryside well.'

'Why did you video yourself raping her?' Dania said.

'Ach, so I could relive it. Why else?' He looked steadily at her. 'Go on, hate me. You'll find it's not too difficult.'

'Let's come now to Euna Montcrieff,' Owen said, turning to the page in the file. 'You were the photographer at her sister's wedding.'

'The Montcrieffs had seen my landscape work and asked me to be the official.' His eyes took on that distant look, as though he were seeing it all again. 'Euna had caught my eye right from the off, with that dark hair and pale skin. Aye, from then on, it was a waiting game. I was in the bar and saw my chance when the children piled out of the hotel. I strolled out, and followed her into the woodland. The other children were still in the garden, making an unholy racket.' A smile crept on to his lips. 'She was so trusting. She even held my hand as we walked through the trees to the Hyundai. But, then, she'd seen me take the wedding photos. Of course she believed me when I said we could go somewhere for a special photoshoot. Just the two of us.'

'And you came back in time to be interviewed,' Dania said.

'Aye.' He held her gaze. 'I knew that, with Euna, it had to be quick.'

'And Morag Pinkerton?'

He closed his eyes. 'Ah, the one with the blue eyes and long blonde hair. She was a dream.'

'Where did you first see her?'

'I was taking photographs at Camperdown Wildlife Centre earlier in the day. It was a Monday, I remember now. I hung around and heard her mother call her Morag and say something about a sleepover. I followed them to their car. With all the vehicles coming and going, they didn't see me tail them to their house.' He grinned. 'It was so near to Harestane Road that I told myself it was Fate.'

'So, you waited on the street until she came out later that evening?' Owen asked.

'I drove around for a wee bit. I reckoned the sleepover would be nearer eight o'clock. She came out of the house just after seven. Aye, and I nearly missed her.'

'How did you get her into the car?'

'Thanks to her mother, I knew her name, which is a huge bonus. I had a flash of inspiration and told her I remembered her from the school photo. I've taken all the school photos this year, and I reckoned she might remember me.'

'And did she?'

'Aye, right enough.'

'And did you give her all that guff about making her famous?'

'She didn't want to come at first. Said she had a sleep date. I decided not to push it. I knew where she lived, and another chance would come along. I was driving off when she called out to me.'

'So she knew your name?' Dania said.

'I'd told her who I was.'

'Bit risky, if you were prepared to drive off.'

'Ach, away. What would she tell her folks? She'd run into the school photographer, Jamie Reid?'

'She might have told them you'd offered to take her for a photoshoot.'

He considered this. 'Somehow, I think she'd have held her wheesht about that.'

'And the text she sent to the people she'd be staying with?' Owen said, wiping his face with his hand.

'She told me she'd have to let them know she couldn't come. Said it would be rude otherwise. I watched what she entered on her phone. It was short and sweet, with no mention of me or what we'd be doing. When she turned away to find the seatbelt – it was caught up round the back of the seat – I slipped the phone out of her pocket and switched it off.'

'When did you scatter her clothes?' Dania said.

'Not until the wee hours of Wednesday morning.'

Dania folded her arms. 'So what was all that with the mask?'

'Aye, well, you know, a bit of fun.' He smiled slyly. 'I wanted to see if I could set a few hares running.'

'Is that why you put Morag's body up in the treehouse?'

The smile widened. 'I watched you, you know. You and that other detective. You didn't have a scooby that I was hiding in the bushes, did you?' He must have seen the look on her face, because he added, 'You could have fallen and broken your neck.'

Dania thought back to that day. She'd seen no one. 'How did you know we were there?'

'I was driving past and saw the police car. I parked a short distance away and crept back. In time to see you and the other officer going over the wall.'

She felt a sudden anger. It was her turn to ball her fists. 'You're a bastard, Jamie,' she said thickly.

After a glance at her, Owen said, 'Let's come now to Katie Macalister.'

Jamie picked at his nails. 'Aye, I was photographing around Tentsmuir yesterday. I wanted to get pictures of those anti-tank defences – what are they called? Dragon's Teeth.' He nodded at Dania. 'Did you know that it was Polish soldiers who manned the defences there during the war?'

'I did. They built them in nineteen forty-one, in case the Germans attacked from Norway.'

'So I was in the forest,' Jamie went on, 'and I heard children's voices. I hid behind a tree. One of the lassies went into the forest for a pee. As she was pulling up her jeans, I stepped out and pretended to take photos of the woodland. She was well interested. Aye, interested enough to ask me what I was doing. Told me straight out that her name was Katie.'

Dania's own experience of Katie had been enough to show her how strong-willed the girl was. If she'd wanted to go off with Jamie, she'd have needed little persuading.

'I asked if I could borrow her phone and she said they'd all had to hand them in to the club supervisor.'

'Convenient,' Owen said.

'I gave her the usual about looking for a model. I was taking photos for a big London exhibition. Told her we'd only be gone for a wee while, and I'd bring her right back. Ach, it was as easy as that.'

'And how do you feel now?' Dania said. 'Now that you've been arrested?'

He didn't answer immediately. 'You may find this strange, but it's a relief to be able to tell somebody.'

'Did you ever think you'd get caught?'

'I pushed away thoughts like that. I'm a professional coward, you see. A fully paid-up member.' There was a vacant expression in his eyes. 'But I don't think I'd ever be able to stop.'

'Then it's just as well we found you,' Owen said nastily.

'What will happen to me now?'

'We need to interview you again, to fill in some details. After that, we'll type up a statement for you to sign.'

'Then what? I go to trial?'

'In due course.'

He gazed at Dania. 'What are you thinking?' he said eventually.

She returned the gaze. 'That we should reconsider bringing back hanging.'

'Someone will have to tell Pam,' he said suddenly. 'I don't suppose you could find a way of keeping all this from her?'

Dania stared, incredulous. The press were beating down the doors . . .

'Interview terminated at ten forty-five a.m.,' Owen said, looking at the ceiling.

As Dania and Owen left the interview room, there weren't the usual cheers and back-slapping that greeted officers who'd succeeded in securing a confession. If anything, the mood was more sombre than usual.

'The DCI wants a word,' Honor murmured, taking Dania aside. 'She doesn't look too happy.'

Dania nodded and left. She'd been expecting this. Better get it over with. And she'd rehearsed mentally what she would say.

She hurried to Jackie Ireland's room. The door was open. The woman was bent over her desk. Dania was lifting her hand to knock when she glanced up and saw her.

'DI Gorska. Come in and shut the door.' She nodded to the chair.

DI Gorska. Not Dania.

Jackie opened the folder on her desk. 'I've had the doctor's report on Jamie Reid. As you know, we sent him to the hospital after booking him because he was limping and seemed to be in great pain. He was kept in overnight.' She picked up her pen. 'I need you to tell me what happened.'

'He resisted arrest and I had to use force. It was unavoidable, I'm afraid.'

'And you kicked him in the groin?'

'I used my knee.'

'And kicked him in the ribs when he was down?'

'He was reaching for something in his pocket. I thought he might have had a weapon.'

'The doctor says he was badly bruised. But no broken ribs, thankfully.'

Dania said nothing.

'And where was DC Downie while this was happening?'

'He was in the bedroom, calming the girl.'

'DC Downie gives a different account.'

Dania tried to look surprised.

'He states that you were the one in the bedroom with Katie, and he was in the corridor. He said he lost it and hit Jamie Reid.'

'He's trying to look out for me, that's all.'

'Interestingly, Jamie told the doctor it was Hamish. He couldn't remember his name, but he gave an accurate description.'

'He would have said that because he doesn't want to admit that a woman roughed him up.' She looked squarely at the DCI. 'You know what men are.'

Jackie stared at her for a long moment. 'Let's hope he doesn't make a formal complaint. He'll have other, more important, things on his mind, and may let the matter rest. Although if he doesn't, there'll have to be an investigation.' She closed the folder. 'And that will be followed by disciplinary action.'

CHAPTER 30

'I'm sorry I haven't been in touch before now, Father,' Dania said, leaning back in the armchair. 'Work has a habit of getting in the way.'

'I understand, my child.' He started to pour the coffee, but his hand shook so much that he spilt it into the saucer.

'Let me do that,' Dania said, taking the pot from him.

She watched him as she poured. Something was wrong. Father Kliment was always so self-assured. And he couldn't be worried about the concerts he was yet to ask her about, as he knew she'd say yes because she always did. No, this was something else. And it was serious enough to have aged him ten years: the loose skin under his eyes sagged more than usual, and his silver hair was a mess.

She tried not to show her alarm as she added milk and his three heaped teaspoons of sugar. After a glance at his face, she added a fourth.

'How is Marek, these days?' he said, sitting up.

'Marek's the same as always. He's working on a big story.'

'Oh?'

'Nothing he can tell me about.' She poured coffee for herself. 'And I can't tell him about my investigations, either. Whenever we meet, we sort of dance round each other trying to find things to talk about.'

'There must be times when your investigations cross.'

'That happens more often than you might imagine.'

'I see that you've caught the lunatic who's been abducting girls.'

'You've been reading the papers, Father.'

'It's hard to miss it. I heard it on the radio.'

'That just leaves my cold case. Cameron Affleck.' She shook her head. 'I can't rest until I get justice for him.'

The priest set down his cup and took off his glasses. He laid them on the sofa and wiped his eyes. His expression was one of anxiety, bordering on dread.

'You've been trying hard not to tell me something, Father,' she said gently. 'What is it?'

It was a while before he spoke. 'A long time ago, I heard a man's confession.' He stopped and covered his face with his hands.

A confession? She felt a sudden lurch in her stomach. 'And what did this man tell you?' she said slowly.

He let his hands drop. 'You cannot ask me that. When a penitent confesses during the Sacrament of Penance, the Seal of Confession can never be broken. Remember that it is Christ who forgives the sin. I am a mere mediator. I cannot reveal what a penitent has confessed to Him.'

'I understand what you're saying, Father. But why have you waited this long to tell me?'

'It was seeing the photograph of that beautiful child in the newspaper. His smile. Something stirred in me. I thought of the life that had been taken, the family who grieved for him, not knowing what had become of him.'

She set her cup down. Her thoughts were spooling round in her head. She knew from her Catholic upbringing that the words that follow the sign of the cross – 'Bless me, Father, for I have sinned' – set in motion a process that ends in absolution. It is the power that every priest exercises when he raises his hand over the contrite sinner and says, 'I absolve thee from thy sins, in the name of the Father, and of the Son, and of the Holy Spirit. Amen.' She sat, paralysed, as she realised that Father Kliment knew the name of Cameron's killer. And she also knew that he would never give it up.

As if reading her thoughts, he said, 'When I absolved him, it was under the Sacramental Seal. I can say no more.'

His nerves were strung to breaking point. Now was not the time to press him. But she had to ask: 'Why are you telling me this, Father?'

'Because I can no longer bear this burden alone.'

'And you wish me to share it with you?'

He seemed to shrink into himself. 'At the time, I did wonder about stopping the confession and contacting the bishop for guidance,' he muttered, 'but the man was desperate. I couldn't refuse him.' He gazed at Dania, his eyes empty. 'He knew he had committed a mortal sin. He had to receive sacramental absolution, or he could never again take Holy Communion.'

She stared at Father Kliment. She felt physically sick as she appreciated the predicament she was now in. Here was a priest who knew who had murdered Cameron but was forbidden by his office to reveal the name. She felt suddenly unmoored, unable to see a way forward.

'Father, I have to go,' she said, dragging herself to her feet. 'Don't get up. I'll see myself out.'

He said nothing as she left the room.

On the street, in the half-light of late evening, she pulled out her phone. There was only one person she could talk to about this.

★ ★ ★

'Come in, Danka,' Marek said, ushering her into the living room. 'I hope you don't mind my saying, but you look terrible.'

'Only a brother can get away with a remark like that,' she said, trying a smile.

'A glass of vodka?'

'Bring the whole bottle.'

He raised an eyebrow. 'Like that, is it? The spare bed is made up, by the way.'

'Before I forget, I've brought you a present.' She took something out of her bag and handed it to him. 'It's homemade jam. Rhubarb and strawberries.'

'Did you make this?' he said, in amazement. His sister had neither the time nor the patience to cook, let alone make jam.

'Someone gave it to me.'

It had come at an excellent time. He was out of the cherry jam he usually bought at the Polski Sklep. 'I'll get the vodka,' he said, with a smile.

In the kitchen, he searched for the Żubrówka, but found he was out of it. How had he let that happen? He took a bottle of Wyborowa out of the freezer, cut a lemon into quarters and carried everything into the living room.

'Tell me what's bothering you,' he said, pouring. He didn't look up. 'Is it about Jamie?' he added softly.

'It isn't. But I'm guessing you might want to talk about that.'

'There's nothing to say, is there?'

Since learning of his friend's arrest, Marek had found himself unable to function, stumbling about like a drunk man. He'd rung the Lodge, saying he needed a couple of days off, without saying why. Fortunately, it was Allie who'd taken the call. She'd been sympathetic and told him not to return until the following week. He'd tried Pam's mobile, but she wasn't answering. Nor did she seem to want to return his calls. It was as the details slowly filtered

out that he began to appreciate what sort of a man his friend
Jamie was.

'There's something I need to ask you, Marek. Is Jamie a Roman
Catholic?'

'I really don't know. I think he may be Church of Scotland.'

'But you're not absolutely sure?'

'When it comes to Jamie, I'm no longer absolutely sure about
anything.' He squeezed a piece of lemon into his vodka and drank
it. 'Have you asked him?' he added, pouring more.

'I doubt he'd tell me the truth. He lied about knowing
Cameron Affleck.'

'Do you think he locked the boy in that doocot?' When she
didn't reply, he added, 'And what does his being a Catholic have
to do with it?'

She hesitated, and then it came out so quickly that she tripped
over the words. He listened, forgetting the vodka, as she told him
about her visit to Father Kliment.

'I don't know what to do,' she said finally.

'So Father Kliment knows the identity of the boy's killer,'
Marek said, playing with his glass. 'Can't he be compelled to tell
you? In a case like this, surely even a priest isn't expected to keep
silent.'

'That's just it. There's no distinction based on the nature of the
sin. Technically, Father Kliment shouldn't have told me this much.
Just by saying that there *was* a confession is crossing the line.' She
sipped at her vodka. 'From what I remember of the Code of
Canon Law, if he violates the seal of the confessional *directly*, he'll
be excommunicated. I think that means if he gives up the name
of the penitent.'

Marek looked at her thoughtfully. 'All right, so what if he
violates the seal *indirectly*? I presume that means he doesn't give
up the name, but gives you some sort of clue.'

'In that case, he's punished but not excommunicated.'

'Punished how?'

'I've no idea,' she said, in frustration. 'The bishop decides.'

'In the past, it would have been bread and water for a week.'

'More like forty lashes.'

'Did he tell you anything useful? Anything at all?'

'He said the penitent was a man.'

Marek smiled. 'Well, that's something, at least. It rules out half the population.'

She glared at him, then downed the rest of the Wyborowa. 'What I can't understand is why he told me about the confession, knowing he couldn't give up the identity of the penitent.'

'Well, it's obvious, isn't it?'

'Not to me.'

Marek folded his arms. 'He's prepared to help you find this man. But not give you his name.'

'Even if it means punishment?'

'He'll accept punishment, whatever form it takes.' He smiled ruefully. 'I suspect he'd accept forty lashes. But he won't do anything that would result in excommunication. His faith is too important to him.'

She sat up slowly. 'So I need to coax the clues out of him.'

'It won't be easy, especially if he's in a bad way. Push him too far, and he'll clam up. Or his nerves will get the better of him.'

'I don't know if I'm up to it,' she said, in a small voice.

'Of course you are. He thinks the world of you.'

'He does?'

'He's always telling me about the concerts you've agreed to give at the hospital.'

'But I haven't agreed to anything.'

Marek gazed at her steadily. 'You have now.' He saw her look of dismay, and added, 'Tell you what, shall I make some *kanapki*? I know how you like my open sandwiches.'

Her expression brightened. '*Kanapki*? What are you going to put on them?'

'I bought *kindziuk* at the Polski Sklep today.'

'What is it? I've never heard of it.'

'Sausage stuffed with minced meat and bacon. It's smoked and dried. And it's heavenly.' He got to his feet. 'A couple of those each, followed by toast and that jam you brought me, and then we'll plan your course of action.'

Dania bowed her head at Sunday Mass, listening to Father Kliment speak the words that signalled the end of the service. She was hoping to catch him afterwards but, seeing the uncertainty in his eyes as he gave her Communion, she guessed he might make himself unavailable. It therefore came as a surprise when she found him waiting for her after the service.

'Dania,' he said, taking her to one side, 'could we have a talk?'

'Of course. Now?'

'Let me take off my cassock.'

'I'll wait for you at the gates, then.'

She watched him go, daring to hope that he might have had a change of heart. But one look at his face as he returned told her otherwise.

'I won't keep you, Dania,' he said. 'There's a little girl at the hospital. An excellent pianist like yourself. She has terminal cancer, and the doctors haven't given her long. I wonder if you'd take her for a masterclass. There's a piano at the hospital. The other children could watch.' He gazed anxiously through his glasses. 'I know how busy you are. But would you do this?'

The question barely merited an answer. 'Of *course* I'll do it. Send me the details, and I'll get it arranged. Would you like to be there, too?'

He clasped his hands, as though in prayer. 'I knew that would be your response. God will bless you, my child,' he said, glowing with happiness.

She smiled, and he smiled back. Her instinct was to ask him for something in return – the name of Cameron's killer – but she remembered Marek's advice about not pushing him. 'I'll be going then, Father. Don't forget to email me those details.'

He gripped her arm and said, in a whisper, 'He used to come regularly to confession.'

She felt the heat rush through her body. She nodded slowly, as if this were the vital piece of information she needed.

'And then he stopped.'

People were arriving for the next service. Wilkie's Lane was always such a bottleneck with its line of parked cars and ultra-narrow pavement. She stepped aside to let them enter.

The priest was gazing at her without blinking. It seemed that the moment was lost. She was about to thank him and move away when he said, 'It was five months before he came back.' He lowered his voice. 'That was when he told me what he'd done.'

'You know who it is, don't you, Father?' she said softly. 'You recognised his voice.'

He didn't reply. But seeing the expression in his eyes, she knew the truth of it.

Without another word, he turned and hurried into St Joseph's.

CHAPTER 31

Dania was sitting gazing at her computer screen, unable to concentrate. Most of the staff were out, officially celebrating the arrest of the killer rapist, but she had declined Owen's invitation. It was less the interview she'd had with the DCI – with the possibility of disciplinary action – and more that Cameron Affleck's murderer was still out there. She'd pulled Jamie out of the cells and demanded to know why he'd lied about photographing Cameron, adding that unless he gave an account of himself, she would be charging him with the boy's abduction and murder. Jamie's reaction had startled her and made her doubt herself. Yes, he'd said, thumping the table angrily, he'd lied about photographing Cameron, but who wouldn't, given the circumstances? The last thing he'd wanted was to be under any sort of an investigation, especially since his house *and* his mother's might be searched. Surely Dania could see that. No, he was prepared to admit to killing the girls, but he absolutely categorically denied having taken Cameron. When she'd asked him if he wanted to confess his sins to a priest, he'd stared at her open-mouthed.

Her investigation had stalled and she couldn't see a way of restarting it. At the Met, she'd heard talk about a legendary DCI whose favourite expression was: Find the motive, and you find the murderer. But who would chain up a child in a doocot and leave him to starve? What possible motive could there be, except perhaps revenge? *Everyone has enemies, Inspector.* Gregor Affleck's words. Yet the interviews of his Mason friends had led nowhere.

Experience had shown that, in the absence of motive, gathering the evidence was the only course of action. Motive came later. She would have to go back to the beginning and see what, if anything, she'd missed. All detectives, even experienced ones, overlooked clues that were staring them in the face, and until she'd convinced herself that everything had been thoroughly considered, she couldn't move on. She exhaled loudly, her frustration mounting.

Hamish had stayed to finish a long-overdue report before catching up with Owen and the others. He glanced up. 'Something I can help with, ma'am?'

'I need to look at Cameron's case again. From the start. I've got to find a way of joining the dots. The problem is that I don't know where they are.'

He threw her a crooked smile. 'Maybe a second pair of eyes would help find those dots.'

He must have seen how grateful she was because he brought his chair round to her desk.

'Let's start at the beginning, and examine the evidence,' she said. 'By that, I mean everything we found in the doocot.'

'Aye, sounds like a plan.'

She pulled up the photographs and, as the screen filled with the images of Cameron's remains, she found herself back there with Honor, reliving the moment when she realised that this was a child, and someone had left him there to die.

'Old lavatory chains,' Hamish murmured. 'You don't see them now, right enough.'

They had been through this. The killer could have picked up the chains off a skip for some amateur DIY. Yet the neat job of brazing suggested he wasn't an amateur. Their only lead was Bill Baxter, but his alibi had checked out: on the Sunday Cameron was taken, Baxter had been in Dumfries, visiting his cousin and her family.

'And these are the images from Kimmie's lab,' Dania said.

The tattered remains of the boy's clothes and his mouldy shoes were laid out on a sheet of plastic. Everything was falling to bits when they'd found it and was completely in bits after Kimmie's tests. They went through her report line by line. The one thing that could have helped them – DNA that wasn't Cameron's – had degraded in the thirteen years inside the doocot to such an extent that it was useless.

Dania's gaze wandered over what was left of the jacket and trousers, the tie with its barely visible crest, and rested on the paisley-patterned handkerchief.

'Know what I reckon, ma'am?' Hamish said, folding his arms. 'Bill Baxter. He could still be in the frame. He could have set up that alibi with his cousin.'

'He could, but I'm inclined to eliminate him.' She thought back to their visit to Lundie. And how Baxter had believed the lad's abduction was somehow his fault. 'He didn't deny he'd been a welder, or that he'd spent time painting with Cameron. But you could be right. He might be smart enough to think that, by drawing attention to himself, suspicion won't fall on him.'

'If all else fails, shall I interview the cousin again?'

'Why not?' she said wearily. 'If all else fails.'

She was scrolling to the reports of the interviews when Hamish said, 'Just a moment, ma'am. Can we go back to those photos of Kimmie's?'

'You've seen something?' she said, bringing up the first image. 'Shall I zoom in on anything in particular?'

He brought his face close to the screen. 'That paisley handker-chief.'

'What of it?' she said, enlarging it.

'We thought the killer had taken it from the lad and pushed it into his mouth to keep him quiet.'

'That's right.'

'Now that I see it again, it seems an odd choice for a lad that age. Paisley. It's a wee bit old-fashioned, isn't it?' He sat back. 'Know what I think, ma'am? It belonged to the killer.'

'But the killer wouldn't have left anything of his in the doocot. The risk of it leading the police to him would be too great.'

'Maybe he didn't use it as a gag. It might have fallen out of his pocket by accident. I take it Kimmie didn't find another hankie among the lad's clothes?'

'She didn't. Wait a minute, though. Mrs Spence showed me what was in his wardrobe. There was a jacket he'd worn when he was younger. It had a white hankie in the breast pocket. All the Affleck men have them, now I think about it.' Dania pulled up Chirnside's report, and found the photo of Cameron holding the school trophy. She centred it on his breast pocket, zooming in until the image began to pixelate. 'That's the best I can do.'

But it was enough. A tiny triangle that was lighter than the rest of the material was just visible above the line of the pocket.

'That's the tip of a handkerchief,' she said.

'There's not much to go on but it doesn't look like paisley to me.'

'So why didn't Cameron have a white handkerchief in his jacket the Sunday he was taken?'

'Maybe in all the kerfuffle it got dropped somewhere between the house and the doocot. Or he didn't fold one into his pocket. And if he didn't have a handkerchief, the killer would have had no choice but to use his own.'

And, as soon as he'd said it, she knew it was true.

She gazed at Hamish in admiration. 'That paisley belongs to whoever put Cameron in there. You did well to spot that.'

'Worth getting it into the media, ma'am?'

'Definitely. Someone may recognise it.'

He hurried back to his desk. But as he tapped away, frowning in concentration, Dania found her excitement evaporating. Who would remember a paisley handkerchief after so much time?

Dania let herself into her flat on Victoria Road. She'd decided against bothering with lunch, as she needed to get in some piano practice. Instead, she'd bought a sandwich at the Overgate and eaten it as she walked home. Her mood was one of despondency. The paisley-patterned handkerchief had appeared on television, and would also be in the evening papers, but she doubted anything would come of it.

She sat at the Bechstein Concert 8 and gazed at the framed photograph of Chopin in Warsaw's Łazienki Park. The bronze statue was a replica of the original, which, as a symbol of Polish nationalism, had been blown up by the Germans in 1940. Whenever Dania saw it, she was reminded of her grandmother's story about how, the day after the explosion, a note had appeared on the pile of rubble. The wording was slightly different each time she had told the story, but it went along the lines of 'I don't know who blew me up, but I know why. It was so that I won't play my famous funeral march at the funeral of your leader.' After the war, a replica was cast from the original mould, which had somehow survived the near-total destruction of the city.

She launched into the Polonaise from the film, *Pan Tadeusz*. Like all Polish children, Dania had studied *Pan Tadeusz*, an epic poem by the romantic writer Adam Mickiewicz, which told of a time in history after the Polish-Lithuanian Commonwealth had been partitioned and erased from the map of Europe. The music had been composed twenty years earlier by Wojciech Kilar and was usually performed by an orchestra. The consul general had asked for it at the 11 November concert, so she'd written a piano version. She finished it in under five minutes and had to admit that the orchestral version was far better. It was a pity they couldn't fit an orchestra into the rooms in Edinburgh.

The consul general had agreed with her suggestion of playing something by Liszt, and, thankfully, had left the choice up to her. It would be Liebestraum No. 3, a piece she knew so well that she could almost play it with her eyes closed. It started easily enough – and this part she often did play with her eyes closed – but a minute in, she had to concentrate, summoning all her reserves as the music grew more animated. Suddenly, halfway through, after the second key change, she stopped and stared at the wall.

Something had surfaced from her subconscious. It was still at the half-formed stage but she knew it held the key to her investigation. She got up slowly and paced the room, trying not to let anything distract her.

A series of loud thumps came from behind the wall. It was the computer scientist who lived in the neighbouring flat. As someone who worked from home, he was her audience whenever she practised. They'd run into each other on the stairs, and he'd confessed to being a great fan of classical music, and had even suggested one or two pieces she could play. He'd also suggested they get together for a drink sometime.

The thumping again. 'Don't stop!' came the muffled shout.

She hurried into the kitchen and sat at the tiny table. And, as if recalling a dream, she remembered Mrs Spence's words.

He took a tumble down the stairs. He was in a coma for five months.

And what had Father Kliment said?

He used to come regularly to confession. It was five months before he came back.

Five months. Five months . . .

And then she saw them all – the joined-up dots. Sandy Spence, for reasons unknown, had kidnapped Cameron and chained him in a doocot. But before he could implement whatever plan he'd hatched, he'd suffered an accident that put him in a coma. For five months. She tried to imagine how he'd felt on waking, learning that five months had passed, and realising that the boy was long dead. No wonder he'd rushed to seek out a priest.

She ran into the living room. Her neighbour must have heard her, because he started to bang on the wall, shouting to her to carry on playing. She pulled out her phone and called the station.

'Hamish. Take a uniform and pick up Sandy Spence. He lives somewhere in Blackness.'

'On what charge, ma'am?'

'I'll explain later. If he or his wife put up a fuss, say that we just want to ask him a few questions. Is Honor there?'

'Arrived this minute. Shall I put her on?'

'Ask her to meet me at my flat with a squad car. It's possible the Spences are at the Afflecks'.'

'Will do, ma'am.' He rang off.

And, as Dania stood listening to her neighbour beating his fist against the wall, she knew she had finally come to the end of her quest to find Cameron Affleck's killer. But, instead of the soaring exhilaration she always experienced at this point in an investigation, she felt a sudden, inexplicable sadness.

CHAPTER 32

'These are for you,' Marek said, placing the bunch of red carnations in Allie's hands.

'They're beautiful. Thank you.' She buried her face in the flowers. 'Carnations smell marvellous, don't they?' She pulled one out and broke off the stem, and then inserted the flower into the lapel of Marek's cream jacket. 'Perfect,' she said, standing back, her head tilted to the side.

'Shall I find a vase?'

'There'll be one in the kitchen. Oh, I should have asked.' She looked searchingly at him. 'Are you all right? When you phoned last week, I did wonder if something had happened.'

'I may as well tell you. The man who took those girls.' He hesitated. 'I knew him.'

'My God. How awful for you.'

He waved a hand as though it no longer mattered. 'Let's see to those flowers, shall we?'

In the kitchen, she filled a white vase with water. 'I've got the key, by the way.'

'The key to the cellar?' He threw a glance at the door. Noises off suggested that someone was in the building. It would be the Master: in all the time Marek had worked at the Lodge, he'd never seen another Mason.

She turned off the tap. 'Niall will be going out soon for the rest of the day.'

He gazed at her in admiration, wondering how she'd managed to get the key. If gemstones were hidden in the cellar, Niall would keep the key on him. She didn't volunteer the information and Marek thought it best not to ask. He imagined her slipping the man a barbiturate and waiting until he'd fallen asleep before riffling through his pockets.

She carried the vase into the hall and set it on her desk. Marek took his seat in the archives and continued to work on the database.

There were footsteps and then voices in the hall. He stopped typing and listened. The Master was telling Allie that he'd be back the following day and she was now in charge. A moment later, there was the sound of the front door opening and closing.

She popped her head round the door. 'So, Franek, are we doing this?'

He got to his feet. His heart was galloping.

'Better take your jacket off.' She studied his light-blue shirt and beige chinos. 'Pity I haven't got a boiler suit or something you could wear over those.'

'It's all washable.'

'Right. Come on, then.'

She lifted the flap of her bag and rummaged around inside. 'Here it is,' she said, handing him a key. She paused, frowning. 'There may not be any electricity down there. I'll see if I can find a torch in the kitchen. I'll be back in a tick.'

He watched her go, thinking that even a tick was a long time to be away from her.

She returned with a large torch. 'Will this do, do you think?'

He switched it on and off. 'It's fine.'

The key fitted the lock perfectly, but he had to do a bit of fiddling before he could get it to turn. It made him suspect that no one had been in the cellar for some time. If that were the case, searching the place would be a wasted effort.

The door opened. A set of wooden steps led down into darkness.

'Shall we?' he said.

'You first. But take the key with you. And I'll close the door behind us.'

He switched on the torch.

The beam illuminated a large room. Stacks of old furniture occupied much of the space. But the rest was taken up with wine racks laden with dusty bottles.

'Wow,' Allie said, peering down. 'No wonder the Masons look happy after their meetings.'

'Doesn't the wine belong to Gregor?'

'I don't think so,' she said, frowning. 'He wouldn't have left it here.'

'Perhaps he doesn't have enough space where he lives.'

She nodded, but didn't look convinced.

They descended the steps slowly until they reached the cold flagging. Marek shone the torch over the wall. 'Yes, there's electricity,' he said, his voice sounding hollow. He flicked the switch, bathing the cavern in a dim, eerie light.

'So the place is falling down and it's not safe?' he said, indicating the solid curve of the ceiling.

'Sounds like we were fed a whole load of porkies.' She glanced at the racks. 'But I can see why the Master wanted to keep us out of here.'

'Okay, let's see what we've got.'

He was no expert, but these were vintage wines, mainly from France.

'I don't suppose Niall would put the emeralds into these, would he?' Allie said, lifting a bottle of claret and peering through the dark glass.

Marek looked scandalised. 'I sincerely hope not.'

'Then where would he have hidden them?' she said, turning round slowly. 'In among that lot?' she added, nodding at the furniture.

'I doubt it. Not if he needed to get at them quickly.'

They wandered around the cellar, examining everything, but it soon became apparent that, wherever Niall had hidden the gems, it wasn't there.

'What that?' Allie said, in a voice full of disgust. 'There. In the corner.'

Marek directed the beam into the shadows, illuminating a series of mousetraps with tiny desiccated corpses in the metal jaws. As he turned away, the light caught something on the wall.

'Look, Allie,' he murmured. 'I think there's another door.'

It was so well hidden that they might not have found it. If the gems were behind it, then, as a hiding place, it was ideal.

He gripped the knob and turned it, causing flakes of rust to fall on to the floor. He twisted the knob firmly, but it didn't budge.

'Try the key,' she said. 'Maybe it opens this door as well.'

He had more difficulty with this lock, but in the end succeeded in turning the key. The door opened soundlessly.

'See?' she said gleefully. 'I'm not useless, after all.'

She made to hurry inside, but he grabbed her arm and pulled her back. She gave a little cry.

'I'm sorry, Allie,' he said, releasing her. 'I didn't mean to hurt you.'

'I'm fine. You took me by surprise, that's all.'

'Let me check it out first. It could be that this is where the ceiling's falling in.'

He took a cautious step forward, playing the beam over the walls. The long tunnel was lined with grimy yellowing tiles, the grouting as hard as concrete. It seemed to disappear into the near distance, where the ground sloped downward. Given how deep they already were, he was reluctant to go further, but Allie was suddenly behind him, peering over his shoulder.

'Good heavens,' she murmured.

'I don't think we should go in.'

'Why not?'

'It may not be safe.'

'It looks perfectly solid to me.'

'It may be flooded further on.'

'Yes, I see. Well, of course in that case, we'll turn back. But don't you think it's worth a look?'

'Okay, but if it's unsafe, we turn back. No ifs or buts. Agreed?'

'Agreed.'

Something made him take the key out of the lock and slip it into his pocket. It wasn't that he thought the Master would return and lock them in, but simply that it made him feel less exposed.

He was conscious of the sound of their movements as they crept along the tunnel. The thought came to him that the battery might die on them, and he wished now that he had a more powerful torch. But they'd be able to find their way back if he kept one hand on the wall and the other gripping Allie's.

He tried to calculate where the tunnel was taking them. The door to the cellar was at the end of the hall, there were the steps, and then they'd turned left. The relative distances made him suspect they were walking parallel to Guthrie Street in a direction away from the Marketgait.

They began their descent, the gradient taking them deeper underground. It grew colder, and Marek was starting to regret not bringing his jacket. A minute later, the ground levelled off.

'Any idea how far we've gone?' Allie said, her voice sounding strange.

'Hard to tell. Look, we're climbing now.'

'Why do you think Gregor had a tunnel built?'

'Are you sure it was Gregor? Maybe the Lodge has been in the family for generations.'

'What's that?' she said suddenly.

Marek moved the beam. The tunnel ended abruptly at a door.

'Bingo,' she said softly. 'The emeralds must be behind that.'

'I don't think so, Allie. Look again.'

Several thick planks had been nailed across the door in such a way that it would have taken a sturdy axe to smash through them.

Her disappointment was almost palpable. 'Why did someone do that?'

'No idea. But those rusty nails suggest it was a long time ago.' He glanced at her. 'Wherever the Master's hidden those gems, it's not behind that door.'

'Damn.' She turned away, her shoulders slumped.

He was about to follow her when he thought he heard a sound.

'Wait,' he said. He put his ear to the door. A faint humming came from behind it.

She started to speak, but he lifted a finger in a gesture of silence.

He strained to listen. And there it was again, faint but distinct.

He played the beam over the door, looking for a crack in the wood. Near the top, under the frame, there was a long split.

'What is it?' she said.

'I think I might be able to see what's behind it if I can get some of this off.'

He took the key and started to chip at the wood. Time had done its work and the shards splintered easily, leaving a crack the thickness of his finger. It was difficult to shine the torch and simultaneously peer inside, but he managed it by angling the beam.

At first, he could see nothing, but gradually he made out a shape that might have been a man in a black suit. He was standing sideways on, and looking straight ahead. Marek moved the torch a fraction, and the light caught something that glittered. He directed the beam further down, seeing a white band round the man's waist. No, it was an apron. The man was a Mason!

Marek pulled the torch away, and stepped back, stunned. Another second, and the Mason might have turned and seen light filtering through the door.

'What is it?' Allie said. 'What can you see?'

He put a finger to his lips and made a gesture to indicate that they needed to get out of there. She nodded, and they retraced their steps to the cellar. He closed the door and locked it.

Her voice was insistent. 'What did you see, Franek?'

'I caught a glimpse, nothing more. But I think it was a Mason.'

She stared in apparent disbelief.

'Is there another Lodge near here?' he said.

'There are several in Dundee. But I know of none that are nearby. You're sure that's what you saw? A Mason?'

'Would a Lodge hold secret meetings underground?'

'I'm sure they would. The more secret the better, I'd say.'

He was beginning to doubt himself. 'Let's get out of here before someone finds us.'

They returned to the hall.

He locked the door. 'So, no emeralds in the cellar,' he said, handing her the key. 'I'm out of ideas, I'm afraid.'

'I can't believe that's the end of it.' She seemed close to tears. 'Where would anyone hide jewels in this place?' she said, in frustration.

'Jewels,' he murmured, his gaze falling on the cabinet.

It was too obvious. And yet . . .

Marek examined the gleaming medals and other regalia. It was hard to tell whether any had been moved or were otherwise different. But hiding in plain sight was always a good bet.

He crouched down and ran his hand under the cabinet, feeling rough wood along its length.

'What are you looking for?' Allie said.

'I'm wondering if there's a catch, or a way of removing the bottom board.'

'You think there might be a secret hiding place or something?'

'It's possible.'

He tried at the top with the same negative result. The only other place was the back. He studied the side of the cabinet and saw immediately that there were a good couple of inches between the inner back panel and the wall.

'Here goes,' he said. He placed his hands under the cabinet and lifted it without disturbing the contents. Then, balancing it on two legs and taking care not to tip the thing over, he swung it out.

Someone had cut a large square out of the back panel and attached a hinge. Whoever it was had added a V-shaped notch so the square could be opened out easily.

He beckoned her over. 'Look at this, Allie.'

Her eyes widened. 'Open it,' she said softly.

He inserted his finger under the notch and lifted back the square.

Inside, taped to the inner panel, was a brown plastic package.

They looked at one another. Allie reached in and pulled the package away. She handed it to Marek.

'I need scissors,' he said. 'Or a knife.'

'The kitchen.' She ran in and returned with a pair of scissors.

He cut away the duct tape and packaging, revealing a folded, waxed paper bag with the printed word CHIVOR. Inside were a large number of uncut stones, each the size of a walnut. The clarity of the gems and their deep bluish-green colour told him that what he was holding was worth millions.

'It's all true, then,' Allie murmured.

'Did you ever doubt it?'

'When we drew a blank in the cellar, I did begin to wonder whether Murray hadn't found the emeralds after all.'

'We'll need to call the police, Allie.'

'Do we have to? I mean, can't I have just one?' She must have seen him hesitate because she added, 'I need to get away from here, Franek, if I'm to have any chance of living something like a normal life.'

The distress in her voice alarmed him. 'What do you mean?' he said.

'There's something you need to know.' She played with her fingers. 'You see, I wasn't telling the truth when I said that my husband had died.' She gazed into his eyes. 'My husband is Ross Affleck. And he's a monster.'

'Gregor's son?'

'I have to get away from him.' She rolled up her sleeves. 'Look what he does to me.'

Marek felt the air leave his lungs. Some of the bruises were old and yellowing, but others were more recent. No wonder she cried out whenever anyone touched her.

'He does this to me whenever I behave in a way he doesn't like. Most of the time, I've no idea what I'm doing to anger him.'

'Why haven't you gone to the police?' Marek said, feeling his blood rise.

'I can't,' she wailed. 'He's a Mason. For all I know, there are Masons in the police force. Or in the courts. I can't take the risk. You do understand that, don't you?'

Yes, Marek understood. One of his recent assignments had been about abuse in marriage. He'd interviewed a dozen women, all of whom had been terrified that their husbands would be acquitted or, if found guilty, would be given ridiculously short sentences. So they'd kept quiet.

'This Ross,' he said, his voice level. 'Where does he live?'

Her look of anguish was replaced by one of terror. 'Don't go after him, Franek,' she cried. 'He'll kill you.'

'Not if I kill him first.'

'Oh, don't talk like that. Promise me you won't go after him.' She gripped his fingers. 'Promise me!'

He gazed into her green eyes, wanting only for her terror to disappear. 'I promise.'

'Swear to me!'

'I swear, Allie.'

She relaxed then and released him. 'So, you see why I need to disappear.'

He nodded, realising that this meant the end of his scoop. If he involved the police, Allie would be questioned – something she might not deal with well in her present state – and in the meantime she'd be living with that bastard of a husband. If you could call that living. No, he wouldn't do that to her, even though by withholding what he'd uncovered, he would be breaking the law.

He pressed the bag into her hands. 'Take these. All of them. And get as far away from here as you can.'

She stared at the bag, and then at him. 'I can have them all?'

'I'll put the cabinet back exactly as it was. It may be a while before the Master comes looking. That'll give you some time.' He squeezed her hands. 'Have you got any money?'

'I can take what we owe Murray. It's not a lot but it will get me started.'

He fetched his jacket from the archives room and felt in the pocket for his wallet. 'Here, take this.' He pulled out all the notes and thrust them into her hand, curling her fingers round them.

Her expression softened. 'Oh Franek, where were you before I met my husband?'

'I'm here now,' he said hopefully.

'I'm sorry I lied to you about so many things. I was in a corner, you see.'

'There's always the truth.' He smiled. 'As a last resort.'

'You need to leave here, too. The Master is likely to suspect you when he finds the emeralds have vanished. Whatever they did to Murray, they could do to you.'

'Don't worry about me,' he said, brushing her hair back from her forehead. 'I can look after myself.'

She held up the bag of emeralds. 'Thank you. Thanks for everything.'

'I didn't do it for thanks. I happen to be in love with you.' He took a breath. 'You'd better go now.'

She gazed at him longer than was necessary. Then she picked up her shoulder bag and pushed the emeralds inside. From the desk drawer, she withdrew a brown envelope, which he presumed was Murray's cash. She powered down the computer and, with a final glance around, made for the door.

She paused and looked back at him. 'I won't forget this, Franek.'

Yes, you will, he thought, as the door closed behind her.

CHAPTER 33

There was no reply to Dania's knock at the Afflecks'. She waited and tried again, with the same result. Hamish had just radioed to say that there'd been no one at the Spences' flat, so she was pinning her hopes on the couple being at the house on Albany Road.

'Maybe she and her husband are out for lunch,' Honor said.

'Or they're not answering.'

'You think they saw that handkerchief?'

'It may have been a mistake to get it into the media straight away. Come on, let's try round the back.'

'They haven't got a guard dog, have they?'

'Not that I recall.'

They slipped the latch on the side gate and followed the path to the kitchen door. Dania peered through the window. Mrs Spence was sitting at the table with her hands over her face.

Dania opened the door.

The woman lowered her hands and gazed up at the detectives. Her face was taut with tension.

They took the seats opposite.

'Mrs Spence, I think you know why we're here,' Dania said.

She nodded in silence.

'Where is your husband?'

'He's at home.'

Dania exchanged a glance with Honor. Sandy must have gone out. No matter. Hamish and the uniforms had taken up position and would apprehend him on his return.

The woman began to speak. 'I was at home this morning. I saw the neckerchief on the midday news.' She swallowed. 'At first I thought, Aye, well, there's someone else who has the exact same one as Sandy. He was in the kitchen, having his lentil soup, so I called him in. He took one look at the telly and collapsed.' Her voice grew hard. 'That's when I knew.'

'And you hadn't suspected before?'

'Why would I? He was a good man.' She looked at her hands. 'My Christian conscience compels me to tell you what he told me.'

'I think I can guess some of it. But I need you to give me a full account.'

Mrs Spence smoothed her hair. 'Sandy ran his own wee business. He was a plumber and pipefitter. With his own van,' she added proudly. 'The work didn't always come in but we managed somehow. At that time, he was doing a job in this area. Aye, and it was a long one, refitting a house.' She lapsed into silence.

'And he often saw Cameron playing in the garden?' Dania ventured.

'He'd met Cameron here, in this house. He would drop by now and again for a cup of tea and a natter. Mr Gregor didn't mind. Nor did Mrs Affleck.'

'So he knew about the doocot key, and where it was kept.'

'Aye, that he did.' There was a note of pleading in her voice. 'You ken where we live, Inspector. We haven't got much money, not enough for a comfortable retirement. Sandy came up with a plan. And he didn't let me in on it.'

'You sure about that?' Honor said.

'As God is my witness,' she cried, gripping her crucifix, 'I knew nothing about this until he told me today.'

331

'Please go on, Mrs Spence,' Dania said, throwing Honor a warning glance.

'He prepared the doocot, putting in the chains and that, well in advance of the day. He'd intended to ask Mr Gregor for money.' Her hands were trembling. 'And then he would release the lad.'

Dania knew now how it had happened. But she had to hear it from the woman.

'That Sunday in June, he knew I'd be visiting my mother. He parked the van where he would get a good view of the house. He reckoned no one would pay it much heed because they'd seen it in that road so many times. Then he waited. I think he hoped an idea would come to him.' She seemed to brace herself. 'He knew that only Mrs Affleck and Cameron were at home because I'd told him the menfolk would be at the museum.' She bowed her head, and added, in an anguished voice, 'So, you see, it was my fault what happened to that lad.'

Dania leant across and gripped the woman's hand. 'You can't say that, Mrs Spence. How could you have known?'

She gazed at Dania, her eyes empty. 'When Cameron didn't show, he decided to chance it. He went round the back of the house and in through the kitchen door.'

'It was unlocked?'

'Aye, Mrs Affleck must have come in that way. They often went in and out through the kitchen. Anyway, the door into the living room was open and he saw the lad there, playing with his toys. But there was no sign of Mrs Affleck. He knew that, if he was going to do it, he'd have to do it then. He told Cameron that Mr Gregor had asked him to bring him to the museum to see the animals. The lad loved that place,' she added wistfully.

'And they went out through the front door?'

'I reckon Sandy was for going out the way he came in, but the lad ran to the front door and tried to move the bolts. Of course, he couldn't reach them. Sandy was worried that Mrs Affleck might appear at any moment so he drew the bolts himself and opened the door.' She fell silent.

'And when Cameron found they weren't going to the museum?' Dania prompted.

'He kicked up an almighty fuss. Fortunately, there was no one near the doocot. I reckon everyone at Inchture was at the kirk.' She paused. 'Sandy said the lad was making enough noise to wake the dead. He chained him up, and then took his neckerchief off and pushed it into the lad's mouth because he couldn't stand all the hollering.'

'And locked him in, in case someone came nosing around.'

'He'd intended to speak to Mr Gregor the same day. He was sure the man would pay up. Aye, the lad would be out in a matter of hours, and Sandy and I would be far away from here. But when I came back from my mother's, I found him at the foot of the stairs. He'd tripped and hit his head. He was in a coma for so long that I considered having the life-support switched off. I was on the point of giving my consent when the next day, as though he'd read my thoughts, he came out of it. He was a changed man. I put it down to the accident. Ach, who wouldn't be changed after a fall like that?' She gave her head a little shake. 'He couldn't work. His business folded, and he took to the drink. After a while, he turned to carpentry. Made toys. Boats, mainly. Like Cameron's.'

Dania tried to imagine Sandy's state of mind. As a practising Roman Catholic, the first thing he would have done was run to Father Kliment.

'Obviously, by the time he came out of the coma, the lad was dead,' the woman was saying. 'He told me he couldn't bring himself to go and look.' Her eyes filmed over, and the tears started down her cheeks.

333

'Mrs Spence, did Sandy say what he did with the key to the doocot?'

She pressed a handkerchief to her eyes. 'Aye, he buried it outside.'

'Did he say where, exactly?'

'By the monkey puzzle tree. It's not buried too deeply.'

After a brief silence, Dania said, 'Is there anything else you'd like to tell us?'

'What will happen to Sandy?'

'He'll be charged with kidnapping,' she said, watching the woman. 'And also with culpable homicide.'

'Not murder?'

'There was no intent.'

'And what will happen then?'

'It'll be a custodial sentence. The judge will decide how long.'

The woman's shoulders drooped.

'Is there somewhere you can go, Mrs Spence?' If she went home, she might well witness her husband's arrest, and Dania wanted to spare her that. 'Do you have a close friend nearby?'

'There's just Sandy and me.' She drew herself up. 'But I should stay here. I'm working this afternoon.'

Dania glanced at Honor. The girl shook her head. She was thinking the same: the Afflecks would be coming home and might not appreciate seeing the wife of Cameron's killer in their house. Although Sandy's arrest hadn't yet made the news, it soon would.

'How about I take you to see Father Kliment?' Dania said.

The woman seemed to consider this. 'Aye, that's a good idea. He'll know how to counsel me. He's always been good that way. I'll tell him everything I've told you.' She frowned. 'It will come as a huge shock to him.'

Dania returned the woman's gaze. *Not as big a shock as you might think.* 'Perhaps you should take your belongings with you, Mrs Spence.'

'I won't be coming back here, will I?' She looked around the kitchen where she'd spent more of her life than in her own home, then struggled to her feet. 'There's just my coat and bag.'

CHAPTER 34

Niall Affleck threw open the door to the Lodge. 'Ross! Thank God you're here.'

'What's wrong?' Ross said, before the door had even closed. He'd got the phone call while he was at the museum. His uncle, normally a cool-headed man, sounded close to the edge and, given what was at stake, he thought it best to deal with this personally.

Niall looked like a man demented. 'This whole thing is unravelling, and no mistake.'

'What do you mean?'

'I arrived here a short while ago and found the place deserted. Filarski's meant to be on shift. I don't like it, Ross. His laptop is still on.'

'Filarski?' he said, his anger rising dangerously quickly. 'Did you say Filarski? Franek Filarski?'

'Aye, the archivist. He's been working here for about a month. He's taken over from Murray.'

Ross stared at his uncle. So Filarski was the new archivist! He and Kenny had been scouring Dundee trying to find the man, and he'd been at the Lodge the whole time. The situation couldn't have been more farcical. Had everything not started to spiral out of control, he would have thrown back his head and laughed.

'Kenny and I have been looking everywhere for him. He was asking questions round at Murray's place.'

There was an edge of panic to Niall's voice. 'How do you know?'

'His next-door neighbour told us.'

'Do you think he was in with Murray?'

'Ach, he must have been. Aye, I can see it now. Murray disappeared, so Filarski took his place, hoping to get his hands on the emeralds.'

'You need to find him. And do it now.'

'Right enough. The problem is how?'

'For God's sake, how hard can it be?' Niall glanced at the computer. 'His address will be on the database, surely.'

A quick search uncovered Filarski's address. 'I have to say that Allie keeps a tidy system,' Niall said. He paused. 'You don't suppose she's in on it?'

Ross sneered. 'Allie? She hasn't the brains.'

'Where is she?'

'Right now? I passed her on the way to the museum. She's working with Kenny. We've had a commission, and we need to get on with it.'

'But you'll make this a priority? Finding Filarski?'

'Aye, I'll find him.' He stared at his uncle. 'And I'll deal with him.'

Gilie Wallace was in Dudhope Park, north of the Lochee Road, looking out over the river. He was standing beside the cannon, which faced the Tay in case of an invasion from Fife. This was a favourite spot, not for the stunning view but because it was an out-of-the-way place and therefore ideal for meeting clients. And today he was meeting a client who commanded attention. Never mind that the man was always late.

He pulled the packet of Superkings out of his trousers, drew one out with his teeth, and lit it, inhaling deeply. He closed his eyes, savouring the nicotine hit, so was unprepared for the thick, deep voice in his ear.

'I've been looking for you for the last twenty-four hours.'

Gilie jumped. 'I was visiting my sick mother.'

Ross smiled. It was the sort of smile that made Gilie's bowels turn to water. 'Of course you were,' he said.

'So how can I help you? Or have you come for a wee blether?'

'A wee blether? Aye, right.' He stared out over the river. 'I'm looking for someone. His name's Filarski. Franek Filarski.'

Gilie pulled on the cigarette. 'Never heard of him.'

'Are you sure? Or is this your opening bid?'

'I'm sure. I know many Poles in this town, but not that one.'

'Maybe one of the Poles you know knows Franek Filarski.' Ross reached into the pocket of his black trousers and drew out an envelope. 'Ask around.' He held it out. 'Do it.'

The menace in his voice wasn't lost on Gilie. 'You've tried the obvious, I take it. The phone directory. Social media.'

Ross threw him a look of contempt, which Gilie reckoned was all the answer he was going to get.

'It would help if I knew a wee bitty more about this Polak, ken.'

'He's an archivist.'

He was glad he was facing the Tay, or Ross would have seen his expression. 'An archivist?' He kept his tone conversational. 'Where does he work?'

'Until recently, at the Lodge. We put an advert in the *Courier* and he applied. But he's vanished. And the address he gave us was false.'

'Why do you want to find him? Did he scarper with your ledgers, then?'

Ross turned to face him. 'Why I want to find him is none of your business.'

He nodded contritely. Ross was not a man to antagonise.

'So you'll ask around.' It was a statement. 'And if you find him in the next twenty-four hours, or tell me where *I* can find him, there'll be a big fat bonus for you.'

He took a breath. Up to now, he'd been prepared to keep Marek out of it, but the mention of the bonus sent his moral compass spinning out of control. 'I can tell you where he is,' he said softly.

'I thought you said you'd never heard the name.'

'Franek Filarski isn't his real name. It's Marek Gorski. He's a journalist at the *Courier.*'

Something shifted in Ross's expression. 'How do you know this?'

Gilie thought rapidly. He didn't want to reveal his association with Marek in case whatever fate Ross had in mind for the Pole would be visited on him. 'I have a contact there, ken. He mentioned that this Gorski was about to go in undercover as an archivist.'

Ross gripped his throat, pulling him close. 'And you didn't think to tell me?'

'He didn't say *where* he was going in undercover, just that he was going in somewhere as an archivist,' Gilie said, choking.

Ross released him. 'Two undercover archivists. It must be the same man.'

'Aye, that's what I reckon, too.'

'Marek Gorski,' he said, with a thin smile. 'I'm obliged to you, Gilie.' He nodded and left.

'What about that bonus, eh?' Gilie shouted after his retreating figure.

'It's in the post,' Ross shouted back, without turning round.

Gilie threw the remains of his fag on to the ground. 'In the post,' he muttered. 'The wee shite doesn't know where I live.'

There were many places where Ross could take up position and keep a watch on the DC Thomson offices, but the statue of Burns was as good as any. From there, he had an uninterrupted view of the revolving doors into the building. He settled himself on the plinth and unfolded the previous day's *Tele*. He pretended to read, keeping half an eye on the comings and goings at the entrance.

It had taken Kenny a matter of minutes to find Marek Gorski online. Ross had never clapped eyes on the man as, the few times he'd called in to see the Master, the door to the archives had been closed. But when he saw the photo of the handsome Pole, he did wonder whether Gorski and Allie mightn't have had a thing going. There was that day when she'd spent much of the morning at Jock's, right enough. He never did find out if she'd gone there alone. Or maybe she'd never left the Lodge and simply hadn't answered when he rang. When you're having sex in a distant room, the last thing you hear is the sound of a phone. But he dismissed the thought: whatever come-on this Marek Gorski might have given her, she had more sense. And, anyway, she was one of those women who weren't interested in sex.

It was nearly six, and the only people who'd entered or left DC Thomson's were women. He was getting to his feet when he caught a movement at the swing doors. A tall, fair-haired man was leaving the building. He strolled down the steps and, with a glance around, headed towards Reform Street.

Ross waited until Gorski would be a good distance ahead, and then followed him. He was easy to pick out, not just because of his height and build, but because he was wearing a well-tailored light-blue suit and everyone else was in T-shirts and shorts. At the High Street, he turned right and continued westward, crossing the busy dual carriageway at Debenhams. Ross tailed him along the Perth Road to the junction with Union Street, where the Pole vanished.

Taking care not to be seen, he peered along the street. It sloped down towards the river, narrowing to a lane. On the right was a line of four-storey buildings. Slowing his pace, he followed the Pole to where the lane stopped at a double ribbed-metal gate with a 'No Entry' sign. Gorski disappeared into the end building.

The open door led into a short hallway with an echoing stair-well. Ross glanced up, seeing a flash of light blue. There was no need to follow him: the buzzer listing confirmed that a Marek Gorski lived on the top floor.

Ross smiled. He pulled out his phone as he left the building.

'What time is it, eh?' Kenny said.

'Forty-two seconds later than when you last asked me.'

'And you're sure he's in?'

'The top-floor light's on,' Ross said patiently.

They were sitting in the black van, in the car park on Union Place, facing the street. The sun had set a couple of hours earlier and the sky was a deep inky blue.

'Ach, we may as well get on with it,' Ross said, unclipping his seatbelt. 'Ready?'

'You're sure he'll let us in?'

'It worked with Murray. Come on, let's go.'

They left the van and walked the short distance to the build-ing. In the hallway, Ross pressed the buzzer next to Gorski's name.

'Yes?' came the distant voice.

'Police, sir,' Ross said politely. 'Could we have a word?'

'At this hour?' A crackly pause. 'Can't it wait until morning?'

'I'm afraid it's an urgent matter. It concerns Mrs Allie Affleck.'

'Oh, God,' came the breathy voice. 'You'd better come up.'

'Thank you, sir.'

They took the stairs. 'See?' Ross said. 'Easy.'

He had decided against showing their IDs. The false warrants had fooled Murray, who had left meekly enough, thinking he was being arrested. But a journalist might spot they were fakes. He might even be well enough connected with the polis to know that Ross and Kenny were imposters.

'Now mind what I told you,' Ross said, as they reached the top floor. 'We only need him to open the door. Don't bother footering around for your warrant or anything.'

Kenny nodded.

Gorski must have heard their footsteps because he flung the door open. 'What's happened to Allie?' he cried. He looked from one to the other with an anguished expression. His gaze rested on Kenny, and the expression changed to one of recognition.

Without a moment's hesitation, Ross pulled the cosh out of his pocket and brought it down heavily on Gorski's head. The man's legs buckled.

'Come on, help me,' he said to Kenny.

Kenny lifted the Pole up by his arms and helped Ross half pull, half carry him down the stairs and out to the street. They dragged him to the back of the van and hoisted him in. Kenny scrambled in after him.

Ross started the engine, cursing under his breath. He knew that look. Somehow Gorski had seen Kenny before. It could only have been at the Lodge, unless he'd paid a visit to the Natural History Museum and spotted him there, although that seemed unlikely: they and their father usually entered and left via the back. Ach, it hardly mattered now. Aye, and in a short while it wouldn't matter at all.

Marek rolled over on the floor of the van. His head hurt like a bastard, and all he wanted to do was sleep. He drifted in and out of consciousness. In his few moments of lucidity, he thought about Allie. Who were these men, and what had they done to her? Had her husband, Ross, sent them? But he couldn't think about that now. He had to concentrate on staying awake. And staying alive.

After what seemed like an age but was probably no more than a few minutes, the van pulled up and the driver cut the engine. Marek half opened his eyes. In front of him was a dark, looming shape. The door opened and light flooded in, and he realised that one of the men had been in the back with him. He decided to play dead. Or at least play unconscious.

A voice came from outside. 'Push him out.'

The man inside rolled Marek over until he reached the edge, then shoved him hard. He landed badly, scraping his cheek, but managed not to cry out.

'Help me get him up.'

They grabbed his arms and dragged him a short distance. The long row of lights and the smell of river water told him he was on the Tay Road Bridge. He choked down his growing feeling of panic. If they threw him in, he might survive, especially if he was near the Dundee end, where the bridge was not as high. He was a strong swimmer, and his powerful lungs would ensure he survived the plunge through the water. But he had a sudden presentiment that they weren't just going to throw him in.

'Stand him up.'

With a feeling of unreality, he felt the noose slipped over his neck and then tightened.

'Hold him while I tie this.'

Whoever was securing the other end of the long rope to the railings took his time. 'Okay, let's do it,' he said finally.

Marek felt dangerously detached from what was happening. They bent him over the railings and gripped his legs. As they tipped him over, he managed to work his hands under the noose before the rope tightened. He knew he wouldn't have time to pull it over his head, so he made his hands into fists and braced himself for the shock of the drop.

The pain in his hands and across the back of his neck was like a searing burn. What was worse was the sharp jolt as his body came to a shuddering stop. He felt a sudden terror that he might not have the strength to pull the noose off himself. One wrong move would be fatal. He was swinging back and forth, trying to keep his fists clenched when, without warning, the weight on his fists lessened, and he was dropping again.

A second later, he hit the water, his descent slowing, but not rapidly enough to stop him bumping against the bottom. The cold seeped into his bones. He felt pressure in his ears, and his chest burnt with the effort of holding his breath. In the darkness, he groped around, intending to push himself away, but his hands came into contact with something soft. He scrabbled about, feeling fingers, a hand, an arm, then a head and tangled hair. With a sudden rush of fear, he kicked out, disturbing what was lying on the sandy bed, and tried to swim upwards.

Had he reached the surface? He couldn't tell. There was nothing but the dark, creeping in at the corner of his vision. Unable to hold his breath any longer, he took a huge gulp, feeling a surge of blood to his head as his mouth filled with water. His final thought before the circle of blackness closed in was not for Allie. It was for his sister, Danka.

CHAPTER 35

Ross lay back, sweating and breathing heavily. The redhead was kneeling over him, moving rhythmically. He was reaching his climax when the mobile rang. Fuck! He was tempted to ignore it, but the girl had stopped and was looking at him questioningly. He felt the orgasm recede before time, and closed his eyes, swearing softly. No matter, he'd soon have another. But he had to answer the phone. It could be Kenny with news. He pushed the girl away so hard that she lost her balance and fell off the bed with a cry. She pulled herself up, yelling at him in a foreign language.

He grabbed the phone off the bedside cabinet and peered at the display. It wasn't a number he recognised.

'Ross Affleck,' he said, in a gruff voice.

'Ross?' It was Allie. She was sobbing. 'Ross!'

He sat up sharply. 'What is it?' He could hear traffic in the background. 'And where the hell are you? You're supposed to be at work.'

'Oh, Ross, something awful's happened.'

Where the fuck did she get . . . 'Whose phone is that?' he growled.

'I've borrowed it from someone. I had to call you.' She was wailing now. 'Ross, you've got to help me.'

'Okay, calm down. I said calm down!' He glanced at the red-head. She was pulling on her jeans. He thought about ordering her back into bed, but he had to deal with this thing with Allie. She sounded crazy. He ran a hand through his hair. Christ, he'd never known her like this. She was usually so submissive.

'I'm going to the police,' she said, in a trembling voice.

The polis? That was the last thing they needed. 'No, no, don't do anything rash. Ach, just tell me what's happened. Where *are* you?'

'It's Kenny. He – he . . .'

'Kenny?' What did his little brother have to do with this?

'I was helping him in the workshop.'

Ross got slowly to his feet. 'Are you at the workshop now?'

'No, of course not. I had to get away. But he—'

'He what, Allie?'

The redhead was standing in front of him, her hand out, palm up. When he did nothing, she rubbed her fingers together to signify he had to pay her. He tucked the phone under his chin and searched around for his trousers. The wallet was bulging with money. He took out a few notes and thrust them at her. While she was counting, he gripped her arm and dragged her across the room. She shouted something at him, but he shoved her into the corridor and slammed the door.

He sat on the bed. 'Start at the beginning, Allie, and tell me what happened.'

'I was at the museum,' she said, sobbing again. 'Kenny came to the reception and asked me to help him in the workshop – you know, with the deer? But as soon as I was through the door, he grabbed me and pushed me on to the table. He was like a wild man.' Another sob. 'He's never been like that before. Oh, I know he looks at me all the time as though he wants me, but he's never touched me, except that one time when he grabbed my breasts, but he apologised straight after.' A pause. 'Ross, are you there?'

He felt his anger swell. He had to clear his throat before speaking. 'Aye, I'm here.'

'I tried to fight him off but he's so much stronger. He put his hand under my skirt.'

'Did he have sex with you?' Ross said, in a hoarse voice.

'Not at first. He put his fingers inside my knickers. Then he undid his belt and pulled down his trousers. I was struggling all the time to get him off me but he was too strong. He forced my legs apart.' A sob. 'He didn't use a condom. It wasn't my fault, Ross, it wasn't my fault.'

He closed his eyes. 'You don't listen, do you, you little bitch? Of course it was your fault,' he added savagely. 'Tell me where the hell you are. I won't ask you again.'

'I'm sorry, Ross, I've got to give the lady her phone back.' The line disconnected.

He tried ringing her back, but there was no answer. A wave of anger coursed through him. He sat, motionless, trying to tamp down the rising mental image of Allie lying on a table in the workshop with Kenny on top of her. *He didn't use a condom.* Jesus, she could be pregnant, she was near the middle of her cycle. He was boiling with rage now, his thoughts turning to Kenny and how he'd taken advantage of his older brother's absence. And then, just as suddenly, his anger evaporated, to be replaced with an icy resolve. He dressed, combed his hair back, and left the hotel room.

Allie was standing on the Tay Bridge in the central walkway reserved for cyclists and pedestrians, gazing east towards Broughty Ferry castle. She turned and walked slowly back into Dundee. The pay-as-you-go rang, as she'd known it would, but she didn't answer. It would be Ross, trying to call her back. No, she would let him think the mobile belonged to someone else, and she'd borrowed it in an emergency. As soon as there was a break in the traffic, she hurled the phone into the river. She could easily buy another. She'd sold her engagement and wedding rings, and she also had Franek's money, and the cash she'd set aside to pay Murray.

So far, things were going according to plan. She knew what Ross's next move would be as if she'd written the script herself. His brother, Kenny, had defiled the nest, and for that he would be punished. Of course Kenny would vigorously protest his innocence, provided Ross gave him the chance. It was that remark about the condom that had clinched it. Ross had been monitoring her periods and had sex with her nonstop when she was most likely to conceive. He'd made no secret of the fact that he wanted her to produce a son and heir. 'The next generation to continue the family business,' he would say, zipping himself up. She smiled. The stupid man wasn't aware of that slit in the mattress where she kept her contraceptives.

Yes, with this revelation about Kenny, it wasn't just Ross's manhood that was under threat. It was the paternity of a possible child. But Kenny, for all his faults, was no rapist. She imagined the scene – Ross thundering into the workshop, demanding an explanation, Kenny taken by surprise, perhaps admitting under duress that they'd had sex, but stressing it had been consensual. Which it had. She'd had to psych herself up to it, anxious in case he proved to be even rougher than Ross. But he'd been delightfully gentle, and she'd found herself enjoying the experience, especially when she closed her eyes and imagined it was Franek. When it was over and he'd moved off her, hungrily kissing her face and neck, she'd taken the opportunity to slip her crumpled knickers into his trousers pocket. With luck, he wouldn't find them. With even more luck, Ross would.

She reached the end of the walkway and rode the lift down to street level. It would soon be time to set the last part of her plan into motion. She felt the corners of her mouth lift. It would be the grand finale. And she would be there for every second of it.

CHAPTER 36

'What do you reckon, then?' the uniform said to his younger companion.

They were staring at the figure of a man lying face down at the edge of the water. Someone taking an early-morning stroll along Marine Parade had spotted the partly submerged body, and immediately called the police.

'Do you think he could still be alive?' the younger one said, watching the body rise and fall as the water flowed round it.

'Ach, look at the state of him. He's dead, no question. We need to pull him out. Come on.'

They climbed over the rail and stepped into the shallow water. It was an effort to haul the man out but they managed. They laid him on the ground near the car park and turned him over.

'Nice clothes, eh,' the older one said. 'Any ID?'

The other uniform covered his nose and mouth with his sleeve, and thrust a hand into the pocket of the sodden jacket. His fingers closed on something inside a plastic bag. It was a bottle with a screw cap. He could just make out the white pills and the typed word FENTANYL on the label. They'd all been to the meetings, and heard the experts talk about this new horror drug, and what it had done in the US. And could do here. 'This is one for the Drugs Squad,' he said. He tried the other pocket and then checked the trousers. 'Nah. No ID.' He glanced up. 'Do you reckon he got bladdered and fell off the bridge?'

The older uniform shook his head. He indicated the noose round the corpse's neck. 'This was no accident, son.'

Niall Affleck was hurriedly emptying the office safe. After Ross's call confirming they'd dealt with Filarski, he'd decided it was no longer advisable to stay. After all, who knew what wheels Murray or Filarski had set in motion before they came to work at the Lodge? They could have been police informants, playing the long game in the hope of finding the evidence to implicate him. And flush out his source. Aye, but that they would never do. By the time the police came for him, he would be out of the country and in a faraway land with a new ID. He'd had the foresight to prepare for such an eventuality a long time before.

The illegal emerald trade had been funding the civil conflict in Colombia for decades, and the Afflecks had profited handsomely from it. But it was only he, Niall, who had the details of the source – a high-ranking government official – and was in sole contact with him. When a shipment arrived, he would hide the stones in the Lodge, and Gregor and the boys would find the buyers, using the contacts Gregor had built up over the years. The emeralds had been an excellent source of income, right enough, but all love affairs come to an end. Aye, and who was to say that he couldn't start up elsewhere? But perhaps it was time to retire, both from the smuggling and from writing novels, which brought in hardly enough for him to feed himself. No, once he'd sold the batch hidden at the back of the glass cabinet, he would live out his days in obscene luxury.

He crammed the last of the dollars into his satchel and closed the safe. There was enough there to get him to his new location, but that was about it. His entire wealth was tied up in his Broughty Ferry house and contents, which included some pricey artwork. He couldn't hang around to sell his estate so, the day before, he'd put everything in order by signing the papers that gifted it all to the Masons in perpetuity. He no longer needed it. The emeralds behind the cabinet would ensure he was made for life.

All that remained was to pick up the packet of stones, and then he was out of there. A glance at his watch told him he had plenty of time to make his London flight.

He whistled happily as he left the office.

Marek woke to the sound of seagulls, and the feel of something rough against his cheek. He opened his eyes to see an evil-looking German Shepherd resting its front paws on his chest. The dog regarded him for a second, then resumed licking his face. Marek tried to push the animal away but lacked the strength. He lay back, gazing into the empty sky, letting the hot tongue scratch his face while he tried to remember how he'd got there.

Memory slowly returned. Two men had kidnapped him. And then taken him to the Tay Road Bridge. After that, things became hazy. He had a fleeting recollection of falling deep into the water, and seeing something at the bottom, but he couldn't remember what. Somehow he'd made it to the surface, refilled his lungs, and started to swim. He must have reached the shore and pulled himself up before blacking out. But what he now wanted to remember – and couldn't – were the faces of the men who'd taken him.

'Rosie!' The voice was a woman's. 'Come here!'

The dog bounded away. With a huge effort, Marek hauled himself up to a sitting position.

'Good Lord in Heaven.' The woman leant over him. She had soft brown eyes and coiffed blue-grey hair. 'Are you all right?'

'I'm not sure.'

'Can you get up?'

'I won't know until I try.'

He struggled to his feet, only then aware of the noose round his neck. The woman couldn't take her eyes off it.

'What on earth happened to you, laddie? Was it one of those stag parties?'

It seemed the simplest way out of his predicament. 'Unfortunately, yes.'

She nodded in sympathy.

'Where am I?' he said, looking around.

'These are the docks. HMS *Unicorn* is in that direction. Aye, you're not far from the city centre.' She studied him thoughtfully. 'Can you get home by yourself?'

He tried a smile. 'I think so. I live not far from here.'

'All right, then. Take care.' She strode off, Rosie loping along beside her.

Marek pulled off the noose and threw the long rope away. After rubbing and working the stiffness out of his limbs, he limped along the shore towards the bridge. He shivered despite the heat in the air. From the glances directed his way, he suspected he looked a mess. He ran his hands over his hair, flattening it, and felt a sudden dull pain from where he'd been hit. Bastards. He'd need to inform the police. But first, he'd get himself home, take a shower, and eat something. His exertions had left him ravenous.

He reached the busy road that led to Perth and Coupar Angus and followed it towards the V&A and the city centre. By the time he made it to his building, he was exhausted. Somehow, he managed to stagger up the stairs. The door to his flat was open, although a quick look round suggested that nothing had been disturbed. He lay on the sofa, puzzling over the events of the previous night, and trying to remember the faces of his kidnappers. As he adjusted his weight, he felt something hard inside his trousers pocket. He reached in and drew out a package wrapped in plastic. It was a bottle with a screw cap. He brought it to his face and squinted at the contents. White pills. And on the bottle, clearly visible through the plastic, was a label with the word FENTANYL in large letters.

And then he remembered one of the men shoving something into his pocket as he lay in the back of the van. And it was now obvious why. The police, finding the body of a man with a noose round his neck and fentanyl in his pocket, would be led down entirely the wrong track.

'And that's all you can remember, sir?'

Marek ran his hands over his face. 'I know it's not much to go on, but I can't give you a better description. I can't recall much about last night.'

The officer from the Drugs Squad was looking at him in a way he didn't like. Suspicion lingered in the dark eyes, making Marek conclude he didn't completely believe him.

'You're lucky to be alive. Had you gone over the side further along the bridge, you wouldn't have survived the fall. And you've no idea why they wanted to kill you?'

'I've made many enemies in the past, one way or another. It's possible someone wanted to settle an old score.' He nodded at the bottle of fentanyl on the table. 'And lead you down the garden path with that.'

He was starting to regret having gone to the police. He'd decided before setting out for West Bell Street that he wouldn't bring Allie into this. She might still be in Dundee, and he wanted to give her a chance to get away. But the officer's next question floored him.

'Do you know a Murray Johnson?'

'Murray?'

He'd given himself away. The officer's expression changed. 'When did you last see him, sir?'

'I've never met him.'

'Aye, but you know the name.'

There was still a way he could keep Allie out of it. 'I'm doing an investigative piece on fentanyl. I heard that Murray Johnson was a dealer, so I went to his place hoping to sniff out a story. His neighbour told me she hadn't seen him for nearly two weeks.'

The officer opened his file. 'We've interviewed this neighbour, Lorraine Barrie. She told us that someone by the name of Franek Filarski came looking for Murray.' He glanced up. 'That wouldn't be you, would it?'

Marek lifted a hand. 'You must understand that when I'm undercover I don't use my real name.'

The man seemed satisfied. 'Mrs Barrie's story corroborates yours.' He closed the file. 'We're as keen as you are to track down who's bringing in fentanyl. One of my colleagues informed me that you've helped us in the past, Mr Gorski. I hope you'll continue to do so.'

'Of course. If I find anything, you'll be the first to know.' He nodded at the bottle. 'Can you get dabs off that?'

'Forensics checked it,' the officer said. 'It's clean.' He picked up the bottle. 'The name Murray Johnson is the first solid lead we've had. My guess is he was the middle man. What we want is the head honcho.'

'Perhaps if Murray shows up, he can help you find him.'

'He showed up this morning.'

Marek tried to keep the dismay out of his voice. If they

355

questioned Murray, he might crack and lead them to the emer-alds. And to Allie. 'What did he say?'

'He didn't say anything. His body was found washed up on Marine Parade. According to the pathologist, he'd been dead for a wee while.'

'And you're sure it's Murray?' Marek said slowly.

'Aye, we had a good description of him in MisPers. We were able to track down his boyfriend. He identified him.' The officer gathered his papers and stood up. 'There's something you need to know, Mr Gorski. Murray Johnson also had a noose round his neck and a bottle of fentanyl in his pocket.'

Marek got slowly to his feet, his legs weakening as the impli-cation of the words hit him.

'He was found not far away from where you landed up.' The man studied him. 'I would lie low, if I were you, until we find these people. If they learn you're still alive, they may try again.'

CHAPTER 37

Allie was standing in the roof garden of the recently opened multi-storey hotel at Carnoustie. The hotel had been built to cater for players and spectators coming to the world-famous golf links, and therefore the obvious place for it was on Links Parade. She'd learnt from Ross that there'd been an attempt to block it at the planning-permission stage, but the builder – one of the Masons from the Lodge – knew the Masons on the council and had got it through. From the Parade, it was an eyesore, dwarfing the houses and other hotels. But from the roof garden, it gave an unparalleled view of the golf course and Carnoustie Bay.

The hotel owners had made the best of the roof space with a tasteful arrangement of flowerbeds, shrubs and garden furniture. Allie had chosen this spot because she'd learnt there were always people here, either propping up the bar, lounging on recliners or sitting reading under the striped sunshades. Like her, not all were guests at the hotel. The bar's reputation and the view over the water drew people from Dundee and even Fife. And the restaurant had one Michelin star.

She was resting her hands on the railing, watching the tiny players on the golf course, when the waiter-barman approached. He was a huge man with fair hair and restless eyes.

'Would you like a drink, madam?'

'Mineral water, thanks,' she said, smiling.

He nodded and left.

She glanced at her watch. It was time. She rummaged in her bag for the new pay-as-you-go and called his number.

'Ross Affleck?' came the growl.

'Ross? It's Allie,' she said tonelessly.

'Allie? Where the hell are you?'

This time, she was prepared to tell him. 'I'm in that new hotel in Carnoustie,' she said, in a small voice. 'You know, the one you told me about?'

'What the fuck are you doing there?' A pause, in which she could almost hear him grind his teeth. 'I've been looking everywhere for you, you daft bitch. Why haven't you come home?'

'I'm frightened of Kenny.'

'Aye, well, you needn't be. Kenny won't be bothering you again.'

'But how can you be sure?'

'He's gone. For good. And he won't be coming back.'

She paused long enough for Ross to say, 'Are you still there?'

'Yes, I'm here.' She took a loud breath for his benefit. 'All right. I'm ready to come home. I need you to come and fetch me.'

'Why are you in Carnoustie?' he said suspiciously.

'I wanted to get as far away from Kenny as I could. I hitched rides, and this is as far as I got.'

'Do you know how dangerous hitching is?'

'Don't shout at me, Ross. I was desperate.'

'All right, all right.' Another pause. 'I'll meet you in the lounge.'

'I'm in the roof garden. I've bought myself a drink and I've no money to pay for it. The barman's lent me his phone so I can talk to you.'

'Jesus,' he muttered. 'Ach, okay, I'll be there as soon as I can. And stay put.' He rang off.

The barman watched her put away the phone. He'd left the water on the table beside her. She took a sip and waited.

Twenty minutes later, she saw the black Volkswagen pull up outside the hotel. So typical of Ross. He ignored the double yellow lines as though he owned the place, slammed out of the car and headed for the entrance. She turned, surveying the garden. There were about a dozen people there.

The barman was putting down the phone. He came out from behind the counter. 'Ladies and gentlemen,' he said, 'we're about to test the fire alarm.'

There were groans from the guests.

'I know it's an inconvenience, but it's a legal requirement. You'll have to use the fire stairs to get down. I suggest you go now to avoid the residents on the other floors. Otherwise, there'll be a huge crush.'

'Can we use the lift?' someone said.

'I'm afraid not.' He raised his voice. 'Once you get to the ground floor, the fire door will take you out directly to the car park at the back. Assemble there and someone will come and look after you.'

The guests seemed resigned. They picked up their belongings and made for the fire exit.

Allie pulled off her long black wig and thrust it into her bag just as the lift doors were opening. Ross strode in, pushing past the crowd. He looked around and, seeing Allie, scowled and marched over to the bar.

'How much?' he said to the barman.

'I beg your pardon?'

He nodded towards Allie. 'How much for that woman's drinks?'

'They're on the house, sir. The lady's only had mineral water.'

He turned to Allie. She hadn't moved from the railings. 'Pick up your bag, and let's go,' he said thickly.

'No, Ross, I'm not coming with you.'

His expression darkened. 'What did you say?' he said softly.

'I'm not coming with you. I'm leaving you.'

He laughed unpleasantly. 'You stupid bitch. You can't leave me.'

'I can. And I am.'

He took a step towards her. The barman slipped out from behind the bar and pressed a button that put the lift out of action.

'What are you saying, Allie?' Ross said slowly. 'That you don't love me?'

It was her turn to laugh. 'Love? I doubt you know the meaning of the word.'

He seemed mystified. 'I turned myself inside out and upside down for you. I gave you everything.'

'You gave me nothing, Ross.' Her voice grew hard. 'You see, I know about Murray. You and Kenny killed him, didn't you? On whose orders? No, let me guess. It was your uncle Niall. Murray had stumbled across your little scam with the emeralds.' She was enjoying Ross's reaction. 'You went to his flat and took him away. Then you sent an email from his account saying he was leaving Dundee. How am I doing?'

His stunned expression gave her her answer. He glanced at the barman, who was leaning against the wall, his arms crossed.

'You don't know what you're talking about, you daft bitch.'

'Oh, but I think I do.'

'Murray just did a flit.'

'Not according to his partner, Blackie. He came to the Lodge looking for him.'

'You've had a wee shock, lass, and you're not thinking straight. It was that business with Kenny.'

'Yes, about that. You've killed him too, haven't you?'

His eyes flared. 'He raped you,' he said, in a hoarse voice.

'Actually, he didn't. It was consensual.' The look on her husband's face was everything she'd hoped for. 'He told you that's what happened, and of course you didn't believe him.' She was enjoying herself. 'Well, it's true. I led him on. And you know something? I rather liked it.'

Ross made a lunge towards her, but the barman leapt forward and gripped his arm. 'I wouldn't do that if I were you, sir. I'm better built for a fight.'

'I could take you on the best day you ever had,' Ross snapped, shaking himself loose. He turned to Allie. 'Why did you tell me he raped you, you lying bitch?'

'Because I knew how you'd react. I knew you'd kill him. And that's what I wanted. Because I didn't want him coming after me for what I'm going to do to you.'

He stared at her in amazement. She saw the emotions come and go on his face as he understood what she was telling him.

He roared suddenly, and hurled himself at her. She stepped smartly aside and, in the split second it took him to try to grab her, she reached into her bag and pulled out the electroshock device. The stupid man had thought she didn't know he kept it in the unlocked bedside cabinet, an oversight that was about to cost him dearly. She'd recharged the thing the night before and checked that the security switch was off. Before he could react, she plunged the device into his groin.

He shrieked, his legs buckling, and thrust his hands between his legs. He gazed up at her, an appeal in his eyes. 'I loved you, Allie,' he whimpered.

She waited for him to haul himself up, and then jabbed the electrodes into his chest. He dropped to his knees without a sound.

She threw the device into her bag, and she and the barman dragged Ross to his feet. His eyes were glazed, but he was still

361

breathing. They bent him over the railing. At the barman's signal, she reached down and grabbed Ross's right leg, the barman gripping his left.

'On the count of three,' he said firmly.

She nodded.

'One, two, *three!*'

They tipped Ross over.

She watched him fall. Halfway down, he seemed to realise what was happening because his arms and legs started to flail. He'd hardly had time to fill his lungs for the scream when he hit the ground.

She gazed at the barman. 'Thanks, Blackie,' she said. 'I couldn't have done it without you.'

Almost on cue, the fire alarm sounded.

'Come on,' he said. 'We need to see ourselves out of here.'

She pulled the wig out of her bag and put it on along with her sunglasses. Then, joining the residents who were vacating their bedrooms, they hurried down the steps to the ground-floor fire exit, and inserted themselves into the crowd spilling out of the hotel.

'This way,' he shouted in her ear. 'I've got the car.'

He drove her into Dundee, and pulled up at the railway station, leaving the engine running. They sat for a few moments, watching people weave in and out of the building.

'What will you do now, Blackie?'

'I need to get back before anyone notices I'm missing.' He threw her a lopsided smile. 'But what with the fire drill and the body on the pavement, there'll be a right bourach. I'll have no trouble slipping back inside.'

'And the CCTV at the hotel?'

'I've arranged for it to be on the blink these last couple of days. I reckon no one will be asking why it was down this morning.'

'It was good of you to arrange that fire drill.'

'Aye, it was long overdue. All I had to do was whisper the idea into the manager's lug.' He studied her. 'What about you? Have you thought about what you'll be doing?'

'I'm going to get as far away from here as I can.'

'You okay for money?'

'I've got enough to get me started.' It was a lie. Thanks to Franek, she had enough for the rest of her life. Her online sleuthing had paid off: an old friend of her father's was in the jewellery business in London and had already lined up a buyer for the emeralds.

'And how do you feel?' Blackie said.

How did she feel? The experiences she'd had with Ross were the kind that marked the soul. But she was a survivor. She smiled. 'I feel fine.'

And, as she waved Blackie off and strolled into the station to buy her ticket to London, she realised it was true.

Marek was at home watching television. The evening news had come on, the main item being the tragic accident that had befallen Ross Affleck. The name caused Marek to sit up so sharply that he spilt vodka down his shirt.

The female reporter was standing some distance away from the new golf hotel at Carnoustie, where white-suited forensics staff were working silently behind police tape.

'A number of guests remembered Ross Affleck getting out of the lift and pushing past them,' the reporter was saying. 'They thought it strange that, while they were heading for the fire exit, he was wanting to get on to the roof. One guest said he had a determined look in his eyes, as though there was something he desperately needed to do.' The reporter nodded behind her.

'Falling from such a height, he would have had no chance.' She smiled suddenly at someone off camera. 'I'm joined now by the manager of the roof garden, Blackie Cowan.'

Blackie Cowan. Blackie! The rest of the vodka fell on to Marek's shirt.

'Mr Cowan, can you tell us what you saw?'

'Aye, well, there's not much to say. This guest, Ross Affleck, barrelled out of the lift as I was moving people towards the fire exit. I had to make sure everyone was getting safely down the stairs and, by the time I'd turned back to the garden to fetch him, he was gone.'

'You didn't see him go over the edge?' the reporter said, clearly disappointed.

'I'm afraid not.'

'Was there anyone else on the roof at that time?'

'No one. It was my responsibility to make sure of that.'

'What do you think was going through Ross Affleck's mind?'

'I haven't a scooby. I didn't see his face.' He shrugged. 'I thought he'd left something on the roof and wanted to go back for it. The guests do that sometimes. They can't find their handbags or wallets, and they take these risks.'

'Is there anything else you can tell us?'

'I'm afraid not.'

'Well, thank you, Mr Cowan.'

He nodded at the camera and left.

Marek sat back, his mind in a whirl. So Blackie had been there. With Ross. That couldn't have been a coincidence.

The reporter was speaking again. 'This tragedy comes close on the heels of another tragedy for the Affleck family. The remains of Ross's youngest brother, Cameron, who disappeared in two thousand and five, were found not long ago in the old doocot in Inchture. And Ross's brother, Kenny, has been reported missing

364

by his father, Gregor Affleck, owner of the Affleck Natural History Museum in Lochee.'

The image changed to show headshots of the three Affleck brothers. Marek recognised little Cameron with his curly hair. But it was the faces of the two older brothers that gripped his attention. And suddenly he remembered where he'd seen them before: they were the men who'd kidnapped him and thrown him off the Tay Road Bridge. The one with the scowl had to be Ross, Allie's abusive husband. The other, whom he'd last seen being inducted into the degree of Fellowcraft, was Kenny.

The reporter was concluding her account. 'We tried to get a statement from Mr Gregor Affleck, but no one at the family home was available for comment.'

'What do you think?' Marek said.

The video recording he and Allie had made at the Lodge had just come to an end. His boss was gazing slack-jawed at the screen. 'We can't use this,' he said, folding his arms.

'Why not?'

'Because I recognise some of the people in it. They're pillars of our society. And also great supporters of our publications. They won't take kindly to being outed like this. Especially as the recording was made without their permission.'

Marek ran a hand through his hair, saying nothing.

'What about your informant's tip, and the scoop you were going to get?'

'It didn't work out.'

'Ach, well, those are the breaks.' He looked at Marek with sympathy. 'Remind me. Wasn't it drugs?'

'I didn't get anywhere with that.'

'Aye, but I think you did. Listen, remember that jumper, Ross Affleck?'

Marek looked at his boss. 'What about him?' he said slowly.

'His brother Kenny was found this morning. Washed up on the Ferry beach. But get this. There was a bottle of fentanyl pills in his pocket.'

'Kenny? The one who was reported missing?'

'Kenny Affleck. And you know that man who was pulled out of the Tay a while back? Murray Johnson?' He tapped Marek's desk. 'That's two dead people found with fentanyl pills on them.'

And it was nearly three, thought Marek.

'There's your story. Find out how these pills are coming into Dundee.'

He said nothing. The two people who could have told him – Ross and Kenny Affleck – were both dead.

His boss looked at him for a long moment. 'It must have been tricky to get that recording. Aye, you did fine well.' He glanced at the screen, and then at him. 'But I want you to erase it.'

So mote it be, thought Marek, as he pressed delete.

CHAPTER 38

Dania walked briskly along the Arbroath Road towards the Victorian Gothic entrance. She was late, because her meeting with the DCI had overrun. Jamie Reid, awaiting trial, was persisting in his claim that Hamish had beaten him up, and was making a formal complaint. It was the one thing both women had hoped wouldn't happen. And a headache they would now have to deal with.

Inside the entrance to the Eastern Cemetery was a board with the ground plan. It took Dania another five minutes before she found the grave. People were already moving away.

Gregor Affleck was standing, head bowed, holding a bouquet of roses. He stepped forward and placed it on the grave. The simple granite headstone bore the words: 'Davina Affleck. Loving wife and mother'. Next to it was a freshly turned mound of earth. Cameron's headstone would be erected in due course.

'Mr Affleck?' Dania said, touching his elbow.

He turned, and she was shocked to see how he'd altered in the short time she'd known him. But, then, losing all of your sons would break anyone.

'Inspector,' he said, in a voice that was rougher than she remembered. 'Good of you to come.'

'I'm sorry I couldn't get here earlier.'

367

He waved a hand as if to indicate this was of no importance. 'The main thing is that you came.'

She glanced behind her at the mourners making their way to the entrance. These would be his friends from the Lodge and their wives. She looked for Niall in the crowd but couldn't find him.

'And how are you keeping, Mr Affleck? If that's not an impertinent question.'

'I've lost my entire family, Inspector. Aye, even my brother Niall has moved on.' He smiled thinly. 'And I'm looking for a new housekeeper.'

'Has Mrs Spence left, then?'

'She could hardly stay, poor lass. Which reminds me. How are you getting on with finding her man?'

'We're still looking.' Dania gazed into the distance where some of the older headstones were listing alarmingly. 'I only met him once, but he doesn't strike me as someone who would do a runner.'

'What do you think's happened to him?'

'I suspect he's lying in some nearby woodland, having drunk himself to death.'

'Aye, right enough. The few times I saw him lately, he reeked of the drink.'

'You never suspected him of taking Cameron?'

'Good Lord, no.' He glanced at her. 'I haven't asked you how you came to the conclusion he did it. Did Mrs Spence see that neckerchief and come forward? I mind now that Sandy was always wearing it.'

'No one came forward.'

'So what made you suspect him?'

'He confessed to his priest.'

'And the priest told you?'

'He's not allowed to. But he gave me a clue that led us to Sandy.'

'Perhaps you could thank this priest for me.'

'I'm afraid he's left Dundee.'

'Aye, why is that?'

'He spoke to his bishop. He's been recalled.'

After a pause, Gregor said, 'I reckon that not finding Spence must have soured your triumph. But I should emphasise that, as far as I'm concerned, you've done your job.' He looked at the little mound of earth. 'Please do tell me when you find him. I would like to attend his trial.'

'And we finally found the key to the doocot.'

'Where was it?' he said, in surprise.

'Under the monkey puzzle tree, where Sandy had buried it.'

'It will be rusted through.'

'Would you like me to send it over?'

'No need. I'm having the doocot razed to the ground.' He was silent for a while. 'It's not hard to see why the good citizens of Dundee used to come here for their Sunday-afternoon strolls,' he said, gesturing to the meandering paths lined with trees and flowering shrubs.

'If it weren't for the headstones, it could be a park.'

'Aye, right enough. I come here regularly to visit my wife's grave.' He lowered his head. 'And I'll be here again once Ross and Kenny's bodies are released.'

'I'm truly sorry, Mr Affleck. There's nothing I can say, so I won't even try.'

'I expect you're involved in the case of Kenny's murder. Although it was another officer who came to interview me about that.'

'We're working closely with the Drugs Squad.'

Gregor stared at the headstone. 'I can't believe he was taking drugs. They say that what was found in his pocket when they pulled him out of the river was orders of magnitude stronger than what we usually see on our streets.'

'It's called fentanyl.'

'And I don't believe for one second that Ross killed himself,' he said angrily. 'Ach, why would he? He had everything to live for.'

Ross Affleck's suicide during a fire drill had puzzled Dania. 'I believe there was an eyewitness,' she said.

'So I heard.'

'We've spoken to his wife, Allie.'

'Aye, her parents told me she'd moved to London, intending to make a new life.'

'We needed to establish her movements on the Friday Ross died.'

Gregor looked stunned. 'You're not suggesting she had anything to do with his death?'

'You must understand that we had to interview her. Especially as she left Dundee so suddenly.'

'Aye, right enough. I can see that.'

'She told us the last time she'd seen Ross was the Thursday. The day before he died.' Dania paused. 'She said she'd told him she was leaving him.'

'But that's impossible!'

'Impossible that she was going to leave him?'

'They were happily married. And trying for a bairn, Ross told me. Why would she go?'

Dania had met the pretty, confident blonde in the American bar in the Savoy. When she'd asked the woman why she'd decided to leave her husband, she'd replied that there was no single compelling reason, only that she realised she'd made a mistake and he wasn't the man for her. She'd lowered her gaze, adding that Ross had been gutted, and had begged her almost on his knees to stay. He'd wanted children, you see, but she simply wasn't cut out for motherhood. And yes, of course, she was devastated that he'd committed suicide, she'd never dreamt he'd do anything awful like that, but what could she say? Surely the detective inspector wasn't blaming her for that. No, she didn't have an alibi for the time of her husband's death. She'd been at home, packing. Yes, she'd been alone: for some reason Mrs Spence was away.

'And you say your brother's left the city, too?' Dania said.

Gregor drew his brows together. 'Niall was always blethering on about going abroad. Something to do with getting peace and quiet to write his novels.'

'I see. Oh, I nearly forgot.' She pulled a plastic bag out of her pocket and handed it to Gregor.

'Cameron's watch,' he said, fingering the maroon strap through the plastic. 'Where did you find it?'

'One of my officers, Honor Randall, came up with the idea of using the internet to track it down. We put an image of it online, and someone came forward. It appears that Sandy had sold it.'

'And where did you get the image?'

'It's in our records. DI Chirnside, the officer originally assigned to the case, had uploaded a photograph of Cameron. He's wearing the watch. Do you remember the photo? He's holding a trophy.'

Gregor's face broke into a smile. 'Aye, he won that at school. It was for a recitation of Rabbie Burns's "To A Mouse". Do you know it?'

'I've heard it.'

'Wee Cameron had it off by heart.' He looked at the watch. 'This is all I have left of him. And my memories.' He straightened. 'Aye, right enough. And my memories.' He clutched the watch to his chest, then slipped it into his pocket. 'Well, I'll be saying goodbye, Inspector Gorska,' he said, pronouncing it correctly.

And, with a nod, he walked stiffly away.

EPILOGUE

Gregor Affleck let himself into the workshop and hung up his coat next to the row of aprons. The place was silent. Only the hum of the machines told a visitor that this had once been a bustle of activity. The tables were bare, except for the various dioramas his sons had been constructing. At some stage, he would have to finish them, although he lacked Kenny's deft touch. He checked the dials on the freeze-dry vessels. But he was simply going through the motions: his heart was no longer in his work. Some time soon, he would have to consider either selling up or taking on staff and carrying on. His preference was for selling the business, and he would have put it on the market by now had it not been for what was behind the locked door in the basement. Which reminded him that he needed to get himself down there.

The museum's office was at the back of the workshop. Ignoring the mail that had piled up, he clawed under the desk drawer to where his grandfather Mungo had made a hiding place for the key.

Behind the heavy curtain, a flight of stone steps led down to the musty basement, which was crammed with broken animal forms and other taxidermy paraphernalia. He switched on the light and pushed past the clutter to the door hidden behind the stacks of crates. The key, which turned smoothly, let him into a special room. Hardly anyone knew of this room's existence. There were two doors in: the one through which he'd just entered, and another at the end of the long, tiled tunnel that led from the Lodge cellar. But that door was no longer in use: Mungo had nailed planks across it many years before.

As he entered, locking the door behind him, he heard the loud hum from the dehumidifier, which, rather than remove the dusty, spicy smell, seemed to enhance it.

Mungo had liked to sit in this room, and had installed a cabinet where he kept his finest whiskies. Gregor had seen no reason not to continue the tradition. He removed the bottle of twenty-five-year-old Lagavulin and, after running his handkerchief over a whisky glass, poured himself a generous measure.

The wooden chair creaked under his weight. He sat sipping the Scotch, contemplating the bodies of his grandfather's victims. Aye, they were all there, standing on a raised plinth, dressed in their Mason's regalia.

It was his father who had let him and Niall into the secret that Mungo had found an original method for dealing with his enemies. He had begun by burying them, or throwing them into the Tay, then laying a trail that suggested they'd left the country. But he knew that if their bodies were ever discovered, they would lead the police to him. It wasn't long before he'd found another way.

Some years earlier, he'd taken a wee trip to Sicily, and seen the dried and embalmed bodies of the good citizens of Palermo on display in the catacombs. The rows of finely dressed corpses, some upright, others lying on shelves, had prompted him to make enquiries as to the method of preservation. On his return, he'd set about investigating whether he could use the technique in the taxidermy business, but he'd rapidly concluded that fur inhibits the process. The procedure was only suitable for animals with bare skin. Which included humans. His first experiments, which required drying in a chamber that he designed himself, then treating and injecting the body with zinc salts and salicylic acid, were conducted on pigs. Decomposition had set in immediately. But he soon perfected the technique, in particular finding a way of shortening the drying process from years to months.

Gregor had never discovered which of his ancestors had built the tunnel between the building that was now the Lodge and the old jute mill. The victims that Mungo intended to 'disappear' were wheeled from the Lodge cellar through the white-tiled passageway into the museum's basement. There they were dried and processed, their bodies preserved in a dehumidified environment, which was now computer-controlled. In the event of a power cut, a liquid-fuel generator took over.

It was many decades since the last Mason had been embalmed, and Gregor was forced to admit that his grandfather could have patented his technique had he been so minded. The bodies were amazingly lifelike because Mungo had replaced their eyes with glass. As Gregor sat nursing his whisky, he could almost feel their glares of admonishment.

His gaze drifted to the body lying in the huge drying chamber. It would be many months before Sandy Spence was ready to join the men on display. Aye, Gregor had been lucky there, right enough. As soon as he'd seen the paisley neckerchief on the lunchtime news and heard where it had been found, he'd known in an instant who had abducted Cameron. He was not a man to sit on his hands, so he'd lifted the phone immediately and ordered Ross and Kenny to take him. They'd held him somewhere secure, he hadn't asked where, and then, under cover of darkness or what passed for it in summer, they'd brought his body to the basement.

Gregor set down the whisky and hauled himself to his feet. He consulted a chart, made a slight adjustment to the dial on the drying chamber, then returned to the chair.

He downed the rest of the Scotch, and poured another, then another. Before his brain began to cloud, he tried to remember the stations of his life. He'd first seen Davina at the kirk. She'd been there with her parents, frowning in concentration as she listened to the minister. After the service, while her folks were gabbing to their friends, he'd walked over and formally introduced himself. She was a primary-school teacher, and after they were engaged, she'd told her pupils that at the wedding the groom would be wearing a suit with tails. The children had dutifully produced drawings of Gregor in evening wear, complete with assorted animal tails. How the two of them had chuckled at that. His smile faded as he recalled his final sight of Davina, growing cold in his arms, the empty bottle of sleeping pills in her hand.

He'd never really been interested in money for its own sake. He'd gone into Niall's emerald-smuggling racket because he'd wanted to secure his boys' futures. Although the museum and the taxidermy business had provided for the Afflecks in the past, their fortunes had changed, and they'd needed another source of income.

The first shipment had arrived inside glass eyes. Thereafter, they came hidden in the wooden forms used for mounting animals. Where Niall stashed them, Gregor had never discovered. But he and his sons had had little difficulty in finding a market, and the gemstones had made them all indecently wealthy. Now, with Niall gone, the shipments had come to a premature end. Ach, perhaps it was just as well. His brother was something of a lightweight, and they'd all lived in constant fear of discovery. Yet the speed with which he'd left the city was odd. He hadn't even stayed long enough to dispose of his estate, gifting it instead to the Lodge. And what had become of that last batch of emeralds? He must have taken it with him. There was no other explanation. Aye, well, good luck to him.

Gregor poured himself another whisky, reflecting upon his unexpected change in fortune. Davina and his three sons were dead, Niall had left for God-knows-where. Even Allie was gone. She'd been his hope for grandchildren, for continuing the succession. But that wouldn't happen now. With Gregor, the Affleck line had come to an end.

He continued to drink until the bottle was empty. His eyelids flickered and grew heavy. There was a sudden dull ache, like a band tightening round his chest, and numbness spread along his arms to his hands.

The glass slipped from his fingers. He didn't even hear it hit the floor.

ACKNOWLEDGEMENTS

I owe a huge debt of gratitude to Jenny Brown and Krystyna Green, both for their support and for reading this novel and suggesting ways in which it could be improved. I am also deeply grateful to Hazel Orme for doing such a magnificent job of editing. Any errors in the text are mine and not hers. My heartfelt thanks go also to the team at Little, Brown – Krystyna Green, Amanda Keats, Clara Diaz, Brionee Fenlon, Matthew Burne and Kim Bishop – for all their hard work in getting this novel to publication.